# QUEST FOR ROSHAN

## ENORA ONLINE: BOOK TWO

### ARLO ADAMS

# PROLOGUE

## Two Years Ago

Black grime covered her gloves as Roshan raised the rock pick and chipped away at the hard stone that encased her quarry. Dust and pellets burst from the surface. When the recesses around the glassy face of the gem curved deep enough to work the pick tip into the gap, she pried gently, and then with more force. Sweat stung one of her eyes as the stone jiggled in its seat.

The ruby popped free then dropped into her left hand. She considered its weight as she bounced it a few times in her palm. After shaking off her gloves, she pinched the rock between two fingers to admire it. Her thumbs swiped away the muck, revealing its red luster and, although the light of her Illumination spell wouldn't do it the same justice as sunlight, its clarity was undebatable.

A good stone. Her master might even smile.

It was he who sent her here daily to advance her Gemology skill. Roshan had but one goal—to retrieve a single stone. Not that each day presented a return, but she'd had good luck of late. Though her people worked the large mines a mile to the north, this concealed cave behind a rock outcropping had evaded their notice, and her master kept it that way so she could work in peace.

Master Mitwah believed the consistent use of her *Inner Illumination* spell against the darkness helped bring her into alignment with Solara's blessed Light through focused work. He credited the journeys with calming her mind. Roshan believed the skill points she received by using the spell for prolonged periods had been the early goal, but she'd stopped seeing advancement long ago. She kept this fact to herself, and her master never asked. Luckily, professions didn't cap with her level, like magic.

Warlords of the region banished the use of magic decades ago when a demon invasion brought blight to the eastern lands by the beckoning of the shadow warlock Arturus. So she channeled Solara's energy only in the privacy of her master's temple. Had Roshan's father known, he would have stormed the temple, dragged her away, then driven the priest from the village.

When she reached the bottom of the cave's embankment, she peeked around the outcropping to ensure there were no children playing nearby, no wandering vendors, and no one from Clan Fortwan who might have found the ruby cave where she found peace each day. Roshan was grateful she didn't have to pass through her village to return to the temple. People would ask questions about the dusty bag and her sweaty brow. When she'd shared her concerns about being discovered with her master—and that it was inevitable—he'd given her the same answer she received to most of her questions.

"Have faith the goddess will provide, and her bounties shall be yours."

A better answer would've been that villagers didn't push their luck with in-depth questioning of their religious guides, and Roshan was an apprentice to become exactly that.

The door opened as she reached for the handle, and a figure standing inside smiled up at her. The light behind her cast her shadow across his hooded head, revealing only his chin and a mouthful of aging teeth as he hunched there.

"Roshan," Master Mitwah greeted. "The Light blesses you this day. Please, come in."

"Thank you, master." She passed by the shorter man then stood in the narrow aisle between the benches lining either side of the temple. "Solara blesses us with a ruby, today. She leveled my mining skill another point."

"Glorious!" Master Mitwah raised his hands in excitation. "Soon you will be a master in the field."

The door closed, washing the place in a dim gray, reminding her that the seeing spell had expired. She began to recast it.

As if reading her mind, he gripped her wrist gently. "This day, the darkness will serve."

Though she couldn't imagine why one would stumble around with limited sight, she acquiesced to the man who'd risked so much to bring her into the Light. Meeting his gaze, she extended her fist, then splayed the fingers to reveal the irregularly shaped gem.

"Oh, a beautiful one, Roshan. You must have contemplated Solara's blessings for some time to extract one of this size."

She repressed a smile and nodded reverently. "Solara always rewards my focused meditation."

He led her along the dusty temple floor to a door behind the altar, beyond which was the private space he called home. Roshan waited as he withdrew a rusted key from his pocket then slipped it into a hole most wouldn't notice near the bottom of the door. A bolt clanked, then the creaky hinges protested as he pushed his way through. Master Mitwah turned. "Enter, for it is a special day."

Her eyes flared wide before she could suppress the response.

He flicked the fingers of an impatient hand. "Come, come, Roshan. The darkness inside is but a shroud from wandering eyes. After these years together, have we not established trust?"

The toes of her worn shoes halted near the threshold. A narrow stairwell circled into the shadowy depths below. It was unexpected—she'd envisioned walls of shelves stacked with volumes on the opposite side of that door, perhaps a chair with an oil lantern by which her master read.

"Come child, for today you are a woman of seventeen. Your rite of passage awaits." After two steps down, he turned. "Remove your shoes. You will not need them."

She slipped off her ragged footwear then stepped onto the cool stone stairs. Goose pimples formed on her exposed forearms. Orange light flickered on the wall from a source somewhere below as the foreboding cold caused a shiver to shimmied up her spine.

Though her master descended with his back turned, he registered her discomfort. "Your senses have become strong under Solara's guidance. Give fear no quarter, no matter what you see or sense."

Chills erupted as she stepped off the final stair. She might have smiled at the tomes filling shelves, similar to what she'd imagined, if not for three shadowy figures seated atop decorative pillows on the floor. All wore robes, but the hoods of travel cloaks rested on the strangers' shoulders and backs as they sat around an oil lamp, cross-legged with eyes closed. Cinched bags rested next to each of their knees. On a table off to one side was a small chest, its lid open. As she passed, Roshan spied its velvety interior.

Empty.

A man of pallid skin sat furthest from her. To his left was a woman with long obsidian locks flowing into her lap. Opposite her was a man tanned of the sun, much like the people of Roshan's clan, but with bright yellow hair. His angular jaw ended in a strong chin over broad shoulders.

Master Mitwah paced over to a space in the wall between two of the waist-high shelves where a white garment hung. He slipped it off the hook, crossed to her, bowed his head, then presented it with both hands.

Roshan blinked her eyes at it then read its description.

### Robe of Apprenticeship
Level 5
*Slot: Chest*
*Type: Armor*
*Quality: Uncommon*
*Durability: 20 of 20*
*+20 maximum mana*
*+5 to light spells*
*+5% resistance to magical attacks*

"Today you are a woman, worthy of indoctrination into the priesthood, Roshan of Clan Fortwan. While you celebrate the years passed with your father and sister, rejoice in your future. You will bathe in Solara's Light," he flicked up an eyebrow, "and in the appreciation of a master who could not be prouder of the woman you have become."

Three years prior, she might have screamed with exhilaration at such an unexpected gift, but Master Mitwah didn't cater to outbursts, and she wouldn't embarrass him in the company of these strangers.

"Thank you so much, Master."

"You are welcome, Roshan. As the others meditate, please don your robe. Though you will only wear it in the confines of this room until your destiny someday calls, I hope it will bring you much growth in the Light."

Roshan shivered again and glanced at the silent figures as she accepted the robe. She dared not inspect them, for such violations without their explicit leave would be uncouth, but her curiosity bordered on explosive when she focused on the one furthest from her in the circle.

Though he was humanoid, the tips of two long teeth protruding from the top row pressed indentations in his bottom lip. She sensed suddenly that he, and not the dank basement air, was the source of her chill upon entering the room.

*A shadow creature! A true vampire!*

The gray pallor of his face contrasted with spots of color in his cheeks. He opened his eyes and turned his purple irises in her direction. His expression remained level as he gave a curt nod and closed them again. The corners of his mouth hinted at a smile.

When she was sure none of them watched, Roshan stripped to her underthings and donned the robe. Its power infused her blood the moment it draped over her. She tied it off in the front, noting how it split from her mid thighs, leaving her legs exposed. Wonderment as to its revealing nature washed across her thoughts, but she reasoned the split allowed better mobility. If this robe was based on the designs used by the healers of yore, it only made sense.

Master Mitwah opened his eyes then gestured to the

unoccupied pillow on the floor beside him, across from the vampire.

She sat and tucked the robe under her to prevent her shame.

Master Mitwah spoke in a clear but hushed tone as he addressed them all. "As we act in the shadow to serve the Light, I'm struck by the irony of my task. Roshan, of the ancient and esteemed Clan Fortwan, today becomes an entrusted servant of our goddess, Solara. With the blessings she is about to receive, she becomes a woman in the eyes of our goddess and will henceforth stand accountable for her actions.

"I have counseled my protégé in the responsibilities of entering the priesthood, and she professes awareness of her responsibilities to the goddess from this day forth. Say you so, Roshan?"

She nodded reverently, excitement warming her blood with each pump of her heart. "So I say, in the name of Solara."

"And you acknowledge that, for as long as you draw breath, the ritual you undertake shan't be revealed from thine lips, for your magic binding to Solara is a personal and blessed thing between you and the energies of Enora?"

*That, and channeling mana would have me executed.*

She'd practiced these lines with her master enough times for them to roll from her tongue, and yet they felt foreign on her lips among new company.

"Never shall the sacred ritual be known outside these walls by my words, Master Mitwah."

"Then let the blessings be given that allow you to grow in the power of the Light."

The woman of fiery locks next to her blinked each eye as if inspecting her without permission. Roshan squinted over to her master at this offense, but he nodded acceptance as one side of his lips ticked up. Somehow his expression set her mind at ease.

At a sudden pulsing in the muscles of her arms and legs, Roshan tensed and jerked. Master Mitwah reached out and placed a hand on her bent knee, again nodding. The room tilted and eased straight. The woman nodded at Master Mitwah.

Relief filled her as the imposing sensation passed, leaving behind it a surging fullness in her chest.

The long-toothed man opened his eyes just as the woman closed hers. Again, her head pulsed in acceptance of his blessing, but a cold sensation filled her veins this time. Mitwah squeezed her knee harder, as if in reinforcement and support, then pulled his hand away. Roshan couldn't recall her master ever touching her, except when grasping her hands, but she found his support calming. The pale man lowered his head.

The man of coppery complexion ticked his head up and began his work, and she was filled by an even stronger surge of empowerment.

Then, the ceremony for which she'd waited, though among unexpected company, was over.

"I bestow upon you the title of Apprentice," Master Mitwah said with a smile. "Welcome to the priesthood."

"Thank you, Master."

Master Mitwah stood and gestured for the others to follow as he paced toward the steps. "Roshan, wait here as I show our guests out."

She nodded, but it occurred to her as the other priests and the priestess fell in line behind him to climb the narrow stairs, that Master Mitwah had not introduced them. Her attention leapt to their bags when she heard the distinctive clatter of gems jostled together.

*The gems I've harvested all these years?*

Setting the thought aside and trusting in the wisdom of the man who'd taken her under his wing and taught her patience and bravery, she closed her eyes and meditated in prayer to the esteemed goddess of the Light. A new sense of power coursed through every vein.

1

Roshan, gone.

She moved farther away with every passing moment we spent in that gods-forsaken forest. The governor's men who'd burst into the inn room and taken her woke my wrath. Now I intended to administer some rather ugly justice. When I caught up to her, people were going to fucking die.

In the meantime, I had aggression to disburse.

My hands choked the staff like a baseball bat. I rolled it in tiny circles over my shoulder as I eyed my target, stepped into the motion, then swung for the fences.

"Of all the *stupid—*"

*Thwak!*

"—shit I've done in my life!"

Text floated above my target's head as it launched from the tree branch and careened into the thick underbrush with a squeal.

*Critical hit!*

I eyed the bottom center of my heads-up display, or HUD, which I'd customized so combat messages displayed three lines of text at a time.

*Mortal Wound!*
*You have vanquished a Level 1 Squirrel.*
*13 XP*
*You have gained +1 to your Stealth skill.*
*Dark Alignment +1*
*Alignment: Light +47*

When I'd first changed the text log, messages swamped my screen. Even though the blur of the outside world cleared when I focused beyond them, the clutter proved annoying. The way the lines of text rolled like turning scrolls was cool, but I liked this new layout better. Tweaking it so I only received preferred messages took an hour of trial and error in the gods-forsaken woods.

But who needed to see the damage inflicted in a cumbersome log when floating combat text above my target's head reported the same?

My OCD fired on all cylinders.

"A squirrel, my love?"

I shot a glance over one shoulder at my half-elf companion, who ambled along the narrow dirt path about twenty feet away.

"Hey, at least I got a stealth rank-up."

*Even if I lost a point of alignment.*

"That's wonderful." But Priya's tone contradicted her words. Errant shadows cast by the tree canopy above danced across her angular but delicate features. She nudged a rock with the toe of her boot. "But they've done nothing to offend. Besides, they're cute. Why kill cute things?"

Another target clutched a nut between its greedy little paws on the ground nearby. I activated my stealth and advanced on the little bugger, this time envisioning a wild croquet stroke.

"Because I'm pissed off."

I wound up, stepped into my swing and—

*Thwak!*

*Critical hit!*
*You have vanquished a Level 1 squirrel.*
*11 XP*
*Dark Alignment +1*
*Alignment: Light +46*
*Priya's disposition with you has decreased by 1.*
*Current disposition: Beloved*
*499/500*

Priya cringed. "Yes, I sense that, but I don't believe these innocent creatures are the source of your anger. Hmm?" A thin eyebrow ticked up on one side.

I huffed and high-stepped over a tangled mess of ground cover. "Fucking vines."

"The yearning in my chest is distressing enough without your unnecessary violence toward inconsequential foes."

A creeping sense of emptiness tempered the anger I used to suppress my longing for Roshan. Priya's emotions had me bouncing back and forth between hers and mine.

The trait first manifested when we resurrected in the village that morning. Priya's compounded sense of fear and loss had crawled through my gut as I embraced her. At first I'd thought it was just empathy. Then, when she'd become angry, a tightness filled my chest, my teeth clinched, and I realized a supernatural bond had formed.

*More surprises. Thanks, Enora.*

Death was *traumatic* enough, and the resurrection sickness was no ballgame, either. According to the A.I. who welcomed us back to the world, the sickness would get worse each time we experienced it. That wasn't an attractive proposition, considering I'd quaked like a car crash victim the first time. But then Priya had resurrected next to me and the strange, unnamed magic crashed over us in an invisible wave—a real clincher to what had already started out a shitty day.

"I grew up in these woods, Gemini. I hunt the wildlife because it feeds me. I don't share the royal appreciation of hunting for sport, nor do I take out my anger on innocent beasts."

But it wasn't like I was killing real animals, here. It was a game world. These things re-spawned.

She caught up and fell in step next to me though she required much longer strides to keep pace. I slowed as a question occurred.

"Are you telling me you've never noticed the animals in the forest reappear after you kill them?"

Her dimpled chin jerked up as if I'd yanked her thought train to a halt by the caboose. "Reappear? What nonsense is that?"

*Wait a chicken-roasting second! Priya lives in these woods. Hunted here for years. How was it she didn't notice beasts spawning again after she'd hunted them?*

I reminded myself Priya couldn't conceive of video games. She lacked the technological reference. No matter her apparent intelligence and intuition, she wasn't primed for that kind of thinking. She'd been born in Enora—not created by coders, but as offspring of digital beings coded many generations before. She wasn't some static NPC who handed out quests and stood idle while she awaited the next player to arrive for a reward or seek the same quest as the last.

But I was from the outside world. Simple game concepts such as spawning creatures in an area where their last iteration died were commonplace. This illustrated a major difference between us and reminded me there were rules against certain disclosures between players and their NPC companions. The system warned when I trod dangerous ground and, while I could change an illicit subject with a few words to skirt the hefty XP penalty, screwing around often wasn't worth the cost. And guessing wrong could be catastrophic. This discussion, however, was all about in-game mechanics. I wouldn't have to mention the outside world or my previous life.

*But let's keep an eye out for prompts, hey?*

I scanned the forest floor and low branches for a new target to use for a demonstration. The game certainly couldn't penalize me for what it allowed NPCs to see for themselves.

A few days ago, I would've sucked the juice out of a two-pound lemon for a few level-one mobs to kill, but there'd been no damned squirrels then, so my first combat involved the pincers of a four-foot-tall spider two levels higher than me.

And I hated spiders.

*I wonder if Enora added these furry little shits after she saw how close I came to biting it. I mean, isn't that what an A.I. would do? Adapt the game for future players based on the hardships of the previous? Give them a little breathing room as they acclimated themselves to a new reality?*

"Come here, babe." I released her hand and motioned for her to stand idle. I activated stealth and approached another squirrel.

*He chokes up the bat, steps into his swing, and...*
*Thwak!*

*Critical hit!*
*You have vanquished a level 1 squirrel.*
*12 XP*
*Dark Alignment +1*
*Alignment: Light +45*
*Priya's disposition with you has decreased by 1.*
*Current disposition: Beloved*
*498/500*

Without hesitation, Priya threw out a double-thumbs-up—a gesture she'd learned from me during one of my sarcastic moments—and adopted a tone of feigned appreciation.

"Oh *yes*, my liege." She added a slow gentle clap reserved for golf fans in my old world. "Bravo, your lordship. Heroics such as there must be immortalized in the finest of poetic prose."

She slapped a hand to her chest and beat it with splayed fingers

"How my heart erupts at your majestic chivalry."

She threw in a long, idolizing sigh.

"How I shall elicit wonder from my grandchildren at the retelling of this tale."

She snapped her fingers and her eyes flared.

"I shall write to King Luttrell! His majesty would be remiss to deny you commendation for the defense of his kingdom against such fearsome beasts."

Reaching into the brush, I fished the squirrel out by the tail and dropped it on the ground between us. I raised an index finger and flicked my wrist to point at the carcass. "Watch, oh, Queen of Snark."

"Queen of what?"

I thrusted two fingers toward my eyes, then the squirrel corpse.

"Will his lordship stare it back to life? Is Roshan not our lone priestess who can raise the dead? What power hast thou hidden?"

"Your refined language is about to stick in your throat and make you choke."

About a minute passed before the animal faded and vanished.

Priya's head slammed into reverse. "How did you do that?"

"You've lived in the forest for how long?" I asked, shaking my head.

"All my life, but I only remember these last years, as you well know. Now answer me!"

I waxed creative. "When an animal dies, it journeys into the Nether—or whatever you'd call it—and Solara recycles its energy. I noticed it when I first killed a beast here." The second part was a white lie to forego questions about my origins for which I had no acceptable answers.

Or legal ones.

There was a certain irony in how my narrative supported preexisting beliefs, a central tenant to theology on Earth. Once agnostic, I now lived in a world where I knew god existed... she just happened to be digital.

Priya's expression screwed up in confusion, but her strange vibe pricking at my mind communicated distress.

I pointed at the tree branch where I'd struck the squirrel, though I wasn't certain that was the spawn point. When I'd killed a porcupunk nearby just days before, it'd faded back into existence near the same bush where it'd initially appeared, so I dared an educated guess.

"Patience."

She dropped her hands. We stared. The longer we stood there, the more I feared I'd look like an idiot. Warm relief washed over me a moment later when a squirrel appeared on the branch from which I'd evicted the previous tenant. A smile tugged at the corners of my mouth.

Priya's hand clutched her robe so it wrinkled in the center of her chest. "You are a witch!"

The squirrel's twitching nose froze and its head snapped around at her outburst. It scurried to a safer height.

"I think the male version is a warlock."

"Not funny!" Priya growled. "How did you do that?"

"All I did was wallop a squirrel. How is it you've lived here your whole life and have never noticed this?"

"You take your gift of recollection for granted while mine measures the years of a child's, unless you've forgotten."

I winced and rubbed my hand in a small circle between her shoulder blades. "I forget about your memory. I'm sorry."

She nodded, and we paced up the trail.

*Priya's disposition with you has increased by 2.*
*Current disposition: Beloved*
*500/500*

Before Crohl had swiped her from these woods and swept her underground to do his lord's bidding, Priya had been kidnapped by another minion of the dark underlord

Caym, with whom I'd shared select threats via a magic picture frame two days earlier.

The story nagged at me. If Caym wanted her, why not just have her taken to his stronghold, fiery pit, or wherever he dwelled in the first place? If the shadow essence she contained was of such value to him, then why not just get it done? Why not carry the glass globe in which Crohl imprisoned her to his dark domain? Was it because Crohl had used her as a taskmaster to manage the beings who tunneled beneath the Dark Wood? Was the journey long?

Priya's memory of her captivity was spotty and of little help. Her unsteady energy tugged at my chest. It was like having two people in one body. I busied her mind with a question in hopes a distraction would lighten the load she was unwittingly dropping on my psyche.

"Do you skin animals immediately after you kill them?"

She nodded. "Zhara taught me."

"Walk me through it."

"Your expressions are strange. Are you asking me to tell you how I skin animals?"

I nodded.

"I place my hand on the slain beast, say a word of thanks to Solara, then skin it with a knife. On our first few hunts, my stomach hadn't taken well to the plentiful blood from my misshapen knife strokes. The wretched scent made me sick. But repetition and practice both desensitized me and lessened my mistakes. Moving fast helped, too, as I found myself focused more on the process than my disgust. It's best to act with purpose and accuracy. Otherwise, other predators might sniff out my work before it's done."

"What about your magic ward? Isn't it supposed to keep predators at bay?"

Priya huffed. "Yes, silly man. But it seems unfair to use

it against defenseless animals. Where's the sport in that?" Her lips pursed.

"I thought you weren't into the royal hunting for sport."

"That is a totally different thing. I'm talking about working for what I eat. It's a question of honor."

"Hmm. I can respect that."

But it still didn't answer my question, so I rolled it over in my brain. If she cut into a beast before it vanished, its corpse might stick around longer, and she might not see the remnants disappear. Skinned animals might not vanish at all. My insatiable curiosity to understand everything about my new worlds' S.O.P.s created more questions than answers.

"Did you usually hunt in the same areas? Did you ever go back and find their corpses picked clean by predators?"

"I'm not a monster, Gemini!" She slapped the back of my hand.

I tilted my head to one side. "What do you mean?"

"I don't leave them in the open to rot! I bury them!"

This wasn't my day. My shoulders dropped as I let out a long sigh. Why add to her distress? Clocking squirrels with the staff wasn't brightening my mood over losing my healer and friend, anyway.

A squirrel chose that moment to skitter across the path about twenty feet ahead.

Holding Roshan's staff in both hands, my gaze skimmed the knotted weapon.

### ***Staff of Endless Bounties***

*Level 8*
*Slot: Weapon*
*Type: Two-handed Staff*
*Quality: Uncommon*

*Durability: 47 of 50*
*Damage: 10-14*
*Light magic +3*
*Increases the chance you will find magic items by 9%*
*Intensifies the power of light spells by 2%*
*Soulbound to Roshan, Clan Fortwan*

Roshan had been the only one of us with the foresight to secure her weapon before crawling into bed at the inn. It slid through the opening in the top and into the black void. My inventory pane popped up on the right and confirmed it was stashed.

"I didn't mean to bark at you," Priya said. "About burying the animals."

"I'm sorry, too. I was just distracting myself with the squirrels. I guess I'm trying to distract you from my stupidity, too."

"You're not stupid, Gemini." Her tone indicated I was an idiot for thinking I was an idiot. "Roshan decided her binding could wait until morning. You wanted her to have time to think about her point allocations. No one before showed her this kind of respect. They made decisions for her. Empathy and stupidity do not equate.

That made me feel a little better, but didn't quite satiate my hunger for self-abuse because I'd made other mistakes. "We're only traipsing along this path for the second time and giving those sell-sword bastards who took Roshan a gaping head start because I didn't bind us to the inn." I kicked at a rock, missed, then stumbled.

*You have learned a new skill!*
### Idiot
*Whenever you do stupid things, you appear stupid.*

*Your **Idiot** skill is rank 1.*
*Charisma -1*
*Effect Duration: 10 minutes*

I peered up at the leaves blocking the sky.
*Fuck you, too, lady.*
Maybe the A.I. was trying to cheer me up.
Priya gripped my hand. With another long sigh, I gave hers a consoling squeeze. Her tension barely waned, and it was unfortunate I could tell.

"Blaming yourself won't get us there any faster. And what of me? I lay in that bed with you, reveling in the warmth of my companions one moment, unprepared for conflict at the next. Why didn't I use my Sleep spell? My weakness has cast our companion into peril because I lay unready to fight for her. Solara blesses me with such inspiring companions and I..." she pressed a finger of her free hand to her lips, searching for the right words.

*Shit the bed? Flubbed it? You got nothing on me, sister.*

I was thankful our link was emotional and she couldn't read my mind. "Take your own advice. Blaming yourself won't bring her back. Would you kill a dragon with your bare fists?"

She shook her head. "The depravity of the human spirit continues to astound me. Despite Zhara's warnings, I still find myself surprised by acts of men who sell their decency for power and coin. Men like Crohl." She turned those sea-blue eyes on me as she pushed out her bottom lip. "The innkeeper seemed so kind. Are you certain he was complicit?"

*For a woman whose mind was wiped, she has a hell of a vocabulary.*

The thought reminded me of a unique quest in my log:

### *Not on the Up-And-Up*

*Your wonderings about Zhara's true motives could serve you.
Find out the true nature of Zhara's relationship with Priya
Skyy.*
*Level: N/A*
*XP: Commensurate with your level at the time of completion
A blessing granting you one full level*

A quest promising a whole level enticed me, but I didn't even know where to start. Maybe there would be bread-crumbs to follow.

Meantime, I gazed at Priya and considered amnesia victims in my old world. People lost their memories but still knew how to tie their shoes and use words they'd always spoken. Enorians like my companion seemed governed by similar rules, even if magic caused her fugue.

"Gem?"

"What's that?" I asked. "Oh, right. The innkeeper. Hell, yes. I'm sure someone involved him, whether under threat or by choice, motivated by coin or a promise of the *governor's* favor. Simple logic proves it. There was no ruckus prior to their arrival. Did you notice the door didn't splinter when they kicked it in? It was all for show. They had a key."

"You speak true, my liege."

"I wish you'd call me Gemini more often."

Priya swung my hand in longer arcs. "But my pure adoration for my lord guides my tongue to respect thee." She planted a clumsy kiss on my cheek and chuckled at her mockery. "I *do* adore you."

Adored in two days. I'd have scoffed at the idea if I didn't reciprocate. I wondered if our love at the cave or the inn the previous night had played a role in this sharing of emotions. Bonded us, somehow. "I feel the same, although adore is too weak a word."

A new emotion bled into the surrounding air.

"Does it give you pause, Gemini, the speed at which we have become endeared to each other? Is it unusual?" A nervous wrinkling crept across her forehead. "I sense hesitation in you."

*So much for hiding that.*

I reminded myself I no longer lived in a world where pretension was as natural as the wind, where people had to do their mental mating dances before they could profess feelings for one another. I'd weirded out enough women in my former life to appreciate one where two beautiful creatures could adore me in a couple hours. But I couldn't say any of that to Priya.

"Did my poisoned wood-elf lips leave a burn?"

I jerked away the two fingers pressed against the spot on my cheek where Priya had planted her kiss.

"Your lips leave the blessings of your warmth indelibly tattooed on my soul."

She spat projectile laughter. "Pffft. You swell with poop."

"Do you mean to say, I'm full of shit?"

"Yes." She nodded with enthusiasm. "That's what I meant."

"Well, your 'pure adoration for your lord' swells equally with feces."

I noticed a trend in Priya's speech patterns. Though she still spat formal usages with regularity, she'd added more contractions to her dialogue. I wondered whether that was adaptive programming inserted into binary genetic code generations ago.

I was a nerd like that.

I popped her on the bottom. "Besides, I've been accused of worse."

Priya jumped, rubbed her round backside, and scowled. "Bastard."

Something skittered across the trail and I flinched.

### *Squirrel*
*Level 1*

"No more squirrels," Priya said.

"I'm not going to kill the squirrel."

"Thank you."

A new emotional wave punched me in the gut. "I can feel you worrying about her."

"I do worry. Is that strange?"

"Hell, no. I'm sick over it." I slipped my arm around her waist, and she grasped my hand. "If it makes you feel any better, I think the governor wants his Eastern prize intact. The ruffian I found manhandling her at the lake—you know, the one she stabbed—hadn't wanted to leave a mark. He'd as much as said so. At the Inn, the governor's men weren't rough with her, either. I think we can take small comfort in the extremes they've gone to *not* to harm her. As a bounty, I think a concubine is worth more without scars and bruises."

Priya stopped in the trail's center, spun out of my grasp, and scowled. "How can you speak as if it's a trifle that a woman would be kidnapped, dragged so far from her home, then sold into bondage? That such a majestic creature would be treated like a rare artifact and not scratched to keep her value?"

"You mistake my emotional suppression for indifference." I kept my tone low. "Don't equate me with those bastards. You've been walking on this trail for hours with me, feeling what I feel."

"Shit," Priya said.

It might have been the first time I heard her use a cuss word, unless one counted bastard, which I didn't.

"You're right." She patted my cheek. "Would you accept pleasure tonight in penance for my atrocious disregard?"

"No apology necessary."

*The fuck are you saying?*

"Good. But you still must leave the squirrels alone."

I activated stealth, jumped to the side, then crept behind her.

*You have gained +1 to your stealth skill.*

"Whoa! I skilled up!"

Priya's ears twitched and she turned, squinted, then shoved me. "Got you!"

"Nice. But hey, I gained a skill-up sneaking around you. You're not even an enemy."

"You mean to say, you needn't have killed these squirrels?"

"You would focus on that. I just told you I advanced."

Priya smiled. Correlating feelings to thoughts would take getting used to, but the shit-eating grin was unmistakable.

"You were screwing with me."

She nodded. "Now, come. I'll assist you. Pass me by, undetected."

It seems we were both hunting distractions.

I faded from view again and slipped into the bushes at the foot of a nearby tree. When she paced ahead, her blonde curls danced on her shoulders as she swiveled her head to search for me over each shoulder. I slipped past her a few feet ahead.

*+1 Stamina*

"Bonus," I muttered.

Priya lunged and shoved me with both hands. One ankle crossed the other, and my ass hit the dirt. Hard. I huffed, awaiting a burst of high-pitched laughter and the accompanying shoulder bouncing. When it didn't happen, I peered up to find her high elven cheekbones tugging at her cheeks, her eyes wide, her mouth agape.

Priya extended her finger. "Gem."

I stole a glance over my shoulder but saw only the thin line of bare earth dividing swaths of low grass. Then a scratching sound drew my attention, and my eyes panned from the trail into the trees where they settled on a massive knot on the side of a nearby oak.

*Did that just move?*

I craned my neck forward and tilted my head to one side. My ears itched as a low, vibrating hum filled them. The sound crackled and became a dry growl. Chips of bark crumbled to the ground in a shower as a clawed hand ripped away from the wide trunk and the head I'd mistaken for a huge knot twisted. Two orange eyes glared in my direction.

The creature descended headfirst, with long claws leaving deep gashes in the tree's woody flesh. Scaly gray skin stretched around hard muscles working across the thick shoulder blades of the hairless beast.

"What the..." I started.

"It's a—"

### *Vellick*

*Level 10 Beast*

*These tree-dwelling beasts boast pigment in their scales that act as camouflage. Often called "Tree Demons" by natives because of their glowing eyes and humanoid forms, they are not undead or underworld creatures.*

For once the system message provided some details about my target, but I found I'd rather not have known.

The newer Bow of the Light constructed for me by the Matron of the Wood hadn't been soulbound because Enora was a burning pain in my ass where nothing was simple. So, when I scurried to my feet and whipped around, it was my low-level bow I shrugged off my shoulder and down my arm. Luckily, I'd stuffed it in my bag for sale to a vendor in Brumhill before the actions of assholes altered my plans.

The vellick dropped the final few feet to the ground hands first, then planted its clawed feet. It crouched there, glowing orange eyes flicking between Priya and me. When it pushed itself onto its hind legs, it stood half-a-foot taller than I. Its long, wiry arms ended in scaly hands with long fingers reaching to its knees like an ape. Before our eyes, the hue of its skin transitioned from bark gray to grass green.

Just as my fingers brushed an arrow fletching at my hip, it leapt.

I dodged to one side, but too late. Pain ripped its way up my torso. Warm blood spread across my shirt. My bow clattered to the ground. Pivoting to face the creature, I quickly scanned the bottom of my HUD.

*Vellick performs* **Rake**
*-49 HP*
*-13 HP (bleed)*

It stood between Priya and me, but focused on me.

"Run, Priya." I muttered.

She scurried off the trail without further coaxing.

The creature sniffed through a flat nose, little more than two holes on a bump. It tilted its head to one side, sniffed again, then scanned me from high to low. The beast stretched its arms out to its sides and clicked its claws against its palm in sequence. Over its shoulder, Priya scaled a tree with a deft nimbleness I hadn't expected but probably should have.

Afraid reaching for my bow would bring the lanky thing down on me, I clutched the rapier shoved into my belt. It was a low-level weapon but it was what I had.

*You are now a level 10 Fighter*

The beast launched just as the weapon came free. Rather than trying to evade, I lunged and shoved the rapier out in front of me. The beast spun in a blur, avoiding the blade, and razor claws sliced into my left shoulder.

*Vellick performs* **Rake**
*-40 HP*
*-14 (bleed)*
*-9 (bleed)*
*Health: 47%*

*Shit!*

My health was dropping way too fast. I lunged backward to evade the reach of those long arms as it swiped again. Pain seared my muscles, rendering every movement a struggle. My adversary swung wide, and I ducked. The wind from its attack breezed through my hair as I took another step back and poked with the rapier to keep it at bay.

"What the hell do you want?" But I already knew the answer. Even though the vellick appeared to be humanoid, my HUD referred to it as a beast. It wanted one thing.

To kill me.

*Health:* 44%

So far, it was doing a bang-up job! Giving it a real college try!

The beast feinted toward me, and when its eyes followed my poorly placed jab with the point of my rapier, its body easily darted out of the way. It had measured me and lured me into a stupid move. It lunged around the blade and swiped in an upstroke. Only by the grace of extra points I'd spent on Dexterity did I escape what would've been a deathblow to my throat.

I circled the beast as blood poured from my torso. Coldness enveloped my shoulder and ran down my arm, leaving it numb.

A long hiss emanated from the vellick's nostrils, and clear fluid ran down to its scaly, lipless mouth.

I stabbed again, but it dodged.

"Gah! My fucking shoulder!"

We circled, and I leaned hard toward the left. My muscles seized again so I couldn't stand erect. What I would've given for a proper sword and the training to use it. The rapier would not do the job, and I sure as hell couldn't get to my bow, draw an arrow, then fire before the vellick was on me.

*Mental note: Weapons training. Now.*

A frame of orange, flashing light circled my vision. The

function I'd found in my combat options told me when I dropped below forty percent HP. There's was no way I'd miss that.

*Health: 37%*

A dim light grew over the creature's shoulder, but I dared not divert my eyes. Despite the pain, I shook with the adrenal response bringing my body into hyper focus. The beast swung a long arm, and I ducked, but my body refused to cooperate with the extra stress through my slashed anatomy, and I landed on my backside.

*I should've summoned Click, dammit. Note to self, always summon your pet when in the wilds!*

To its credit, the system didn't give me any idiot points.

*Health: 27%*

The creature dropped its arms and stood tall, staring down at me. Another hiss erupted from its nostrils and its mouth gaped into a black grin displaying long yellow fangs. He was beyond the reach of my rapier as I sat on my duff, but I was also out of his range and wanted to keep it that way.

I cast a spell with a two-second casting time. The creature stared at me contemplatively and then tried to step forward.

*You cast **Vine Entrapment.***

Thick vines erupted from the grassy earth and encircled the beast's legs.

*Vellick is bound.*

A piercing squeal of rage erupted from the beast's gaping jaws as I threw my free arm across my chest wound and struggled to my feet. The light behind the beast vanished, and the vellick's head dropped. It hovered in a circle from toes to heels and back as the vines grasped its legs to the knees. Little green Zs chained above its head.

*Priya casts **Sleep.***
*Vellick is sleeping.*

My gaze shot to the tree she'd climbed to find her scurrying down, easily gripping branches then dropping the final few feet.

Health: 17%

She sped across the path and onto the grassy land before me. "Get a health potion!"

As I nodded and reached into my bag, she began to pull her shirt over her head.

"What are you doing?" I asked.

*Sleep effect ends.*

The vellick's eyes blinked open. They flared with anger, and it hissed. I gaped over Priya's shoulder as my vines untethered from the beast and slithered into the earth. A clawed, scaly hand raised high over Priya's head as the beast prepared to strike.

My legs tensed as my instincts urged me to lunge forward and push Priya out of the way, but then a bright glow of golden light reflected off the vellick's face. The monster dropped its arm to its side with a leathery slap and stared. A low whine that sounded like a whimpering dog's escaped its throat.

I sighed and sucked down a large health potion. "You're a genius."

With her arms crossed over her breasts as her glowing ward sedated the beast, she shook her head in derision.

"If I was a genius, I would have exposed my ward in the first place. What now?"

I peered down at my HUD.

*Health: 67%*

I raised the rapier and stepped around her. "Now I'll run the bastard through."

"You will do no such thing," a low, feminine voice said behind me.

I spun around, rapier at the ready, then froze. The tall woman with flowing blonde hair not unlike my companion's peered past me at the charmed beast.

Priya and I spoke her name simultaneously.

"Zhara."

2

The Matron of the Wood swept an indifferent hand in front of the vellick's face and the creature turned away. It sank its claws into the bark of a thick pine with needles that glowed, turned a final time to peer at Priya's ward, and then at Zhara. Although the muscles of its hard face didn't curve into expressions, its eyes shone with desire.

"Go, for you are one of mine, beast." Zhara said. A dull yellow glow filled her eyes.

The vellick turned and climbed the tree.

"If that thing is one of yours, I might have misconstrued you," I said.

"Come," the Matron said. "My home is close."

*I guess that's the end of that discussion.*

As we paced away from the scene of yet another near-death experience, Zhara cast a *healing over time* spell to aid in my recovery. It was like being washed in a warm honey bath, but it only ticked twice before my jagged cuts sealed.

"Where did you come from?" I asked.

"I think you know the answer to that question."

I sighed. "How come that thing wasn't here the first time I passed through these woods?"

I suspected I'd already addressed the answer, internally.

*Because Enora adapted to my level.*

Zhara had a different answer. "The vellick feed on other tree-dwellers and rarely come to ground. Priya's ward and your own essence presented ample reason to make an exception."

"Then why does my interface say they enjoy human flesh?"

"It is not my place to question Solara, nor is it yours, boy."

"What does Solara have to do with it?"

"Where do you think your interface comes from?"

I sighed. Everything came from Solara. Solara was Enora.

She swirled a finger in the air. "Continue your prowling practice. It would seem you need it."

"Gee, thanks."

She shrugged. "It would do my conscience service to see the man I entrusted with my family approach his quest with seriousness. A perilous road winds ahead."

I activated stealth and scurried behind Priya. "Happy now?"

Zhara didn't answer.

"He can practice later," Priya said. Though she apparently couldn't see me as she peered over her shoulder, she addressed me next. "We are almost there, Gemini."

I pushed my lips close to her ear. "Cool!"

She about jumped out of her boots. Throwing a hand against her chest, she turned, detected me—breaking my stealth—then sneered.

"I enjoy aiding you in your skill development, but

spooking me is unacceptable... my *liege*. Grow up!"

"Okay, I'll stop spooking you if you stop calling me your *liege*. Deal?" I thrust my hand out.

Priya shook her head. Taut muscles suppressed her smile and rendered our emotional link extraneous. She slapped my hand away. "I decline your offer. You are my bound lord. You saved my life, and we have cemented our bond with our love... twice. Now, as you like to say, deal with it." She turned her attention back to the narrow path. Ahead, Zhara's long golden curls blew in the wind, and we scurried to catch up.

Then, in a true expression of my maturity, I goosed Priya's ass, activated my stealth, and returned to the vine-covered overgrowth just off the trail. I loved touching her butt.

Priya jumped and grabbed her backside. "Roshan is right about you! You're incorrigible... my *liege*."

"The two of you are like children," Zhara mumbled. "How will you ever drive darkness from the world while you gallivant like adolescent wolves who've discovered the second use of their loins?"

I rounded the next curve and stopped next to the largest oak I'd ever seen. The first time I'd encountered it had been at night. The second time, I almost passed it by as if it held some kind of subliminal camouflage. But now that I knew what I was looking for, it was like a skyscraper among townhouses.

This was Zhara's place.

I hid near the tree, waiting for Priya to round the corner so I could pounce again, but as she came around and I stepped closer to the trail, Zhara appeared. Her gaze homed in on me, then she threw a hand against my chest and shoved me.

"Ah!" Spinning, I stumbled on tangled ground cover then face planted. Grumbling as I wiped pebbles and soil off my elbows, I peered down at my dirt-covered clothes.

*Your idiot skill has increased to rank 2.*
*-1 Charisma (2)*
*Effect duration: 10 minutes*

*So much for a high dexterity rating.*

When I got to my hands and knees, I glared at the Matron of the Wood over one shoulder. The mystical woman stood tall, with her shoulders back, her bare breasts covered only by wavy locks of thick golden hair. Her full lips wore a smile, and a fleshy bark colored the same as the tree behind her shrouded her fruit.

"Therefore, you must practice."

I spat dirt then ran my forearm over my lips. "Thank you, Zhara."

"Now, why does an assassin wield a staff?" Zhara asked.

Considering I'd stowed the staff in my bag before the vellick attack, I knew Zhara had seen us coming from quite the distance. I wondered what ability allowed this sight and at the limits of its range, but then my thoughts turned to why she hadn't helped sooner.

The way she answered questions, I lacked the patience to ask. This day had been shitty enough. But that didn't mean I had to answer hers, either.

"I have my reasons," I replied.

I used my interface to check Zhara out.

**Zhara**
*Matron of The Wood*
*Level??*

*Guardian of the Tree of Solara and keeper of the mana-rich
ley lines intersecting the Dark Wood, Zhara is the beloved
servant of the goddess herself.*

Zhara flashed me a look and projected one of her tele-
kinetic thoughts into my head.

*Surely, I present better options for your eyes than what
your interface offers.*

Did I mention Zhara was a persistent flirt?

She turned to Priya. "Visits on consecutive days? Such
honor you bestow on your old—"

"Am I unwelcome, aunt?" Priya interrupted, snickering
at me as I untangled my feet from the vines.

Priya called herself a half-wood-elf, but my interface
labeled her simply a half-elf. When I ran a check on Zhara,
it didn't display her race.

The servant of Solara threw her hair over her shoulders
to reveal her fleshy handfuls, so my eyes gravitated there.

Although Priya wasn't the jealous type, the shot of
emotion she fired across my bow when she detected my
lusty gaze was unmistakable.

*Shit. She's already wielding it like a weapon.*

I glanced away to find my companion squinting at me as
she stepped into Zhara's waiting arms.

Zhara rocked Priya back and forth in her grasp as Priya
lay her head high on her aunt's chest. Though the familial
resemblance was undeniable, Zhara stood more than a head
taller. Priya had her beat on the curves, though.

A halo of light enveloped them and though it didn't
extend to me, the tension in my shoulders slipped away and
a calming breath left my lungs.

I checked Priya's avatar on my HUD as a new icon of a
golden halo appeared.

### *Quiet Grace*
*Calms the target for one hour*
*+5 Magic Affinity*
*+5 Magical Defense*

As the calm washed over me, I wondered if this was the same spell she'd cast the first time I spied her in these woods as I woke during a thunderstorm. Then I recalled I never received the buff. Only Priya enjoyed the Magic affinity and defense increases, now. Checking my hands for a glow, I tilted my head in wonderment.

Then it hit me why I was feeling an effect not cast on me.

*Priya's the conduit. When her emotions calmed, I relaxed.*

"I sensed your distress, Priya," she said. "And yours, Gemini. Tell me, has it something to do with Roshan's absence? And the fact Priya is not adorned in her robe?"

Accusatory tones aside, Priya's red robe would either be waiting at the inn in Brumhill, have been sold, or have been stolen by the men who thought they'd ended her life. No one would expect her to return from the dead to recover the article. But if it was still there, that innkeeper could bet his ass she would reunite with it, as I would with my armor and the fancy new bow, made by Zhara herself in reward for erasing the darkness from the Tomb of the Lost.

I cocked my chin at Zhara.

"It would be nice if the gifts you gave us were soul-bound, just for future reference."

"Did Priya's betrothed fail to protect his companions at a critical time?"

*Hey, fuck you lady.*

Zhara's head swiveled toward me, though her arms held

Priya close. Her eyes flashed a white bloom, and I feared I was in for my second lesson about respect that day, having already learned one from the chiding of Enora, herself.

*Enora, Solara—depended on who was talking.*

"I will forgive your loose thoughts because I sense the depth of your feelings for Roshan." She waved a dismissive hand. "I should not have poked your predictable male ego." She glared at me, daring me to refuse the gift of her forgiveness. I envisioned a baseball diamond to confuse her. Zhara cocked her head to one side and beamed. Then she pursed her lips and turned her gaze to the top of Priya's head, which she kissed.

"So, it is as I've feared. Roshan was taken from you."

*As if you didn't already know this.*

She ignored my silent jab.

Priya stepped out of her aunt's grasp with pink cheeks and, the tension she'd carried in her shoulders eased. For that, I was thankful.

Zhara grasped my emotions like I did Priya's. "I find your gratitude appealing, Gemini. You are welcome." She sighed. "I suppose not all is lost, since it was you who made my dear child immortal. Come into my embrace." The Matron threw her long arms out with expectation.

Priya stepped aside but wore a wary glare as I stepped forward. I smiled contentedly as I hugged Zhara, just to screw with her. I squeezed good and hard, too. Then a warm glow surrounded us, and I felt my shoulders relax.

*You have received a blessing from Zhara!*
*Quiet Grace*
*+5 Magic Affinity*
*+5 Magical Defense*
*Duration: 1 Hour*

"Stop charming my beloved, Aunt Zhara. And get out of his head. I see the way your eyes talk to each other." She turned her dark glare on me. "You are sharing thoughts."

"Fine." Zhara rolled her eyes. "My gift to you, love. Henceforth, Gemini and I will speak with only our mouths."

An inaudible thump somewhere in my brain told me Zhara had vacated, but another door swung wide open as a new thought occurred.

*'Aunt' Zhara. How is it that she's Priya's aunt if she's a thousand years old? Is she a great, great, great aunt? How's that work?*

I'd just brushed over a blank area of canvas on the painting that was the mystery of Zhara and Priya, but the larger picture eluded me. It was like standing blind in a dark room as my fingers traced a shape my brain should've been able to interpret but couldn't grasp.

"You should get your own man," Priya mumbled.

"You should learn to share, greedy wench."

Priya threw up her middle finger—another gesture she'd learned from me—and I winced. But Zhara's face just wrinkled in confusion.

"Did you just call me a prostitute?" Priya asked.

The Matron raised one shoulder and tilted her head toward it. "I was hoping my smile displayed my jest, love."

"If you two are finished sniping at each other, Priya and I have a friend to retrieve from the clutches of an ass hat up north."

"Ah, yes," Zhara said. "Very sad. As I shared your pleasure whilst the two of you were off fornicating in the cave—"

"Gross!" Priya said.

"—I channeled your virile energy to help Roshan

convey the Nature discipline of the Light.

"Yes, I remember how you stroked her back as she channeled said energy," Priya said. "You are so horny, aunt. Can you not please yourself?"

"You try living in the middle of a forest, where the only passersby are rare lost youths with no mind for how to wield their tools for a matron's pleasure!" She threw me a glance. "Present company excluded." Her gaze traveled to my pants.

I felt a little tick inside my head again. Zhara wanted to hear my thoughts. It bugged me how she so easily broke her word to Priya. Morals didn't seem high on the immortal's list. Or, human ideas of morals. I envisioned yellow strawberries to block her mind intrusion.

"Zhara!" Priya barked, slapping her aunt's shoulder.

"It isn't like he showed no interest! Did your beloved not tell you that one of his possible quest rewards was an encounter with me? I forwent my physical desires in deference to you. Perhaps you could accept my grace for what it is!"

*I get the impression your grace is measured by your desires.*

Zhara smiled, but kept her attention on Priya so as not to give away her foray back into my brain.

"Tuning into my private moments is uncouth, at best," Priya said. "And it's just a wee bit creepy, don't you think?"

"Well, maybe if you're a *prude*. The young are overly sentimental about natural things."

"You're impossible," Priya said, but she dropped her shoulders and chuckled.

Priya was fucking awesome. Lax. Chill.

Zhara sighed. "If you two ever change your minds, I would love to have Gemini for a little visit."

"Not going to happen," Priya said. "Anyone but you."

"Ugh! Fine!" Zhara thrust her hands on her hips and turned my way. "You say they're taking Roshan to the governor, yes? Is this the *ass hat* of which you speak?"

"You've heard of him?" Priya asked.

"I might not leave the forest, but I'm not lost here, child. I have ways of learning what's going on in the world."

"Do you charm all the wanderers for information and sex?" I asked.

She shrugged. "Yes."

Priya gave her head a derisive shake. "Why am I not surprised?"

"Otherwise they might shoot at me."

"You're immortal!"

"Why do you two seem so different than yesterday?" I asked.

"Shut up!" they yelled in unison.

*Whoa! Okaaay...*

Zhara winked at me, reminding me she could read my thoughts like a cheap comic. I flinched. One reading my mind, the other monitoring my emotions, I itched to get the hell out of there and cut my challenges in half.

"The governor will not leave his stronghold. If he wants Roshan for his own, he will have sent many men to collect her. I wouldn't be surprised if they had a procession of carts and an armed escort. They couldn't let bandits defile his virgin prize."

It occurred to me that the thieves who kidnapped Roshan had been planning to meet the governor's men in Brumhill. They'd been so close to the finish line and their reward before we'd killed them. When the kidnappers didn't show, the mercenaries would have questioned the innkeeper. Roshan's eastern features—and extreme hotness

—made her unforgettable. She stood out. The innkeeper would have remembered her.

Zhara continued. "The roads from Brumhill to the north have become perilous, and most traveling merchants of means now take the round-about-way through the Blackstone Mountains in the West. They pay the dwarves a toll rather than take the direct route. For a king's regent, the governor doesn't do much to keep his own thoroughfares safe."

I shook my head. "Sounds incompetent. I'm not surprised."

The Matron of The Wood tapped her lips as she peered up at the lush tree canopy. "So, if they took Roshan this morning in Brumhill, it will take the governor's men a day to reach Warrington—assuming their convoy is too large for bandits to risk trifling with. From Warrington, it will take a day to reach Trowlsby. After that, count on at least six days to pass through the Plague Barrens."

I mouthed *Plague Barrens* in an unspoken question to Priya. She shrugged.

"Then they must climb the Gynas Peaks before entering the governor's seat in Modesta. While purchasable horses aren't common in Brumhill, you could catch them in Warrington, but more likely Trowlsby."

I cleared my throat. "What if they went the other way? Through the dwarves' mountains?"

"They would follow the governor's own roads. Trust me, Gemini, they will be well-equipped for conflict. Do you have gold for horses in Warrington?"

"Depends on what horses cost."

Priya shook her head. "I dwell in a forest and still know the price of horses is beyond our reach. It's like my Gemini crawled out from under a rock."

I had no response to that.

Zhara shook her head. "The price will have risen commensurately with the peril of the roads. I'd bet it has doubled." Zhara closed her eyes and pressed her lips into a thin, white line. A low hum filled my ears. Light lined the slits where her eyelids met. Leaves rustled.

I opened my mouth to say something, but I stopped when Priya raised a finger and shook her head.

Zhara's eyelids opened, and her eyes glowed white. "A merchant with a horse and cart. You could offer security for her return trip to the North." The glow dimmed and azure irises returned.

*You have been offered a quest:*
### *Thumbing a Ride*
*Objective: Find a vendor and hitch a ride to Warrington.*
*Reward: 1,500 XP*
*Would you like to accept this quest?*
*Yes/No*

I accepted the quest.

"Thank you, aunt."

"You are welcome, beloved niece. Be safe on your travels." She turned. "Come now, Gemini, give us a kiss goodbye."

Knowing the Matron was goading her niece as much as saying goodbye, I still inched forward. Priya passed me and stepped onto the trail. She spoke in a sing-song voice over her shoulder.

"Kiss her and you will only have Click's lips to enjoy until we retrieve Roshan."

I settled for a hug.

## 3

Brumhill.

Yesterday, the town was a shining beacon of my future. Sightings of the first beings I'd encountered outside the Dark Wood had filled me with a surge of enthusiasm. But without Roshan, it was a game world truck stop I planned to pass through with expediency.

First, I had business. Deal with the traitorous innkeeper, retrieve our gear, visit a weapons shop, inquire about a crash course in training, get the fuck out.

Guards in ratty half-chain armor slouched against the jagged stone bricks of a low wall. That there were only two told me the innkeeper had kept the goings on in his establishment the previous night close to his vest. The lack of increased guard count proved he expected no trouble for his complicity in a kidnapping and the murders of two visitors.

He would have pain.

In his mind, we were deceased. I wondered if he had to have our corpses removed. Were they buried? Did they wink out of existence like dead squirrels? Or did my victims vanish because I was a player and Priya's stay as NPCs?

I spared the low stone walls only a slight glance as I stated my business. We passed through unmolested, except from the guard's gaze which had given Priya a requisite going over. No doubt, he enjoyed the way her curvy body complimented the high-cut shorts and midriff-revealing top I'd found in my bag at the resurrection hub in the village earlier that day.

*Gods. We've lost half a day. They'll have departed by now. How far ahead is Roshan?*

The sun was high as we approached the Brumhill Inn. I set my hand on the door handle but rethought my plan. It wasn't complicated—I should be in and out. But everything depended on what the innkeeper knew and whether our bodies had vanished upon our deaths. If they had, the suspicions of foul magic might have prompted the inn keeper to rent security. I wasn't sure if that was how they did things in Brumhill and, if so, whether they'd hire farmhands or off-duty town guards. But when the rubber hit the road, I craved my gear, and more human obstructions would equal a higher body count. No more fucking around. I didn't suffer the Dark Levels to have a bunch of hicks impede me.

"You should wait out here and let me handle this. You're eager to use your new sleep spell, I get that. But I need him awake."

Priya laughed. "If you think I'm waiting outside, you dream vividly, adventurer."

"Funny how when you disagree with me, it's 'adventurer.'"

She ignored my quip. "Sleep is not my only spell."

"Right. Did you expect to find demonic minions inside who you would cast into a dark void?" I flicked a querulous eyebrow. "No? Then why don't you—"

"Be a good girl and wait?" She fired her patented squint

at me. I found it less endearing than usual at the moment. "I'm the one with negotiating skills, and you might need a negotiator."

"Honey, love, sweetie..."

Her lips practically vanished.

"Okay, fine. Come in. But I don't plan on negotiating. I'm here to get our gear and leave a message that people shouldn't cross us. Then we'll vacate this dark hole before that sun falls behind yon rolling hills." I pointed northwest.

"Sounds like a wonderful plan. It will set my soul alight to witness its execution with your highest level of competency." She pulled open the inn door and waved me inside. "Illuminate me with your skill."

"You're snarky today," I muttered as I passed through. "What did I get myself into?"

"Perhaps you will find out when I ravage your body in our bedrolls tonight."

"Okay, snarky works."

The sparsely-decorated lobby was vacant. I leaned over the low counter and peeked into a small room in the rear. My low-level bow slid off my shoulder, and I retrieved a simple wooden arrow from my older quiver. I slipped around the counter then waited next to the inner door.

Nocking an arrow, I drew back and aimed at the doorway. "Call him."

Priya dropped her chin in feigned amusement. "Oh, now my lord has a use for me?" She pressed her hand against her cleavage, not understanding how stressing her precious mounds destroyed any chance she'd annoy me.

"You wanted to come in. Make yourself useful."

She rolled her eyes and rose onto her tip toes to beckon toward the back. "Hello?" She wiggled her shoulders, feigning the tone of a damsel in need of aid.

"Ah, yes. Hello, miss. May I—"

The innkeeper broke the threshold between his office and the front desk and the tip of my arrow dug an impression into his cheek. As my bowstring creaked its desire for release, I sneered. "Hello, traitor."

The innkeeper raised his hands and rolled his eyes toward me in slow motion. Then he turned his attention to Priya.

Her smile was *priceless*.

"Um, m-may I h-help you?" His gaze bounced between us. "No? No. I suppose not. Um, you can take my silver. There's not much, I'm afraid. I—"

"Look again, dimwit. We were just here last night."

Sweat beaded on his balding head as he studied Priya's curves.

"Why do you still look confused? You see women like her every day?"

"Well, many beautiful—"

Priya threw her best squint. "Now he's annoying me." She glared. "Picture a red robe."

His face peeled back into a horrified expression as recognition dawned. "Oh, my. But... that's impossible!" His voice took on a strange twang. "Adventurer or not, you were dead too long to resurrect! Is it a scam? I'm the victim of a ruse!"

"Impressive," Priya said. "The way you don that accent when under duress. Do you find it serves you well with country folk? I judge, by your expression, the answer is *no*. So, how about we drop the pretense, hey?"

*Damn! You go, Priya.*

The innkeeper nodded. "Apologies, my lady, but I didn't hear the wood in your words. I would never take advantage of—"

"The wood in my words." She threw her head back and cackled, but the laugher died as abruptly as it came when she launched a death glare. "What a creative way to say he didn't perceive the bumpkin in my utterances."

I stretched my bowstring, so the wood creaked. "Measure your words, scum."

Priya set her elbows atop the faded maple of the aged counter. "My dear man, the only ruse was that you would provide us safe sleeping quarters. Those men killed us, with your help. The problem—and by *problem*, I mean *your* problem—is we didn't *stay* dead."

"This isn't possible. This... are... are you demons?"

When the short, fat, bald, ugly man turned his cheek toward me, I showed him as many teeth as my lips would allow.

"The legends are true?"

I shrugged non-committal. The fuck did I care what he believed? "Tell me you still have my gear."

The horrified stretch of his facial muscles relaxed and morphed into a more hopeful expression. "Oh, yes! Yes! In the back here! The mercs only wanted the woman!"

"Mercs?" Priya asked.

"Short for mercenaries," I replied.

She flared her eyes and donned a tone of teasing melodrama. "Such a man of the world are you, *my lord*. What great command thou holds over the lingo." She fanned herself then shifted her gaze and flicked a finger toward the innkeeper as if a thought occurred. "Why does he linger?"

The innkeeper's eyebrows inched up. "What? Why?"

Priya cupped a hand to her hip. "Get our gear, you duck fucker! Snap, snap!" She snapped her fingers. "We have places to be!"

The man twisted his head to peer at me, pressing the

arrow firmer against his cheek. I scowled. When he stepped toward the back room, I peered at Priya and mouthed, *Duck fucker?*

She shrugged.

The innkeeper was true to his word. He'd kept every article—including the new bow and arrows Zhara had given me before I reached Level 10. As we continued our short interrogation, the innkeeper explained that he'd planned to sell the items later today.

I used the opportunity to find out more about possible dealers in Brumhill. "To whom?"

"There are some less-desirables in a local watering hole who'd have been interested."

That sounded useless. If they were undesirable to him, they'd likely cut our throats for our coin, and I didn't want to linger, even less cause a scene that might draw the ire of the local authorities.

I thanked my lucky stars the mercenaries hadn't paid the gear any attention. Maybe they weren't mercs, but actual guardsmen of the governor's. It was more likely they left the gear as a reward for his loyalty, but if he admitted as much, I might have killed him, and that would screw up my alignment meter. So, I didn't ask.

I'd enjoy plausible deniability if I let him live. What demons would return from the dead but leave their betrayer alive?

He agreed with me.

Priya donned her robe in a wide lobby in my world. As she draped it over the skimpier clothes available in my bag that morning, it warmed me to see my Little Blonde Riding Hood returned to true form.

"Okay, one last thing," I said to the innkeeper.

"Anything. Name it!"

I remembered stumbling on this twentieth century show called *Happy Days*. There'd been this episode where the amiable protagonist, Richie Cunningham, had pissed off the supposed tough guy, Arthur Fonzerelli, and ended up at odds with him over a girl. So, "The Fonz" decided preserving his reputation would mean sticking Richie with a jagged pipe in the men's room at a local hangout called Arnold's, where high school students liked to eat hamburgers. This was before high school was virtual. We're talking way back.

Since the Fonz had to keep up appearances but Richie was his friend, he showed the courtesy to ask what body part he should jab. Well, just as Richie tried to make a run for it, someone pushed open the door to the restroom and slammed the door into his eye, leaving a real shiner. So, Fonzie decided he'd let everyone assume he punched Richie. He hadn't wanted to hurt his friend, anyway. The bruise gave him an excuse to take it easy on him.

When considering the innkeeper's hopeful expression, I saw an aged Richie Cunningham. He was no friend of mine, but he was a product of his lot in life. What would've happened to him if he'd denied the governor's men access?

Sometimes I hated my conscience. But an untimely vision of Roshan's face boiled the blood in my cheeks. She wouldn't want me to hurt him, despite his treachery. There would have to be compromise.

So, I crew the string on my bow and asked, "Where do you want the arrow?"

"What?"

"You say 'what' a lot. I'm asking you where you would like me to shoot you, to leave a reminder of what fate might befall you if you betray us."

He scurried back a couple steps and held out jazz

hands. "If you shoot me, I must commission a healer. Then they'll ask who shot me. What would I say?"

*Gah. The Fonz wasn't thinking about legal problems, either! Talk about your plot holes.*

I shared a glance with Priya.

She shrugged. "He has a point. We don't want pursuers."

"Hmm. You're right..." I shouldered the bow and deliberated while I scratched my chin. "Okay, asshole, listen up. Do I have your attention?"

He nodded, but his gaze shifted to Priya's face, then down to her tits.

*Mistake.*

I slapped him. If there was anything I hated about my previous life, it was when those with power bullied those without it, but considering how I'd fantasized about cutting this bastard's throat all morning long and into the afternoon, a good cuffing seemed a fair compromise.

"I asked if *I* had your attention, not if *she* did." I grinned and widened my eyes to project an extra dose of crazy, "I can understand why she would captivate you. But if you see women like her every day, you should be able to *focus!*" I thumped his forehead to stress the last word. He nodded and locked his wide eyes with mine. "Good! Now. What stories might you spread about our return from the dead?"

He blinked, and I could almost hear rusted parts turning in his skull. He wasn't the sharpest arrowhead in the quiver.

"None?" he replied.

"You asking me or telling me?"

"Um... telling you, sir?"

I glanced at Priya. "Damn, babe, he gets it."

Again, my shadow-infused lover shrugged. Roshan

often rolled her eyes when she shrugged like that. I seethed at the thought. My hands shook as I refrained from cuffing him harder.

But Priya stomped around the counter and stared at him, "One last thing."

"Yes, ma'am?"

She cocked up her chin. "Close your eyes."

"What?"

Though she glared at him, I was the target of her words. "I swear to the gods I'm gonna let you shoot him. I drew the string tighter.

"No, no no no!" the innkeeper said. He squeezed his eyes closed so deep wrinkles appeared near his temples.

Priya's tone took on the even timbre of a storyteller at a campfire. "I want you to imagine a beautiful eastern creature stolen from her home by ruffians then dragged across the sea. A devout follower of the Light, she is a vision of beauty, of only nineteen years. A priestess in the School of the Light, she must endure a journey across rough waters, surrounded by people dying of plague, including a member of her own clan. Imagine her, this innocent professor of all that is good."

Though her burning emotions rose my chest, her words had painted Roshan's troubles in my head, and I soaked up my recollection of her like a withered chamois dropped in a bucket of water.

"Can you see her, the woman we brought here when we checked in to our room?"

The innkeeper nodded.

"Good."

Priya balled up her fist and walloped him in the eye.

Hard.

*Priya attacks the innkeeper.*
*Innkeeper*
*-6 HP*

Priya shook her hand. "I should have known such a dimwit would possess such a hard skull!"

I nodded. "Thick-headed assholes often do. You need a healing potion?"

She glared at my snark, but the hint of a smile touched her lips.

To his credit, the innkeeper covered one side of his face but didn't dare peel himself from the wall. He stared at me through the other eye, injured pride evident on his face.

I leveled my gaze at him. "If anyone asks, you ran into a door. Got it?"

He nodded.

"Make yourself sound clumsy and stupid. Are we agreed?"

More nods.

"That's for letting them take our friend. Be glad you're not dead."

"I'm thankful, sir." He nodded. "Grateful, indeed. I am terrible. The worst of humanity. My betrayal is unforgivable."

We paced toward the door, eyeing him as he lobbed feigned expressions of gratitude while covering half his face with one hand. I stopped at the threshold and pivoted to face him a final time. "Hey, innkeeper."

"Yes, my lord?"

*This time, I relished the title.*

I snapped my fingers and pointed at him. He moved his hand and focused on me with both eyes. A tear fell from the bloodshot one. I channeled The Fonz. "If my healer winds up dead, Priya will use you to rank up her skinning skill, you dig?"

His lips parted as if to reply, but he bowed his head in a curt nod.

*Sparing the innkeeper has earned you 50 points of Light.*
*Alignment: Light + 387*

We paced into the dusty street. I ignored Priya's gaze for a few beats then turned, raising my eyebrows. "What?"

She peered up at me. "I know what you wanted to do to him."

"You're the one who cleaned his clock."

"Yes, but I sensed your intent. I have not acclimated to our bond enough to put the feeling into words, but... Let me rephrase." She stopped and turned to glance up and down the dusty road.

I faced her.

"Roshan, my friend, consumed my thoughts. My only wish was to retrieve her, but... the way you controlled your urge to murder that man filled me—*fills* me—with such... desire."

"I like you, Priya."

She scanned the street a second time. "So, I guess we're camping outside of town tonight?"

I nodded. "Probably a good idea. We should play it safe."

"Can we go now?"

*Yum.*

4

A quick exit wasn't in the cards, though.

Our fingers interlocked as we progressed up the main thoroughfare en route to the north gate. A breeze pushed dust devils up the deserted road, reminding me of one of the old westerns my Dad used to make me watch with him. Visions of horse hooves kicking airy dirt into the wind touched my mind as the occasional pang over my parents' absence thumped in my chest. I expected a tumbleweed to roll by at any second.

The quiet brought the air of an impending gunslinger showdown, and I peered over my shoulder, wondering if we'd overdone it with the proprietor of the Brumhill Inn.

*You're being paranoid.*

The squeak of a swinging metal sign drew my attention. I tugged Priya's hand. "Hey, that's a by-gods armor shop. We should check it out."

She held out her arms. "What, you don't like my armor?"

I ran my gaze up and down her form, playing along.

"Yes. I love the way it exposes your sexy, strong calves. It lends visions of what hides beneath."

"You confuse me with your descriptions. I will never understand from where you conjure your words or how you use them. It's so... garbled."

"And yet you've already shown such an affinity for turning phrases you learn from me." I smiled.

She smirked and pushed a hip out. "I doubt it. Now, will you interpret for me?"

"Gladly. What I said was, 'You're not wearing any armor.'"

"Ah." She shrugged. "That might be true, but I'm comfortable."

"Great. Come with me and you'll remain alive. Unless you enjoyed having your throat slit."

"I was naked. In bed. With *you!*"

"Yeah, but you can have your throat slit in normal combat, too."

Priya shivered. "Point taken, but you shouldn't make light of such things." She led me into the shop.

"Greetings, my lord, and lady!"

I looked up and threw a habitual courtesy wave to a man with a walrus mustache. Then I remembered where I was. This was my first Enoran vendor!

He wore a fitted brown shirt closed all the way to his neck by tiny metal clasps. Black cotton pants cut into rotund hips. A slight belly spilled over his waistline, though his clothes accommodated it. He stood in a corner brushing a metal chest piece fit for a gorilla.

**Branson Breeder**
*Level 45 Vendor*
*Proprietor*

*Unfortunate name.*

Breeder stepped down from a short stool I hadn't noticed behind his counter. The armor's stand screeched across the stone floor as he dragged it to the wall and aligned it between two lesser pieces loaded with dents and scratches. With a final meticulous straightening, he waddled over to us.

He stood maybe a half-head taller than Priya. His otherwise manicured salt-and-pepper mustache seemed to have a dangling tentacle.

Breeder bowed his head, revealing a perfect circle of bald skin centered on the crown of his skull.

I tapped my chin. "You seem to have... no, there, no... right in the middle, there, buddy, a..."

He pulled the tentacle free, revealing it was just a noodle.

Cool. Enora had noodles. My stomach grumbled.

His voice squeaked with cheer. "Thank you, kind sir! I suppose that's been there for hours." He stroked his 'stache self-consciously. "Glad I haven't had many patrons today!" He tapped his chin and chuckled. "Well, that's not good for a man of business, but..."

"Right." Considering how unpopulated the shit hole town appeared, low foot traffic made sense. "So, hey..."

"Hello!" His smile beamed.

"Yeah. Um. So, I'm a Woodsman?"

"Well, that was almost like you were asking me a question, sir." He slapped my shoulder. "But I jest. Come, let me show you a fine piece, carved out of Zhara's own forest!"

If Priya or I swiveled our heads in each other's direction any faster, we might have snapped our necks and had to resurrect all the way back in the village again. It occurred that if we died again, we'd resurrect in the village and be forced to make our hours-long trek for a second time.

As if she'd read my thoughts, my companion peered up at me and whispered, "We should've bound to the inn."

I choked on my own spit.

Priya slapped my back.

"Can you read minds, like your aunt?"

"No. And she reads feelings."

"Keep telling yourself that."

"Wait. Why do you ask?"

"Um, I'd just been thinking about resurrection... never mind." I turned to Breeder. "So, you know of Zhara?"

"Oh, yes! Our own local immortal. She is the source of much lore and casts her warm light across our fair town. At first, I doubted she even existed, but several descriptions of striking similarity about mystical encounters grace my shop and our town. The tellers of these tales describe a beautiful creature, bathed in the Light of Solara herself... though I'd never journey into those horrendous woods, myself, as I'm sure you understand."

Priya squinted. I wondered if she knew she was doing it.

"But," he closed to a conspiratorial distance, "did you know she even prances around the forest devoid of clothing? It's supposed to be quite a sight."

A low growl rumbled deep in Priya's chest. Like an angry purr.

Breeder, who I doubt lived up to his name, disappeared behind a display of metal gear. When he reemerged, he carried a stack of leather items. Pieces tumbled to form a pyramid.

"While I look these over, could you check for gear we could conceal beneath the lady's robe? I'm thinking piercing protection. Oh, and magic resistance would be awesome, too."

He threw up a stiff finger. "A discerning mind, I see!" Tapping the finger to his lips, he peered at Priya's robe.

I was rifling through the stuff he'd set on the counter for maybe ten seconds before I realized he was still standing there. I peered up at him.

"I don't mean to be rude, madam, but um... the fit of your robe leaves..."

Priya sighed, unclasped her robe, and flashed her under-things. The surprise I would've expected on the shop owner's face at her exposed curves never formed. But her bare midriff and deep cleavage combined with the perfect rounding of her full hips woke every animal sense inside me.

She flashed a bashful smile, and I realized she'd sensed my hunger.

*I have to get used to that.*

In contrast to my own desires, the shopkeeper's methodical gander was pro.

Breeder muttered, as if to himself. "Hmm. Full around the hips. Tighter around the waist. Yes. Hmm. Then the full bust. Got it!" He pitched his voice louder. "Thank you, ma'am." He walked away.

As I turned to Priya, she widened the gap in her robe a little, flicked an eyebrow at me, and mouthed the word:

*Later.*

"I really, really like you."

She smiled, straightened her hips, and fastened the robe.

I eyed the leather pyramid.

### *Bowman's Hand Guard of Dexterity*

*Level 10*
*Slot: Hands*
*Type: Armor*
*Quality: Uncommon*
*Durability 18 of 18*
*+3 Dexterity*
*+2 to ranged attack*

Gazing at calluses forming on my draw fingers—forming in a game world, I might add—I eyed the strap that would lock around my wrist with a silver buckle.

*Good stats for a small item.*

I set it down in what would be my 'inquire' pile and moved to the next item.

### Magic Quiver of Replenishment

*Level 9*
*Slot: Ammunition*
*Type: Ammunition Container*
*Quality: Uncommon*
*Durability: 32 of 35*
*With each arrow fired, there is a twenty percent chance of replacement.*

"Holy crap," I said.

Priya leaned in and set her cheek against my bicep. "Hmm? What's that?"

I explained.

"Hmm. Sounds expensive."

I dropped the quiver atop the hand guard and picked up a scroll. "Is that all you can say about a twenty percent chance at a free arrow every time I fire?"

"Oh, it's wonderful, but I doubt you have the coin."

She was probably right.

### *Scroll of Dexterity*
*Type: Magic Scroll*
*+2 Dexterity applied to reader's attributes. This
enhancement is permanent.*
*Requires Light Magic rank 20*

*Dammit, if Roshan was here, I could use this.*

Although equipping her staff and switching classes
would've made me a Level 10 Light priest, I still didn't meet
the Light Magic rank requirement to use the scroll.

I put it in the Inquire pile, noting it would further moti-
vate me to retrieve her. As if I needed more motivation.
Every cognizant moment my healer was away from me set a
fire burning in the pit of my stomach.

I set a pair of non-magical leg protectors with a 5 armor
class rating in the Inquire pile as Breeder returned. He
slapped two hard leather items onto the counter. At first
glance, they struck me as something better made for S&M
play, which wasn't my thing.

"Ooooh!" Priya moaned as she approached. She
unclasped her robe and pulled the chest protector close to
model it.

"Looks like a fine fit." She nodded at Breeder with
appreciation. "Our proprietor has a good eye."

"Thank you, ma'am. I think my many years of experience serve."

I cocked my chin at the other item. "Priya, try the, um,
privates protector."

She giggled and held it over herself.

I nodded. "Okay, kind of skimpy and all, but if it takes
an arrow, it should hold."

"Since when don't you like skimpy?" She asked.

"Hey, if it doesn't bother you... I don't want to objectify you is all... well, more than I already do."

"Objectify?" She squinted, this time in thought. "Does that mean you don't want to treat me like a possession?"

"That's right."

"Ah, a gentleman adventurer," Breeder interjected. "So refreshing."

"Well, it's too late for that. I'm yours." She kissed my cheek. "But I appreciate the sentiment."

Roshan had spewed strong words about the concept of being considered a possession the night she and I spent in Priya's dome in the forest. I smiled at the memory but ached inside.

Priya dangled the straps of the chest protector over her fingers at Breeder, not bothering to re-clasp her robe. "Is there somewhere I can try these on?"

"My lady. Step into the back there. No one will see."

"How much for these things?" I asked when Priya stepped away.

Breeder tapped his lips and tilted his head. He eyed me and returned his gaze to the items.

"I can't go lower than seven gold for the hand guard."

"Seven!" Priya yelled from somewhere in the back. "In my lifetime I might never see seven!"

*Note to self—the elf has good ears.*

I shook my head. "And she's supposed to be the negotiator."

Breeder laughed. "For the scroll, since it is a permanent upgrade, I would expect fifty gold. But if you buy the hand guard and the quiver, I can reduce it to forty."

"Right. How much for the quiver, though?"

"Well, that's the real piece here, isn't it?" He held it up

and knocked it with his knuckles. "Elven construction." He flipped it around. "Wide storage box, holds fifty standard arrows." He dangled the strap by one finger and lifted it up and down several times. "Light. You'll never know it's on your shoulder, I guarantee you." He cocked his head sideways. "Or your hip, in your case. Hm. That's a very good place to store your arrows."

"Thank you," I said.

He dropped the quiver and ran two fingers over it. "And you must consider the magic properties. One in five arrows returned to you?"

"Mister Breeder. Not to be rude, but I already checked the stats. So, price?"

"Seventy gold."

My butt cheeks tensed.

*But I want!*

I reached into my bag and scanned my inventory.

"There has to be something of value. Maybe a trade?"

Breeder pumped a fist to his chest and bounced on the balls of his feet. "I've been known to barter."

Three consecutive slots in my inventory caused my eyes to bulge. I withdrew the items I'd stolen from a sacrificial altar in the underground dungeon where I'd found Priya.

### *Gold Ceremonial Offering Plate*
*This plate could be of high value.*

### *Ivory, Jewel-encrusted Ceremonial Chalice x 2*
*This chalice could be of high value.*

Breeder eyed the items, threw a hand to his chest, and stepped backward. He dropped the hand as quickly as he'd raised it and cleared his throat.

*I should play poker with this guy. I could clean him out.*

"I know they're not armor or a weapon, but do you know anyone who might be interested? I got them while adventuring in the kobold depths beneath Zhara's forest."

"The Tomb of the Lost?" Breeder asked.

"Oh, you've heard of it?"

"It's on every map of the Dark Wood. An ancient, dark place."

"Not so much, anymore." I flashed him a sideways smile. "I wiggled one of the chalices. Anyway, I think someone used them for blood sacrifices or such dark intents, but they look clean."

He inched forward and raising a hand, dipped a finger toward the plate. "May I?"

"Of course." I smiled.

He analyzed each piece with a meticulous eye then produced a small tube. Reading the confusion on my face, he tapped it.

"A focusing lens. Common in the jeweler's trade."

I seemed to remember Roshan mentioning such an implement when we found the chalices. She'd lacked one at the time, but by her naked eye claimed they might be of value. Breeder's response seemed to validate her suspicions.

A well-timed fib seemed prudent. "Yes, one of my companions is in that trade and checked these out for me when we got them."

"Ah. I see." Peering through the lens, he checked each gem in-turn. "Hmm. Mmm. Yes. Ah, yes. Mmm-hmm."

"Well?"

"Honestly, sir," Breeder said when he finished assessing the goods, "These items might be a little out of my range." He set them down and stepped back.

I frowned. "Oh, is there someone else in town who might—?"

"Ah!" He raised a finger. "If you'll pardon me sir, I wasn't finished. I don't have the gold on-hand, but I know people in the area who would pay. Perhaps I can give you credit for these items and we can barter for the ones you desire?"

"Okay. What kind of deal can you give me on the quiver?"

"Sir, the quiver's bottom price is seventy."

I shook my head. "Best I can do is fifty."

I was blind to currency values in this world. I knew the cost of nothing, and Breeder had tagged none of his items, so I had no standards for calculation. But haggling was haggling, and it was time to test the Enoran waters.

He tilted his head back as his mouth formed an O and shook his head. "No, no no no no no. You jest. I could not go beloooooow... sixty-three. Bottom price."

Priya appeared with her robe flailing open, the black leather protector wrapping around her bust as if tailored for it.

She marched over to the stone counter and lifted the quiver. "You want how much for this? Tell me you didn't say sixty-three! No. Uh-uh. Put it back, sir." She turned her face away from him and held it out, but when Breeder reached for it, she reeled it in and tapped it with her index finger. "Look at these scratches. And this, here, is that blood? It's not even new. What's the durability? Hmm?" She widened her eyes, but she didn't wait for a response. "No way. I wouldn't pay over fifty for it."

Breeder squinted at her. Priya returned it.

*Let the stare down begin.*

I could've heard a feather rustle against felt.

"Elven construction," Breeder murmured.

Then Priya unloaded the big guns.

"Aunt Zhara would rip a branch from her tree and tan my hide if I paid over fifty gold for that when I could scamper back into the forest," she made a walking gesture with two fingers, "and have her make me one like it for free."

"Your..." Breeder stepped back, the squint gone from his eyes. "Your... Did you say..." his eyes flicked to me.

I shrugged.

His facial muscles went slack as he scanned us. The expression morphed into a scowl. "I enjoy a good game as much as the next man, but I do not stomach swindlers! Blasphemous ones, even less! I have my limits!" He stabbed a finger at the gold plate. "Tomb of the Lost, indeed! Aunt Zhara, indeed! Take your ill-gained possessions and leave my shop at once!"

I jerked at the outburst, but Priya tilted her head to one side, considering Breeder as if he were some new species of toothless canine with one eye and a shiny coat.

She leaned over the counter, encouraging her assets to swell over the chest protector. "You think I'm lying?"

"Young lady! You cannot persuade or distract me with your flesh-revealing tactics."

"These aren't tactics, my friend. This is just how I lean. Besides, if you aren't distracted, why are we talking about them?"

Breeder huffed and squinted one eye so it almost closed.

She leaned closer and whispered. "I will wager with you I can prove what I say."

"Oh?" He thrust his hands upon his narrow hips. His gaze lingered on me for a moment and an eyebrow ticked up as if he'd read something in my expression. "Yes! Fine! I will play this game! You prove to my satisfaction you are related to the wood goddess Zhara, and I will sell it to you for... for... fifty gold!"

He waved a dismissive hand and returned it to his hip.

Priya pushed her robe over one shoulder as if she planned to show the proprietor the tattoo of the magic tree in which Zhara lived glowing across her back and, though I had little doubt the tattoo's leaves shuddering as if a breeze blew across her flesh would set him straight, using the hypnotic state it induced bordered on unfair.

I gripped Priya's forearm.

"Allow me."

I could meet the aim without her disrobing. I retrieved the low-level bow from my bag and slammed it on the counter.

For my entertainment, I read the stats, knowing the proprietor had the same ability. How else would he make a living?

***Longbow of the Light***

*Level 10*

*Slot: Weapon*

*Type: Ranged*

*Quality: Unique*

*Durability: Unbreakable*

*No durability loss*

*Ranged Damage: 21-34*

*+10 to accuracy*

*+10 piercing damage*

*+10 ranged attack*

*Unique: Constructed by Zhara, Matron of The Wood.*

*Bam, bitch!*

"Made for me by Zhara as a gift for my completion of a quest and the rescue of her beloved niece."

I didn't know if I'd ever seen a face transition through every emotion in the human toolbox in mere seconds before, but as Breeder's regressed from *defiant*, to *perplexed*, to *baffled*, and to *horrified*, I was sure that was the closest I would ever come. For the icing on the cake, I dropped my quiver on the counter.

### *Light Quiver of the Matron's Tree of Life*
*No Level Requirement*
*Slot: Ammunition*
*Type: Ammunition Container*
*Quality: Unique*
*Durability: Unbreakable*
*No Durability loss*
*Unique: Constructed by Zhara Matron of The Wood.*

"'Signed in lightning script," Breeder muttered. "This is..."

"Pretty fucking great, right?" I flashed him a smile.

"Pretty... um... yes." His eyes widened as his gaze reacquired Priya. "But this proves nothing!"

"Huh?" I asked stupidly.

"These are quest rewards, yes? All this proves is you have performed tasks for the Matron."

"Can I?" Priya asked.

I threw my hands up.

She shrugged off the protector and turned. The room glowed as her tattoo came to life. I closed my eyes to avoid its effects, but was still warmed by its glow. When the warmth diminished, I blinked them open.

Breeder rushed forward, gripped her hand, then

covered it in dry kisses. He shook his head. "My lady! I offer my most humble of apologies. Please don't let the niece of the Matron of The Wood be at odds with me. I pray you!"

Priya stared at her hand as he kissed it, then she peered at me and smirked. When he finished his subservient display, she flicked off a noodle left behind and cringed.

*Karma, I guess.*

Breeder's back went straight as a board. "Fifty gold! It is done!"

Priya turned her nose up and continued snapping the clasps on her robe.

His head bobbed. "Fifty gold, and you will accept these items adorning your goddess-like form at my expense! Bless you and the immortal soul of your beloved aunt!"

Priya lowered her tone as her eyes inspected the shop's ceiling. "And for the rest?"

It was all I could do not to bust out laughing or piss myself.

Breeder's lips moved as he eyed the chalices, the gold plate, and the items I'd put in my ask pile.

"I offer you these items, including the scroll, the quiver, the hand guard, and the clothing upon Miss Priya's blessed form, in exchange for the chalices and the plate. I offer ninety gold in additional store credit for you to shop with me later. I will also provide you a writ in case you wish to spend it in one of my other shops to the north. I wish I had more coin on hand to accommodate you, but—"

"One-hundred in credit," Priya said. "Twenty gold in hard coin, now."

She'd almost fainted just days before when I told her I had seven gold. Talk about adaptive.

Breeder shrugged, causing me to wonder if we'd gotten the better end of the deal.

"Done! I shall mark it down!" He reached into the pocket of his ugly green shirt and snapped coins onto the counter, speaking as another part of his brain counted. "Twenty gold! Eighty in store credit! And, if I might be so bold, please pass my eternal good tidings to your beloved relation." He withdrew a thick piece of parchment, scribbled, then folded it inside another piece. He grabbed the candle burning on the shelf behind him, melted a ball of red wax, sealed it, and pressed a stamp into the wax. "Present this to either of my sons in Trowlsby or the king's own seat, and they will extend you credit and every courtesy."

Priya might as well have been an heiress with an expense account.

"Very well." Priya pushed out her hand and let it hang limp from her wrist.

*I've underestimated the guile of my companion. The elf is a monster.*

Breeder grabbed the offered hand and kissed each knuckle.

Priya patted his head like he was a gods-damned dog until he finished. And his blinding grin said her touch thrilled him. I thought he might lick her face or roll onto his back and expose his belly for a good scratching.

I missed my cat.

As much as I was enjoying the display of her dominance, a glance at her robe brought me back to what lured me to the shop.

"Hey, Breeder. Do you have binding scrolls?"

"I'm afraid not. There's a shop nearby that might, but they're uncommon this far south. It might waste your time. Prices will be high. If your destination is to the north, there are more magic users and scribes capable of producing such artifacts, the closer you get to the university."

Another possession I'd seen in my bag while retrieving the chalices reminded me of another goal I'd hoped to achieve while I was here.

"Is there anyone here or to the north who can train me in sword skills? I need a basic run-through, nothing extensive."

Breeder lowered his tone and leaned into the counter.

"I can do better than that, for one who keeps the company of Zhara's blood." If he'd kissed Priya's ass any harder, he might have left a hickey. "There is such a... being in Brumhill, but I doubt he'll appreciate your rush. He's a stickler for form and diligence." He eyed Priya. "But I'm certain he would hear your request.

He pushed away from the counter and pointed to the street. "Turn left down the second alley, just before the north gate. The lone door at the end is the one you seek. Here..." He reached into the pocket of his vest and withdrew a silver token with no discerning marks. "To the family of Zhara, this comes free of charge. I often do business with the proprietor who houses this man. Ask to see Guiles." He leaned even further toward us. "You will not want to let the town guard know you seek weapon training in the town limits."

"Why is that, Mister Breeder?" Priya asked.

Breeder flashed her a smile as if his name upon her lips was a blessing. "Because they scheme against outsiders, and I would not have my new friends taken advantage of. They're not esteemed swordsmen themselves, but they charge high rates. Besides, rumors abound as to travelers in the past who fell on ill tidings along the northern road after seeking their training."

I nodded. "So the scumbags rip them off then follow to clean them out. Thanks for the warning."

Dropping the token into my pants pocket, I donned the magic quiver and pulled the old one off. As I raised my bag to drop it into one of my few open slots, I glanced at the man across the counter. His eyes lingered on the item. Holding Breeder's initial doubt and accompanying outburst against him would have been unfair and, considering the spoils of our visit to his shop, he'd treated us with abundant respect and trusted me with a token that would gain me access to some weapon training at no known gain to himself. Breeder was likable.

I reached across the counter. "Accept this gift, made by Zhara's own hand."

Breeder's slapped the counter with both hands as his legs buckled. I reached out and grabbed his shoulder. My companion, however, remained true to her role of the heiress. She didn't so much as flinch.

*Call Priya a fucking liar, will ya?*

I stopped at the door and peered back at Breeder, who was all smiles as he watched us go. Reaching into my bag, I grasped the Return Stone deposited there when I'd reached level ten.

*Would you like to bind your soul to Breeder's Arms?*
*Yes/No?*

I selected 'Yes.' If we resurrected, this option was better than the inn.

We'd started the day with blades at our necks, but we'd finished it with gear granting a modest boost to our stats. Things were looking up.

I reached for Priya's hand as we walked, but only managed to brush her fingers.

She turned her nose up, slipped her hand away, and

adopted a nasal tone. "Do you think I didn't hear?" Adding bass, she mimicked my voice and shook her head back and forth. "And she's supposed to be the negotiator." She paced ahead of me. "Of all the insulting..."

"Priya..."

"Humph!" She marched on.

"Priya, I was setting you up to finish the negotiations! Hey, I thought we were a team!"

"You're worse than him, Gemini. At least he shows a little respect. You... you're... humph!"

I jogged forward, wrapped my arms around her waist, raised her kicking into the air, and spun her in a circle.

"Ah! Gemini! What are you doing! Put me down!"

I laughed and dropped her to her feet. "You forget I can sense the humor spilling out of you. Stop screwing with me."

She smiled and ran a finger down my Adam's apple. I locked my arms around her waist and pulled her closer.

"But your words still offend me, my lord."

"Then let me make it up for you in our bedrolls tonight, in the way you offered me apology earlier." I brushed my lips against hers. "I will feed your desperate wanting."

"Oh? What is this wanting that so encumbers?" The fingers swirled in the divot at the bottom of my neck.

I whispered in her ear.

She swooned.

<hr>

We picked a sunny patch of grass beneath a tree near the north gate to eat leftover pheasant from my hunt in the woods a couple nights before. I'd planned on reheating it over a campfire, but I found myself famished by the time we were back on the dusty street outside Breeder's shop. We ate it cold, but it was still delicious.

Appetite was a funny thing in Enora. Though I didn't need to eat three times per day, I found that when my stomach set to grumbling, it was better to feed it than to get persistent reminders. When I'd asked Priya how often she ate, she'd answered once per day, but not every day. Then she'd sucked her fingertips clean, rolled sideways, and straddled me, as if bored by the topic.

She threw her arms over my shoulders then settled her pelvis on mine and stared at me, her sea blue irises mesmerizing. Her full, muscular backside was a welcome weight on my quads.

I set my hands on her hips. "Well, hello, there."

But Priya had more serious inclinations. "Tell me our bond doesn't have you regretting the day you saved me from Crohl."

I pulled my head back so I could focus on her features. "Why would you say that? You can't be getting that vibe off me."

Could she?

She shook her head. "I'm still interpreting your emotions at a given moment. There were times today I had little doubt about your moods." She looked down as she spoke. "Though this bond gave my heart pause this morning, our sharing has become comfortable for me with the setting sun."

I delayed, trying to search myself for any truth in her suspicions. "Why would it would be different for me?"

She drew a deep breath, her chest rising and falling. "It's not that I *think* that. I share your sense of loss over Roshan, so that's an easy one. But I need to know this new bond doesn't add to your strain over losing our priestess.

There is such richness in your emotions for her, and I respect them. At the same time, I adore the very distinct warmth you hold for me. It pleases me each time your body and mind express it. I love that sensation because I know it's uniquely molded for me."

"Then what's the problem?"

She pressed a finger to my lips. "Let me finish. It's hard to form words describing emotions, sometimes. Your heart pauses. There is a hesitation at the sudden reminders that our emotional bond flourishes... when we share."

"I see."

She shook her head and patted my cheek. "I'm not sure you do. The entire time I was captive beneath the ground with Crohl, I longed for my hearth near Magellan. But since you and Roshan liberated me and we left it behind, I've not yearned for home. I spent only one night there after my captivity, and yet I have no desire to return to the Dark Wood.

"That our destinies are intertwined is a welcome gift. But I couldn't have foreseen this link between us and wouldn't have you feel indebted when the debt is mine to pay. It is you who saved me. So, I'm asking you. Is your sense of duty compelling you forth despite the discomfort our bond presents you? Would it be better if you forged forward alone, retrieved her, then came back for me? Do I threaten your focus?"

The women of my old life were distracted by technology, but the elven woman astride my lap was tuned to me emotionally. Our communication was intimate and direct. The concept of a handheld device or sending text messages was foreign to her. I'd found a party chat tab in my expanded interface when I reached level ten, but I hoped to use it as little as possible.

Eye contact was better.

The current emotion radiating off her was vibrant and strong and, though I was new to all this, I had little doubt it was her yearning hope I would answer 'no.' Despite her generous offer to step aside, Priya wanted to be with me. And that was pure gold I planned to bank.

I hadn't missed home for a single moment since she'd entered my life, and separating from her would not do. In one long day, we'd become enhanced by this new bond. We were a team, we were a couple, and we'd written ourselves into each other's story.

A toothy smile crossed my lips.

Priya's face turned pink. "Is that my answer?"

"No, this is." I ran my fingers through the golden locks hanging in rivulets past her shoulders and pulled her head close. "I'll never let you out of my sight."

I kissed my half-elf companion, and then again. Time passed despite us, and when I peered up, the sun had fallen beyond the jagged northwestern peaks, sweeping the town in the black of their shadows.

She touched her fingertips to her lips. "I like this answer, very much."

5

Priya and I gazed at the blanket of a million stars as the moons converged. The slight dizziness as I paced with my attention turned to the sky reminded me how authentic my virtual existence was. One day I'd live in this world with few thoughts as to its origins. The biological replications were indistinguishable from my physical existence on earth, and this was one of many times I found my heart pounding with that realization.

Which was also a simulated biological function that compounded the effect.

When I'd entered Brumhill that afternoon, I thought we'd be camping somewhere north of town by nightfall, but another commonality between Enora and Earth was that my plans seldom came to their intended fruition. My lack of knowledge about the world I now called home stacked the odds further against me.

The road ahead would be rocky. Come hell or high water, I would follow it to Roshan. But what I would do when I got to her was still up in the air.

"She will probably stop for the day in the next town to the North."

Priya's intuition for my emotions was sharpening.

"If it's as Aunt Zhara says, they will have to rest and water their horses. And if the quest you shared with me is any indicator, we must advance in our skills if we hope to reclaim her when we've closed the distance. Remember the conflict with the vellick."

"Wise words. But the way you respond when I haven't said a word is spooky."

"Your longing is strong."

I slipped an arm around her waist. "Is it bothering you now? That I long for Roshan?"

Priya chuckled. "We've covered this. Your feelings for me are my own as are mine for Roshan. You know, she told me that night in my home that the Light is love and that you have room for both of us in your heart is a sign of your capacity for the Light."

*Whoa.*

Our boots kicked up dust painted white by twin moons as we crossed the main thoroughfare then turned down the alley to find the promised door at the opposite end. I raised my hand to knock, but my knuckles fell short as a metal slot slid open, revealing a set of yellow irises surrounded by umber skin.

The token Breeder gifted me clanked on the metal inside the slot. "I'm looking for a fella named Guiles."

A heavy bolt thunked and hinges creaked as the thick door swung open to reveal a stout man with a tan born of heritage more than sunlight. Those yellow eyes seemed to glow in the dark.

My guess was he was half-dwarf, but I always thought of dwarves as dark-dwellers and couldn't guess what genetics might have painted his dark skin and, seeing as he appeared the hard type, I didn't want him to misinterpret the wink to bring up my interface's HUD and inspect him.

Stale brew dominated the dim interior. At one end of the unfinished bar, a hulking figure wearing a tattered straw sunhat peered over his shoulder, eyeing us the whole way. He scanned Priya from top-to-bottom, and what her robe didn't obstruct from his view, I did. Guards outside the town glaring at the radiant beauty pacing next to me were one thing, but judging from the hunched postures and dark dispositions of the riffraff eyeing us, I didn't credit them with the good judgment to settle for what their gazes gave them.

The only logic I saw in locking the door was to keep these guys inside.

I scanned the tavern for polished armor, fine weapons, anything that would identify higher level sorts of whom I should be wary, but I'd spied no one who impressed me by the time our guide led us into a room in the back.

Then that changed.

He sat alone at a table that took up half the small recess. Though he concealed his legs beneath the polished wood, he had the wingspan of an NBA center and I had little doubt he would tower over me if he stood. His broad shoulders looked fit to carry boulders on his back. A thick, braided beard twisted beneath his chin to reach halfway down his barrel chest. A golden loop pierced the cartilage of his septum beneath a crooked nose.

The great sword leaning against the wall within easy reach of those thick arms stood taller than Priya. A ruby the size of an eagle's egg gleamed inside its pommel. I wondered if the gem was for show or if it offered magic properties. I was about to inspect it when our escort spoke.

"These two want to see you," the half-dwarf growled, cocking his chin up at me as he passed back into the main bar area to saunter back to his stool behind the door.

The giant stared at the hand I offered across the table with a bored expression. The low, single word he spoke shook my bones.

"Sit."

*If a grizzly could talk that's what it would sound like.*

He raised a wooden goblet framed in bronze and slurped as we took our seats. When he slammed it back on the table, foam spilled over. He didn't seem concerned.

I spoke in a low tone. "We need sword training." I glanced at his massive weapon. "Breeder tells me you're the guy who can provide it."

Priya nodded over at me. "Love the deep voice, hon. Top-notch."

*Ugh.*

Her humor was contagious. "Hey, thanks, babe. I thought it might add a little flair."

The giant's gaze darted from me to Priya's cleavage and back. "Funny ones, eh?" He slurped from the mug again. "I don't like funny ones. Swordsmanship is for serious people. Who's to say I won't take your gold, drag you out into the wilds, and stomp on ya? I bet the buzzards would think you *taste* funny, too."

"Well, look at you," Priya said. "You're witty, yourself. That's a nice bit of salesmanship, there."

"Well, love," the giant said, "I might care a little if something as sweet as you gets pecked into a bird's belly, but this one?" He cocked his chin in my direction. "Can't see how he's gonna survive long even with my help. Looks kind of *soft,* what with his bow, an' all." Leaning forward, he set his elbows on the table and pushed the goblet away with a forearm thicker than my bicep. "What you think, big guy? You got the stuff to survive out there?"

I winked with each eye, not caring he'd know why.

### Brugh
*Human*
Level ?? Warrior


I cleared my throat. "Guess you'd be a better judge than me."

"Hmm. Might that I would."

I leaned forward and set my own elbows on the table, mirroring his posture. "But it's really none of your damned business."

"What's that?"

I raised one shoulder in a half-shrug. "Way I see it is, I'm here to buy a service. I don't need my hand held. I don't want special treatment. But I'm not sure I want to study under a dimwit lacking the respect to look me in the eye." I cocked my head toward Priya. "She's not for sale, and you aren't even the guy I'm looking for, *Brugh*. So how about we dispense with the cloak-and-dagger shit and get on with it?"

The giant's attention flicked to his sword, then back at me, and for a second there, I thought he would reach for it. My mind leapt to my daggers. A scenario flashed in my head.

I'd flip the table toward him. He'd cast it aside in time to see my daggers lunging toward his throat. I'd open him up like a practiced surgeon, then throw the bar on the thick door behind him and slip put the back way.

*Or he'd crush me like a bug within seconds without the sword, and I'd find myself back at Breeder's place when I resurrected. But fantasies are nice.*

His laughter echoed off the walls of the small room like the horn of a big rig on a highway. I jerked as his thick hand slammed the table in amusement, but Priya sat stony like she hadn't even noticed.

"They'll do," he called over his shoulder. He reached back and threw up the heavy bar without having to stand. The door hinges squealed under the weight of the thick oak, revealing a wiry figure a head taller than Priya, with flowing white hair mismatched to his young, golden skin, and a matching Fu Manchu forming a V on his chin. His ears curved up into a point.

Just inside the door, he beckoned. "Come with me."

### *Guiles*
*Elf*
Level ?? Weapons Trainer

I stood and peered at the massive man as he polished off his goblet and slammed it on the table.

"Hey, I'm just the filter, fella, but you keep glaring at me like that and maybe we'll find out if you're as tough as you talk."

"Thanks, Brugh," the elf said.

"Sure, Guiles. Do me a favor and make it hard on the jester."

"We'll see." The elven dude's thin lips almost hinted at a smile as he surveyed me. He jerked his head toward the alley then held the door open with his narrow back as Priya and I passed through.

After the door slammed, and the security bar thunked back into place, the elf extended a hand.

I grasped it. His grip was warm, firm. Stronger than his slender form indicated it would be.

"I'm Guiles." He led us down the alley toward a distant gate on the west side of town.

Despite the pounding in my chest from the whole ordeal moments before, I bordered on giddy at the sight of my first full-blooded elf in Enora. This was bad ass. *Elves* were bad ass.

"Gemini." I thrust a thumb to my left. "This is Priya."

Guiles nodded at her. "Sister."

She returned the nod, but I felt confusion fuming off her and thought it stemmed from his use of the familial title.

"You'll forgive the pretense, but people don't take to unregistered trainers in the eastern half of the Kingdom. My elven heritage adds inconvenience. Though the king doesn't seem to disapprove of the other races, his regents aren't so open-minded."

"Hmph," Priya said. "I serve no king, Luttrell nor other."

"A proclamation best whispered, if you'll forgive me, my lady," the elf said, peering over his shoulder. "Our king is but a figurehead, like his father before him, but he has powerful allies who listen from afar."

Priya's shoulder barely twitched. "Sure."

"The town guard has a racket in subpar weapons training, so we'll keep to the alleys."

I nodded. "Breeder mentioned their side action. How'd you get hitched up to the barbarian?"

"Don't let *him* hear you call him that." His gaze shifted up and down my form. "You don't look suited to survive a backbreaker." He chuckled and turned his attention back to the alley. "To answer your question, Brugh and I used to adventure together, years ago."

"Aside from the white hair, you don't look like you were doing much of anything years ago."

"My kind keep a youthful appearance but live long lives."

Priya huffed. "Gemini, we have to get you out more."

"It's okay, Priya. I easily forgive ignorance of an unfamiliar culture." The elf smiled and Priya returned it. "My, but you are a dashing one, if you'll give me leave to say it."

I shrugged my approval. "She is dashing."

"I was asking the lady's leave. Is she your slave?"

I admonished myself for my sexist attitude. "Definitely not my slave."

Priya slid her arm in mine and leaned close. "But assuredly his betrothed."

"Hmmm. I see." He changed tacts. "So, Breeder warned me you might show up. He was strange. The way he spoke of you... he said I would find you worth my time but wouldn't say why. He was almost glowing."

Well, at least he didn't give up our secrets.

"Yes, I was hoping to skill up before we hit the road tonight."

"Tonight?" The elf stopped and waved a hand. "Oh, my." He clicked his tongue. "Young adventurers. Always in such a hurry."

"I have pressing concerns."

"Then I hope you are skilled with that bow and those daggers because the proper wielding of a sword is not something you'll learn in a couple hours."

"Then how about the highlights?" I did my best to project my embarrassment. "It's not like I plan to use it as my primary weapon, but I've found myself disarmed of my bow and daggers, both. Then we had an encounter with a vellick this morning, and I found its reach challenging. A third go-to weapon of better reach could prove useful."

"A vellick? The tree demons? What level?"

"I don't recall."

"Was it taller than you?"

I nodded.

"Well, if you survived, you must have worth as a fighter."

I didn't correct him.

"So, you'll help with the sword?"

"It would be more useful to train on the weapons you already wield." He waved his hand in that same dismissive gesture. "I train beginners for a week minimum, fees paid in advance. I don't send seedlings out to die. That is a service better left to the town guards and, believe me, they provide it. I could see how the concept might be foreign to you in these corrupt parts, but I have a conscience."

I sighed.

Priya stepped forward and cupped her hands together. "I don't suppose you train daggers, master elf?"

"My lady, when I adventured with "the barbarian" as your friend described him, I was the disabler of traps and creeper of shadows in my party."

I leaned in. "You're an assassin?"

The elf chuckled. "I once was, a long time ago." His facial muscles went slack. Then he vanished. Purple fumes rose in his wake.

Priya and I shared a glance.

My shoulder jerked forward as he shoved it from behind. "I am a rogue." The curved blade of a long dagger with tiny jagged indentions on the backside appeared inches from my eyes.

"Damn, you're quick."

Guiles sheathed the weapon in an effortless blur. The simple motion spoke of a man who'd performed it thousands of times.

"Yes, well, I served in the shadow art for many years."

I glanced at the inspection function on my HUD again, to find the description had changed.

### Guiles
*Elf*
*Level 50 Rogue*

"Fifty?" I muttered.

Guiles nodded. "Again, I used to adventure. Let's say I retired early. Constant peril isn't all it's cracked up to be. Circumstances prevented me returning to my home in the northern forests, so I chose the birthplace of my long-time companion as a substitute."

I considered questioning why he couldn't return home, but it was none of my business, and the last thing I wanted was to appear rude. I didn't know the customs or conventions of his world. "I don't get the impression many would challenge a companion like Brugh."

The elf raised a single finger. "Ah, but you did."

I shrugged.

Priya cocked her head toward me. "My friend exudes courage of the mind and the body. He's worth your time, I assure you."

Guiles nodded, but his words contradicted the gesture. "Bravery is only a short step from stupidity when challenging Brugh, but I could tell he warmed to you."

"If that's warm, I wouldn't want to see him pissed off."

Again, Guiles gave that easy nod. "No, you wouldn't."

"Well, don't let Gemini's low-level fool you. He saved me from a caster beneath the Dark Wood and rescued a Light priestess kidnapped from the Eastern continent on the same day. By the time he was Level Five, no less. He is the most decent man I have ever known and chivalrous to the last."

"My," the elf said. "Aren't you a charismatic one? As you are one of my kin, I believe what you say." He turned his blue eyes on me, blinking them in succession, checking my stats. "You have learned the stealth fade and some rudimentary skill with your daggers. I can teach you a new skill if you feel it would serve."

"What skill is that?"

"You witnessed it. Shadow Merge."

"Yes, I'd love to learn that one."

"The price is a little steep for a new adventurer."

"How much?" Priya interrupted.

Guiles smiled so the teeth on the right side of his mouth flashed white against the dimness of the alley. "The cost is six gold."

Priya rubbed her chin and rolled her eyes toward the distant sky as if considering.

"Spare me," Guiles said. "When you are among family, it's bad form to haggle. The fact is, I like the two of you. You strike me as untouched by the cynicism and greed of the region. If you go north, to Warrington, you will pay three times as much from shady trainers who'd just as soon rob a new adventurer as train one."

Priya smirked. "Pay the elf."

I chuckled. "She's a real negotiator."

She flicked a finger at Guiles. "He's Level 50 and probably older than both of us, combined! What do you expect from me?"

I paid the elf.

He eyed the gold as my hand withdrew from the bag.

"Hmm, a magic bag—are your parents rich? Are you of noble blood?"

Speaking about my parents, who weren't of this world, could violate the player's agreement, so I shook my head and avoided the topic. At least I knew my mind was *in the game*, pun intended. "I don't remember my parents. Everything I have, I earned in the last three days." A pang of guilt accompanied an image of their faces in my mind, despite my reasoning for the lie.

"My goodness, you must have luck, then. It's a much-underestimated attribute."

My eyebrow ticked up. "There's a luck attribute?" I switched to my character sheet on my HUD "How'd I miss that?"

He shook his head. "No. Who has ever heard such a silly thing? But there is such a thing as luck! For instance, you were lucky to have met me." He smiled. All-teeth. "Now, close your eyes, and I'll teach you Shadow Merge."

The elf's hand clutched my forehead with his thumb and forefinger pressing my temples. I still wasn't one-hundred percent sure I could trust Guiles, but Priya was watching him and would let me know if foulness were afoot.

Then again, Priya lived in a forest. But Guiles could've robbed me and left me for dead if that was his intent, and I doubted Breeder would lead us into a trap.

"I want you to imagine a dense cloud in front of you."

"Got it," I said.

"Now, I want you to imagine stepping through that cloud."

"Okay?"

"Now imagine yourself vanishing from existence."

"That's dark, dude."

*He didn't understand how close I'd come to doing that the day before.*

"Focus on the mental energy you create when activating your stealth skill. Do you have it?"

"Yes." A chill ran up my spine as a tingling tickled my forehead around his fingertips.

"Open your eyes."

For just a flash, there was a purple haze in my field of vision. Then a few Hendrix chords echoed in that place in the brain reserved for nostalgia.

*You have learned a new skill!*
### *Shadow Merge*
*Level 10*
*Cost: 10 Stamina*
*Cool-down: 30 Seconds*
*Step into the shadows and journey instantly through the netherworld to reappear behind your opponent.*

Guiles peered into my eyes, standing on his tiptoes, and I likened him to a doctor giving me an exam.

"Okay, now, focus on me."

I did.

"For the sake of comparison, fade into stealth."

I focused and transitioned to my semi-transparent state.

"Oh, goodness."

"What?" I said.

He slapped my chest, breaking my stealth and making me visible, but he didn't remove his hand. "Who taught you how to fade? Hmm?" He paused. I wasn't sure how to answer since I'd learned the skill by hiding from an enemy. When I stayed silent, he continued. "I insist you go back and demand they return your gold. Better yet," he smiled, "give me the name and I shall eviscerate them for you."

Priya and I glanced at each other.

"I jest, but you must learn to transition faster than that. You fade slower than a sunset. It's like watching fog dissipate. If you were a cloud—"

"I get it! I get it!"

"I didn't mean to bruise your ego. Whoever taught you—"

*Screw it. This guy liked to talk, and we had places to be.*

"I taught myself."

Guiles dropped a hand on one hip and pursed his lips. "Well, that makes sense! I taught myself just yesterday how to flap my arms like a gull and fly high in the clouds."

"I did." I raised a hand. "Hand to G—Solara."

"Deception. While I understand the authorities frown on unsanctioned skill advancement, you need not worry about concealing your trainer's identity. No one will learn of your illegal training from me, for I offer you the same. I didn't even want to know who trained you."

I raised a shoulder in a half-shrug. "I taught myself, dude."

The elf glared at me.

I tilted my head to the side. "Why is that unusual?"

His hand dropped from his hip and he leaned toward me, raising an eyebrow that peaked in the center. "You're claiming you had no trainer? That you learned to fade into stealth on your own?"

*Common theme in Enora: People don't believe you are anything special.*

I nodded my head. "I first managed it while hiding from an enemy."

The rogue stepped closer, piercing me with his gaze, though one side of his mouth curved. "Tell me this lie again so I might see it in your eyes."

"Ooh, this is fun," Priya said.

"For whom?" I asked her.

"Did you witness this, sister?" Guiles asked.

"Nah, it was before he met me."

The elf's gaze was starting to make me uncomfortable, especially at that proximity. I widened my eyes for effect.

"No one taught me."

Guiles's eyes flicked back and forth, like he was peering through my sclera to see my brain. He stepped back and folded his arms across his chest.

"Well, if that doesn't just beat the dragon bare-fisted. You..."

I tilted my head toward my other shoulder. "I what?"

"Any child can hide among the bushes. But you have the *fade*. It's a skill born of the ether." He continued to gaze at me, but spoke to my companion. "Tell, me, Priya..."

She raised both eyebrows. "Yes?"

"You said you are this man's *betrothed*. Are you married?"

"Well, no. I don't subscribe to..." She peered up at me. "Yes. I suppose we are. Why, just today we started sharing emotions. That's a marriage of sorts." Her smile broadened in realization, and her happiness swelled in my chest.

"The *elven* bond?" His eyes widened as they flicked back at me. "You sense Priya's emotions?"

Priya interrupted. "I don't know why that's strange. I shared it with my aunt upon waking in the woods years ago until she blocked it. She's stingy with her feelings, so I never got used to it. But now that Gemini and I share it, I plan to make the most—"

*Zhara?*

"Why didn't you tell me you shared this with—" I began.

"Impossible!" Guiles interrupted. He shook his head in

derision. "Such stories live only in lore. A human who manipulates the ether and shares the elven sense? The two of you..." He ticked one finger back and forth in the air. "It's rude to fool with strangers. Perhaps Brugh was wrong about you." The elven rogue turned his head to peer back up the alley and seemed poise to bolt.

Guiles was the second person in Brumhill to imply we were liars. It was getting on my nerves. The sense I got from Priya was that she felt the same way, but for her often-snarky demeanor and impatient disposition, she surprised me with an even tone when she responded.

"I assure you we speak the truth, *brother*. It manifested earlier today when we res—"

I cleared my throat to cut Priya off. Talk of resurrection might screw us. She took the hint.

After a suspicious glance at each of us, Guiles's gaze flickered down at Priya's robe, then he winked them in succession and gazed at her.

"Bound to Gemini Fowler?" he muttered.

His eyes shifted between us, unable to find rest.

She nodded and answered as if he'd asked a question, though I knew it hadn't been his intent. "Um... Yes?"

Priya. Snarky. Cute. But this elf's prying was tweaking my nerves.

"I mean, you are *soulbound* to him."

She waved a dismissive hand. "Oh, that. He spent more than..." she trailed off, reconsidering what she'd been about to share. Since she'd lived in the Dark Wood and hadn't practiced much social interaction, her tendency to blurt out unthinking words was forgivable. But we were going to need to discuss it. Enora was stacking up to be a place where loose lips could sink our ships.

*And I plan to keep our boat afloat.*

The elf flicked a crooked finger at me. "Spent? Were you going to say he spent attribute points for you? Now you try to convince me he is your attribute trainer? At Level 10?"

"My what?" Priya asked. But I knew she was just buying time to think. She didn't want to say something stupid.

"Do you people speak the common tongue?" He huffed out a quick breath of air. "I am asking you if this man, your soul-bound companion, can increase your Strength, Intellect, Wisdom, and other stats without your need to labor for it... in reward for level advancement."

Priya feigned innocence. "Oh, why didn't you just say so?"

Guiles rolled his eyes.

I empathized.

She glanced at me.

I nodded. "You might as well go ahead. He's already figured it out."

"Yes. He raises my attributes. I suspect my aunt could have as well. But she wouldn't do it."

"Your relation is a trainer, too? Sanctioned or illicit?"

Priya threw a hand out, palm up, "Well, she didn't even *tell* me she *could* do it. She can do everything else, so I *assume* she can do what Gemini does. Now that I've learned I can gain spells by increasing my skills, I suspect she feared I'd learn shadow magic." She flipped her hand and smirked. "She's always going on about shadow magic this, and shadow magic that."

Guiles surprised me when he nodded with sympathy. "There are similar sentiments on the Eastern continent. I've never understood why people withhold the gifts given their children. It contradicts logic. The pains of our history should encourage us to use those blessed with magic as tools to prevent evil deeds. I'm afraid your aunt's disposition toward the dark arts is shared by many." He shook his head as if to clear his thoughts. "This still doesn't explain how a low-level like—Gemini, was it?—trains your skills. I've never met a skill trainer without a specialty profession."

We shrugged in unison.

Guiles lips shrunk. "I am not one to become easily frustrated, but what you say is... improbable. Yet, I detect no dishonesty in either of you. How long have you been together?"

Priya eyed me questioningly. "Is it two days or three?"

I went for snarky in my response. "What, you haven't counted every minute? Mean I nothing to you?"

"Two days?" Guiles asked. He turned a blank stare on Priya. "But someone has spent all your points. You say your aunt hasn't trained you, and yet your attributes are at their cap for your level."

Apparently, Guiles's interface was more detailed than Priya's. I wondered if the interface expanded its capabilities as he gained levels.

"Do you really want me to answer that little quandary?" I asked. "You seem frustrated."

Guiles sighed. "Priya, how did you meet this man?"

"I told you. A shadow caster captured me. A servant to an evil underlord."

I filled in the blank. "Caym."

Priya turned her eyes on me. "Come to think of it, it makes sense my aunt would warn me against shadow magic, right?"

"Bah! You speak like being kidnapped by an underlord's minion is commonplace. I've heard some tall tales..."

"Sounds crazy, right?" Priya chuckled. "Not my first

brush with evil, I'm afraid. Anyway, Gemini came along the other day, rescued me, and enamored me to him with his *epic heroism*," She flashed me a sarcastic wink.

I contended it was Priya who'd rescued me by sucking Crohl into the globe, but there was no point arguing. The elf already thought we were liars, and I didn't want to complicate things. I wanted to learn swordsmanship.

"How did you come to rescue her?"

I adopted a monotone droll. "Her Aunt Zhara offered me a quest to expunge this dark dude from an underground mini-dungeon, and I found her while I was there."

Guiles nodded and half-smiled. "I miss my questing days, sometimes..." His eyes took on a dreamy gaze of nostalgia, but then his arms jerked and dropped. "Wait. What?" The high-pitched squeal of the second word caused me to peer up and down the alley to ensure he hadn't been detected. "Did you... Did you say... Aunt *Zhara*?" He annunciated the name in two, deliberate syllables.

*Here we go again.*

Priya mocked him. "Do you speak the common tongue?"

6

"What is it about today?" Priya asked, throwing her hands up at me. "Zhara this! Zhara that!"

"I've heard it all! I don't know how you conceal these lies from me, but you know nothing of Zhara's blessings on us!" Guiles stomped up the alley.

"Great." I threw up a hand and let it drop. "Now we've pissed off the weapons trainer."

"Guiles?" Priya beckoned. "Brother?"

He stopped and turned.

Shaking her head with a complimentary eye roll, Priya unclasped her robe in fluid, practiced flicks of her fingers, shrugged it off her shoulders, and slapped it against my chest. Sexy things jiggled.

"Um, honey? What'cha doin'?"

Priya ignored me. Running a hand through her curly golden locks to raise them from her neck, she turned.

"Unhook me."

"Are we going to do this every single time someone—?"

The glare she threw over her shoulder left little room for argument. I snuck a glance at Guiles, who peered back in our direction with his head tilted to one side. The elf's face stretched in unmistakable confusion, but he said nothing. I unsnapped the fancy new torso-hugging armor, knowing full well the undergarments she'd worn weren't there anymore.

"Do you mean to disrobe in the interest of—"

"Just wait. I shall placate your curiosities." Priya pressed the protector to her chest and turned as the split in the back fell open. I forgot to close my eyes. The tattoo was dim, but as the air touched it, the ward glowed, washing the elf's face and the alley walls in bright gold. The leaves shimmered, and the trunk shone a brilliant white.

I loved that tattoo. It was bad ass.

Utter softness stroked my consciousness. Warmth washed over the flesh of my arms beneath my shirtsleeves. For the first time, I could drag my gaze from the ward when Guiles's shoulders dropped, and he halted his slow pace forward. I found my attention drawn back to the ward.

Priya peered at Guiles over her bare shoulder. "What do you think, *brother* elf? Lack understanding of Zhara's blessings, do I?"

Then she turned so I could reattach the hooks, just to find me in a semi-hypnotic state. "Gem?"

"Oh!" I barked, shaking off the effect. Although it was like trying to draw myself out of heated quicksand, I set my fumbling fingers to work. But then my eyes fell to the ward's glow again and my lips tightened as they spread into a smile. My fingers slowed.

Priya turned her head. "Could you maybe go a little slower? I adore the gooseflesh prickling my skin from the night breeze. That chill coursing up my spine adds flavor."

"Sorry!" I threw Guiles an embarrassed glance only to find disappointment washing across the elf's features as the ward's light faded. I muttered to Priya, "Maybe if you didn't rip your clothes off to prove a point…"

She shrugged as I fastened. "I guess I'm just a simple girl from the Wood, used to taking shortcuts."

"Bah. Simple, my ass. And while we're at it, 'girl,' my ass, too."

"Begone from my sight!" Guiles barked.

We both jerked. "What?" Priya and I asked in unison.

Guiles slouched and closed his eyes. "It's an expression of disbelief, not dismissal." He shook his head as he cupped his forehead with his hand as if a migraine was ramping up.

I laughed with relief. "I see. It's like saying *Get the fuck outta here!* when you don't believe something incredible." Considering the ward's influence, I empathized with the sentiment.

Priya slid on her robe. "If not for our bond, I would understand you no better than him."

"I'd never considered Zhara had a family, but this— what is it, exactly?"

"A ward."

"Ah. Well, this *ward* proves you are washed in the Light. Blessed am I to know you, Priya Skyy."

Priya smoothed her garment in the front. "Thank you." She seemed unemotional about the elf's sentiment.

"You will forgive my disbelief. I—"

"Consider it forgotten," she said.

I nodded. "We get a lot of that."

The breeze blowing down the alley calmed, surrounding us in silence.

Guiles broke it. "Did you say Zhara sent you on a *quest* to retrieve Priya? A quest from the Matron of the Wood?"

I shook my head. "She sent me to purge Crohl, though she didn't mention him by name. I've been wondering why she hadn't mentioned Priya was there, as if she didn't know. I have my doubts."

"Strange." He tapped his angular chin, then turned his eyes on me and winked them in succession. Though inspecting me, he spoke to Priya. "How long were you captive?"

"It's hard to say. It seemed like forever."

Guiles's eyebrows furrowed. "While I'm not one to question the guardian, leaving you in the grasp of an under-lord for any period is curious. Caym, you said?"

"She didn't know I was there." Priya threw me a suspicious glare.

"She didn't know you were captive in a place within the Dark Wood?" Guiles scoffed. "You can't be serious."

Priya shot him an evil sneer. "Twice now you've said this. That I can't be serious. If you must know, I had a tendency to disappear and explore the Dark Wood for extended periods to escape the monotony of my guardian treant's rejoicing over my aunt's existence. She didn't suspect anything from my absence because it was more common than not. It's not like we dwelled together, and I didn't visit often—a fact I dreaded each day I was captive. If I'd seen her more often, she might have known I was missing."

"You can't be—" Guiles stopped himself beneath Priya's glare. His words came in a measured tone. "I assure you an *immortal guardian of the Light* knows when her *marked* family blood is imprisoned by her antithetical power."

"Marked?" It took a few seconds to make sense of his words.

"The ward that tamed my will? The mark of the Matron's seat? Do humans teach their children nothing of lore?"

Priya chimed in. "We've established he doesn't remember his parents."

Guiles sighed as his eyes continued to flicker left and right as if reading text in his HUD. When I thought the sun might rise before he spoke again, the elf muttered his internal thoughts just loud enough for us to hear. "I was distracted by the mention of Zhara, but it was plain before my eyes the whole time. He spends her attribute points. She becomes soulbound to him, meaning..." He peered up at me. "You spent all these points, yes?"

I nodded confirmation.

His voice took on an airy, distant quality. "He does not understand he's attuned. You sent him to me."

"Are you okay?" Priya asked, stepping toward Guiles and setting a gentle hand on his shoulder.

"What?" He glanced at her hand on his shoulder, and she jerked it away. The elf waved us down the alley. "Come, we must not linger here."

We fell in next to him.

"Forgive me, friends. I'm just trying to make sense of your tale." His breathing seemed labored, but his taut cheek and wide eyes conveyed excitement. "Gemini, you bound Priya by spending her attribute points. Zhara sent you to cleanse this Crohl from her Wood—or underneath it. Yet, she omitted her niece from the story. If she knew not of her niece's imprisonment, how did she know of the dark presence? No, I don't believe she was unaware of your captivity."

"Are you saying my aunt delivered him to rescue me? That she knew I was there, all along? And what's more, lied about it?"

I suppressed a nod of confirmation at what I'd believed deep down but had just needed to hear from the elf's lips to confirm it. Unfortunately, I forgot about my bond with my companion and my emotional response gave me away.

Priya turned and dropped her jaw at my unspoken suspicion as we paced.

*She's too good at this.*

I cringed.

Guiles gave an exaggerated nod. "That's what I'm telling you."

This time, Priya flinched. "You lack reason. Why would Aunt Zhara wait?"

"Aren't we missing the obvious here?" I asked. "Doesn't the Matron enlist treants and such to do her bidding because she can only travel so far from her tree? What options would she have for rescuing you if I hadn't come along? Does The Matron of the Wood socialize a lot? Are passersby who could've rescued you common?"

*In a world where there are no players?*

Priya rattled off her words like gunfire. "To my great discontent, she often regaled me with stories of travelers drawn to her Light. She predicted a man would be drawn to me in the same way so I might carry on our family line. Relentlessly. Those tales are one reason I left the cave she carved for me and kept my distance." Then she swiveled back to the topic. "You distract me! Why would Aunt Zhara leave me there so long, just to send..." Her eyes widened, and her glare fell hard onto me. Her lips parted as if she would speak, but then she pressed them together for a few heartbeats. Then the patented squint tugged at the skin beneath her eye. "Why you, Gemini?"

"She sees," Guiles said.

Priya turned the gaze on him. "You tread curvy paths en route to making your points, sir."

Guiles shrugged. "I'm a teacher. The best of us ask questions."

A low growl emanated from Priya's chest.

"What is Priya seeing?" I asked.

Priya answered before Guiles could speak. "I am seeing collusion. Guiles is right. My aunt knows everything that goes on in that forest, I was just too blind to believe she would leave me down there in that smelly pit of kobold hell." She tapped her chin with her index finger, much as Guiles had moments earlier. "I'm left with the same query. Why would she send you? What did she know about you?"

"She wrapped a vine around my neck when she learned I'd bound myself to you."

"And yet I sense you don't believe she would've harmed you. Something is foul."

Guiles thrust a finger at me. "You trained Priya into bondage, right?"

Priya squinted. "I don't think I like the way you arranged those words."

Guiles ignored her. He raised his sleeve and wiped away sweat beading on his forehead despite the cool night breeze.

It calmed, and the elf's hair settled across his shoulders as we paced. His lips remained relaxed as he awaited my answer, although I hadn't determined whether I'd give one.

The shopkeeper, Breeder, knew who Priya was. The innkeeper thought we were demons raised from the dead. We'd already told Guiles too much, and he wanted to know more.

But the elf's disposition indicated an unmistakable reverence for Zhara. The inquisitive voice in my head told me to press on, so I cast my earlier thoughts about keeping a low profile to the wind.

"Yes."

His next question came without pause, like a pistol he'd loaded in anticipation. "Do you speak multiple languages?"

The inner voice of prudence spoke up again, and I hesitated. But again, Guiles remained quiet. Patient.

That the elf concealed his weapons training proved he wasn't a pawn of the government. Breeder, who worshipped the ground Priya trudged upon by the time we'd left his shop, had referred us to him. Still, Guiles let Brugh 'filter' us, because he trusted the giant's judgment.

Or maybe it was to avoid traps being laid by the guards.

I inspected him, focusing on one particular attribute. If the newfound patience he exhibited was genuine, he wouldn't mind.

### *Guiles*
*Elf*
*Level 50 Rogue*
*Disposition: Friendly*

*And there it is, folks. Friendly.*

There was something to be said for using the tools provided.

I answered. "I learn languages from neutral or lawful beings when I hear them."

Priya stopped and turned on me. "You *what?*" The second word squeaked like a chair with a loose screw.

Although she'd been confused when I'd spoken to Roshan in her native language in Crohl's lair, I'd suggested we all use Common to ensure we understood each other. But it hadn't occurred to explain I could speak languages upon hearing them.

Guiles saved me from that impending tiff.

"I sense your doubts about the Matron of The Wood, Gemini, but trust me when I say she is the living expression of the Light in this world. You strike me as a man of caution and character, so I can understand why you might not be loose with your trust, especially if she hasn't been forthcoming with you. But Zhara is the guardian of the goddess's source of power in this region. If she chooses deceit to meet Solara's ends, then you should believe she has good cause. Profound reason. We must sometimes operate in the ways of the darkness to defeat it."

He continued. "I also cannot pretend Zhara's choosing you was a product of your good luck or her lack of calculation. Your abilities to train your companions, bind them to you, learn skills independently, and divine languages suggests why she chose you." He shook his head as a genuine smile crossed his lips.

Priya unlocked her gaze from mine and turned them upon the other elf. "So, because my aunt sensed his abilities, she sent him for me."

Guiles nodded and held up a finger. "I'm certain of it."

"Do you know Zhara?" I asked.

"I have never had the pleasure of a meeting, but her lore is extensive. Her influence in this region is undoubtable."

"But if you've never met her, how can you be sure of the reason she sent me for Priya?"

"Because, Gemini, you are a Shénhuà."

"What'd you call me?" I shoved a finger at his chest.

Guiles shook his head as he peered down at my lingering digit. "How do you suffer him?"

Priya flashed me a sideways grin. "I'm still figuring it out."

I folded my arms across my chest and addressed Priya. "You know about these Shénhuà?"

"My aunt annoyed me with the stories, but she never used that name. I dismissed them as tales intended for children." She turned her attention to Guiles. "What does the word mean?"

"Our closest word in Common is *mythic*."

Mythic. That didn't sound so bad. Kind of pimp, really.

Priya snapped her fingers. "That was the word she used!"

Guiles leaned against an empty keg. All thoughts of sword training had vanished from my head.

"If you believe the legends, you're attuned to the energy of Enora. This removes the confinements which bind normal beings. Zhara, in all her wisdom, recognized your affinities and coupled you with her niece before you even met."

"No," I muttered. "She knew I was coming."

7

Wind moaned through the alley and blew Guiles's white hair around his face.

"Priya is bound to you, so she is immortal, yes?"

"I'm standing right here," Priya said.

I might have laughed, but Guiles's question trampled any semblance of humor in me. "You know things."

"You speak in the tone of a man who keeps secrets." Guiles paused for a few beats and nodded. "Wise, indeed. Yes, the immortality of those bound to the Shénhuà is one reason the lore survives the centuries. The return of a mythic is... alas, there is no appropriate word. That I learned of you first is a blessing beyond my deserving."

From his tone I thought he might tear up at any moment.

"Take your time," I said. "I've got all night."

"I apologize. I've just waited a long time."

"Waited?" Priya asked. "Waited for what?"

A smile raised one side of his narrow lips. "It seems Solara has seen fit to reward my faith. I've lingered an eternity in this seedy town for an opportunity such as this. For now, just know your secrets are safe with me, but powerful beings would seek to corrupt someone they see as a potential tool, or kill one they perceive as a threat."

"You've been waiting for this? For us?" True to form, Priya wasn't giving up so easily.

"I didn't know why I waited, but I'm now convinced. The appearance of a mythic in this tiny and insignificant boil proves it. The tale of how I came to be in Brumhill is best saved for another time. For now, I must focus on your esteemed aunt's desires."

"And how might you do that?" I asked.

"By serving you. You came for weapons training."

"That bitch!" Priya barked.

I jerked and fell back a step as her word, coupled with an emotional avalanche, slammed into me. "What in the utter fuck, girl?"

Priya growled, "She left me down there to rot until you came. Crohl hurt creatures by channeling spells through my body! He kept be in a glass ball!" She seethed and half her teeth flashed between tight lips. "There can be only one reason."

I raised an eyebrow. Guiles tilted his head to one side.

"Babies." The low grumble of her voice might have spat poison into the air.

I tried to relax my shoulders and my tone as I replied. "Why do I think you've been having a silent conversation with yourself?"

"No, I spoke of it moments ago when you distracted me. Remember? How Zhara talked of creatures drawn to her light? How one day a man would be drawn to me in the same way, that we might carry on my family line?"

"That's not so unusual, is it? That someone wants to see their family go on. How does that mean—"

"She offered you her body in reward for purging Crohl, right?"

Upon returning to the tree she guarded with Priya in tow, I'd suspected that Zhara had never planned on making good on that promise, no matter how she flirted. I had the distinct impression she'd been leading me around by my dick. There was a lesson there.

Guiles injected a theory. "Maybe if Gemini survived but you fell to Crohl, she would've mated with him."

"Bitch!" Priya spat the word.

Guiles cringed, drew up his shoulders, and squeezed his eyes closed like he waited for lightning to strike.

She glared into my eyes. "I bet he's right. She would've made babies with you and given nary another thought to her precious Priya. But since you won the day..."

"It seems she had larger things in mind for you than just reproducing," Guiles said. "She sent the two of you forth with her blessing, yes? To advance yourselves?"

"That was our idea," Priya said. Then she eyed me with suspicion. "Wasn't it?"

I showed her both palms. "I am not in cahoots with your Aunt Zhara."

"Well, she will not manipulate me." Priya pinched her lips together and squinted. Her boots swished across the dusty alley floor as she paced around us, muttering. "I'll feed you Tyne Leaf soup once a week. She'll see!" Her voice dropped to a mutter too low for me to hear as she paced in a circle around us.

I leaned toward Guiles. "What kind of soup? Is she going to poison me?"

"Tyne Leaf. So you can't get her pregnant. It seems she's missed the point."

"Any permanent effect? You know? On my guys?" I flicked my eyes downward.

It would be just my luck I end up in a land with two beautiful women who wanted me and my banana shriveled up.

*Again, thinking with your cock. When will you learn?*

Guiles shook his head and rolled his eyes. "It seems you've also missed the point." He sighed. "Nothing permanent. Your *guys* should be fine."

"Good. Whew." I feigned wiping sweat from my brow.

Instead of chuckling, Guiles raised one shoulder in a half-shrug. "Of course, powerful alchemists *can* use Tyne Leaf as a poison when its mixed with other ingredients."

I sighed, then I recalled something he'd said a moment ago. "Wait. What do you mean, we've missed the point?"

The question had barely passed my lips when Priya turned to face us, and her continuing verbalization of her thoughts grew louder.

"—what she thinks when our line ends and she has to find another"—She glanced at Guiles—"What did you call him? That word for mythic?"

Guiles rolled his eyes. "Shénhuà"

"Yeah, that. Let's see what she thinks of that!"

I cleared my throat. "This all presumes I'm something more special than I am. I'm just this guy, you know?"

"Pfft!" they rattled their lips in unison.

*The Douglas Adams nerds at my old job would've gotten a kick out of my reference. Maybe Enora was recording.*

Guiles gestured toward a grassy area just beyond the end of the alley on the right. "Let me recount some history from my library before you decide what you are." Though he hadn't stated it in the form of a question, his gaze showed he was waiting for confirmation.

"Library?"

"Yes, Elves appreciate history. We keep quite the collection back home, and I've copied much of it to my interface repository." He tapped his temple.

"Oh, right."

Again, the full-blooded elf sighed. "You didn't know you could stash documents in your interface."

"No. I didn't."

"I'll show you later. Come, let's sit."

Having concluded her muttering for the time being, Priya followed us to the grassy area near an unmanned, rusted gate. We sat across from Guiles, and I peered at the blanket of stars above. A check of my interface showed it was after 2100 hours.

*You have been offered a quest:*
### *A Tale of Fate*
*Listen to Guiles's history of the legendary Shénhuà.*
*Rewards*
*500 XP*
*Entry in your Enoran Book of Lore*
*Would you like to accept this quest?*
*Yes/No*

It sounded like free XP to me!

Having calmed, Priya set a hand on my leg.

Guiles crossed his legs like a guru. His gaze flicked around as he read inside his own field of vision. "Shénhuà popped up all over Enora millennia ago, starting across the sea in the East. Many believed Solara sent them to bring

Light into the world. Hmm. I guess that part didn't pan out."

"What do you mean, *didn't pan out?*" I asked.

"A longer story for another day."

Coupled with the tale about how he came to be in this sparsely populated town, Guiles seemed to have a penchant for delaying stories he didn't want to tell.

"Not all Shénhuà turned out to be so... shall we say, enlightened. Legends and lore often entail feats of great heroism, but the Shénhuà were awe-inspiring because of their ability to empower others. They bonded beings to themselves in the way you have Priya. Since they could train their companions each time they advanced in level, said companions became powerful."

Priya flicked up a finger. "This! I like the sound of this!"

Guiles gave his head a derisive shake.

"So, they were glorified trainers?" I asked.

"Hmm. Perhaps more background. Throughout time, Solara has matched the energies of trainers and trainees so a maximum five attribute points could be on those who seek training, but the Shénhuà were an exception. Lore has it that a being attuned to Enora's energy could draw limitlessly from ley lines to elevate the skill points of anyone who gained levels.

"Ley lines?" Priya asked.

Guiles nodded. "Neutral lines of magical energy that run underground throughout Enora. The theory is the mystics could access these channels to empower their companions without limits, as long as their companions gained levels. But where one limitation was removed, another was imposed."

I nodded, understanding. "The binding to the mythic.

They could train up attributes to their hearts' contents, but they had to bind the person to themselves."

Guiles snapped his fingers, pointed at me, then gestured alternately to Priya. "Exactly. Just as you have."

I recalled the warning I'd received before I bound Priya to me. The system message had stated there were no limits to the number of NPCs I could bind. My forehead wrinkled as a revelation rocked my mind.

*If I can bind a bunch of NPCs and raise their attributes as they level, we could do raids. We could level like mad. I could build a fucking army. This game is insane!*

My mind conjured grand images of banner text on web pages.

***Survive the Dark Levels in Hard Core mode! Adventure with non-players so real, you'll never want to log out! Build an army! Take over entire regions! Conquer whole continents! Battle for the world!***

I felt woozy. Priya gripped my knee and shot me a glance. I shook my head to cast off her concerns. She grasped my hand as Guiles went on. Her affections made me feel like a middle school kid with his first girlfriend.

"The Shénhuà first appeared on the Eastern continent, then on this one. Later, they spread to the others. Some were professionals who created armor or weapons, others adventured. The Shénhuà came in many races. But they all shared common traits that lead me to believe you are, indeed, the returned."

He ticked them off on his fingers. "You have spent over five attribute points and bound Priya to you. You learn skills naturally. The speaking in multiple tongues was common among the mystics. Add to these that you share an emotional link with Priya otherwise reserved for Elvenkind. That challenges even my elven mind."

*In all its humility.*

"Then, to hang a helmet on it, add on the fact Priya has no class."

My heart paused as I remembered how Priya had taken offense when she misunderstood what Roshan meant when she said Priya had 'no class.' Had that really been only two nights ago?

Guiles continued. "You must choose an adventurer class before points earned via leveling can be spent to rank up your attributes. Otherwise, you'll only gain ranks through your daily exercise of mind and body—the slow, natural way that ensures balance in the world. If just anyone could rank up their skills without limits, they would all be out with swords and bows, or casting magic spells to destroy creatures for experience points! But when bound to a Shénhuà, one could become powerful."

"Where did these mythic people come from?" Priya asked.

Guiles nodded. "That's a question for the ages. As far as anyone can tell? Thin air." He eyed me, to illustrate his point. "No family lines—pauper or royal—were ever established. The mythic were tight-lipped about their heritage. Yet another mark showing your companion's mysticism, since he has no memory of his parents. I wonder if they all shared this amnesia, but it was so long ago and our history doesn't mention it."

And there, despite the lie about my parentage, I found an answer right in front of my stupid face.

Every sign I got from Nokuro Takemoto was that Infinity Designs left this world to evolve naturally after the A.I. took over. So, if these Shénhuà held powers that operated outside the rules governing normal NPC advancement, there was only one explanation.

This inkling in my head blossomed into a full-on flower of conjecture. "Tell me, Guiles, what happened to these Shénhuà?"

"They vanished in much the same way as they appeared. They left behind their castles and their garrisons, their villages and all their followers, abandoning them to their fates. I assume they returned to Solara's eternal kingdom. Or in some cases, Hokrahm's pits of fire."

I pursed my lips and nodded. "Let me guess, they left around two millennia ago?"

Both his eyebrows ticked up this time. "Yes. This is why most have written them off as religious legends. But how did you know when they disappeared if you knew nothing of them?"

*Because that's when beta testing ended, the players logged out, and they fast-forwarded Enora.*

The Purge.

*They'd designed the game so NPCs benefitted most from cooperating with players. Even if NPCs evolve over generations, the skill point limits keep their power in check.*

It was kind of genius. Enora was going to be around for a long time.

"Call it a lucky guess."

"I don't believe you," Guiles said. "But keep your secrets. I wish only to serve Solara's purpose."

Priya did that squinting thing again, and I felt her suspicions bubbling to the surface, but she remained quiet.

8

You have completed a quest.
***A Tale of Fate***
*Listen to Guiles's history of the legendary Shénhuà.*
*Rewards*
*500 XP*
*Your Enoran Book of Lore now includes the entry, 'A History of The Attuned.'*

Puzzle pieces locked into place. Though the players were wiped from the servers after beta testing and the world had been fast-forwarded, their impacts on the world had endured in the lore of the races of Enora.

When I woke in the starting village, Lucera said I would choose whether I took advantage of opportunities, but now I saw that for the half-truth it was. It'd all started when she allowed me one question, and I'd inquired how I could best survive the Dark Levels.

*Make friends.*

Then she'd given me my first quest.

Visit Zhara.

Zhara's quest? Clear out Crohl.

Priya hadn't been mentioned though. Why was that? If the Matron of The Wood knew Priya was a captive and expected I was coming, wasn't she also risking my killing Priya? Why would she?

Because it's a game? Because my decisions should decide my fate... and hers? I didn't think so. This all reeked of a setup.

My mind drifted to the myriad scans of my brain before my transition into this world. Personality tests, question-naires. Nokuro Takemoto had watched my game play in the Light of Babylon before meeting me. Infinity Designs knew all there was to know about how I thought, my reactions to stressful situations. They were all too aware that in other games, I was a stone-cold motherfucker.

When they'd needed to fill in the blanks, they had to go no further than to Nokuro Takemoto's niece.

*Katelyn.*

The woman who'd called her uncle when she found out I was dying and asked for his help. She was the one person I'd spent the most time with in the world, as we played Light of Babylon late into the nights and early mornings. I spent many sleepy days at work due to that woman and the game.

I had no doubt Infinity Designs shared all these scans and profiles of me with Enora, the game A.I.

Although it had been Roshan who'd warned me Priya was a slave to a dark caster so I wouldn't harm her when we'd first encountered the half-elf, Zhara had warned me I might find minions under evil's control. And Enora had already known how I would respond.

Sure, surviving long enough to complete that quest was my responsibility. I had emotional scars to prove I hadn't been given a free ride. But A.I. as smart as Enora could put me in positions where she could reasonably predict the outcomes.

*Enora knows me. For all my professing that Roshan and Priya should have free will, I now have to ask myself if I do.*

When all of this started, I'd wondered why I had to undertake the Dark Levels. If the point was to transfer my consciousness to test the function so they could help the terminally ill, why not just give me a pass? Why risk having me wiped from the servers if I fell in combat?

Nokuro had set that squarely on the A.I.'s shoulders, saying Enora had taken over the world and refused to make allowances other players wouldn't enjoy. Taking everything into account, however, I suspected I might have been given only half the story.

*Consider the timeline.*

Enora was amazing, it's citizens the most realistic recreations of sentient life I could ever have imagined. Yet two years more would pass before players entered the game. That was six in Enoran time.

*Why wait?*

"Something happened," I muttered.

"What, honey?" Priya asked.

I shook my head and raised a finger. "Give me a sec."

The two elves shared a glance, but my mind journeyed elsewhere. I filled in holes in the jigsaw puzzle of my new life.

*Why isn't Nokuro releasing the game?*

He said the purge removed player impact from the world. If players bound companions but then disappeared, I bet their spawn point disappeared with them. The NPCs would die off if they had nowhere to re-spawn. Their immortality would be erased. So Nokuro hadn't lied, exactly, although the player influence lived on in lore and history.

*All the players who enter this world will be Shénhuà. Hell, it makes for great storytelling. Start at level one. Survive hard core. Recruit NPCs. Build an army. Blah, blah.*

*But why wait two more years?*

I recalled words Enora spoke after my lone resurrection that morning.

*"The last time I allowed a human into my world, Hokrahm tempted him and a creature of utter darkness thrived, bringing blight and pain to Solara's faithful. I hold high hopes you will not follow in his footsteps."*

Had she meant another human *lived* here? Had someone else's consciousness been transferred?

*"Nokuro Takemoto believed bringing another human player here might balance the corruption and make Enora a place millions of players could enjoy."*

*Balance the corruption. They'd already given me the answer. Someone in Enora had poisoned the well and Nokuro sent me in here to clean up their fucking mess, to get the world back in balance. But Enora wanted me to prove myself, so I'd had to survive the Dark Levels first.*

The worst part was, Nokuro could've just told me. It wasn't like I had a lot of options. I'd been dying.

*What if Enora wouldn't let him tell me? She could easily read my mind to see if he'd violated such an agreement. The A.I. warned me it would analyze my thoughts for the first ten levels.*

Guiles spoke up. "I understand your amazement. What you've learned about yourself is not easily absorbed. Especially since Solara has changed the rules."

"What do you mean?"

"Oh," Guiles said, patting his abs. "I thought it would

be obvious. The attuned could not bear children. Solara rendered them sterile."

"What the fuck are you saying right now?" I asked.

Guiles's head turned. "Priya, you've had only Gemini to your bed?"

*Oh, shit.*

She nodded, but then shrugged. "Well, him and Roshan."

"I assume Roshan is a female name?"

*Oh, fucking golden gravy.*

Priya nodded. Confusion washed off of her as my own waned.

Guiles's eyebrow ticked the highest I'd seen it as his eyes danced between Priya and me.

"I'm sorry. I thought you'd known. It's not my place to bear such tidings as I have just met you..."

I shook my head and cupped it with one hand, like Guiles had earlier.

"You should check your companion tab, Gemini."

I was one step ahead of him.

***Priya Skyy***
*Half-Elf*
*Level 9*
*(No class)*

**Attributes**

*Strength: 8**
*Dexterity: 3**
*Intelligence: 16*
*Wisdom: 10*
*Constitution: 14*
*Charisma: 8**

### *Combat Skills*

Ranged: 4

Unarmed: 1

Blunt: 3

Melee: 5

### *Defensive Skills:*

Dodge: 4

### *Weapon Skills*

Bow: 14*

Blunt: 7

### *Spells:*

### *Shadow Void*

Level 8

Required Affinity: Shadow Magic

The caster opens a portal to the underworld and banishes chaotically aligned creatures within two levels into the void.

Cast Time: 3 seconds

Cost: 100 Mana

Cool-down: 30 Minutes

### *Sleep*

Level 9

Required Affinity: Shadow Magic

The caster calls forth dark essence to force a single adversary to slumber for up to one minute.

Damage will end the effect.

### *Occupational Skills:*

Not to be confused with combat professions, occupational skills allow people to earn a wage, run a business, build foundations, or create weapons, armor, and potions to supplement adventuring.

Carpentry: 18

Forestry: 41

*Skinning: 15*

*Cooking: 17*

**Affinities:**

*Shadow Magic: 100%*

*Elemental Magic: 57%*

*Languages:*

*Elven*

*Common*

**Disposition**:

*Beloved*

*Due to your beloved status, you may spend four attribute points per level for Priya Skyy.*

"Look next to her name," Guiles said. "Focus there."

### *Priya Skyy**

Another asterisk I'd casually mistaken for one I'd found next to her age. The one that came without a tooltip.

I focused on the asterisk. Text popped up on the screen, and my heart thumped hard in my chest. My throat swelled.

"What is it, Gem?"

*This doesn't happen in VMMORPGS!*

My mind ventured to the forest two days before just before Priya and I had gone off to a cave together. Zhara had cast a spell on Priya.

*'My niece shall not bleed.* Her greatest lie of all.

My mind echoed Priya's earlier sentiment.

*That bitch.*

"Gemini? You're starting to—as you say it—freak me out."

I shook my head in disbelief. I raised my head and

found a glowing smile adorning Guiles's face. I suddenly wanted to choke him.

Priya's tone grew more desperate. "Gem, your gaping mouth will catch bugs."

For the third time in the last minute I read the tool tip that popped up when I focused on the asterisk.

***Priya Skyy*****
*Pregnant*

9

Conflict. My brain versus my body.

"She did this!" Priya barked, jumping to her feet.

*She's pacing again.*

I was so gut-punched over the prospect of being a father after having spent less than a week in Enora, that the feeling stifled the anger pouring off Priya.

Then I was pacing, and we orbited Guiles at varied distances like planets around a star.

I guessed Infinity Designs could add:

**Have a family!**

to the aforementioned banner ad.

Would players want that level of reality? When all was said and done, wasn't it just a game to them? How would it fly in-game if a player logged out on their family and returned three days later, Enoran time? Would an angry NPC mother's nagging ruin the gaming experience? Hell, could female gamers have babies in-game?

No. No way. The more likely explanation was that I could reproduce because I wasn't human, anymore. In this sense, Enora was treating me like a resident, not an alien. Now *that* made sense.

*What if it's a gift?*

Now there was an interesting thought.

*What if Takemoto worked with the A.I. to give me this opportunity? Hell, that makes even more sense when I think about critically ill people being sent to a non-game world to live out their lives. Could I be the test bed for them to have children? That theory reaches far beyond Enora. Far beyond me.*

Priya's expletive-filled tirade went on for another minute, but Guiles sat with his legs crossed, eyes forward. Patient.

Something told me Zhara would get an earful, someday. Besides, I wasn't sure the magical woman in the woods was to blame. After all, it was Priya's and my dirty dance in that cave that created this situation.

*That's right. Keep what you can't change in perspective.*

"I need to prioritize," I thought aloud. "Roshan needs us. That's our first concern."

Priya continued muttering under her breath, and I wondered how much her cursing of the Matron of The Wood had to do with the prospect of being a mother. So, when she slowed her vitriolic prattling, I shrouded my voice in sweetness and tried to equal it on an emotional level to influence her. The shit was hard work.

"Sweetheart? You still with me?"

The emotional bridge did its thing.

"Oh!" Our orbits halted as we stared at each other. She pressed her hands to her cheeks. "Gemini! Tell me you aren't angry." She dropped a hand onto her flat stomach over her robe. "I know it's all so sudden, but..." Raising her gaze, she tilted her head and one side of her lips curved up into a hesitant smile.

To my surprise, I wasn't angry. Shocked, yes. Angry? No. And right now we needed to focus on Roshan, which meant I needed to focus on weapon skills. We needed to remain calm and stay on track. Luckily, Priya's smile proved contagious.

"Why would I be mad about fathering a child with the most beautiful elf in Enora?"

Priya took two lunging steps, flung her arms around my neck to hoist herself up, then wrapped her legs around my waist. Suction tapped at my cheek and neck as she planted tiny kisses. "How could I talk about Tyne Leaf soup with you, my love? Who else in this world would I want to father my offspring?"

Feeling her body pressed next to me brought a brand new set of sensations. Though overcome by the prospect of being a parent—the prospect it was even *possible*—Priya's new emotions bathed me in a weird cross of calm and excitement. She dropped her feet to the ground, and I lay my cheek atop her head and smiled.

Guiles wore a half-smile of his own, assuming the casual stance of an elf who was in no hurry.

I pulled back from Priya and tapped my wrist to indicate the time. But her confused expression reminded me wristwatches were a foreign concept. I sighed at my stupidity. "Roshan awaits. So, skill training and then the rest?"

She dropped her shoulders. "So, business now, talk later?"

I nodded. "Absolutely."

She kissed me. "And more."

Guiles's eyes danced back and forth between us. Then

he spoke, though more to himself than the rest of us. "A thing of legends. The child of an immortal and a mythic."

I cleared my throat. "Let's get cracking."

Guiles nodded and led us into a wide swatch of open grass framed by narrow dirt paths with buildings on three sides and the low city wall on the fourth. "Time to try the ability I taught you. Now, pretend I am the cloud I had you imagine. Step through me."

"That easy?"

He snapped. "Don't think! Do!"

I shrugged, imagined the sensation I experienced when entering stealth, and stepped toward him, expecting we'd bang heads.

I suddenly stared at the side of a building with scraggly lines dotted like stucco. A black icon of an eye appeared in the periphery of my interface. Guiles tapped my shoulder and I swung around. The symbol vanished. He stared up at me.

*Say whaaaaat?*

Weirdo that I was, I wished I'd tried rogue as a class in earlier games so I'd have something to compare to. "Holy rocking shit! Did I step right through you?"

"Yes, but I didn't mention you should twist as you step through the cloud. This would have left you facing my back so you can perform a Sneak Attack, Spine Snap, or Backstab skill. What you did is a good method of evasion, though, so keep it in your mental toolbox. You should practice on a tree to level those skills. Shadow Merge moves you forward no matter when you use it, but you must have a subject to step through." He held up a finger to belay my celebration. "Also know, if you picture that cloud when you activate your simple stealth and remain still, you will vanish quicker. Try this now."

I waited for the cool-down timer to reset, and reactivated the skill, this time thinking of myself disappearing in a cloud.

"That's useful," Priya said. "Notably faster. My betrothed will become a very bad-butted mother-humper."

"You mean badass motherfucker."

She waved a dismissive hand. "Maybe I was trying to be less vulgar." A mischievous expression crossed her face. "Perhaps you could use this new skill on Zhara and give her something else from behind... in the wrong hole."

"I would not recommend it," Guiles said with a deadpan expression.

"Gross," I muttered.

Guiles pressed forward. "Gemini, your dagger skill is only fifteen. I don't know what you've been waiting for. Ugh." He lowered his voice to a mutter. "I discover a Shénhuà with a barely double-digit dagger skill who calls himself an assassin." He shook his head and spoke out loud again. "Come. I can help you raise it and give exercises for when you move on. I have target dummies this way, but a tree will do on the road."

Guiles doubled my dagger skill to 30 in about an hour. I was pissed to learn I could've stabbed trees in the Dark Wood to accomplish the same. Upon the first ranking, to sixteen, I auto-learned a new skill.

### *Combat Flurry*

*Level 10*
*Unleash a barrage of dagger strikes.*
*Requires: Daggers, skill rank 16*
*Duration: 5 seconds*
*Cost: 30 Stamina*
*Cool-down: 30 Seconds*

*Unleash a barrage of attacks on your attackers' ventral side.*
*100% damage increase to main-hand weapon strikes*
*50% damage increase to off-hand weapon strikes*

I reminded myself that ventral was the front. So, Combat Flurry was a face-to-face skill. Since assassin skills cost stamina, I'd need to focus more attribute points into Constitution to increase that pool. Combat alone had impact upon my stamina, and I had to ask myself whether it was worth being a rogue, since that one attribute-suck stole from my ability to pump other attributes later.

Then, at dagger skill rank 20, I'd learned another ability:

**Spine Snap** (1st Tier)
*Wedge your dagger between your enemy's vertebrae and twist.*
*Requires: Daggers, skill rank 20*
*Stealth skill*
*Cost: 30 Stamina*
*Cast Time: Instant*
*Damage: 500% Weapon Damage*
*+15% increased chance of Critical Hit for 5 seconds*

*Five-hundred percent weapon damage! Now we're talking.*

Guiles showed little concern for who or what I was as we progressed. As a trainer, he'd changed his focus to how much he could help in the short time we had together. I appreciated the professionalism and worked hard to keep my mind on the tasks at hand, but thoughts attacked me with inevitable fury.

*You're going to have a kid.*

I activated Combat Flurry. My hands weighed nothing as they became charged with energy, and I swung my daggers in blurred strikes against the target dummy's wood.

*You've been set up.*

Thankfully, Guiles kicked into trainer mode, rattling off commands as I executed the flurries. My distractions floated away.

"Keep your back straight so the energy channels smoothly through you. Tighten your strikes so you have more control over the region you assault. Keep your hands in front of your chest, inside your shoulders, so you land more strikes per use of the skill."

I tightened my attack area and the daggers almost punched the target on their own.

"Yes, use jabbing motions until you have learned to control the acceleration. Later, you can add in slashing motions, which will increase the chance of your opponent blocking your strikes, but you'll notice the way your slashes swing your arms further from your target as you follow through. The strikes are more likely to open arteries and cause mortal wounds. The further your arms have to travel back to your target, the fewer strikes you land during the limited duration of the skill and the more open you leave yourself for counter, but when well-timed, dividends are paid by slashed arteries. Punch with your blades until you're ready for that."

He stepped from behind the target and unsheathed his dagger.

"Now, evade."

**Guiles** *challenges you to a duel.*
*Accept?*
*Yes/No*

My heartbeat doubled as I peered down at the very dangerous elf in front of me, but the matching adrenaline surge almost tickled my brain with excitement. I nodded and focused on 'Yes.'

A wide square of orange light shot down from above and a translucent wall surrounded us. I estimated it stretched thirty feet in a circle, and we stood near its center.

"Um, is that going to draw attention?"

Guiles shook his head. "Only we can see it, since we're the duelers. Oh, and Priya, since she's in your party."

Priya's avatar had appeared in the corner of my HUD ever since we bonded. It seemed we were permanently in a party. I wondered how that would work if I ever partied with other players, but thoughts like that were just more distractions.

He stepped forward and lowered his chin. "You need only dodge, for now."

I'd expected Guiles would be quick, but I hadn't seen his hands coming at all. Luckily, the duel function mitigated the pain so his blades were pinpricks instead of all-encompassing nightmare slices. He tore me to pieces in two seconds.

*__Guiles__ has defeated you in a duel.*

"You are not a monk. A punching stance will not serve. Elude strikes by twisting at your waist and hips instead of hunching." He grasped my hips and illustrated. "This will increase your ability to evade and increase your dodge rank faster. Stay always in motion, so no enemy has a clear shot at you."

He illustrated and I emulated. When he was satisfied, we switched it up.

We dueled again, and this time I straightened my spine as I performed simple strikes with my daggers. Sweat dripped from my forehead. I activated Combat Flurry, and Guiles took it easy on me so I could adjust. What few strikes landed did little damage.

Counting off the ticks to my stamina as I continued to swing the weapons, I estimated the recovery of two stamina every five seconds, totaling twelve stamina every half-a-minute. This meant Combat Flurry, if activated every cooldown cycle, would eat away 36 stamina per minute.

My Constitution rank was fifteen. As I'd figured out by now, the initial point of every attribute was worth 100 points in the correlating pool. One Intellect equaled 100 mana. One Constitution equaled 100 hit points. That one point of Constitution was also worth 100 stamina. Each added point was worth ten.

At least Enora kept that simple.

But Stamina was unique, as I could earn additional points through labor. My first boost come as I jogged through the forest my first second day in Enora, chasing Click to where we found Roshan. The second point had come as I practiced stealth sneaking up on squirrels on our return from the village. Priya'd gained a Stamina point when we made love in the inn. We'd laughed hard at that. I looked forward to leveling the skill that way, too.

Adding the 100 for the base point to the 140 provided by 14 additional points, then adding the two naturally-earned points, my total stamina, as illustrated by a tiny number atop the bar, was 260. The rate at which Stamina burned during combat or running was so confusing, I'd given up on trying to do the math and used my intuition along with fatigue sensations to balance its depletion.

Since I could only control it by feel, my best chance at

controlling resource losses was to understand I would exhaust 36 Stamina per minute if I kept Combat Flurry active between cool-downs. Then I'd have to add in other assassin skills, like Spine Snap, to get an idea of how often to use each ability.

One thing was certain. The quicker I took down an enemy, the less the stamina expenditure. That would always be the best plan. Long-term combat at melee range was a bad idea for non-tanks, anyway. Some facts were true in all games.

I returned to the practice dummy, which was really just a post with a cross board, and activated Combat Flurry. I tried to focus my strikes in one area while keeping my back straight as instructed. It seemed unnatural, straightening my spine as I punched, because my inclination was to bounce my head side-to-side like a boxer, but a straight back increased my lateral mobility when the excess energy of Combat Flurry filled me.

"Punch! Yes!" Guiles barked. "Center mass only!"

When the ability ended and went on cool-down, I worked my way behind the target and launched a Spine Snap

The wood splintered, and Guiles yelled, "Good!"

I barely heard him because my attention was locked on my interface, watching the Stamina consumption of the Spine Snap skill. It cost me 30 stamina, as promised. It also had a 15-second cool-down, so I could, in theory, expend as much as 120 Stamina per minute if I used it at the exact second it was available.

Watching my stamina meter, I stopped and sucked air. The meter slowly filled.

"Good," Guiles said. "Now, tell me your best single-target rotation."

I nodded. "Assuming my Stamina is full…"

"No, best to subtract twenty right at the top. We are almost never at full Stamina unless we are sitting on our duffs drinking ale."

"Okay, um," I paused, trying to rework the numbers as I huffed and puffed.

Guiles shook his head. "If you are to lead, you must learn to think while your body is under duress. Spit the numbers at me. Don't stop thinking. Never stop thinking."

"Minus 20 Stamina, I start with 240. I open with Spine Snap. That drops my Stamina to 210. Backstab on the tail of Spine Snap brings me down to… 180 stamina. Then I auto-attack until I work back around my enemy and use combat flurry. That should bring me to somewhere between… 150 and 160 Stamina. Then I Shadow Merge at a cost of ten and try to recover a few ticks, if my enemy isn't dead. I'm left with about 140 to 150 stamina, considering regular loss with movement."

Guiles smirked at Priya. She returned it with a sideways smile.

"Well?" I asked, still huffing and puffing.

"It's a fine rotation," Guiles said. I smiled, but he held up a finger. "If you were a Level 20 rogue instead of a Level 10 assassin. You have left yourself no room for error. Let me ask you, what is the weapon damage bonus of Spine Snap?"

"500% main-hand bonus." I reported this memorized fact with pride.

"And what's the damage of Backstab?"

I eyed my interface. "150% main-hand weapon damage."

"And Combat Flurry gives you 125% weapon damage per second over three seconds if you are using weapons that give you attack speeds of less than half a second—which you are not, but I'll be generous—and you split the difference between your main and off-hand damage output."

I shrugged my acquiescence.

"You have burned off over 100 of your Stamina and have not accounted for the mass amounts you will lose from movement during combat. Subtract another 50 to 100 for that. If you have a second opponent to deal with and you are lucky enough to stay on your feet, you've left yourself either huffing and puffing on the ground or spent your last Stamina on Shadow Merge—if you have the Stamina remaining—and *then* left yourself huffing and puffing on the ground, but at least you'll be invisible." He shrugged and shoved his hands in his pockets. Then he kicked a rock and focused on it as it bounced away. "I suppose the latter is preferable... if you must be on your back." Guiles turned and glared at me as if daring me to contradict him.

I waited as my wind returned.

"Tell me, if you spent 30 Stamina on Spine Snap, as you said, Shadow Merged for 10 stamina as your opponent turned, and then Spine Snapped him again, what is your total damage output versus Stamina lost?"

I rolled my eyes upward to do the math. "70 Stamina—a total of 1,000% weapon damage."

"Now, add in a Backstab and tell me your advantages."

"My advantages?" I squinted as I worked through it. "I've done 1,150 weapon damage—not counting for armor reductions—and left myself with about..." I nodded. "Okay, I see the damage difference, but my stamina is still low as fuck."

"Correct!" He winked at Priya and lowered his voice to a conspiratorial tone. "He sees."

"Yes, oh great one, I see more damage and worry I might still be on the ground."

"I will address that. But first, what's the other advantage of my proposed rotation?"

Though I tried to parse his words and come to some logical conclusion, I was missing it.

When I didn't answer, he said, "Using my rotation, your enemy never saw you until you unloaded all of that damage. It was all from behind."

"Oh! Well, shit. That makes sense."

"Ah! But what you don't see is that when you vanish and wait for your enemy to turn for the second Spine Snap, you could *regain a few points of Stamina.* Stay behind your opponent and he might not know what hit him until it is too late. But my crucial message is this, Gemini. Are you listening?"

I nodded, though I tired of the superior tone.

*You tire of it, and yet you're speaking to an NPC right now. He's amazing.*

"If you come this close to spending such a crucial amount of a resource against a single target, do something else."

"Like what?" I asked.

"At Level 20, if you become a rogue, your Stamina will no longer fuel your attacks. Rogues gain an energy bar, instead. Therefore, many of us choose not to build up high constitutions in the first place, because we know high amounts of hit points are useless when compared to quick, devastating damage." He raised an eyebrow. "And few successful rogues double as tanks. Ninja's are another matter, but I digress."

*Ninja's? Monks? I was learning more about classes in Enora from this encounter than any time before.*

Guiles continued. "The energy bar is a game-changer

that a proper trainer would've alerted you to. Of course, you didn't have a trainer... until now."

"Energy bar. Well, shit, that would have been nice to know. So, what is it I should do?"

He nodded. "Save your assassin skills for when you require the element of surprise. And then, I would only use them on a single target, I would Shadow Merge after my first attack, prowl behind that target until all my stamina returned, then attack again."

"Won't waiting allow for my enemy's hit points to recover?"

"Not as fast as your Stamina."

*Ding!*

"Still, at your current level, range is a better ally than deception."

"Then why spend all this time on my dagger skills?"

"To get you a new skill for later use, give you a secondary class to fall back on that wasn't so weak you'd face annihilation, and because any fool can shoot arrows and level his or her bow skill and ranged attack. Trust me. Until Level 20, be a Woodsman, Shénhuà. Practice your assassin skills and train your daggers often when not in combat. If you can get one-handed swords, practice with those, too. But focus on your ranged skills and you can spend your attribute points between Levels 11 and 20 on Dexterity instead of overspending them on Constitution."

Which changed my plans of moments ago in a damned hurry. This guy rocked.

He eyed Priya.

"What?" she asked.

The way he twisted his lips to one side, I could tell he was pondering.

"What?" Priya repeated.

"Remember what a unique pairing you are. Though we have spoken in passing the Shénhuà myths for thousands of years, and although I've just learned of the Skyy familial line, I have little doubt profound changes are due to our world. What they are, I can't imagine. But I trained you in this way because I think it's the most efficient way to move you toward your destiny."

"Is there more?" I asked.

"Hmm? Oh!" He leveled his tone after a quick breath. "Yes. I couldn't resist double-checking the niece of a living immortal, and I noticed something interesting."

"What's that?" Priya asked.

"While I think Gemini has done a commendable job distributing your attributes, you are otherwise a blank slate."

"What do you mean?"

"I see you can cast out minor demons and put others to Sleep. Those are common spells rewarded with typical leveling. But the early levels of Shadow Magic require either reading scrolls or finding specialized training to pick up the spells. Though your aunt's refusal to train you is an open wound I don't want to exacerbate, consider the beauty of your clean canvas. The two of you can work together to sculpt you into whatever you desire."

"How can we get more?" I sensed impatience in my lover and companion, but her tone didn't convey it.

Guiles's eyebrow arched.

"Spells?" Priya clarified. "How might I rain hell down on the deserving?"

When she'd agreed it was time for business, she'd meant it. Guiles and I shared a glance.

"Another trait lore conveys of the mystics is their ability to switch classes. Simple beings as myself have no such gifts, so I chose Rogue as my specialty. But seeing as I've dabbled in the non-class-specific abilities of Shadow Magic, I can train you one such spell. But you should still choose a class soon, for class spells can be very powerful."

"What's the spell?" Priya's eyes lit with enthusiasm.

"It's called Lightning Pulse."

"What the fuck?" I asked.

"What the fuck?" Priya echoed.

*I love her.*

"You cast electric orbs from your fingertips, then they bounce from one person to the next. When you level to the second iteration of Lightening Pulse, it gives you a chance to stun enemies. But at your current level, I cannot give that to you. Seek a trainer at Level 30. In the meantime, would you like the first spell?"

"Yes, Lord Guiles. I would love that!"

I shoved my hand into my bag, stoked he was about to give my baby her first offensive spell. "How much do you need for that?"

"This one is on me. For the niece of Zhara."

"No offense." Priya reached out as if to clutch him, but didn't follow through. "We'll pay. I'm not accepting further favors based on my aunt's benevolence, at the moment."

"Then consider it a gift of support against the bastard Governor of Knall."

"How did you know we were at odds with him?" I asked.

"My hearing is keen, and I monitor the goings on of this tiny, silent town. Your other companion's plight is no secret to me. Now that I see her kidnapping in perspective, I wish I'd intervened."

"You couldn't have known. So, you're not a fan of the governor?"

"Another story for another day, my new friend. Suffice

it to say, I abhor slavery. Harems built of willing partici-pants are one thing, but when one takes a woman's..."

"Fruits?" I asked, again thinking of Roshan.

"As adequate a words as any. I find it offensive to the highest degree, for my line includes seventeen daughters, forty-seven granddaughters, and ninety-six great-grand-daughters."

"Man, you're old as fuck." I chuckled. "That's quite the tree you're building. Lots of branches."

Guiles nodded. "An apt metaphor, though not as mesmerizing a tree as depicted on the ward adorning your precious companion's body."

Priya slapped my shoulder. "Let's forgo the family tree metaphors for the time being."

Her humor filled me with the Light. "Understood, my princess of the wood."

"Ooooh." She wrapped an arm around me. "I like it when you call me your princess."

Guiles trained my saucy little tree climber in Light-ening Pulse and because of her boosted intellect for her current level, that shit came on hot. The three posts he'd set up for practice were left burnt, splintered shard-sticks. A direct damage spell added to her repertoire was priceless.

Too bad it took a quarter of her mana pool, but at least her Wisdom rating was decent and would replenish it.

My jaw dropped the first time she cast it. "How the hell? That seems like a lot of damage!"

"Her affinity for Shadow Magic is quite the contradic-tion to her heritage. And quite powerful."

A clanking sound echoed down an alley on the opposite side of the clearing. My attention shot to Guiles, who threw a quick glance over his shoulder.

"Stealth," he said. "Now. Priya, run up the alley and hide yourself among the empty barrels."

Guiles disappeared like he'd winked out of existence. I envisioned a purple cloud and vanished. But Priya lingered for just a second too long to peer in the direction from which the sound had come.

"Hey! You there!"

She froze.

"What's got a little tart like you out this time of night?" the shorter of the two guards asked. He wore a chain shirt and a leather helmet tilted to one side. His partner stood half-a-head taller, and a mace dangled from his belt.

Priya peered around. "Um... I'm out for a walk?"

The taller guard stepped forward and towered over her. His gaze wandered down her cleavage, along the curves of her powerful legs, and back up again.

### *Slate Plorgen*
*Human*
*Level 10 Fighter*
*Town Guard*

"It's not safe for a lady out this time of night. You could fall upon some unsavory types—or worse, they could fall upon you. Why, there's a place right up yon alley filled with the kinds who might take advantage of such a sweet thing as yourself."

"I can look out for myself," Priya said, squinting up at him.

"Ha!" The shorter one barked as he circled around to Priya's side. "Can ya, now?"

### *Wick Glymer*

*Human*
*Level 8 Fighter*
*Town Guard*

Wick gave Priya's shoulder a little two-fingered shove. "Hear that, Slate? She thinks she can do for herself."

"Aye, with my own ears. I'm impressed." His head swiveled to one side as I circled around him. His facial muscles slackened before hardening as he turned his gaze back on my companion. "Those target dummies, I see? They belong to you?"

Priya shook her head. "Nope, I was just passing by."

Slate continued, unabated. "Because training's guard business. It's against the law to unsheathe weapons or cast magic in the town limits without the mayor's leave and guard supervision. You wouldn't be out here breakin' the law, now would ya? Got any weapons? We should check."

I circled them.

Priya's voice vibrated as she spoke. "Who, me? No. I'm just a simple girl from the woods."

I suppressed laughter.

"Hear that, Slate? This one says she's from the woods."

"Bah!" Slate barked. "I'm not deaf, ya idgit!"

Wick took a step back at the burst of vocal energy.

"So, you aren't from Brumhill. Got nobody with you, then?" Slate asked.

I definitely didn't like where this was going.

Guiles's voice echoed from somewhere nearby, an ominous whisper. "She has people."

The guards spun around, squinting into the night. Priya took a step backward while their backs were turned. I circled behind them again.

"Who's that?" Wick blurted.

This time, the voice came from the opposite direction. "Leave this one be, and I'm sure Solara would find her way to reward your decency."

They spun again, this time in different directions. Slate snapped his mace free of his belt, and Wick withdrew a short sword.

"Show yourself in the king's name!" Slate bellowed, his voice echoing off the walls around the clearing and down the alley.

"You serve the king like I serve Hokrahm, idiot," Guiles said. "Begone with you before I open your veins."

The two guards stared at each other, then turned back-to-back and circled, their weapons held out. Slate's head whipped around.

"Wait, where'd the girl go?"

I turned to find Priya had vanished.

A voice whispered in my ear. "Follow me."

Turning, I still couldn't locate Guiles. I twisted around, peering over both shoulders, but it was like he wasn't there.

*You have received a Party Invite!*
***Guiles*** *invites you to a party.*
*Accept?*
*Yes/No*

I accepted with a real shit-eater of a grin as I realized this was the first time someone had invited me to a party in Enora. The fact two guards circled like dopes with shaky grasps on their weapons did little to assuage my giddiness.

A lifelike representation of Guiles appeared in a circle on the upper-left side of my HUD. Priya's face slid below his.

***Guiles*** *has joined the party.*
***Priya Skyy*** *has joined the party.*

Bars representing mana, health, and stamina appeared next to their avatar faces. I'd seen Click represented the same way when summoned, but the fresh look of real people in my party interface brought a fresh surge of excitement.

Text appeared on the bottom left of my HUD.

*Party:* [*Guiles:*] Come now. Let's not linger.

I focused on the chat bar, thought the words I wanted to use, and grinned when it worked:

*Party:* [*G3m1n1:*] Roger that, chief. Where are you?

Peering over my shoulder, I spied the ghostly frame of the elf and waved.

*Party:* [*G3m1n1*]: Nvm. Got it. Lead the way.

Guiles waved me toward the alley from which the guards had appeared.

"Come on, then!" Slate said. "You want to do this, or not?"

I thought he'd drop the mace, the way it quaked in his hand, but I didn't allow myself a chuckle because my lower level meant he'd spot me if I made a sound.

We crept up the alley. Unlike the last, it was devoid of crates and barrels and seemed as if someone actually kept it clear. I imagined the long building on my left might be a row house or something resembling apartments.

*Party: [Priya:]* Hello?
*Party: [Priya:]* Oh! Cool! I figured it out! So, this is how you talk when you want to keep quiet?
*Party: [Guiles:]* *Eye Roll*
*Party: [G3m1n1:]* See what I have to deal with?
*Part: [Priya:]* Fuck you, both. I'm just a simple girl from the Wood. Stop picking on me.
*Party: [G3m1n1:]* <3
*Party: [Priya:]* Are you calling me an ass? A boob? What's that???

Guiles snickered.

*Party: [G3m1n1:]* Noob.

At the end of the long building, Guiles gestured left. He broke stealth as we turned up another alley, so I followed suit.

We almost ran smack into Priya, who stood in the alley, hands on hips, glaring at me. "You like making fun of people?"

"It was a sideways heart. A love symbol."

Priya blushed. "Oops."

Guiles escorted us to the northern gate and past a sleeping guard with his helmet tilted over his eyes.

"I wish you both success in what Solara has planned for you." He bowed. "Be forever happy and contented in the Light."

*The exact words Priya and Zhara shared in parting.*

I expected a display of animosity as Priya turned her gaze on him, but she'd bowed and taken his hand despite the emotions I sensed in her.

"Thank you, master trainer. Be forever happy and contented in the Light."

I repeated the farewell, and we looked to the northern road outside the gates of Brumhill. It was a winding, hilly path glowing under the light of one white and one orange moon.

We'd planned on camping in the rocks on the east side of the road about half a mile up, in a place Guiles suggested could not be seen from the road. But in illustration of my earlier sentiments about fools making plans in foreign territory and expecting them to come to fruition, our objective changed when we crested the first hill on the road outside Brumhill and spied five men trying to molest a giant cat.

## 10

Well, not a cat, exactly.

Facing Brumhill stood a horse hitched to a cart with a dingy tarp. On the dusty shoulder, standing in the cart's moon-cast shadow, I counted five figures. Swords dangled in two of their sheaths. Another wielded a crossbow. The final two had their backs to us. Beyond them, a grove led to a high granite formation in the distance.

As we eased closer to the situation, what I'd mistaken for a feline morphed into a tall woman sporting a tail curving higher than her shoulders. Surrounded, she wielded either a dagger or a short sword. I couldn't be sure which because something wonky about my illumination spell caused shadows to become magnitudes darker and moonlight to paint round ghosts in my vision. I likened the sensation to glancing under the sun at midday and having to squint to see into the shadows.

Priya's elven vision meant she didn't require a spell. She whispered, "I dislike these odds."

I nodded agreement.

"We should kill them."

My head swiveled so fast, bones in my neck clicked.

Thunder rolled in the distance as if to stress Priya's words, and I peered north to find a high cumulonimbus blooming above a line of black clouds threatening to move in and shroud the twin moons.

"Why jump to killing? You could talk them down with your negotiating skills."

"They terrorize that... woman. I dislike them. Besides, we need all the XP we can get."

"How do you know she—"

"How do I know *what*?" She knelt next to me on the dusty road. "That she didn't attack them? Are you going to suggest...?"

"Shit."

"What?" Priya asked.

"Remember what Zhara suggested? That we might hitch a ride with a vendor in a cart?"

"See? We were destined to kill them."

"Okay. XP then." I waved my hand as if I was trying to bat a bug to the ground. Time to get my gamer face on and stop letting the fear pervading my consciousness during my first ten levels create hesitance I'd never shown in previous virtual worlds.

I assessed the crowd's spacing and considered Guiles's recommendation that I fight from a distance until I reached higher level. But the way they encircled the figure, I wasn't confident enough in my ranged abilities to guarantee her safety. "I'll take a closer look. Give me time to get into position before you make your way down. Try to keep low." My gaze traced her form high to low and back. "Shouldn't be a problem for you."

Priya slapped my hand. "Mean bastard. You didn't mind my height when you were tossing me—"

"Right. True enough!" I whispered. My chest vibrated with chuckles.

Her face relaxed and her bottom lip pushed upward. "You have forgotten our bond."

I jerked. "What? I would never forget it. What are you talking about?"

"I can feel you, Gemini. Your protective instincts. It's like the news of our blessing leaves you with desires to leave me behind so you can deal with the danger alone."

*Shit.*

"I won't be helpless. I will fight next to you until I am squatting in delivery." She gripped my chin. "Let us speak no more of it."

"Bullshit," I said. "We should discuss it. But for now, you're right. You're able and willing. So, off we go." I gave her a curt nod then kissed her nose in a way I hadn't realized annoyed her until I sensed it.

I activated stealth. "Can you see me?"

She shook her head.

With a thought, I sent her a party invite, although her avatar already appeared in my interface. She accepted. A minuscule blue line I hadn't noticed before circled the representation of her face.

"Now I see you."

"Great. I'll come up behind the farthest one and you can distract them. We need to spread them out. Don't come out firing until we do. I don't want that... cat woman getting hurt."

Priya's full lips pinched together as she sneered. "I like this plan very much. But we should still kill them."

Thunder cracked. A flash of lightning painted the clouds in the distance. All heads turned in that direction, and I was glad the clouds hadn't been above us. But neither the crackle of sound nor the flash was the source of the shiver that crept up my spine. Priya's longing to kill these men came on like... hunger.

I drew my daggers. My special boots rendered my footfalls silent as I approached.

"C'mon, little kitty!" one bastard pled. "Give us a little a taste."

"Don't call me kitty, you rotten man. If you come any closer, your tongue will taste only your sour blood."

I flicked my eyes toward the speaker. Block text flashed inside the HUD near his head in response to the new output settings I'd discovered in my interface options.

### Brint
*Human Bandit*
*Level 9*

"Why so stingy, love? It's not like no one's been there before. Girl like you, out here on your own."

*Party: [G3m1n1:] Is that guy saying sexual assault is common out here?*

*Party: [Priya:] I grind my teeth at the thought of it. They all die.*

*Party: [G3m1n1:] You said that already. Just keep your trigger finger loose. I don't want to get into the habit of killing everybody without tactics or considering the consequences. We should find out who they are, if we can.*

"If you see but a girl, step forward and meet the blade of a woman!" The feline woman's words were tough, but her voice wavered. Her knife jerked toward each of three bandits before her, repeating the cycle to keep them at bay. The two behind her inched forward, but she wheeled on them and hissed as she pumped the blade. Her hand quaked as I passed the group on the side opposite the cart.

"C'mon, love. We haven't had the pleasure of a woman in a long time. You think them Brumhill guards are gonna care what we do with your kind? Just come easy, and we'll be gentle. Right? Can't be the first time, can it?"

*Something told me these guys would die.*

The powerful white horse hitched to the cart grumbled, its oaky eye twitching at the crowd nearby. I tiptoed around the group then slid behind the bandit farthest from the woman so I'd have the best angle to view Priya's approach. As I took position behind the man I designated Asshole Number One, his head swiveled to my side as if he'd heard something. The icon of a black eye on my interface blinked with a yellow hue, so I froze in place, until he turned his head forward again, and the full stealth effect took hold again and it became solid.

*That is so damned cool.*

Priya crept in the shadows of a tree line leading toward the meadow. I counted us lucky her red robe didn't stand out at night, but the sheen of her golden hair did little for stealthiness. Luckily, the men focused on their quarry, and I understood why.

The strange woman's nose was short and slightly upturned, but human like the rest of her facial features. Evenly-spaced eyes blinked long eyelashes. A round, tiny chin curved into an oval-shaped face with high, round cheekbones.

Instead of a coat of hair I'd expected to find on closer inspection, smooth flesh covered her chest, abs, and long legs. If it weren't for the tail and the ears perched atop her head, I wouldn't have known she wasn't human. Tight muscles adorned broad-but-feminine shoulders. It was difficult to tell from my position, but I suspected she stood almost as tall as me.

I assumed these rapist fucks targeted her as a matter of convenience, but her face must have really spurned them on. She was exotic.

"Okay, kitty, if you want to play rough—"

Priya inched away from the shadows, close enough I could see her cornflower irises. I held up my palm then she stopped. I twirled a finger in the air.

She nodded. "Um, boys?"

All heads turned toward her. The guy to my left raised his crossbow.

"I think maybe you should leave her alone." The confidence I'd become accustomed to was absent in the half-elf's tone. The bravado she'd transmitted as we'd separated had transitioned to a demureness I didn't recognize. There was little doubt in my mind the lack of command in her words wouldn't inspire fear in the men, but we only needed a distraction. Just enough heads turned to get the captive woman out of the center of the circle so we could open things up.

The man closest to Priya moaned as he caught sight of her. "What do we got here, then? What's your name, sweet meat?" This particular asshole sounded like a medieval drunkard trying to pick up a tavern winch. His head jerked in all directions, searching for any hidden companions.

Like me.

The clouds passed in front of the moon, darkening the

scene further. I set my daggers to my target's throat and was popped out of stealth mode.

The dirt bag with cold steel to his neck jolted. He did the talking for me. "Uh, fellas?"

Ugly mugs whipped in our direction as I pressed the blades tighter against his throat, ready to open him up if his friends got cocky. I scanned them to imagine how the encounter might go down. The one standing near the center with a crossbow now aimed loosely in my direction was a wrench in my calculations. A ranged attacker could really screw things up for us if I gave up the meat shield.

"What's this, then?" the apparent leader said. He was a tall one with wide shoulders, but a pooch hung over his belt.

I almost smiled at the little pinprick of evolution. Enora had her eccentricities. I cocked my chin up. "Step away from the lady."

No one moved, including the cat-like woman. I'd hoped she would move when I presented the second distraction. The leader's neck craned in my direction.

"By my count, you shouldn't be giving orders. Why should we move?"

I inserted command in my voice for Priya's benefit. "Because if you don't, we will drop you like the sacks of shit you are."

The cat lady's eyebrow ticked up, though the rest of her facial features stretched. Her eyes shifted, and her white-knuckled grip on the knife steadied.

"Yeah, bub, but you don't got ahold of me," their leader pointed his blade at himself. Then he pointed it at the guy in front of me. "You got ahold of 'at one."

A low rumble of thunder rolled toward us. The single cold raindrop pricked the nape of my neck.

"Boss, hey, come on," Asshole Number One said.

The boss shrugged. "How about this? You kill him, and we all jump on you and shred you to pieces? Then we get what we came for and enjoy the bonus bitch you brought with ya." He flicked the point of his knife over a shoulder to indicate Priya. Then he cocked his head toward me and Asshole Number One. "I don't like him much, anyway. Mouthy, that one. Quite the jester, except he ain't funny."

*Leave it to me to pick the one guy they don't care about.*

The boss leaned forward. The two men closest to Priya stepped around the woman with the tail, but the one on the left kept a cautious watch on her knife as they inched along to flank me. I envisioned my attacks, counting out the steps in my mind, imagining myself zooming around the circle, dropping one target after another with my Shadow Merge, Spine Snap, Backstab, and Combat Flurry abilities.

I smiled my fullest and adopted my best impression of his broken hillbilly accent. "How about this, brother? How about I cut this one, vanish from sight, stab the one next to you in the back, shoot that one with his own crossbow, and then, to tidy things up, I'll carve your spine out slowly through your chest?"

A hum filled the air, followed by resonant crackling.

All eyes turned toward Priya behind the cat woman. Her fingers twisted into claws and jagged blue energy crackled between their tips.

"Bah!" the leader spat at the knife-wielding woman's feet.

Priya spoke from behind the cat woman, keeping her tone low as the crackling glow of electricity painted her features. "Sister, step back here with me." Spreading her hands further apart and aiming them at the men standing on either side, she sneered. "You all stay right where you are, or I'll *blast* you!"

The cat lady's features morphed between fear and gratitude as she slipped backward with her forehead furrowed and her tail rising to curl over her shoulder. That was one way to get her to move. Ask.

The guy standing next to the boss scratched his head, then hell broke loose.

The shadows beside the cart flickered as flashes of bright purple kinetic energy ripped from the half elf's clawed hands and shot two-foot orbs of white-hot energy slamming into the head scratcher's chest. Bolts tore out of her target's body and through his back, then blasted the leader, blowing him against the cart.

*Priya casts Lightning Pulse.*

*Asshole Number Three*
*Mortal Wound!*
*-121 HP*

*Lightning Pulse jumps to Asshole Number Two.*

*Asshole Number Two*
*Mortal Wound!*
*-111 HP*

*Lightning Pulse jumps to Brint.*

*Brint*
*Mortal Wound!*
*-108 HP*

"Holy shit!" I had no time to appreciate the A.I.'s humor because I jerked in surprise at the electrical onslaught, and my daggers severed Asshole Number One's jugular artery. Blood erupted in a geyser and splattered. My hostage slapped his hands to his throat and uttered a nasty, wet gurgling sound. His knees buckled, then he thumped to the ground where he teetered on them.

I raised my shoulder in a half-shrug, set my boot in my victim's back, and helped him finish his face plant. His body jerked once and died.

*You have killed Asshole Number One.*
*Level 8*
*176 XP*

I scanned the area. Three men lay convulsing with electric ripples rolling over their bodies. My guy was what the boss might have called, *'deader 'n shit.'* The fifth man stood untouched equidistant from us, his head pivoting back and forth.

I glanced at the crossbow clutched in his hands.

Prompts blinked on my screen as his companions died and the XP tallied up. The boss had been a lower level, but I hadn't expected Priya's spell to unleash that kind of damage.

When the crossbowman turned his attention back toward me, the cat woman's arm swept out in a blur as she lunged forward. When she stepped back, her knife buried halfway to the hilt in the bowman's forehead warbled. His crossbow pivoted in his hand, fired a bolt into his boot, then fumbled from his fingers to rattle in the grass.

"Oooh!" Priya and I bellowed in unison as we leaned back.

The man's eyes crossed and glared in wide horror at the knife handle as his knees unlocked and he folded to the ground, face first. As gravity would have it, his forehead landed on the hilt and shoved it deeper into his skull.

I spread my hands out to encompass the scene and peered up at Priya. "Nice shootin', Tex."

Her lips creased down in a toothy frown and she threw up her hands. "Oops?"

The crossbowman's legs kicked a final time. A brilliant light flashed around Priya, and a new gold prompt exploded onto the center of my screen. The exclamation point shrank and slid off to the right-hand side, awaiting my focus.

Priya flashed me a smile full of clenched teeth and pumped her fists. "Ding!"

Since the cat woman hadn't seen the leveling theatric, she jumped to one side at the half-elf's outburst. I was focused on text in my interface.

*Your rescue of the mishon has earned you 50 Light points.*
*Alignment: Light + 437*
*New Alignment: Good*
*Solara smiles upon you and acknowledges your efforts to bring Light to the world.*
*Next Threshold: Light x 500*
*Rank Title: Esteemed*
*You have received a blessing!*
*+2 Charisma*

*A bonus for doing good deeds! Roshan would appreciate that.*

The woman with the tail swept her arms to either side. "What in the *hell* is going on around here? Where did you come from? Who are you?"

Her voice was deeper than I'd expected. If a tiger could growl with a smooth timbre, I'd have likened it to that. A rich sound, pleasant to my ears. Short, round-tipped ears perched atop a head of fiery red hair, and an eight-pack thrived beneath a dingy cotton half-shirt with white buttons. Wrinkled knee-length shorts adorned her lower half.

Wiping the blood off my daggers on the sleeve of the closest corpse, I shrugged. "It's complicated. You want the long answer or the short one?"

The cat woman stared at me, silent.

I sighed. "We were leaving town when we saw you with these wastes of oxygen."

"Wastes of... what is ox-y-gen?"

"Air. The stuff you breathe." I peered up at the sky as drizzle tapped at my neck from behind. *Well, shit. Here it comes and we haven't found shelter.*

"A strange word."

"You'll find he has many," Priya said.

I shrugged. "I'd improved my stealth skill and hoped we could approach without tipping anyone off. Then shorty there—" I flicked the point of my dagger toward her.

"I am not short!"

"Priya, darling. You're not tall."

The woman turned. "I thought you were called, 'Tex.'"

"Yes, more of his nonsensical words."

I continued. "Priya snuck up on the other side so we could pounce if we needed to." I glanced at the corpses. "I might have sent them packing, if they'd been trying to rob you. Maybe we'd have just thwarted them, you know? But when they confirmed their plan to do things to you, well, that burned me up. Men who think they can have their ways because no one is watching. You get me?"

I sheathed my daggers and peered up at the sprinkling rain, enjoying the cool pricks of water on my forehead. I stuck out my tongue to catch droplets. When I returned my gaze to the women, their glares were identical. "Oh, sorry. I love rain. Wait, where was I?"

Priya picked up my flow. "Then my fingers kind of" — her arms flew up into a V— "*blew up,* setting off this chain of events."

"Right." I smiled at the stranger. "Questions? Sorry you asked?"

The cat woman shook her head and bowed, showing me the tops of her ears. "Your response was a muddled, interrupted diatribe of which I could make little sense." Her voice had a throaty quality. "But thank you for coming to my aid. As you said, they intended to defile me." She raised her arms, drew back a foot, and kicked the corpse closest to her. "One at a time!"

I stepped over a corpse and extended my hand as I paced toward the stranger. "I'm Gemini Fowler."

The cat-like woman peered down. Her head tilted to one side and her suspicious gaze crept up my arm to my face. When she gripped it, her grasp was firm.

"Desini Sherre." Her tongue rolled on the Rs in a soft purr. Then Priya offered her hand, and Desini gripped it with both of hers. "I don't know how to thank you." She stood two heads taller than the half-elf and her broader shoulders almost hid her from my view.

"You already did.," I said. "Like, twice. That's plenty. No worries."

"You're babbling, fool," Priya sniped.

I smirked.

Desini peered down the road leading to Brumhill. "To accost me so close to town. So brazen have they become. I might have sprinted for the gates if I thought the guards would help. Or if I didn't think I'd take a crossbow bolt in my back. Gah!" She kicked the corpse again. Then again. "Not that a little blood would've deterred them." Two fingers absently traced a thin white line on one side of her neck.

"Why wouldn't the guards help?" I asked, though it came out more like a growl. "I know they run gambits on the down low, but this?"

"Your strange accent makes sense now. You are not from here, are you?" She gave me a good long stare. "This is the Kingdom of Rubal. Are you aware the Governor of Knall rules these lands for King Luttrell? That these small towns, like Brumhill, dislike beast kin—or any non-humans, for that matter?"

"I'm sorry," I said. "No, I'm not from around here. Although I have my own problems with this governor."

Her head jerked back. "I must seem like quite the mouthy bitch to you, and right after you have saved my life, nonetheless." She bowed her head. "Apologies, my lord. I'm not myself."

"It's understandable, considering your stress." I waved a hand at the corpses.

Desini looked back up the road and muttered, "The bastards would probably have joined in."

I scowled, recalling how the guards at the gate that

morning and with Guiles that night had eyed Priya's body without discernible shame.

"Motherf—." Suddenly cognizant that my fingernails were digging into my palms, I relaxed my fists and gave the closest corpse a short-but-hard kick with the toe of my boot. I found it to be a wonderful expender of my negative energy.

Priya interjected. "Well, it explains why a Level 50 adventurer trains weapon skills in back alleys. That a member of a legendary race shrouds himself in this way, even considering the love of adventurers throughout the kingdom, should tell us something."

Desini gave a single curt nod of agreement.

I decided not to point out the legendary race in question was one that coursed in half her blood.

"But he's far from a beast." I glanced at the cat woman. "As are you."

"I agree," Priya said, running her gaze up Desini's tall form. "You're a lovely woman, not a beast. Love the tail."

*Love the tail?*

Desini's tail swayed in the air behind her as if in response to the compliment. She stood with her back straight, her features a picture of athletic prowess. Because of the way her chiseled shoulders contrasted her slim waist and her lower back ramped into her powerful backside, I pictured her leaping like a cat. But the mounds that rolled down her flat, tight abs screamed woman.

The nervous wringing of her fingers at her waist contradicted all those effects.

Priya stepped toward the taller woman and gently cupped her triceps. "I'm sorry they treated you that way." The half-elf's lips spread into a gentle smile. After a long, shared gaze, she wrapped her arms around Desini's waist. Her empathy came on a wave. "I can't imagine what it was like for you."

Desini jolted and shot me a confused look. Then her shoulders dropped, she leaned into the embrace, then wrapped her other arm around my companion.

"Mmmmm," her purring became louder. "I haven't been embraced in a long time. You're not like other humans."

"That's because I'm half-wood-elf."

I thought about saying I was human and wasn't an asshole, either, but the sight of Desini hunching to embrace Priya distracted me. I folded my arms over my chest and tilted my head to one side.

*Tall. Broad shoulders for a female. Long arms.*

A fact I'd taken for granted suddenly punched me. Although the outside world had never quite reached a state of equality between the sexes, game worlds were different. Women were equally proficient in combat and capable of the same carrying capacities.

I now lived in a world like that. That was pretty cool.

Now, as I stood there I couldn't shake a sudden sense that I was studying my future. If not for the experiences with Roshan and Priya in the first few days I'd been here, I might have thought I was getting ahead of myself, but the same two words Lucera had spoken and had served me well in my first ten levels swam through my mind.

*Make friends.*

"We're not like others," I said. "We welcome all kinds into our fold." I bowed as they released the long hug.

Desini's eyes took on a shocked expression. She returned the bow. "You are too kind."

"Not at all," I said with a wave of my hand.

She inventoried the circle of the dead. "Upon reflection, I fear these men would not have left me to tell stories of their misdeeds. I owe you both my life."

"It was our pleasure," I blurted.

"I will, however, ensure I repay this debt. You have saved me much offense, at the least, and my life, at the most." A muscle beneath one of her eyes twitched. "Tell me, how might I serve?"

"I'm not one for holding debts over people."

Priya's face curved into a scowl at the idea I would refuse someone the ability to repay a debt, but that was a lesson I'd already learned and I shook my head at her.

"Let's deal with pressing matters first." I nudged a corpse with my boot.

Priya's scowl melted and her facial muscles stretched taut. After a nod of acceptance, she folded her arms across her chest. An emotional warmth came on the airwaves.

Desini peered into the distance, along the road, and back at me. "You're right. We should probably get these bodies off the road."

"Right."

"Should we bury them?" A short claw snapped from her fingertip, and she scratched it along her round, high cheeks.

I had no idea how long it would take for the men to disappear like other mobs, or if they would at all.

Priya shook her head. "We can move them into the woods, beyond the rocks. Vultures must eat, too."

*But she buries the bodies of the animals she hunts. I guess there's a solid line between innocence and an asshole.*

I nodded. "Okay, but we should make it easier for said wildlife and strip them of their gear."

Desini nodded and hummed. "Mmm. My lord and lady should have spoils in reward for their heroic deeds." She knelt before the boss and opened his burned leather chest piece. I liked how she snapped right to it, but I simultaneously wondered if the piece would remain burned. Could it be repaired? So much to learn.

I went to work on the guy whose throat I'd slit just as sprinkles of rain began to patter atop my head. With a quick glance at the sky, I wondered if headwear was only available at higher levels.

*I should have checked at Breeder's place.*

Prompts lined the right-hand side of my interface, and with each piece of gear discovered, they piled up. I focused on the flashing gold one first.

*Your companion Priya Skyy has reached Level 10!*
*She has gained 4 attribute points.*
*With a beloved disposition, you may spend 4 attribute points*
*on Priya.*

Although I received four attribute points per level, only two of them were elective. The other two were dispensed based on my current class. It was an interesting programming choice that companions could be tailored in ways I couldn't. Guiles had emphasized how the mystics of the past were greatly empowered by their abilities to customize their followers in this way, but the implications hadn't hit me until now.

Where they'd usually been related to stalls and shops where they stood idle and waited for players to come seeking quests, this world turned the role of NPCs on its head. A successful player in Enora would befriend them. I'd never seen an approach to game development like this.

Players could certainly level up without them, but one would have to be a serious loner to even consider it.

Where other games encouraged social interaction—they were called multiplayer for a reason—this one nullified the concept that players would have to make real, human friends to excel in dungeons and raids. I could see how a social outcast might wander into Enora and find fulfillment in relationships with NPCs. My eyes gravitated to Priya's belly.

*And that.*

Priya's natural progression prior to our meeting left her with some nicely balanced secondary stats. I'd stacked her on Intellect and Wisdom two nights ago, in her dome. I'd had sixteen points to play with. Non-players received two attribute points per level. But when NPCs were bound to a player like me, who could spend their points for them, additional points became retroactively available, scaled by their disposition toward me. The mechanics not only encouraged players to take on NPCs, but worked in the other direction as well. When word traveled, would NPCs seek out future players in droves, begging to join their ranks as word spread they could adventure and become immortal?

Priya's Lightning Pulse had fried three low-level bandits with one shot. I tilted my head slowly back and forth as I figured how to best balance the size of her mana pool through Intellect with her mana regeneration, via Wisdom.

"Are you okay?" Desini asked. "Your eyes shift irregularly. Are you head-sick?"

Her hands sat on the chest of one bandit as she hung her speculative gaze on me.

Priya answered. "He's tinkering with my statistics. He gets that look, and soon, his lips will start moving. Don't worry, he doesn't go spacey or anything." She patted down one of the fried victims of her electricity-laden fingers while humming some kind of tune that sounded oddly Celtic. Her head snapped up. "Hey, don't forget the Constitution. I'd like to absorb a couple hits without passing out, right?" She eyed the corpse beneath her. "Doesn't look like I have to worry about casting power yet."

"That's the truth."

I spent two points on Wisdom, two more on Constitution.

***Priya Skyy***
*Half-Elf*
*Level 10*
*(No class)*
***Attributes***
*Strength: 8**
*Dexterity: 3**
*Intelligence: 18*
*Wisdom: 12*
*Constitution: 16*
*Charisma: 8**
***Combat Skills:***
*Ranged: 14*
*Unarmed: 1*
*Blunt: 3*
*Melee: 5*
***Defensive Skills:***
*Dodge: 4*
***Weapon Skills***
*Bow: 14**
*Club: 7*
***Spells:***

### Shadow Void

Shadow Magic

The caster opens a portal to the underworld and banishes chaotically aligned creatures within two levels into the void.

Cost: 100 Mana

Cool-down: 30 Minutes

### Sleep

Level 9

Required Affinity: Shadow Magic

The caster calls forth dark essence to force a single adversary to slumber.

Damage will end the effect.

### Lightning Pulse

Level 10

Required Affinity: Shadow Magic

Fires bolts of lightning at a single target before jumping to up to three additional targets.

### Occupational Skills:

Not to be confused with combat professions, occupational skills allow people to earn a wage, run a business, build Foundations, or create weapons, armor, and potions to supplement adventuring.

Carpentry: 18

Forestry: 41

Skinning: 15

Cooking: 17

### Affinities:

Shadow Magic: 100%

Elemental Magic: 57%

Languages:

Elven

Common

Since I had a magic bag, she didn't have to carry anything, and I didn't want her close enough to enemies that she would need to dodge, I hardly glanced at Strength or Dexterity.

My eyes stopped on her skill list.

"Priya, you have bow skills."

She smirked. "Yes. I know."

"It never occurred to me to ask how you hunted in the Dark Wood. Why did I part with my other bow if you could carry it?"

"I thought the idea was I'd be a magic wielder."

"That doesn't mean it would hurt for you to have a ranged weapon."

"I sense your annoyance. Maybe I don't like walking around with a bow flopping against my back."

"I could've carried it in my bag," I muttered.

She held her hands out in claws in front her and lighting burst between them. Her face glowed in its purplish aura. Her casting bar half-filled then she halted the spell and it disappeared.

"I don't think I'll need a bow."

Point, Priya.

She smiled, then added, "And if I do, I'll borrow yours when the need arises."

"Fine."

*I'm the idiot for not noticing before, anyway.*

I peered over at the feline woman to see how she was progressing with a victim to find her staring back at me, her hands frozen in place, clutching the chest piece she'd removed from one of our victims.

"What is it? Is this making you feel sick? Priya and I can finish if..."

She shook her head in abbreviated swivels. "I'm... perplexed."

"Anything I can help with?"

Priya's head ticked up. "What is it?"

"I mean no disrespect, sir." Her eyes flicked to Priya and back to mine. "But I hear my saviors speaking words like Constitution, Wisdom. These are the words in my Eye Boxes."

"Eye Boxes? You mean, your HUD?"

"HUD?"

*We're about to go in circles.*

"Heads-up display. An interface where you see world and character statistics."

"If this is what you call it, I accept. Yes. But what do you mean, the level gets her four points?" She thrust a thumb at Priya. "And that you are trying to figure out how to... *spend* them? You are a trainer?"

My knees grew sore from being crouched for so long, so I stood.

"You could say that. With your permission, I'd like to check your attributes."

She dropped the ratty chest armor and stood. "Are you asking me to disrobe?" Her back stiffened. "But I thought you were different! Is this how I must repay the debt?"

I laughed. Priya chuckled.

"No, no, no, no," I waved my hands out in front of me. "That would defeat the point of saving you, right? Trust me for one moment, and I'll illustrate. I promise not to lay a hand on you."

Her eyes hid behind slits as they shifted between us. Her tail wagged to one side, and she nodded. Whereas my sight of Guiles's character pane revealed only his name, his race, and his class, Desini's readout gave much more than

I'd expected. My wonderment over the difference was vanquished when I saw her level.

***Desini Sherre***

*Mishon*

*Level 17 Traveling Messenger*

***Attributes:***

*Strength: 10**

*Dexterity: 13**

*Intelligence: 7**

*Wisdom: 6**

*Constitution: 11**

*Charisma: 42**

***Combat Skills:***

*Melee: 14*

***Defensive Skills:***

*Dodge: 24*

***Weapon Skills***

*Unarmed: 14*

*Blunt: 14*

*Bonuses:*

*Resist Magic Attacks: 5*

*Resist Charm Effects: 10*

*Special attribute: Master Negotiator. (Charisma of 40 or higher required.)*

*My goodness! Look at that charisma! Did she really earn all these points the hard way?*

One of Desini's hips jutted to one side. She dropped a hand on it, and her tail raised into the air again, waving from one shoulder to the other. "You seem surprised."

I shook my head. "No. Well, maybe a little. I'd say I'm

more *impressed*. Tell me, Desini, how long have you been a traveling messenger?"

"How did you know I'm a traveling messenger? How do you know I am not transitioning from one place to the next in search of a new home?"

"Ha!" I barked. "No, I don't think so."

Priya clicked her tongue at me. "Tell her and stop being such a..." she paused.

"Dweeb?"

"I don't know that word."

"Nerd?"

She pinched her lips at me.

"It means strange person. Someone socially inept."

"Yes!" Priya exclaimed. "This is the word. Stop being such a *nerd*. She peers at you as if you were born of a stone because you come out with it."

I sighed.

Desini nodded.

"You've naturally earned a lot of attribute advancement. You have a really high charisma rating. Do you negotiate a lot in your line of work?"

Desini's lips parted to speak, but Priya cut her off. "Wait a second," she asked, squinting in Desini's direction. "How high?"

"Are you going to let me tell her, or are you going to feed your competitive streak?"

"More of these strange words." She gave a dismissive wave. "Go ahead, nerd."

I chuckled. "That rating is astounding for your level."

Desini shrugged. "Yes, I know."

"How high?" Priya asked again.

"Wow, honey, you're being really patient," I said.

"Yeah! Tell me about it!" Priya barked.

"It's forty-two."

"Forty-two?" Priya blurted. She blinked her eyes in succession. "I can't see anything."

"Probably because she isn't your companion." I shot Priya a stink eye and spoke to Desini. "Apparently, this gives you the title of Master Negotiator."

"This is accurate," Desini said. "When you are loathed by many because of your race, you must use what attributes Solara gives to survive. Why are you surprised?" She shot me an incriminatory glare. "Do you not think a mishon could advance so? Are we but stupid animals? I thought you said I was not an animal, and yet you—"

"Whoa, whoa, whoa, there!" I said, pumping out my hands in a defensive gesture. "It's not that I have a predisposition about your race—mishon or whatever. It's that I've never seen an attribute that high in someone who hasn't spent a skill point. What I'm saying is, you're amazing! Like a painting of a nature scene waiting only for the focal point to be added."

Her hand dropped from her hip and she straightened, pulling the hem of her tattered half-blouse so the garment straightened, stressing firm curves beneath. "Oh! Well! You display fine taste, my lord." Her throat clicked, and I wondered if she was clearing it or chuckling. I heard a new confidence in her words. "You are wise beyond your years. You'll pardon my outburst?"

"No worries," I said. "You know, with all these attributes you've earned, it's a wonder you haven't visited a trainer and become an adventurer."

She frowned, but didn't reply, so I pressed.

"I mean someone who can spend all these attribute points." A thought occurred. "How long have you been out here alone?"

Her bottom lip inflated. "I don't know. Since the people of my village were... moved. I would say four years?"

*Moved?*

"Sounds lonely." I shook my head. "You've had no companions on the road?"

She shook her head. "Who would have me? I'm a beast to them. They do not engage with me, except in barter if I'm lucky enough to have something they so desire that they can see past my shortcomings. I do my trading behind the shops, so as not to draw attention."

"I'm starting to really hate people," Priya said. "Perhaps we should go back home after we find Roshan."

"You're thinking small, babe. I wasn't sent here to hide from atrocities. Maybe we should change the world, instead."

Priya pushed out her lower lip as she considered me. "You speak logically." An emotion traversed the airwaves and signaled her approval, but there was more. An undertone. A warm one.

I turned back to Desini to address a missing field from her profile. "May I ask how old you are, Desini?"

She nodded. "I am twenty years recently."

"Great tidings on your twentieth year," Priya said.

Desini returned her smile and bowed her head.

"Yeah, happy belated birthday."

"Such strange words," Desini said.

I chuckled. "I get you. No trainer. Humans don't talk to you about such things. Cast out of your home at sixteen, and I'm assuming your people are secluded."

"You know much of me from simple numbers." Her gaze shifted between us. "And how is it you see what Priya cannot?"

"The second part is a long story. As to the first, it's just deductive reasoning."

Priya smirked, paced over and smacked me hard on the ass. "These big words, again!"

"I understood this one," Desini said. "He says he is correlating facts. Deducing."

Priya blushed. "Sorry. Guess I'm a simple girl from the woods."

"You really need to stop saying that. I look at you, babe, and I don't see a girl. I see a woman."

She slapped my ass again. "Stop flirting in front of strangers."

*Stop sending me your sneaky sex vibes, you minx.* I mentally swiped through my interface, grinning.

Desini's disposition registered friendly. That was one tick up from neutral. I was becoming a professional rescuer.

The poor woman had been on her own since before she was what I would call an adult. No one touched her or talked to her unless they wanted something. But her attributes alone showed she wasn't the kind to rest on her laurels.

"Gemini," Priya said, wrapping her hand around my fist. "You'll make your palms bleed. You're grinding your teeth. It makes me grind mine. I don't like it."

Desini took a step backward. "What have I done to irritate him?"

"Nothing, Desini," I said. "I don't like how people treat you. You deserve better."

Her gaze held me for a long minute. "Does he speak true?" She seemed to be asking Priya.

"Always true," Priya said. "Gemini doesn't lie."

*The Player's Agreement has me lying all the fucking time!*

Priya snagged the emotion out of the air and squinted at me.

*Busted.*

Tears welled in Desini's eyes and she clutched her half-blouse. "You... honor me with your kindness."

Priya squeezed my hand, and I relaxed it so she could intertwine our fingers.

Desini swiped away an errant tear, turned her head to one side, and looked away.

"Don't be embarrassed," Priya said. "This is what he does to women. The effect is beyond his clumsy control."

"Bite me," I muttered.

Priya leaned up and pressed soft lips to my cheek.

I muttered, "You're such a hippie."

"What is a hippie?"

"You know, a tree-hugger. A free spirit."

Priya nodded enthusiastically. "Yes, I enjoy the embrace of a good tree." She glanced around as if seeking one out.

The sprinkles transitioned to rain, and we all peered into the sky.

"My friends, where will you rest tonight?"

Priya wrapped her arm in the crook of my elbow. "We planned to camp among the trees. I miss the sounds of my forest."

Desini nodded understanding. "Yes. Nature was my home, too. I cannot sleep among the trees often for my cart doesn't traverse uneven ground well, and I would return to find it looted if I took my horse and slept away." I found her accent grew thicker the longer she spoke in that low, humming purr. She bowed her head. Her words adopted a formal tone. "While I wouldn't wish to stand in the way of your desires, I'd be honored if you would lay your bedrolls with mine and sleep under the cover of my cart. It will keep you dry."

A pleading emotion emitted from Priya, and she squeezed my hand. Though I'd wanted her since she'd straddled me in the clearing at sunset, the clouds showed no hint of breaking and a good night's sleep with our new friend might pay dividends.

At a bare minimum, I needed to resolve the quest to escort Desini back to the North. If luck shone on me, it could go further. My little half-elf minx beckoned forth my hormones, but priorities were priorities.

To Priya's credit, she ignored my disappointment.

"We would be equally honored," Priya replied.

Desini and I dumped the bodies on the other side of a rock formation, in a patch of trees. Then we spent a few minutes getting situated in her cart. There was more than enough width inside for us to unroll our furs next to each other.

Desini tossed a canvas bag forward then smoothed the beige fur she called a bed from the back edge of the cart to the front. I knelt next to the bag near the tied flap behind the rider's bench, trying to allow the two adequate elbow room to prep their bedding. As was my unfortunate nature, I threw a glance at Priya's epic hips as they wiggled from side-to-side. Thus, returned the stirrings to which I was becoming accustomed at the sight of her body.

Desini's hips were slimmer, yet rounded where they jutted from her slim waist. My study of the mishon was more inquisitive than sexual, and I found myself intrigued by the tail that exited through a slit sewn into her shorts. The appendage waved from side to side as she arched her back and smoothed out the fur. When she sat up and turned, I diverted my gaze to the canvas top of the cart. I didn't want her to think I was checking her out. It seemed she'd experienced enough of that.

Through my peripheral vision, I couldn't miss the sight of Desini crossing her arms in front of her as she pulled the half-shirt to expose the bottoms of her breasts. Lowering the shirt and perhaps eyeing me for a moment, I couldn't tell—she pivoted on her knees to turn away. I glanced to find more ripped-but-feminine muscles expressing themselves across her upper back as she removed the blouse.

Priya caught my glance and threw me a knowing gaze. Her lips turned up at the corners, and I felt like the luckiest man in Enora.

The weather worsened as we lay there. The rain was a constant, blasting tympani that left me thankful we hadn't opted for sleeping in the woods. I'd had my share of downpours in the Dark Wood. Tattered though the cart cover was, its thick canvas provided excellent shelter from the rain. Peering at the little dots where the threads were cross-woven, it reminded me of my first sight upon entering Enora—a canvas tent. I wondered how the people of this world spun such a thing into existence and looked forward to finding out someday. I eased into sleep.

I woke in the middle of the night to smooth fur stroking my chest and flesh warming my back. Though I wasn't sure I should've drawn the center spot, Priya had unrolled the fur she'd gifted me in that position, so I'd assumed it was okay. In the humidity accompanying the rain, we'd forgone wrapping our bedrolls over ourselves, and I found Desini stretching in front of me with her back warming my chest as I lay on my side. Her tail twitched between us, nestled along the split of her backside over the shorts.

Peeling my curious gaze from her hard rump, I took a longer gander at her attributes.

***Desini Sherre***

*Mishon*

*Level 17 Traveling Messenger*

***Attributes:***

*Strength: 10**

*Dexterity: 13**

*Intelligence: 7**

*Wisdom: 6**

*Constitution: 11**

*Charisma: 42**

*Desini has 34 unspent attribute points.*

***Combat Skills:***

*Melee: 14*

***Defensive Skills:***

*Dodge: 24*

***Weapon Skills***

*Unarmed: 14*

*Blunt: 14*

*Bonuses:*

*Resist Magic Attacks: 5*

*Resist Charm Effects: 10*

What I'd have given to go wild on her numbers. I mean, the numerical ones.

Priya moaned behind me, and her hand slid across my chest.

"Hmmm." Flipping her fingertips away from my chest, she slid them onto Desini's back.

The mishon twitched and turned her head. Wide eyes shimmered in the dimness, but her taut shoulders relaxed when she peered down and found it was Priya who stroked her gently.

Desini's internal motor hummed with vibration. Her tail twitched and fell on my leg as she slid an arm beneath her and rolled onto her belly.

Whereas Priya and Roshan differed in their demeanors, one commonality between them was how quickly they'd taken to me. Desini hadn't known us for an hour before welcoming us into what equated to her home, but the adoration I'd enjoyed from my other two companions made me sensitive to each diversion of this woman's eyes. Like when we'd been looting bodies and I'd peered up to find her considering me, but her head twisted down and back to her task.

It was an air of suspicion. I couldn't blame her.

As she rolled onto her torso, her shining eyes fell on me as Priya's hand ran in even, languid strokes up and down a small portion of her back. The same arm caressed my waist.

Desini's words about her lack of physical contact, coupled with the memory of the bastards trying to have their ways with her, led me to wonder if having a male this close was the furthest thing from what she needed. Though I couldn't be sure I caused her discomfort, I went with my instincts.

When the purr evened out and her breaths became long and even, I slowly slid away and rolled toward Priya, pushing her onto her back. My companion's eyes popped open in surprise, but they relaxed as she peered up. A smile crept across her face, revealing perfect rows of ivory teeth. She pushed the tip of her tongue between them playfully as she gazed at me, her wanting crossing our emotional link. But that wasn't why I lay atop her.

Her smile faded and she tilted her head on the fur to eye me more speculatively. I sensed her question without the need for words.

I tilted my head toward Desini. She nodded, leaned her head up to set a gentle kiss on my chin, and slid toward Desini so I could sleep on the opposite side.

Relief washed over me as I settled onto my back in the warm spot left by Priya's slight, elven body. I'd had no idea how tense I'd become. As I drifted to sleep with my hand set on her hip, a prompt popped up on my right.

But I ignored it and drifted off.

12

My eyelids fluttered open as rain pattered on the wagon cover and cool air slipped between the slits in the canvas flap at the front. Priya grunted in the throes of sleep beside me. The mishon woman purred. I pushed myself onto one elbow and peered over Priya. My head jerked as I caught unintentional sight of the cat-like creature's naked breast and diverted my gaze.

Feeling a little ill-at-ease, I veered my focus to the prompt I'd ignored as I drifted off in the early morning hours.

***Desini Sherre*** *has become endeared to you.*
*Your decision to give Desini space in lieu of feeding your lesser hungers has pleased Solara.*
*+30 points of Light*
*Alignment: Light + 467*
*Alignment: Good*
*Next Threshold: Light x 500*
*Rank Title: Esteemed*

*It's amazing what a little respect will get you, I suppose.*

The mishon still didn't appear in my Companions Tab. Though Desini stood almost my height and her feminine musculature resembled the chiseled form of a pole vaulter, her body language and the hesitancy I'd detected the night before left me wanting not just to protect, but to empower her.

Then I realized the pure idiocy reflected by my thoughts. She could take care of herself. She'd made it this far. But the mishon carried a heavy baggage of trauma. The best question wasn't whether I could protect her, but if I could help her to carry it.

"Mmmm," Desini purred.

I slid off my fur and slid my butt toward the opening in the tarp.

Desini rolled onto her back and caught me with her piercing stare as I rose to my knees. "Good tidings, Gemini."

I nodded as I fussed with the long-sleeved black shirt I donned beneath my armor. "'Morning, ma'am."

"You seem unsteady." She sat up, and her breasts rose in a single firm motion as if they had implants... or shock absorbers. She made no effort to hide, but I dropped my gaze to my clothing as I clasped hooks.

Priya sat up and scooted toward me on her furs. Her arms slipped around my waist, halting my progress. I smiled over my shoulder and gripped her hands.

"Hey, we'll need to get rolling if we want to catch up to Roshan before she reaches the governor."

"Roshan?" Desini asked.

"Our other companion," I said.

Priya spoke with the air of a storyteller. "She is our Eastern beloved, captured by the foul servants of the governor you mentioned last night."

*Sometimes she sounded like the maiden in a fairy tale.*

"An adventure!" Desini's eyes shot wide with enthusiasm. Then she checked herself, peering down at her lap. "This is why you are at odds with him?" She nodded as if to answer her own question. "I'm sorry to hear this." Her eyes took on a distant look. "Did you say Eastern? Has she big brown eyes slanted down just at the corners? Coppery skin?"

"Yes!" I barked. "Have you seen her?"

"I couldn't miss such an exotic creature. Her contingent was near Warrington South's gate when I set out just yesterday. They'd stopped at the edge of the road, probably to let the lady relieve herself in the trees, as their transports waited in the queue. She wore a fine, pleated garment of green and yellow. They unbound her hands, and I thought perhaps she'd committed a crime. I didn't understand they'd taken her against her will. I probably should have."

"Yesterday morning? How far is Warrington?"

"It is but a day's travel if you make good time, which I usually do with Pickney pulling my wagon."

I made a mental note of the horse's name.

Shoving my fingers through the slit in the canvas I peeked out at the white horse standing beneath the collapsible rain shelter Desini tied to the front of the cart so it covered the animal. This was my first gander at the beast in the daylight. Its powerful hind legs told the story of many journeys and its regular exercise.

Considering all that Zhara had told us about the towns of the region, and since Warrington was only a day out, then the bastards who took Roshan couldn't be too far ahead.

"As I see in your eyes how you both hunger for her return, might I suggest a plan of mutual benefit?" Desini asked.

"Sure!" The response was entirely too enthusiastic, but I had a good idea what was coming.

"I am returning to Warrington after I deliver a message in Brumhill. Perhaps you could accompany me to Brumhill this morning, provide me with security on these treacherous roads, and in exchange, I will carry you north. We can outpace their caravan, and they are likely to stay at least one night in Warrington to water their horses and seek provisions."

Since I'd wanted to return to Breeder's anyway, this gave me an excuse.

"It would be my honor to escort you back to Brumhill and then to Warrington, Desini."

*Quest Completed!*
### *Thumbing a Ride*
*You found a vendor and hitched a ride to Warrington.*
*Reward: 1,500 XP*

The orangish icon with a coat-of-arms I'd come to recognize as a quest offering blinked on the right side of my field of vision. I focused there.

*You have been offered an escort quest:*
### *Mishon Security*
*Guide Desini safely to Warrington.*
*Reward: 5,500 XP*
*Requirement: Desini must survive.*
*Would you like to accept this quest?*
*Yes/No*

"This is of such relief, Gemini." She clapped her hands together as she turned to face Priya, and I found myself thankful for the way her arms covered her chest as each accidental glance of her nudity brought with it a moment of guilt. My baby mama had to be picking up on it. "So perilous have the roads been of late. I am favored with adventurers to accompany me, even if only for a short time. Solara's light shines bright."

"You're a believer?" I asked.

"Isn't everyone?"

I considered her question with the tilting of my head. "No idea. Is everyone?"

"Most I've met, yes. Though some see my worship of her as an animal worshipping the sun, so I'm not allowed near temples."

"Gods-damn people," I said. "But isn't Solara literally the sun?"

Priya smacked my shoulder. "No idiot. It is the symbol of her light. I don't know where you get these silly ideas in your head."

*Desini Sherre is now your companion!*

### *Desini Sherre*
*Mishon*
*Level 17 Traveling Messenger*
**Attributes:**
*Strength: 10**
*Dexterity: 13**
*Intelligence: 7**
*Wisdom: 6**
*Constitution: 11**
*Charisma: 42**
*Desini has 34 unspent attribute points.*

### *Affinities and skills revealed!*

Since you have become Desini's companion, her skills and affinities are visible.

### *Affinities:*

### *Languages:*

Common

Dwarfish

Elven

Gnomish

Mishon

### *Magic*

Light Magic: 20%

Shadow Magic: 15%

Nature Magic: 55%

### *Occupational Skills:*

Not to be confused with combat professions, occupational skills allow people to earn a wage, run a business, build foundations, or create weapons, armor, and potions to supplement adventuring.

Stonework: 13

Woodworking: 11

Animal Husbandry: 22

Cooking: 50

Botany: 50

Skinning: 11

Disposition: Endeared

Endeared disposition means you may distribute two attribute points for each level Desini gains.

You may distribute any existing attribute points (Total: 34).

To increase the number of attribute points this companion receives per level, increase disposition.

"Desini?"

"Yes, Gemini?"

"Would it please you to know I could help you better defend yourself when you're on the road?"

Desini glanced at Priya as if in need of an interpreter.

Priya nodded. "You can trust him. He can increase your attributes."

"Make me stronger? Give me the attributes of adventurers?" Desini clapped a hand over her mouth. "Forgive my display of weakness." Tears filled her eyes. "I'm certain adventurers don't babble like babes."

"It's all good. Would you like my help?"

"I lack gold for attribute training."

"You don't need gold. I only train my companions—people with whom I travel and who show, um, trust with me. Since you've offered to travel with us and we are friends now, I can help a little. In case you leave us in Warrington, I should level what attributes I can, before you go your own way. Five points is better than none. I would like see you better-prepared for challenges ahead."

Desini's facial muscles slackened as her eyebrows slowly raised into an arch. Her words came in a low, slow drawl. "As long as I have been on this road, you might be the first to have called me friend." She shook her head side to side, turning her face down. "And you do it without wanting in your voice." She choked a little and sniffed. "It is a welcome respite. Other men scoff at me in these small towns, but then try to call me friend when we cross paths on the road—to enjoy what they claim should be between friends."

The continued clinching of my jaw and grinding of my teeth left me thankful I no longer had fillings. I required no elven bond to share the emotions flooding off the mishon woman. Desini's tears weren't what showed me the hole in her soul when I peered into those sad green eyes. My experience was. I'd come to Enora familiar with trauma. The pervasive trolls of emotional pain had excavated paths through my brain, aplenty. Maybe kobolds made for a better metaphor.

But my life had been altered in a violent instant on a highway and, though losing my parents left a permanent hole behind, their end had come at a distance.

The gratitude conveyed through her quivering throat told the story of a woman violated in ways I might never comprehend. The kind of trauma that stayed fresh.

In the most fucked up of ways, it highlighted the realism of this world anew.

Desini's story. Hers was a pain that might never dissipate. The kind that kept close to home. I imagined it like a bird on her shoulder, pecking at her ear as she tugged the horse's reigns on the lonely nights out on this road.

*I'm still here, you know. I'll always be right here, ready to peck and remind you. Ready to reminisce every time an unfamiliar cart passes, or with each new rider on horseback, I'll always be right here.*

Text filled the bottom center of my HUD.

*Desini's disposition toward you has increased to enamored.
You may distribute three attribute points for each level
Desini gains as long as you maintain this disposition.
You may distribute any existing attribute points (Total: 34).
To increase the number of attribute points this companion
receives per level, increase disposition.*

I wiped the text away. This wasn't a fucking game.

So balanced was my world that morning that the blades

of my daggers slid into their sheaths behind my back. The motions of retrieving and depositing them was becoming second nature and I mused at how such a simple thing put a bounce in my step. Maybe the increased dagger skills from practicing with Guiles contributed to my accuracy when sheathing them.

We parked the cart just outside the gate then disembarked. Desini's horse nickered. She popped out the short claws on one hand and paced along its length, running her long fingers across its muscular form, leaving narrow streaks in its mane. The animal rumbled contentedly, and she whispered words I couldn't hear. She gave the horse a few solid pats on its neck then turned to where Priya and I waited.

"All set?" I asked.

The mishon's focus turned to the gate less than one-hundred yards away. Though she nodded, I sensed hesitation in the way her gaze flickered to the gate, to the ground, and back.

"They really treat you like dirt, don't they?" I asked.

"Brumhill is worse than Warrington and Trowlsby. It seems the more populated a place, the better I blend." She flipped her tail over her shoulder, grasped it, and shook the tuft of hair on its end at me. "Still, I must keep to the back alleys in all places lest I rouse the ire of those who despise my kind." She revealed a narrow smile.

*Cute.*

"Well, they won't be giving you trouble around us unless they want some back. Right, Priya?"

Priya turned in a mock sneer, curled her hands up like claws, and growled. "Zap!"

Desini missed the joke, as evidenced by her nod of agreement. "Yes, indeed, Priya. The way you dispatched those men was a thing of wonder. I have only dreamed of seeing someone with such affinity for wielding nature's power."

This time it was me who nodded. "Actually, it surprised me, too. Her affinity for Shadow Magic doesn't just increase her ability to learn spells, but apparently their potency."

"Is this uncommon?" Priya asked.

I hunched a shoulder. "How the hell would I know?"

"I have often fantasized about traveling with adventurers," Desini said. "I would take pride in transporting their gear and loot. I've considered undertaking such a business venture, but I doubt I would find any who would take me, even though I could use my negotiating skills to get them the best deals for their spoils."

I stopped, crunching rocks underfoot. "Why would you carry someone else's water with a body like yours?"

Desini cast her arms out and peered down at herself.

"What do you mean, with a body like mine?"

"You're strong. You're athletic. You've obviously kept yourself in shape, or you wouldn't have your attributes. Wouldn't you rather take up a weapon and earn an equal share of the spoils?"

"Who would risk the ire and public scrutiny of taking a mishon for their adventuring companion?" She flipped a dismissive hand. "It's been two generations since my kind battled Solara's enemies."

"We would," Priya and I said at the same time.

Desini stopped. "You jest."

"We don't," Priya said. "If you're interested in such a life, we would welcome someone like you."

Desini's eyes shifted. "Your woman speaks for you?"

"Priya is my equal. If she says it, then it's true."

"Now, you jest."

I shook my head. "Priya has her own mind and her own

mouth for a reason. Decisions made with superior counsel are the best kind. When a question arises and Priya is the expert, she counsels me. I do the same for her."

"Truly?" Desini asked, her eyebrow still raised high in suspicion. "I'm afraid you will encounter many who do not share your views of equality."

*Yeah, well wait until female players invade this world. That's going to be fun to watch.*

"I'm my own man. I don't care what others think of us."

Priya nodded.

"Do you require additional adventurers in your party?" Desini asked.

"Does combat interest you?" I asked. "Are you willing to risk the pain?"

"Compare it to how I live now, my friend."

*Good point.*

"All cultures tell adventure tales going back to the early ages. While I don't understand your power to improve me, I understand the concepts of combat. Before the uprising, my kind took up the sword alongside humans and elves, but after, they discarded us for the trouble our presence caused them in the towns. So, this is something you must consider. If I join you in combat, the people of the towns and cities on this side of the kingdom will disrespect me, and probably you by association."

*Uprising? Seems I need a little history lesson, but it will have to wait.*

"I believe you, but again, I've never been one to care much what others think."

"What role would I fill?"

I nodded. I'd already considered it as I lay in my bedroll the night before. "I think you might make a superb *tank*. It just so happens we need one."

Her head jerked back. "You mean, a front-line fighter? Maybe a swordsman?" Her eyebrows arched high. Excitement tensed her facial muscles. She straightened her spine and pushed her chest out.

I shrugged and nodded as I brought up an abbreviated display of her attributes.

***Desini Sherre***

*Mishon*

*Level 17 Traveling Messenger*

***Attributes:***

*Strength: 10**

*Dexterity: 13**

*Intelligence: 7**

*Wisdom: 6**

*Constitution: 11**

*Charisma: 42**

*Desini has 34 unspent attribute points.*

***Combat Skills:***

*Melee: 14*

***Defensive Skills:***

*Dodge: 44*

***Weapon Skills***

*Unarmed: 14*

*Blunt: 14*

*Bonuses:*

*Resist Magic Attacks: 5*

*Resist Charm Effects: 10*

"Your strength is only three points lower than your dexterity, and you still haven't even tapped your attribute points. Your Constitution is right in the middle. You rock strong shoulders, and I watched how you stood with that knife in your hand last night. You're tall with nice, long arms. A good reach for combat. Plus, you're much higher in level than either of us." I muttered the rest. "And those eyes of yours could charm the fungus out of an ogre's toenails."

Desini giggled, and it was a magical sound, akin to a fairy in a kid's cartoon. "Your tongue spits sweet lies."

"Now she has me thinking of your tongue," Priya teased.

Desini smiled at Priya's sentiment but addressed me. "I will consider your offer, Gemini."

"That's all I can ask."

13

Two familiar faces greeted us at the northern gate. Although not necessarily friendly, they were the same guards we'd encountered upon entering Brumhill with Roshan two days before. They remembered Priya.

Who wouldn't?

"Hello, love," the guard standing at ground level said. He scratched a scraggly black beard and made no attempt to conceal his gander at her epic cleavage before flicking his attention toward me. "Still keeping questionable company, I see."

Priya smiled. "I suppose that depends on how an idiot would define 'questionable'?"

*She zings like a seasoned pro.*

"What's that?" the guard replied, confused.

"We're here to deliver a message to the proprietor of the Crescent Moon," I interjected. The lookout atop the wall threw us a furtive glance at the sound of my voice. The sun shadowed his face as he looked me over. Then he paced down the battlement and out of sight.

"Aye, Leira's place. Who's the message from?"

I blinked. What business was that of his? My face formed its best stony stare in response.

He took the hint after a moment of silence that it was none of his beeswax and changed the subject. "Funny, I don't remember you mentioning you was a messenger when ya stumbled through the south gate with this one and that exotic one the other day." His head cocked back and his ungloved hand flinched as if it might go for his sword's pommel. "Wait now..."

A curse rang out inside my head. He remembered Roshan. Her companions were slaughtered at the inn. So, if we were standing here, alive...

I shook my head. "Exotic one?" I threw Priya a befuddled gaze and, in an epic example of mental agility, she matched it. We were the picture of bewilderment. "I think you have us confused with someone else."

His stare lingered for a moment, then he turned it on Priya. She smiled fully. The guard blinked.

"Oh, right." He waved a hand. "Guess I got muddled there. Must've confused ya for someone else."

I felt like a Jedi using a mind trick on the weak-minded.

### *Turley Blanch*
*Human*
*Level 5 Fighter*

The employment of low-level NPCs in the town met my expectations, but Blanch was even lower than the two we'd crossed paths with the night before.

"Still don't remember you saying anything about being a messenger."

I clinched my fists next to my hips. This guy was

starting to tweak my nerves. We had places to be, a healer to rescue.

"Do people usually tell you their professions? Bit of a nosy one, aren't you? Look man, we're just security. I found work on the road to Warrington. You have a problem with Capitalism?"

If he'd seen Priya and me wandering the roads in Brumhill the previous day, Blanch might catch the lie, but I hadn't remembered seeing any guards patrolling the streets, so I rolled the dice.

"Capital—what?"

I huffed an impatient sigh.

"No point getting your loin covers in a wad with me. If ya don't like answering questions, don't travel with a beast kin." Blanch threw a crooked finger toward Desini, who stood behind us with her head half-bowed. "I've seen you around. You with this lot?"

"Yes, sir."

"She's the messenger. I'm *her* security."

The guard laughed. "Here I guessed you fancied yourself some kind of adventurer."

I returned his gaze, but said nothing.

"All right, you can pass through, but the cat bitch will have to do her business off the main thoroughfare. Human companions don't save ya from the rules. We might not look like much, but we still hold true to our forebears. Keep her on a short leash, or heads'll be busted."

I didn't dignify his name-calling with a response. I wanted to pound him one for being an ass, but it wouldn't serve our purposes—namely, keeping a low profile and getting out of Dodge.

Priya passed in front of me to enter the town and the

guard leaned toward her. "Hey, m'lady? If you ever want the company of a real man come see me, eh?"

Priya cocked her head to one side, eyed him up and down, and then ran a finger under his chin, drawing his head closer. Turley's lips spread, revealing crooked, yellow teeth.

Priya lowered her eyelids. "Or I could cut off a fly's cock and enjoy some girth, instead."

*Dayum!*

The guard raised his hand across his chest as if to backhand Priya. "Off with you before I cuff you one!"

Priya sneered, took half a step back, and raised her hands into claws. Purple fingers of light crackled between her fingers.

*Uh-oh, not good!*

"Ha-ha! Funny hon!" Her electric pulses zapped my palm as I clutched her hands with my own. I winked. "Neat little parlor trick, that one! Okay, like the man said, off with us!"

Right before we crossed the threshold, the guard reached across and gave Priya a shove. "That's what I thought, witch. Listen to your keeper and learn your place."

I clenched my teeth. All I wanted was to get on the road, gain levels, and retrieve Roshan. I didn't want trouble nor did I care about his insults of my manhood. This guy wouldn't be worth the experience I'd get for whacking him. But first he'd called Desini a bitch, then he'd lain his hands on Priya.

And you just didn't put your hands on the baby mama.

I threw a quick glance up at the battlements and verified all was clear. Then reaching back, I grasped a pommel then whipped a dagger to Blanch's throat. With a quick step, I blocked him from the view of the other guard, in case he returned atop the short wall as I entered gamer-who-is-taking-Enora-by-the-balls mode.

"Bad form, my friend. You take my generosity for granted. You might think you're the king of the castle around here because someone with questionable judgment handed you a weapon and assigned you a post, or perhaps you're accustomed to spewing your venom wherever you like, at whomever you like, without repercussions. Could be other men curry to your shoving people around to avoid a scene." I leaned close and sneered. "I've never minded a public display, though. I *tolerate* your snarky mouth because you amount to bug shit and I feel *sorry* for you, but I never stomach bullies for long."

The guard's gaze flitted toward the weapon pinching his throat.

"You ever lay hands on one of mine again, you'll be cutting your daily ration of worm meat without thumbs." I shoved the dagger higher to create emphasis. "Ever loose your tongue to insult my mishon friend again, and I'll cut it out and feed it to my porcupunk. Then I'll burn what's left of you, offer it to the one pacing atop the wall, and tell him it's a pig rump steak. I doubt he'd know the difference, and it's close to the truth. Now, peel your hand off your shitty sword and nod your lumpy head like you understand me, or I'll cake the sand beneath your ratty boots with your spewing blood. I might not look like a lot to you, but you so much as flinch and I'll murder every guard in this piss ant fucking town, starting with you."

Priya stood off to one side, scanning the road entering town at intervals. Desini was just beyond with one hand's fingers splayed on her chest, her mouth agape.

The guard nodded.

I sheathed my blade as I stepped past him. A second later, I slipped back and whispered close to his ear.

"And Blanch?"

The guard blinked, but his eyes never quite met mine.

"Take a bath. Your odor will attract vermin."

*You have lost alignment points for threatening a lower level dimwit.*
*While Solara appreciates defending your party, was all that really necessary?*
*-20 Light*
*Alignment: Light + 447*
*Alignment: Good*
*Solara smiles upon you and acknowledges your efforts to bring Light to the world.*

It seemed Enora was offering me some guidance as to my attitude with this alignment shit. Maybe she was also trying to tame my dark side. If one of the beta testers had gone dark and fucked shit up, I could see why she might try.

I clutched Priya's hand and paced down the dirt road in search of the Crescent Moon.

She squeezed my fingers. "Since I awoke from having my memories stolen, Zhara has entreated me to avoid the plague that is mankind. Often angry and sick with loneliness, I thought I would someday flee the woods and make my own way. But when you defend my honor such as this, I'm glad I waited. I know my words sometimes become loose with you, but I am yours."

Though her emotions warmed my neck, my brain switched on again at the mention of Priya's memory erasure. I remembered my quest to seek the truth about Priya and Zhara. Before I could lend it much thought, Desini paced closer and bumped my shoulder with her own. Her movements made so little sound, I jerked when she appeared.

"Thank you, Gemini. I never expected your honor. Wait, no, that came out wrong. Considering how these people see me, I wouldn't want you to sully your reputation by—"

"Reputation?" I ground to a halt and released Priya's hand so I could face the mishon. "Desini, you're with us, now. You can choose to continue on with us after Warrington or go your own way. In the meantime, you might see me lower my head around ignorant shits like that guard," I tapped her chest just below the neckline, "but that doesn't mean I don't have your best interests at heart. We should watch out for each other as long as we're together."

She nodded. "Agreed. No one shall approach your behind without my warning."

"The time when people treated you like dirt is over. If we're outnumbered, we'll quietly pass by bigots like Blanch. We might even bow when it's prudent. But I will draw my weapons and fight for you when needed. Got it?"

"Yes, master."

I grasped her hands and adopted what I hoped was a softer expression. "I'm no one's master. I own no slaves."

It was Desini's turn to shake her head. "You misunderstand. My people use the word as a term of regard for an esteemed teacher."

Priya cuffed the back of my head. "And you thought you were doing so well!"

I rubbed the spot and squinted at her.

"Are you done giving etiquette lessons?" She grinned.

I turned and pulled Desini along beside me by her hand. "Bite me, Priya."

"It would be my pleasure, my lord. Where shall I clamp down?"

"Gemini," Desini said. "You are holding my hand." The cat-like woman peered around, but averted her eyes from the gazes of passersby. Now that I noticed them, I recalled seeing no one in the main thoroughfare—if a small-town dirt road could be such a thing—the afternoon before.

I wondered if the citizens of Brumhill did business early, akin to the first two centuries in the United States, when the roosters called workers to the fields, when people rose with the sun and sheltered themselves indoors on guard against the perceived evils of night.

"It's not that I mind your touch, master. I'm honored by your friendly affections, but these people will hold you in low esteem."

"I think we've covered this, already."

"But they'll pass lies of your making sex with a beast."

"Does a tail render one a beast?" I asked. "Ears atop her head? A few retractable claws?"

I focused on a woman in clean, white pants and a short-sleeved pullover of fine knit approaching on the opposite side of the street. Pristine white gloves covered her arms to the elbows. A wide-brimmed hat shaded her face from the sun. A wicker basket swinging over one forearm bounced with her determined steps. She seemed out of place.

Though I smiled at her in greeting, her eyes trailed to where my hand clasped Desini's, and her nostrils flared.

Burning with offense at her snobbery, I pulled Desini's hand to my lip and kissed it long and hard. The stranger diverted her gaze, raised her chin, and huffed.

And I fucking loved it. Desini was cool.

My internal considerations brought another thought.

"Desini, how is it you're level seventeen? Where do you gain experience?"

Priya ranked up attributes in myriad ways, like climbing trees... and having sex. But level advancement required experience points and, if Desini spent most of her time traveling between towns on a cart—

"Messenger quests give me experience."

*NPCs do quests? What the hell? I've never even considered that possibility. Roshan never mentioned doing any quests.*

"But I must tell you, when I consider the expenses of time and stress I've incurred alone on the treacherous roads, I don't value the experience gains. I do it to eat. Besides, it's not like trainers will increase a beast's attributes, anyway."

"You're not a beast." I shook my head.

She smiled. "I'm glad you see. Your offer to increase my power is more reason why, as I ponder my profession and lack of companionship, I conclude it makes the most sense to fight my enemies head-on among friends than to live in fear of what threat might wait over the next hill."

*Oh, I like the sound of this. Defending her at the gate, defending Priya, refusing to relinquish her hand under the eyes of snobbery, I was earning some favor when I wasn't even thinking about it. Maybe I would fit in.*

She sighed. "I grow fatigued of delivering messages for coppers and being spoken to like a simpleton."

*And worse fates, no doubt.*

Priya leaned forward to peer across me at Desini. "People suck."

She was really picking up my verbal habits.

"I suspect I'm making powerful enemies by denying this governor his prize. His men have killed us once. Priya and I have to gain levels before we reach Roshan so we can deal with them. I just want you to understand the complexities bundled with joining us. Life won't be easy."

"My existence is already challenging," Desini said. She raised her shoulder in a half-shrug. "At least with you, I would not be lonely... nor afraid."

Priya nodded and gripped my other hand. "Just like I said. I left my loneliness in the Dark Wood when I coupled with Gem."

I'd always hated the abbreviated form of my name until I heard it on Priya's lips.

"So, you won't wait until we're done with Leira?" I asked. "You've decided?"

Desini looked between us, hesitating for a moment, and nodded. "Perhaps it seems silly, but I sense love in the two of you and the way you speak about your lost companion, and I believe destiny has put you in my path. It would honor me to help you retrieve your companion. I know what it is like to be separated from those one loves. If you will have me, I will journey with you beyond Warrington."

*Companion number four! I love this game!*

A familiar sign on the left side of the road drew my gaze. "In that case, membership has its privileges. Come with me."

I led them to the portico outside the shop and stopped on the wooden planks in its shade. Standing with a cool breeze blowing my shirt tail, I released Priya's hand and faced the mishon.

"Since you want to travel with us, I'll equip you for perils we'll face."

Desini's expression morphed into contemplation as her eyes flickered between Priya and me, then to the ground, and finally up again. "I sense uncommon generosity and kindness in you. If you'd spent these years out here, alone, you would understand why these attributes demand my appreciation. There are always people who want the better end of a deal, those would change the rules upon delivery because they know the law will not enforce a contract with a mishon.

"Mine are a proud people who weigh our choices with great care, but to reject opportunities to improve ourselves is to deny Solara's blessings." Desini released my hands, cupped my face, then pressed her lips to mine. "I shall call you family from this day forth." She stepped away and kissed Priya the same way. "I hope you will consider me pack."

*Shouldn't it be litter?*

"Yay!" Priya clapped like a schoolgirl.

Again, I wondered whether Desini's quick decision to join us was more a reflection of programming trumping evolution or a natural disposition because of her situation, but I cast the thought away as I concluded that it didn't fucking matter. We could use her help if we wanted to get Roshan back.

*This isn't a game.*

Priya squeezed my hand as she peered at the door before us. "Can I wait out here instead of suffering Breeder's drooling again?"

14

"**S**ure."

"Ugh." Priya rolled her eyes. "Tread carefully, Desini, for these are the kinds of options he presents. To stand alone on a road in a small town to suffer the speculative gazes of the citizenry or suffer the adorations of a shopkeeper whose relentless babbling causes ringing in your ears."

"You're the one who suggested it."

Desini's lips wrinkled into a smirk. "Can you not imagine worse fates than adoration?"

I raised an eyebrow in Priya's direction. "I guess it's all about perspective, isn't it?"

"Gah. Insufferable. The both of you." She yanked open the door to the shop and stormed inside, though her emotions didn't quite match the level of intensity when they reached me.

"Have we upset her?" Desini asked.

I shook my head. "Not really. Don't worry. We're snarky with each other. She's being a little playful... I think."

We stepped toward the front door of the armor shop and Desini pulled at my hand. "I must enter through the rear."

Over her shoulder, I spied a middle-aged man with a mustache so long it curled on the ends throwing a suspicious glare in our direction. He pulled a younger woman's arm, drawing her close to him as they paced past the shop.

I stepped toward the tall mishon and smiled, crowding her, urging her forward. "No back doors, not here. You'll see."

I held open the door, and Priya stood just inside. She reached for Desini's hand and led her across the threshold. "Come, meet my groveler."

Inside, my gaze gravitated to the racks lining the walls. While the shop wasn't overrun with epic gear, the leather chest protectors, short swords, daggers, and boots were clean and serviceable. I raised a pair of shin protectors and eyed the smooth stitching, wondering if Breeder repaired them himself.

Breeder's pinched voice originated in the back. "I'll be right with you!"

I glanced at Priya and threw her a mischievous grin. She wore a confused expression as she scanned mine for meaning. Then our emotional link filled in the blank as my smile grew and her eyes flared.

"You dare not," she growled.

Nodding, I cocked up my chin and went British. "My dear man! Mister Breeder! I say! The blood of Zhara graces your establishment! Come forth and be blessed by the Light!"

A metallic crash resonated from somewhere out of sight as some number of unseen items rattled to the floor.

"Oh! Oh, my!" A metallic rattle. "Is it Priya? I'm

coming! Oh!" More clattering. "The blessings abound! Is that my beloved Priya!"

"Bastard!" Priya punched me hard in the shoulder. "I dislike you."

I grinned again. "You fucking adore me."

"You will see what happens when you defy me, *Lord Gemini*."

"I'm shaking in my stealth boots."

Priya folded her arms across her chest. "There will be consequences for your chicanery." She peered at me through slits and ran her gaze over Desini's tall, muscular form. "I shall sleep with Desini tonight."

"That's not much of a threat. You slept with her last night."

"And I shall warm her body with my own."

"Now I'm just aroused."

"I will give her pleasure." Priya peered at Desini. "Would you like that, Desini? Would you enjoy relations with the *kin of an immortal*?" She finished with a flourish and shot me her wide, blue eyes.

"Kin of—?"

I'd forgotten Priya's heritage hadn't come up with Desini yet. I shook my head. "Story for later."

Desini ignored my comment. "I would enjoy that very much, Priya."

Our heads swiveled in unison. The mishon stepped closer.

Desini raised an index finger, and a thick, curved claw popped out. "Must we wait until tonight?" She poked a dent in the center of Priya's bottom lip as she purred her words, her accent thick and luscious. "I think you would very much enjoy the sensations I could create within your body. Unlike many cultures, mishon women crave diversity." The claw trailed down as Desini slipped her tongue between her teeth and hummed. Her green eyes followed her claw until it stopped in the slight divot of Priya's chin.

In her gaze was no sign of the reserved woman-beast who'd bowed at the gate and lowered her head as we walked through town. Priya eyed the way Desini chewed her bottom lip as she surveyed Priya's mouth with intense interest.

"Mmmmm." Desini ran the point of her tongue over her lips, as if tasting Priya's remnants. The half-elf's eyes lingered in a closed state. "Your softness is perfection. I would not argue with your claim of immortality, for your beauty will survive the ages."

Priya threw me an amazed glare.

"Hello!" Breeder yelled as he came into view, his hands outstretched.

My own wonderment about what kind of sex-crazed world I'd walked into was cut short when the proprietor appeared.

"Priya! My beloved Priya!" He didn't seem to notice time had come to a screeching halt in his shop.

Desini peered up at the storekeeper then back at Priya. Her words came on a low purr, too quiet for Breeder to hear. "I will anticipate warming your body for the rest of the day, immortal blood." She ran a finger down the center of the robe as she stepped away and whispered to me as she passed, "Joining your party brings great favors, master."

Disbelief painted Priya's features. This might well have been the first time I'd ever seen her at a loss for words.

"Desini?"

"Yes, Gemini?"

"I think I love you."

"I have become quickly fond of you, as well."

What I would have given to view Desini's disposition toward Priya at that moment, or vice versa.

"Breeder!" I barked.

Desini didn't flinch. Priya stood stunned. Our vendor friend jumped at the greeting. Something about screwing with him gave me the happy tingles.

I slipped my arm around my newer companion's waist. She surprised me when she pressed her shoulder against mine and leaned in. Her tail slapped the back of my leg. The numbing rumble of her purr made my arm tingle.

"Master Gemini!" Though he greeted me, his eyes were high beams focused on the half-elf. "How may I serve greatness today?"

"My man! You know how to pour it on thick! I like that about you, Breeder."

"Thank you, sir."

"I'm here with an unusual request."

Breeder threw his hands out. "My lord, if it is mine to grant, you shall have it. Please, tell me how I can serve the Shénhuà and his goddess betrothed?"

Desini swooned suddenly, slipping away from my shoulder and having to set her arms out to right herself.

"Shénhuà?" Her tight, hesitant expression vanished, replaced by something between amazement and sheer horror. Her mouth gaped so wide I could see her uvula hanging from the top of her throat. Lowering herself to one knee, she slapped her hands on my boots. "Can it be? Is this true?"

"Desini."

She peered up, horror-stricken.

I swallowed my irritation. "Up, up, up. On your feet," I reached out and offered my open hands. "Shénhuà or not,

I'm your companion. Treat me like a friend. We can't have you gathering attention."

Her head shook like it was connected to her neck by a ball bearing. "No! No, my lord! Never! If you are Shénhuà, a creature of Her Light, I must kneel!" She dropped again. "That I foul your presence with my lurid hungers is unforgivable. I beg your forgiveness." I snatched the shoulders of her blouse and righted her. Then I spun her around, wrapped my hands around her waist, and pulled her back against me so she faced Breeder. I whispered in her ear. "There is nothing to forgive. Please keep your feet until we have had time to discuss this. We have business here."

"Yes... yes, my lord. Your every desire, my lord."

I sighed and turned my attention back to Breeder, whose astonishment was unmistakable. "I'm guessing you have spoken with Guiles."

"Yes, your holiness."

*Aww bird turds. Not that!*

If I hadn't been the only thing between Desini's standing and crumbling to the floor like a Jenga set, I'd have thrown my arms out to stress my words. "Everyone needs to calm the shit down! I'm just a dude."

Priya still seemed to survey the place where Desini had run her hand across the cleavage. No help would come from there.

I rolled my eyes. "My name is Gemini. Not Lord Gemini, Not Shénhuà Gemini. Not Master Gemini. And certainly *not* His-fucking-holiness, Gemini. Just Gemini. Drop the pretenses and don't believe everything you hear. Okay?"

There was no sign of forthcoming compliance in anyone's face. Priya eyed Desini like a charmed kitten peering at a laser pointer from her perch, ready to pounce.

"Breeder, I'd like you to take Desini in the back and outfit her in whatever I can get with my credit. Plate, if possible, but chain if not. Do whatever's necessary to accommodate the tail, right?"

Breeder peered at Desini. "It is my honor to assist you, Miss Desini. Your blessed company speaks of your prestige. I am impressed. Very impressed, indeed. I shall try to—"

"Mister Breeder!" I really didn't have time for his prattling.

"Yes! Your holiness. Come! Come, Miss Desini. Let's fit you like a true champion."

Desini curved her shoulders in, pulling her fists to her chest, making herself smaller.

*God, she doesn't understand what to do with someone who treats her with respect. She's curling up in a ball.*

Breeder reached out a hand, palm up. "Miss Desini? Come, I won't bite you." Breeder flashed a warm smile.

I gave a curt nod. "On my honor, he won't bite you. But if he gets frisky, you have my leave to bite him."

Breeder gaped. "Your ethereal holiness, I would never!"

*Jesus wept.*

Desini flashed me an uncertain smile and allowed herself to be led away. As they stepped off, I made a wish to the A.I. who governed this world, asking for the chance to run across those who'd disrespected this gentle mishon specimen in the past so I could mold their faces to the treads of my boots.

I called after them. "Hey! Constitution and Strength, in that order, right?"

"Of course, my mythic friend!" Breeder waved over his shoulder! "She shall amass a massive pool of hit points and crush rocks with her bare hands!"

Priya's rapt attention locked on Desini's muscular ass.

"She charms you, doesn't she?" Her voice was distant, enchanted.

*Smitten.*

"She certainly charmed you."

Priya's hand went to her breast and cupped it, and she muttered. "The things I have missed in my life."

"Cut that out, would you? All this up and down will ruin me."

"Sorry," she grunted in an unapologetic tone.

---

Breeder promised the skimpy-but-shining plate mail in which he had clad Desini would protect her against 'raging beasts of all ilks.' I wondered if its defense capabilities extended to include more tactical humanoids who would aim right for her bare midriff or exposed legs. As she raised her arms to peer down, my eyes traced each piece of metal glued to fabric that clung to Desini's muscular curves.

### *Iron Plate of the Lion*
*Level 16*
*Slot: Chest*
*Type: Armor*
*Quality: Rare*
*Durability: 61 of 75*
*+23 Melee Defense*
*+16 Constitution*

### *Layered Hip Guards of the Lion*
*Level 15*
*Slot: Legs*
*Type: Armor*

*Quality: Rare*
*Durability: 70 of 70*
*+13 Melee Defense*
*+11 Constitution*

Though the arm pads strapped above her biceps didn't cover the tops of her shoulders, they bent outward high and low to provide ample protection to her biceps and shoulders. They appeared much lighter than full-blown shoulder pads would've been, and I admitted surprise that they required only Level 15 to equip.

### *Plate Arm Pads of the Lion*
*Level 15*
*Slot: Shoulders*
*Type: Armor*
*Quality: Rare*
*Durability: 70 of 70*
*+13 Melee Defense*
*+11 Constitution*
**Bonus**: *Set Bonus (3 pieces): +9 Strength*

### *Plate Hip Belt*
*Level 15*
*Slot: Waist*
*Type: Armor*
*Quality: Common*
*Durability: 50 of 50*
*+5 Melee Defense*

"Holy crap, Breeder! Where did you get those?"

Breeder laced his fingers in the black suspenders holding up his pants and snapped them. A frown threatened at the corners of his lips beneath the thick mustache. "Your worship, just because I operate in a small town doesn't mean I only offer lesser items. I own two shops, aside from this one. Why, before the road became such a hazard, I moved armor and weapons of the finest quality between my places. One resides in the king's own seat and one in Whimshire in the West. I keep a few select pieces in this shop, just in case." He gripped the lapels of his vest. "I just prefer the small-town feel."

Priya spoke for the first time since her sensual encounter with Desini. "He prefers the shroud of Light cast here by Zhara's presence."

Tugging her shoulder, I grinned and said, "Perhaps I should thump you one on the back of the head like you did when I was disrespectful."

"Do so at your peril, master," Desini interjected with a crooked smile. Had she worn a different expression, the feminine muscles exuding from beneath the shoulder protection of the armor might have given me pause. She was higher level and, dressed in that plate, she might pummel me.

"I admit a certain, shall we say, attraction to Zhara's proximity," Breeder admitted.

Priya bumped me with her hip. "Ha. Now we approach the truth."

"Makes me wonder why this town isn't more crowded," I muttered, but no one seemed to hear.

Breeder set his gaze upon me in the special way only an established vendor could when it came time to haggle. "Of course, my lord, these pieces come at some cost."

Desini peered down at the plate that gleamed despite the few scratches and dents her fingers showed. "It will need repair, master. I would say at least fifty silver's worth.

There's a smith in Warrington who might be up to the task, but we must negotiate the price."

"Ah! A skilled barterer, I see" He glanced at Priya. "Does Master Gemini only hire those with this skill set?"

"I hire no one. These are not my employees, they're my team."

Breeder gestured to a massive metal frame on the back wall. Centered inside was my old quiver, the one constructed by Zhara my first day in Enora. "I fear Miss Desini is correct. I haven't had time to beat the chest plate back into perfect shape, so I will negotiate." He lowered his voice, as if speaking to himself. "Anything I lose in dealing with you will be recoverable." Then he flashed a winning smile. I noticed something caught in his teeth and speculated this was a man who faced challenges with getting his food to where it could digest. "You have the gold credit marked in my ledger."

I peered at Desini and then at Priya.

Priya shrugged. "I know nothing about plate armor."

Desini ran her fingers down the armor, tracing every curve. She shook the breastplate, lifting it up and down, then rolled her shoulders. I guessed she was testing its range of motion, and the side-oriented shoulder guards left her arms free to move unencumbered.

"I don't know how much gold my lord has, but I fear he cannot afford this, despite Mister Breeder's willingness to barter." She smiled at me. "But I am touched you would so adorn me, that my protection is vital to you." She unstrapped the armor.

*All these negotiators who won't negotiate!*

Breeder sighed and glared at me.

"Eighty gold," I said.

Desini's head jerked up.

"Done!" Breeder barked.

Her mouth gaped.

"I assume she can just wear it out?"

"Of course, my lord. The town will cower before her."

"Cool. That leaves me twenty in credit, right? I've got a Level 12 sword in my bag, but she's Level 17. Her rank is 7 in Swordsmanship. I want to have something in reserve when she ranks up in case she outgrows the old sword while we're away from civilization."

"How heavy, my dear?" He scanned Desini's shoulders and peered down her back to her backside. Desini eyed him but didn't object. "You seem... firm, like you could wield a long sword with practice, but I fear a great sword would be a tad much." He looked up. "May I have your leave, madam?"

"Leave to do what?"

"To lay hands upon you to fit you for a sword."

"You would touch me?"

Breeder mistook her meaning, judging by his response. He offered a smile. "I'm a professional, madam. I wouldn't try to fondle you."

Her tension melted away.

"That wasn't what she meant, Breeder," I said. "Most people are bigots and won't touch her."

Breeder's eyebrows shot up. "The politics of the region shame me, sir." He turned his gaze on the mishon. "I assure you, madam, I find such dispositions contrary to the teachings of Solara's priests and hope those who treat you with such rudeness suffer her judgement."

"You may touch me."

As he gripped her shoulders and squeezed his way down her arms, he explained.

"I have a skill that allows me to fit you by feel." He

squeezed. "Hmm. Yes. Very nice. Firm, Miss Desini. You are lovely while very strong. A wonderful combination! Our lord has a refined taste in fighting companions. Or they, in him."

Desini smiled at me over the shopkeeper's shoulder.

I snuck a glance at Priya to find her facing the door, knuckling away a tear.

"You're going soft on me," I muttered.

She slapped my shoulder. "Asshole."

*More like me every day.*

"So, Desini," I said. "You see that not all humans are bigoted, yes?"

"I do, Master Gemini."

*At least she added my name.*

The Level 16 sword and the plate he selected for Desini spent my credit and all but four gold from my stash but came with the promise she could equip it now. It was one-handed, but that was fine. We'd pick her up a shield at some point and make her a good old-fashioned *sword-and-board* tank! Unfortunately, Breeder had no shields in stock. They seemed low in demand, and high prices made them better suited for sale in larger towns. He didn't have any head gear low enough for me, either. That sucked.

### *Sword of the Defender*
*Level 16*
*Slot: Weapon*
*Type: One-handed Sword*
*Slashing Damage: 30-41*
*Quality: Uncommon*
*Durability: 50 of 50*
*+25 Melee Defense*
*+5 Constitution*

I gave the blade a good once over, but its higher level made for clumsy wielding in my untrained hands. I should've known Enora would throw mechanics like that at me.

*You have discovered the class: **Fighter**!*
*You may change your class to Fighter by equipping an appropriate weapon.*
*Do you wish to change your class to Fighter?*
*Yes/No*

I decided on a little experimentation while I held it and focused on yes.

*You are now a Level 10 Fighter.*

### G3m1n1 Fowler
Human
Level 10 Fighter
Strength: 22
Dexterity: 6
Intelligence: 1
Wisdom: 1
Constitution: 19
Charisma: 12

"Sweet!" I blurted. All eyes fell on me. "Sorry, I just changed my class to fighter and realized that it just flipped my Dexterity and Strength attributes, leaving the rest as they were. That's pretty awesome."

It meant when I reached the level where the starter classes stopped their simultaneous advancement, my stats would adjust.

"I assume when you say 'it' flipped your attributes, you meant to say 'Solara.'" Breeder said.

"Yeah," I said. "That's what I meant."

When I handed the sword to Desini, she clutched and twirled it over the back of her hand as if she'd wielded many. That had to be a game thing. A prompt popped up as she gripped the weapon.

*Your companion has equipped:*
### Sword of the Defender
*You may now select the Fighter class for Desini.*
### Warning:
*Unlike players, companions cannot change starter classes. However, at Level 20, you may choose a combat profession for each companion.*

*If you select Fighter for her class, professions available to this companion upon reaching Level 20 will be:*

### Warrior
### Marauder
### Shadow Knight
### Blade Dancer
### Paladin

*If you select the Fighter class for your companion and do not bind the companion to you, your companion will remain a Fighter beyond Level 20.*

I peered at my new companion as her finger traced the flat of the blade in wonder and turned the sword over in a white-knuckled grip.

"Do you like it?"

She nodded. "Mmm. Very much."

Her green eyes flared and gleamed in my direction. I

tried to interpret the determined expression stretching her round cheeks and bringing that glare to those reflective irises. Then I got it.

*Hunger.*

I already felt sorry for anyone who laid hands on this woman.

15

Fifty paces down and across the road from Breeder's, the Crescent Moon operated at the whim of a middle-aged woman with pink and white hair named Leira. Whereas Breeder's shop was utilitarian and plain, this one's dim interior and well-kept wooden finishes spoke of meticulous upkeep. I didn't spy a speck of dust in the place.

The proprietor stood across a polished wood counter from a plump guy who wore the stench of wine and B.O. I waved my hand in front of my face and took a step back. He beat the leather cover of a stacked tome with runic symbols imprinted in gold leaf. "If I can't read it, I can't use it! What do you expect me to do with it?"

Leira crossed her arms and leaned against a shelf behind the counter. Her accent sounded almost-Scottish in inflection. "Mayhap you stick it under the leg of a crooked table? Perhaps you discipline that errant boy of yours with it? It's not my problem ya can't read it, Filton. You bought the book, you gave me twenty silvers. Now *you* own a book, and *I* own twenty silvers." She reached across and knocked his forehead. "So, don't you storm in here trying to intimidate me 'cause ya emptied one too many skins of that throat-numbin' muck ya call wine and need copper to buy something to cleanse yer palate of it!"

Filton sneered and slammed his fist on the counter, causing Priya to jerk next to me as we waited.

I leaned toward Desini. "Should I intervene?"

The mishon whispered, "Leira has magic, and she wouldn't take kindly to someone who treats her like she's helpless in her own place." She shook her head as if to reinforce her words. "No. Leave it, master."

"Okay. And stop calling me that."

"Yes, master."

*Priya's antics are already rubbing off on her.*

Filton tried another tact. "Leira, my friend. How long have we known each other?"

"By my count, 'bout seven minutes too long."

Filton slammed his hand on the counter again.

There was no sign Leira noticed the outburst.

"Fine!" Sweeping the book off the counter he wheeled around and missed running into me by about two inches. "Watch where you're going, beast-lover."

I turned as he passed, staring daggers at his spine since I couldn't stab him with real ones.

Desini nudged me. "You suggested we would walk away when it wasn't in our interest to act. I believe this is one of those times, if you'll grant me leave to say so."

I nodded.

"Ho, Desini," Leira said, eyeing Desini's plate armor. "Interesting attire, today."

"Miss Leira, my heart swells to see you again."

"Thanks." Her voice gave off the raspy quality of a thirty-year, pack-a-day smoker. She didn't seem to care about any swelling in Desini's chest. "I'm noticin' ya came through the front. Think the new outfit entitles you, do ya?"

Desini didn't respond, but I shot the vendor a steely gaze. "Her place in my party entitles her."

Leira shot me a long, stony look, but when she finally spoke again, it was to Desini. "You have a message for me from Tetric?"

"I do, madam." Desini reached behind her and withdrew a letter sealed with blue wax from somewhere in the vicinity of her muscular butt, though I couldn't imagine where she'd stashed it so the seal didn't break. Maybe she had a magic fanny pack I'd missed.

"Good." She snagged the envelope, checked the seal with a suspicious glance at Desini, then flicked it open. Her lips moved while she read the script on the thin parchment. "I see."

"Do you have a return message?" Desini asked.

Leira shook her head. "Sorry. Nothing this time. Here's your silver." She tossed two silver pieces on the counter.

"Thank you, Miss Leira."

"Next time, come in the back like's proper."

Apparently reading my bent expression of sentiments I'd planned keep to myself, Leira turned her clipped phrasing on me. "You got a problem, mister?"

Desini's warning glance was subtle, but I'd be damned if my mouth didn't tend to get me into trouble. She'd spoken to my companion like she was dirt and underpaid her for traveling over a day on dangerous roads. I might not have known a lot about the value of currency in Enora yet, but two silver was short.

"I got ninety-nine problems, but a bitch ain't one."

One of Leira's eyes half-closed as she peered at me. "I'm

not sure I take your meanin', but I get the impression it'd be better for ya if I didn't."

"Is that supposed to scare me?"

Leira burst out laughing.

Desini took a step back.

I took a step forward. "Something funny?"

"Desini, is this one with you?"

"Yes, Miss Leira. He is my companion who saved me from rapists on the road outside of town. A very honorable man."

Leira's head jerked back a tad as she considered me again, from face to waist and back. "I'll forgive his rudeness this time, but in the future, ya bring him in the back like we agreed, or ya don't come."

"I tell you what, *Leira*. I'll do you one better to assuage your concerns over our mutual friend." I reached into my bag and withdrew two gold pieces. At the sight of this, Leira perked up, but I handed them to Desini, whose eyes grew wide and confused. "That should cover about one-hundred trips at *Miss Leira's* current rates. From now on, Leira can find herself a human to move her messages, since that seems to be her obvious preference, and you've found a new job."

I bowed until my forehead almost reached the counter.

If her gaze alone could've banished me to hell, I would've found myself afire in an instant. Maybe when in Rome, one does as the Roman's do, but I was in Enora. I planned on making this place my playground and bending over backward for bigot witches wasn't on my list of things to do.

I was all but certain things would have devolved from there, but the energy inside the shop changed as if on a sudden wind when Priya reached up and lowered her hood, revealing her spiraling shoulder-length locks.

Peering around, the shopkeeper's eyes fell on Priya and froze there. Her head tilted, her eyes flickered in their sockets. Her lips parted, her eyelids flared, then Leira took a step backward and leaned on the counter behind her. I couldn't suppress the suspicious glare I set on the shopkeeper, and I didn't like the expression focused on Priya.

Leira's face relaxed. "Aren't you going to introduce me to your friends, Desini?" Her tone was softer, almost void of the tension it held moments before.

Come to think of it, her accent had vanished, too.

"Of course, Miss Leira. It is my pleasure to introduce you to Gemini—" she turned her attention on me. "Here I have committed to an engagement with you, and I don't recall your surname."

"Fowler," I said.

Desini smiled. "An unusual name. I like it very much."

"Thanks."

She turned her focus back to Leira. "Gemini Fowler. And this is Priya..."

"Skyy," Priya said.

Leira's head ticked back again at my companion's announcement of her last name. I read confusion. She peered at me.

"You know what? I think I like this one, Desini."

My head jerked back this time.

"You're the one Guiles was talking about, aren't ya? The one with the special skills?"

"I don't know what you mean."

She waved a dismissive hand and chuckled. "I got the eye, son." She thrust an index finger at her right eye and leaned forward. The whisper of a cloud, like the beginnings of a cataract, swirled in her cornea. "If only I'd used it a minute sooner. You can't fool me. Here." She reached into a pouch and threw ten more silver on the counter. "That should square us, Desini." The cloud in her eye swirled as she turned it back onto me. "I have a business to run if I want to eat, sir. Small town traditionalists and their snooty ways, you understand."

I shrugged. "Sometimes you stand up, and sometimes you eat, I guess."

"What you don't see, sir, is Desini's use of the front door could get her accosted by the guard or thrown in yon pit for days, especially if Slate caught her."

Slate. I knew that name. Hadn't that been the tall guy, Level 10 or so, who'd caught Priya in the clearing last night when Guiles and I went stealthy?

She twirled a finger toward Desini. "I was protecting the child." Leira bowed her head slightly. "Forgive my petulance."

Priya chuckled. "Who's the teacher now?"

"Oh, fuck you, Priya," I said with a smile.

Leira nodded and eyed Desini's metal gear a second time. "Good for you, Desini. It seems you got a better deal than message delivery. I always hoped you'd find a better way." Then she turned to Priya. "Do you remember me?"

One of Priya's thin blonde eyebrows rose. "Remember you? I'm sorry, have we met?"

"I had the honor of serving as a keeper of lore at the university in Warrington."

"University? Oh, no." Priya said. "Until recently, I lived in The Dark Wood."

Leira tilted her head to one side and her forehead wrinkled. "My mistake. You've lived there your whole life?"

Priya nodded. "Yes. Have you had occasion to visit the Wood? It is possible we met when I was but a child. A shadow wizard cloaked my memory."

Leira's eyes flared, but her expression leveled quickly. Priya and I shared a glance. When we turned our eyes back on the shopkeeper's, her gaze flickered between us.

Priya took a slow step toward the counter. "Perhaps you have met Zhara?"

"Zhara? Oh, well..." Leira's eyes rolled to the ceiling and then seemed to take an inventory of the books lining the shelves on the wall closest to Desini.

*Something is not right, here.*

Desini winced.

Leira took in my whole form. "Yes, I once had occasion to meet Zhara. A majestic creature, for certain. I see now you are her kin."

Priya nodded. "She is my aunt."

"Yes." Leira blinked. "The family resemblance is unmistakable. This why I reacted like I did when you lowered your hood. It was like... seeing a ghost."

*I don't believe a word she's saying right now.*

I probed. "Why did you mention the university?"

Leira peered at me for a long moment and nodded. "The one Guiles and Breeder have spoken of. The returned." It seemed my question hadn't been worth answering.

*Small town gossip. Just what I needed.*

"Um..."

"Your secret is more than safe with me. Breeder, Guiles, and I are devoted followers of the Light. You couldn't be in more secure hands, sir. Again, please forgive my brashness, earlier. I didn't realize until..." her eyes flicked to Priya again, "... well, I didn't understand who I was speaking with."

*Why does she keep looking at Priya like that?*

"As I've had the distinct pleasure of the guardian's

acquaintance, I hope you'll allow me to support your cause with a gift, in the way of apology."

Leira reached beneath the counter and revealed a rolled parchment. My interest would've been piqued under normal circumstances, but the way she'd changed her attitude and her accent, besides how she eyed Priya, brought cautious curiosity, like a beanstalk sprouting in my colon.

"This is a scroll of Mystic Sight. The spell allows you to reveal an area on your map you haven't discovered." She paused and slid her hand away from the scroll. "Or *see* someone in particular. Troop movements, enemies, or mayhap *someone you lost.*"

Okay, so that got everybody's attention.

"Only catch is, it doesn't work underground. You can't reveal all those special treasures in those dark dungeons, but if you have something you want to see within a mile above the soil... you can cast it once per day."

I peered at the scroll and blinked my eyes in succession.

Leira raised her hands on either side. "By all means, Shénhuà. Have a gander for yourself."

### *Mystic sight*

*Level 10*
*All Magic Schools*
*Cast Time: 5 seconds*
*Cool-down: 24 Hours*
*The caster views a 100-yard area from up to one mile away
and reveals the location on the map.*

"Shénhuà," Desini gasped and shook her head, as if hearing it for the first time.

"That is a nice piece of magic," I admitted, softening my tone. "How much gold is that going to cost me?"

"Shénhuà, I said it was a gift."

Priya shook her head at Leira. "What's the catch?"

"Why should there be a catch?" Leira asked.

Priya threw her an epic squint. "Where there is a deal, there is a catch."

"Are you headed north, by chance?" She eyed Desini. "Back to Warrington, love?"

*Now it was 'love.'*

I wasn't certain I wanted Leira to know. "Maybe."

"If you were headed in that direction, I wondered if a quest might suit you?"

"I knew there was a ca—" Priya said.

"Whoa, Nellie!" I interrupted. "Now you're speaking my language. What kind of quest?"

Priya slapped my shoulder, and I turned. "What's up?"

She glared as if she'd burn holes in my face. "What is *up*, my *love*, is that it's rude to interrupt a lady" —she growled the next words— "especially *your* lady, when she is *talking*." She straightened her back, softened her expression, and patted my cheek. "Just for your edification." She tilted her head, showing me all her teeth. "You may now proceed."

I bowed slightly. "Apologies, my lady. I'll endeavor to keep my manners close at hand."

Priya nodded. "Your apology is accepted, your *holiness*."

The corners of Leira's lips turned up slightly. "That's good. You gotta train 'em young or they walk all over ya." Her loose accent had reappeared as if at the snap of fingers.

*Gah!*

My new life was immersed in estrogen. Even my pet was female.

"Now that *the blessed kin of the matron has* granted me leave to inquire, you mentioned a quest."

"Ingrate," Priya whispered.

Leira leaned on the counter. "I made a bargain with a dealer in Warrington to deliver something of... let's call it *magical value* to a mage at the university. This message Desini delivered confirms the person to whom I sent the relic has received it, but the wizard she'd planned on entrusting it to has died. Something about an improper alchemical mixture by an acolyte at the lab there." She waved a hand. "The details are of little importance. But as it is not a thing we can allow to fall into bandit or mercenary hands, I don't want to risk having my contact in Warrington send it back, especially considering the bandits on the roads. It is safe for the time being, but if someone of influence were to buy it off the black market or intercept it? Let's say whole towns could crumble in the chaos."

"Oh, so nothing grand," Priya said. "A little side errand to protect the world, is all."

"Actually, Priya, it might only level one city. The rest of Enora would fare just fine."

## 16

Priya gulped like she swallowed a snail in its shell.

I folded my arms across my chest, but my leather plate wasn't cooperating. So, I lowered them. "What is this relic?"

"It's not the kind of thing I would want to get out."

"But you want me to run blindly north, retrieve it, and do what exactly? Return it to you?"

"Gods, no!"

I jerked a little.

Leira cleared her throat. "Weren't you listening? No, Shénhuà. Since the person I sent it to was a wizard at the university, I judged it would be in safe hands. However, with him dead, I'm not sure who I can trust to ensure it's stowed somewhere safe and kept out of circulation. Or destroyed."

Priya snorted. "Right. You still haven't told us what it is."

Leira sighed. "An entropy crystal."

Priya shot me a confused glance. When I met Desini's gaze, she shrugged.

But I recalled Zhara's interrogation of Crohl in the Dark Wood. She'd asked if the tunnels Crohl's slaves were digging on behalf of Underlord Caym were a search for entropy crystals. I'd wondered what they were, but had gotten distracted.

Entropy was a scientific theory stating that systems tended toward chaos, but I didn't know much more than that. Here, I didn't *need* to. "That sounds unpromising."

Leira nodded and her accent shifted with her tone, throwing me off balance. "Perhaps my demeanor leaves something to be desired, Shénhuà. I apologize again for my gruffness. But it's crucial we set aside any differences resulting from my poor manners so that we can work together for the common good. Now that I realize Zhara has sent her family into the world, I must assume it is to do the work of the Light. Is that a safe assumption?"

*That sounds a lot like she's redirecting.*

Priya and I shared another look.

"Yes. That's right," Priya replied.

"Then I can think of no better pairing—or trio, Desini! —to secure the entropy crystal and ensure it goes some- where safe."

"You say it's about who we are. What makes us so special if we're such low level adventurers? It can't just be that I'm some unproven mythic and she's the family of Zhara. It's not like we've brought the guardian with us. So, slash through the veil and tell us what's running through your mind."

"Gemini," Priya growled in a whisper.

But I was undeterred. I raised an eyebrow at Leira.

*I'm waiting.*

"It is not my place to subvert the will of the guardian of the Tree of Solara," Leira said. "I admit my knowledge of certain secrets, but it is not my place to reveal them. I must have faith that you will learn what your destiny dictates by your own doings."

"That sounds like a raw deal or a poor excuse."

Leira shrugged and threw up her hands. "Put yourself in my slippers. If Priya showed up in your shop after having lived in the woods for so long and Zhara had seen fit to send her into the world without warning, would you assume?"

"What do you mean by 'having lived in the woods for so long?' How long has Priya lived in the woods?"

"You expect me to betray the confidence of the right hand of Solara?"

"Do you expect me to run off and risk our asses retrieving this crystal?"

Her voice adopted a harsh tone. "Your judgement leaves something to be desired. I will not betray the Matron. You may choose whether you accept my quest, but Zhara is a wise being whose sight stretches far beyond my own. I am but a servant and will not sabotage Solara's plan."

"Zhara and Solara aren't the same thing," I said. "Zhara runs around with her tits out, for cripe's sake!"

"Ha!" Leira covered her mouth with both hands. "You know nothing! Zhara is the purveyor of Solara's will! She protects the tree whose roots feed the ley lines across this continent! She ensures Light remains in this world despite the shadow that tries to surround and corrupt it!"

Priya and I shared a third glance. I recalled the dark tunnels beyond the Tomb of the Lost beneath the Dark Wood. Crohl, the task master who'd used my half-elf companion to force demons and kobolds alike to dig. The smoky visage of his master, Underlord Caym framed on one wall as I burst into the room to rescue Roshan. Judging from Priya's expression, I wasn't alone.

"Your path will illuminate when Solara reveals it. I have faith that the quest I offer you plays my part. I don't believe in coincidences."

"Well, it sounds like a big coincidence," I said. "We were just delivering a message."

Leira shook her head. "Allow me to lend you my perspective." Though her tone relayed patience, it was also as if she spoke to a belligerent child. "You and Priya saved Desini from bandits on the road. Desini was here to deliver a message. You escorted her here to deliver that message. Said message informs us that the person with whom I'd planned to entrust a dangerous artifact is dead!" She slammed the counter. "Does that seem like a coincidence to you?"

Zhara's words echoed in my mind.

*Maybe you can provide security for a merchant with a horse and cart. That might be a better aim.*

"Okay, maybe not so much of a coincidence."

Leira nodded. To her credit, she didn't rub it in.

"I'm inclined to accept your quest." I glanced at Priya and she nodded. Desini's face stretched in surprise when I threw her a questioning look, but eventually gave the same, silent reply.

*You have been offered a chain quest.*
### *The Entropy Crystal*
### *Quest One: Retrieve the Entropy Crystal*
*The mysterious Leira has implored you to retrieve a crystal of shadow power from the mage Mora at the university in Warrington.*
*Reward: 12,500 XP*
*Title for completing quest line:* ***Guardian of the Light***

My mind hunted deception.

If Enora didn't interfere in the goings on in her world, how was Zhara permitted to use scrying magic to set us on a path? This wasn't some half-assed game world filled with static quests. Yet, there was Desini. If I believed what I'd been told, the men accosting her as we appeared at the town gates was a coincidence.

From what I'd seen so far, Brumhill was the end point for trade as carts weren't coming and going with regularity. If I trusted what I'd been told about the world evolving without interference, I could only conclude that Zhara's sight—maybe something akin to the spell on the scroll Leira offered but with a greater range—could extend to the bandits on the road to Brumhill and Desini's cart's likelihood to cross their path.

Was the A.I. able to predict events in her world because she knew every NPC? Or at least make extremely accurate guesses? If that was true, how was behavior going to change when players came along and threw a wrench in the whole program?

Also, did Zhara also have knowledge as to the death at the university that rendered this entropy crystal a fresh problem for us to solve? If she could see into the future and across distances, how far ahead did she see? How was she plugged in?

I lacked information needed to draw a logical conclusion, but a quest in my log might lead me down the right path.

### *Not on the Up-And-Up*

*Your wonderings about Zhara's true motives could serve you. Find out the true nature of Zhara and her relationship with Priya Skyy.*

*Level: N/A*
*XP: Commensurate with level at time of completion*
*A blessing giving you one full level after XP is awarded.*

One thing of which I was certain—Leira had recognized Priya when she'd lowered her hood. It hadn't been some familial resemblance that caused her reaction. When I coupled that with the fact she used to serve at the university in Warrington, whatever the university was, I smelled something foul. A deceptive idea crawled somewhere in my brain like a word I couldn't remember sitting on the tip of my tongue. It had to be something to do with the university.

Then it came.

*Leira had told her she'd served at the university to see if Priya recognized her!*

I eyed Leira as she scanned Priya's face. I homed in on her expression, and knew I was right. It wasn't her resemblance to Zhara, Leira was remembering Priya's features. The old caster's expression was of utter familiarity.

*Of a long-lost friend.*

"How long has it been since you left the university?" I asked.

Leira jolted as if awakened from a disconcerting dream. "What?"

"The university in Warrington? When did you leave?"

The muscles around the cloudy eye twitched. "Long, long ago. Decades."

To my surprise, one side of her mouth crept up.

"Why did you leave?"

"You're not so sneaky as you think, Gemini. May I call you Gemini? You won't sneak the information you desire from me. I must leave it to you all. You've been blessed with the family of Zhara, marked by Solara, herself, to take on your merged destinies. Pursue them with faith and mayhap you'll find the answers you seek."

*Marked. The same word Guiles used. 'By Solara, herself.'*

Setting my hand on Priya's back, I rubbed my hand in a gentle circle as I pictured the ward that glowed when exposed to the air, like some kind of magical tattoo.

*But it wasn't drawn with a needle. Zhara didn't use a brush to put it there. It was a mark. Question: If Priya is the niece of the guardian, how is it she has a magical mark?*

I didn't need Leira. Eyeing my HUD, I found the answer I sought in the language used in the quest description.

### *Not on the Up-And-Up*

*Your wonderings about Zhara's true motives could serve you. Find out the true nature of Zhara and her relationship with*
*Priya Skyy.*
*Level: N/A*
*XP: Commensurate with level at time of completion*
*A blessing giving you one full level after XP is awarded.*

*The true nature of Zhara and her relationship with Priya Skyy.*

I didn't understand how I'd missed it before, but now I saw why Leira wouldn't talk to us about Priya. It had been the way Priya had introduced Zhara as her *aunt*. Leira interpreted that to mean Zhara had hidden the truth from Priya. The truth I now harbored with almost absolute certainty. The truth proven by the ward on Priya's back.

It wasn't a tattoo. It was called a "mark."

*A birthmark made by magic or some shit.*

Would the child of Zhara's sibling be born with a glowing ward on her back when it was Zhara who bound with the Tree of Solara? Why would that be? How would that be, in a world that, despite its magic, evolved naturally?

Priya's birthmark required that she be born of the Light, itself, but her primary affinity was in Shadow magic. Which could only mean one thing.

Zhara was Priya's mother. Or was I just spit balling?

A prompt popped up on my HUD.

*Quest Update*
### *Not on the Up-and-Up*
*Complete: Your inquisitive mind has discovered the true nature of Zhara's relationship with Priya Skyy.*
*New Objective: Find someone who knows more about Priya Skyy's past to unveil the secrets Zhara keeps.*

"Well, that's just fucking great," I muttered. All eyes shifted toward me. "Bah. Forget it. Quest update. Stupid shit."

"Quest?" Priya asked. "You're irritated."

I shook my head at Priya. "When it's time, we'll talk. Trust me. Leira?"

"Yes, Shénhuà?"

"If you don't want to answer a direct question, maybe I could ask a theoretical one."

"You may ask, though I guarantee no answer. I tread far from the edge of the precipice that is a betrayal of Zhara's will."

*Zhara carries real weight with people in this town.*

"Yes, you've made that quite clear. How does someone erase another person's memory?"

Leira peered at me for a long moment. The stern expression she wore convinced me I was about to get another short answer, but then it changed, her features softened, and Leira nodded.

"They don't. Powerful magic can shroud a person's memories, but they are never permanently lost. It is a long, tedious process and cannot be reversed by magic."

"You say they're never permanently lost. Can the memories be retrieved?"

Leira shot a glance at Priya and diverted her eyes. Staring down at her counter, she ran her fingers along the dark grains swirling through the wood.

"The effect could be weakened by familiar people and places, or events could serve as triggers to recover the memories."

*Like amnesia in my world. Interesting.*

"Why do you think Priya has yet to recover her memories?"

Leira raised her shoulder in a half-shrug. "How long has it been since she lost them?" She turned her gaze on Priya again, this time in question. It was the most disingenuous expression I'd ever seen.

"I don't know," Priya replied.

"Then I have no answer. I'm afraid this is all I can say, Shénhuà. Please try to understand. I don't want to be vague, but what I see is mine to see because it was willed by a greater being."

*She just diverted us with her question of Priya. She knows the answer. But it might be a long time before I get back to Zhara to ask these questions, and our primary goal is to retrieve Roshan.*

"Fine. Do you have a contact for us to retrieve the crystal?"

"Yes! Desini can take you to Mora, my friend in Warrington." She raised a finger in warning. "Be on guard at all times until the crystal is safe, Shénhuà. Be wary of revealing your identities to strangers."

"You mean everybody."

Leira peered at me for a long, long moment. "May I ask you a question, Shénhuà?" She didn't wait for permission. "How far back do you remember? Have you any idea from where you came?" She rubbed her hands together. "We've heard the stories of the mythics for ages, but we never learned their origin. It would be of great consequence to my studies of our world to know the answer."

I grinned.

"If it is Solara's will that you would know it..."

"Bah!" Leira said, waving a hand. "Fine! Unfair, but fine! Gah! I do not withhold information because I desire it!"

*Payback is so much fun, sometimes.*

"I was joking. I woke up in the forest near Zhara's tree a few days ago. I remember nothing before that."

Leira reached out with one hand, beckoning Priya forward. They clasped hands. "Be well, Priya. I am sure you are in good hands."

I had the distinct impression we were being dismissed. Leira came around the counter and led us to the front door. Her final words were to Desini.

"Your presence among heroes such as these proves my prejudices were ill-founded, and I will find my way to spread the word that it is time for change. It comes slowly, sometimes at great pains, but hold your head high in the presence of your companions. I hope you will grant me your pardon, in time, my lady."

Desini's facial muscles went slack. When her eyes turned to mine, I raised my shoulder in a half-shrug. Though I still wasn't certain how I felt about Leira, I'd convinced myself that I would at least try to live honorably in my second shot at life, presented by Enora.

"Forgiveness is powerful," I said. "Without it, the past is a thorn in our boot."

*Hey, that was pretty damn good!*

"You are absolved, Leira." Desini bowed her head. "May your days be filled with sunlight and your nights by a million stars to gaze upon."

Leira patted Desini's shoulder and turned away from us. "Yes! Go now, my friends! Purge the world of darkness! May your pending babe thrive as long as Zhara herself."

"Babe?" Desini asked.

Priya and I shot each other a glance. Despite all we'd learned and the range of emotions we'd traversed at the Crescent Moon, our lips curved into wide smiles. We really had to catch the mishon up on things.

Desini pointed at Priya's belly. "You can't mean..."

Her face went alight as we stepped out of the shop... and into the glares of five soldiers with their weapons drawn.

## 17

The scraggly-bearded guard I'd threatened at the gate hadn't been as intimidated as I would've hoped. Standing in the rear of a party of five, glaring at me in the long shadow of a tall man in ragged chain mail, a grin crossed his face. It was an expression that said *'ain't so tough now, are ya?'*

"Disarm yourselves and submit to the will of the mayor," the leader said.

I dropped my shoulders. "Ha! Mayor? Right. Who the hell are you?"

"I'm Guntil, head of the Mayor's Guard in Brumhill. You, sir, are under arrest."

"On what charge?"

The man raised his sword. "You threatened a guard."

My eyes flicked back to Blanch.

"Disarm yourselves and submit to the will of the mayor," Guntil repeated.

I checked the leader.

**Guntil Swarn**

*Human*
*Level 9 Fighter*

Guntil stepped forward and raised his sword so I had a great view down the shaft.

Desini lowered her head and muttered, "If he is a guard, where is his insignia?"

"You dare speak, beast?" Guntil said.

Desini's leg twitched as if she might take a step back, but then she straightened her knee and planted the foot on the dusty road. Though her head stayed high, I sensed her inner-struggle from how she clinched her fists to keep them from shaking. I'd done that. Habits died hard.

I shook my head. "She didn't speak to you, Swarn. She spoke to me."

"Beasts should not speak within my earshot!" His head twisted an inch to the side. "Isn't there some law about civilians inspecting members of the guard? How is it a rat of such low level can inspect me?"

Blanch, upon realizing the man was speaking to him, replied in the truest illustration of genius. "Huh?"

"I'm higher level than you," I said. It came off like an elementary school jibe, but I doubted this douche cannon had much in the way of education.

Desini piled on. "If you were the leader of the town guard," she muttered, "wouldn't you know the laws?"

Guntil twisted his sword closer to the mishon. "Shut your mouth, you filthy animal!"

I unsheathed my daggers. "Did you call my friend a 'filthy animal,' motherfucker?"

Guntil's sword was a piece of crap, but it had the redeeming quality of a name resembling its owner.

### *Simple Bastard*
*Level 5*
*Type: Sword*
*2-5 damage*
*Quality: Poor*
*Durability: 6 of 12*

Desini didn't flinch under threat of the blade.

Any sign of the timid woman I'd met the previous night or the sweet, soft one I'd gotten to know today, had vanished in a wink. She stood tall, her shoulders back.

"Gemini, the only guard here is the one we met at the gate this morning. You see his pin, there? On his lapel?" She thrust out a finger above the sword as if it wasn't there. "This man lies." Her eyes settled on the fighter as her eyebrows furrowed. Little wrinkles creased her forehead.

The sudden command in her voice reminded me of when Roshan cursed a skeletal minion back to hell two days before. A flicker of wonderment as to her sudden change dissipated as realization dawned on me.

*She's embracing her new purpose. We're creating monsters up in here!*

I eyed the small, metal pin divided into red and white. Desini clarified, as if challenging the man further. "That is the royal seal. All guards throughout the kingdom wear it." Her hand rested on the pommel of her sword.

Raising his blade closer to Desini, Guntil inched forward, a pair of ratty boots scraping rocks. The tip of his sword waved inches from her face. "Submit and pay the fine for your crime."

"Fine?" I asked. "Is that it? You're shaking us down?"

Peering over his shoulder, I flicked my attention toward the guard standing in the rear.

### *Turley Blanch*
*Human*
*Level 5 Fighter*

When I inspected Guntil, I saw no 'Town Guard' title.

"I see the scam, here." I pointed at Turley. "He's on the take. They pay him to keep a lookout for outsiders to rob. That's why he asked our business before we passed, and he waited until we got paid." I cocked my chin at the guard. "You don't have the sense to wait until we leave town to rob us, idiot? What are you going to do, kill us in the middle of the street?"

"Ah!" Guntil said. "We got us a smart one! Thinks he's got it all figured out. But ol' Turley there can deputize anyone he likes if he's outnumbered. How about this one, *adventurer?* Hand over the bag, or I kill your kitty and leave the real woman to my men. How's that, then?"

"Sure!" I said, stretching my features into the widest, most fake smile I could conjure. I snapped the bag from the clasp and tossed it at his feet. "Go ahead, bud. Have a look inside."

Swarn peered down at the bag with the demeanor of a man expecting a snake to launch from its mouth. The sword quivered in his hand. He knelt and tugged at the bag to loosen the drawstring. A black void appeared in the center. His hand flinched when he reached, and he stretched his fingers with a scowl. The bag was soul-bound. The asshole couldn't access it no matter how he tried unless I was dead. But seeing what would happen when he tried interested me.

He kicked the pouch which rolled to my feet.

"Soulbound! You were right, Turley. We got us a smart

arse." He raised his sword again, this time toward me. "Grant me access or I'll do it the old-fashioned way."

I glanced over my shoulder at Priya. Her hands formed claws, held low at her waist. A ball of lightning floated above one palm. A glance upward revealed her casting bar frozen at 50-percent.

*What the hell?*

She nodded.

I turned and sneered. "Last chance, Guntil. Take your men and go, or bleed out." Gripping the curved handles of my daggers, I crossed them beneath his sword then threw my hands up so it raised into the air. Swarn double-clutched to keep from dropping the weapon.

If I included the conflict with the bandits on the road, this would be the second time I ignored Guiles's advice to stick to Woodsman. But he was too close, and the bow was in my bag. That was the thing with Enora; weapons didn't automatically appear in my hand with a thought.

Guntil peered at me for a long moment, then at Desini. He lowered his sword and stepped back. "Fine."

"Ah!" He lunged and jabbed the weapon toward Desini.

"No!" I yelled.

Desini slid to one side as the sword whooshed above her shoulder, missing her face by inches. One of her boots slid forward in the dust as the mishon rammed her shoulder into Guntil's chest, forcing him back. When she'd created some distance, she stepped back a couple paces and her blade whipped from its slot on her plate half-shorts. But she wasn't a real fighter yet. She stood flat-footed, holding the weapon with both hands clumsily in front of her. I planned to keep the confrontation brief.

*It's XP time, bitch.*

I envisioned a purple cloud, then stepped through space and turned so I reappeared behind Guntil. Guiles would've been proud, and I was exhilarated it had worked. My hand quivered as I slipped the tip of one dagger against the soft spot behind his ear and the other beneath his chain mail, near his kidney.

"You asked for this," I growled as I shoved a dagger into his back and yanked it away. Blood splattered onto the suede tops of my stealth boots. That kind of pissed me off.

*You stab Guntil Swarn in a kidney.*
*Mortal Wound!*

*Guntil Swarn*
*-94 HP*

His sword clattered to the dry, dusty ground. I clutched a handful of his hair around my pommel when Guntil dropped to his knees. Blood dripped from the blade onto the crown of his head. He writhed, threw a hand behind his back and twisted.

I threw a glance over my shoulder at Turley's men. Enora might be my real life now, but it was time to play the game. "As we act in service of the Light, I'll spare the rest of you, but Solara claims this soul for your crimes." My dagger slipped behind his ear and into his skull. It came free with a wet tearing sound as I spun away. His body thudded to the ground as I stepped toward the next man, poised to attack.

My stamina recovered as I stared them down, ready to use it at a moment's notice but wanting to recover as much as possible.

All four men stepped back after a few shared glances,

eyes wide with shock, fanning out as their leader's corpse fell still.

*They're not used to resistance. How many have they robbed, right here in the middle of town?*

I heard the crackling of electricity behind me and turned. Bands of jagged electricity danced between Priya's fingers. I wished she could see how precious her casting sneer was. Cute or not, I wouldn't want to be on the receiving end.

On my other side, Desini gripped the pommel of her short sword in a two-handed, white-knuckled grasp. Her sharp-toothed sneer was *not* cute.

If I was being honest, I wanted to kill all those pricks.

When I turned back to the thieves, they'd sheathed their weapons, all except for Turley. A tall one with a semi-shaven face raised his hands.

"Aye, go on about your way, then. We know when we're outmatched."

The guard, Turley, barked orders. "What are you, a coward? Get them!" He raised his sword, but did it alone.

"Sorry, but we'll take our chances on the road," the tall man said, gazing down at his dead leader with an empty expression. "Blackbard frowns on failure, friend. We didn't sign up for this."

*Blackbard?*

*You have been offered a quest:*
### Blackbard?
*Discover the identity of Blackbard.*
*Reward: 1,000 XP*

The three men paced away, leaving Turley before us,

his knuckles white with his desperate grip on his worn sword.

"You deserve to die," Priya said.

"I would kill him at your command, sacred elf," Desini said. "Command me."

To think I'd almost allowed myself to think I was in charge of this outfit.

"Priya, he's a guard. Like it or not, killing him will mark us." Enora was just the bitch to do that to us.

"Aw," she pouted. "Let me kill him. Please?"

Her emotional tone contrasted her words and dragged my gaze away from Turley. Her lips turned up on one side. An eyebrow cocked ever-so-slightly.

*She's having fun.*

Just beyond Priya, I spied Leira, standing just inside her shop with a short stick in her hand.

*A wand? Guess we don't have to worry who's side she's on.*

I smiled at Priya but hardened my expression before turning back to Turley.

I spoke in a low voice. "We don't have time to talk to your mayor today. I suggest you keep it on the up and up from now on, or next time I come back to town, I might have a chat with him about how one of his men is aiding bandits. Or worse." I recalled Desini's flourish with her sword at Breeder's place and spun one of my daggers over the back of my hand. It was pretty sweet I didn't drop it.

Turley scowled hard at Priya, but when she jerked forward as if she'd cast, he stomped off without another word, kicking up dust in his wake.

Onlookers appeared in the shadows of the shops, including Breeder, who'd come out onto his stoop to watch with rapt interest. I traced his form and spotted the smallest crossbow I'd ever seen in his left hand. I bumped a fist to my chest. Breeder nodded in reply.

*I don't have to worry about him, either.*

*Your decision to spare the lower level outlaws has pleased Solara.*
*You have earned 30 points of Light*
*Alignment: Light + 477*
*Alignment: Good*

When I glanced into the space vacated by Turley moments before, I spied motion down the side road. For just the blink of an eye, a figure appeared in the shadows. I blinked and squinted against the late-morning sun, and spied unmistakable locks of long, platinum hair as he hurried around a corner.

*Breeder, Leira, and Guiles... all watching our backs. Hmm, maybe Enora is also the kind of bitch to give us gifts.*

I waved two fingers at Leira and paced north. My companions fell in behind me. Priya tapped my shoulder.

"Shouldn't we search him, Gem?"

In answer, I spoke to Breeder as we passed. "Don't want anyone getting the wrong idea, so help yourself to the loot."

Breeder smiled. "I will see his body dispensed with so that you garner the least attention possible. Leave it to me."

"Thanks, Breeder."

"You're welcome," he said with a shallow bow. "Might I suggest you take your leave before other guards arrive?"

"I'm surprised you can see us," I said.

Breeder donned a confused expression.

"Because we're already gone."

The shopkeep smiled.

18

We exited town through the eastern gate we hadn't used before. Since she often filled her skins and canteens in a river to the north that ran parallel to the road, Desini suggested we bypass the town well in the interest of a quick exit. The lone guard faced away from the town and spared us only a glance as we passed by.

The storm clouds rolled in again from the Northwest late that morning just as Brumhill passed out of sight behind a hill. Desini steered the horse and Priya rode next to her, fixed on her warm chatter about how nice it was to have companions. I filled my chest with a deep breath of fresh air and tried to enjoy the moment, but then I thought about how Roshan would probably like Desini, too. The mental dominoes tumbled from there.

*I really need to stop bellyaching.*

Text faded as I glanced beyond my HUD to find Priya's gaze wandering along Desini's feminine form, taking it in tiny gulps now that the mishon had removed her new plate for the journey. After the steamy event in Breeder's shop, I suspected Priya would get ravaged this afternoon while I steered the cart, and it didn't bother me in the least. What Priya wanted, I wanted, and jealousy was an unwelcome addition to our party. That Desini even wanted physical affection considering her past seemed like a positive. That she preferred it from a woman just made sense.

*Look at me. I'm all growed up.*

When rain pelted the cart, I looked up from the back to find the mishon extending an awning to cover the riding bench. Priya's hands ran down her back and caressed her tail the second she returned to her seat.

I needed to focus. I was still trying to figure out the best way to distribute our new friend's attributes. Thirty-four points were a bunch, but despite Desini's decision to adventure with us, I might end up distributing only five. Priya and I hadn't sprung the concept of binding on the mishon, and there was still the chance that Desini would balk at the idea.

Where being bound to a man might have given Desini chills a day before, her reaction in the shop upon learning I was a mythic left me hopeful she would sign right up. But her experiences on the road and how people treated her might act as a heavy counterweight.

I wondered how my last girlfriend on earth might handle these situations. After experiencing their authentic personalities and observing how their reactions varied in situations, my companions had become so real that I shivered that I could bind them to my service without permission.

*Not happening.*

At first, I didn't want to earn her agreement to bind on the basis I was some mythical being. I didn't want to pretend to be something I wasn't. But then I questioned whether I was pretending. Enora actually did grant me the abilities to advance these companions. It was baked into the game and, in that way, I was a special being. It was this line of thinking that caused me to check my character sheet and see how I'd advanced, but I noticed something new.

### *Gemini Fowler*
*Shénhuà*
*Level 10 Woodsman*

Instead of *human*, I was now listed as *Shénhuà*. I really was what the game said I was. What Guiles called me. Here, again, was proof I was living someone else's narrative instead of creating my own. But developers always determined the narratives in their games. Quests followed their lore. Why would Enora have been different? An epiphany struck.

*I've been letting Takemoto's description of the game influence how I thought about it. Unique quests, choosing my own path. But just because Enora lets me choose whether or not I accept a quest doesn't mean she doesn't lay a path out before me? If I refused to be led around by the nose, if I left the entropy crystal at the university and left Roshan to her fate, wouldn't I still be able to advance?*

I thought I would.

The stunning realism. Dynamic quests. Sure, those played a part. But I also learned how to tame a beast based on my intuition and experiences in other games. That's how Enora was different. That's how it convinced me I had more control than I'd ever enjoyed.

The reasonable certainty I had the freedom of choice to pick a direction and wander paled against my surety Enora had ideas of her own. If the A.I. guided my fate with real-time quests and the appearances of companions, I was better off following along. Now that I'd survived the dark levels, I was having the time of my life.

Still, I wondered what might change if I refused to follow the path. Enora had said a dark influence had befouled the world in some way and my experience would serve as a test for Infinity Designs, to see if more players could be unleashed on a world the beta testers had almost ruined.

*Maybe one day I'll be in a position where I'm not so starved for XP that I'll try it and find out the extent of my free will. In the meantime...*

I made a note in bold letters in my interface's journal:

*Play the gods-damned game.*

I laughed at myself as I turned my attention back to Desini's character sheet. Distributing five points was child's play. On the chance that she didn't want to be permanently tied to me, we could always pay for trainers to advance her. If she bonded with me, I would deal with the other 34.

But I had to admit to myself her base stats made me itch to add her to our family.

***Desini Sherre***

*Mishon*

*Level 17 Fighter*

*Attributes:*

*Strength: 10**

*Dexterity: 13**

*Intelligence: 7**

*Wisdom: 6**

*Constitution: 11**

*Charisma: 42**

*Desini has 34 unspent attribute points.*

A scan of her potential was like eyeing a thick steak on an empty belly.

*Gah, now I want a steak.*

I knew I wanted to prioritize Strength and Constitution, but her dexterity was almost as high as those two, which increased her chance to dodge. I wondered if a high dexterity was a racial trait because the way she moved and how she carried herself screamed of a natural agility. A certain grace of motion.

Despite her fit core and tight muscles lining her arms and legs, she lacked the brawn of a traditional front-line fighter. That might change as I increased her strength, but it was also possible her physical form wouldn't be altered. Games rarely changed player appearances to reflect attribute changes because they blew hours customizing their avatars to look a certain way, and inflating their muscles might piss them off. But those were players. I didn't know what mechanics applied to NPCs in Enora.

Good armor, a high defense rating, a pile of health, and sufficient strength to inflict damage to keep mobs angry built the core of an effective tank. I didn't want to toy with her stats haphazardly, but the more I scanned the expanded tool tips, the more confident I became that adding dexterity would ensure she took less pummeling. Add to that she already had all the naturally-earned stats, and I had room to play.

I knew little of party dynamics in Enora. It wasn't like I could go out to forums and read about the experiences of other players to build my strategies. The best I could do was make reasonable inferences based on data provided. As a data center engineer, I was no stranger to analysis.

My first step—distribute five points.

If Desini bound with me, I would pyramid her attributes with Constitution at the top to make her withstand more damage, and then Strength so she would cause more damage. Desini had no shield, so I saw Dexterity as a reasonable third attribute to replace the damage mitigation. If I added Dexterity into the regular leveling cycle and she later suffered for it, I'd change focus to Constitution and change battle strategy to accommodate until we made up for it.

But if she left us, I wanted to ensure I gave her the best five points for survivability. So, there would be no Dexterity in those first five-point allocations.

Reviewing the notes I'd made in my interface notepad—a feature like my journal, where I thought the words and they appeared—I nodded to myself and crawled on my knees to the front of the cart.

"Priya, please slide over so I can talk to Desini." The half-elf peered up at me with mock suspicion. "Don't you give me that look. You can play grab ass after we've discussed her attributes."

"*Sure* you want to talk to her about her attributes," she jested.

I slid between them and, though the canopy Desini extended over the bench blocked most of the rain, it still pelted my boots.

I shouted over the downpour to explain the attribute distributions. Desini was mystified at first, but became excited at the prospect of stamina bonuses from a high Constitution. I would've expected that added strength would've goosed her excitement, but it turned out our new companion loved to run the open fields on the western side of the road after a long day sitting on her duff behind her horse. This accounted for the higher stamina than her Constitution's base value allowed. She'd earned it the hard way. More free stamina meant she could run for longer periods.

"I'm so thankful you have these skills."

I nodded, but then frowned.

"What is it?" Desini asked.

Priya set her hand on my knee and whispered, "The five-point thing, right?"

"Right." I figured it was as good a time as any to fill her in. Then I could stop sweating it. "I can distribute five attribute points for you and the change will be permanent."

"But?"

"If I spend any more than that, it will form a special bond between us."

Desini placed her hand on my knee, letting the reigns rest in her lap. "Our friendship grows, but I decide who partakes of my fruit." Her lips spread into a wide smile.

But I shook my head, rejecting her humor. It wasn't the time. "This is serious. If I distribute all of your points, you will be bound to me forever. Literally, for all time."

"Until death?"

I shook my head. "This is the part you'll have a hard time believing. If you bind with me, you won't die. If you fall in battle, you'll resurrect at the last place I bound myself." I read the confusion in her eyes and cleared my throat. "No, that's not right. Okay. Priya and I bound ourselves to Breeder's shop in Brumhill. If we fall, we will resurrect there, along with our soul-bound items."

"You confuse me. Bound this. Bound that. Binding people. Binding places. Binding items."

"Let's focus on the not dying part."

"You don't die? How is this possible? It is foolishness, yes? You jest with me."

"No. No jesting."

Priya leaned across me and patted her knee. "It's true. If you bind to him, you won't die. You'll still experience pain and suffer violent memories when stabbed to death—believe me—but you will revive in a different place. This happened to us two nights ago, and we woke in the forest yesterday. This is the Shénhuà's greatest gift."

The light came on in Desini's eyes. After minutes of contemplation, she nodded. "If you were anyone else, I would call you mad. But as you are Solara's mythic, I must have faith in what you say. This gift is unimaginable and while its value is not to be dismissed, I would thank you to spend the first five points and let me experience these changes before I decide on anything more... permanent."

I nodded and patted her knee. "That's more than fair." Roshan had melted with joy the first time I increased her attributes, so the prospect of doing it for Desini gave me hope she'd share similar physiological results.

When I did, she wavered on the bench. I wrapped an arm around her as she peered down at her biceps. As we watched, the lines around her biceps grew more defined. It was like watching Bruce Banner transition on a miniature scale, except they didn't grow as much as tighten. The mishon peered up at me in awe.

"Magnificent! Never have I imagined such a fate would fall upon me. But I must have your word."

"About?"

"Might I fight by your side as your bound companion without demands of a... sexual nature?"

"You mean, will I expect you to sleep with me if you allow me to bind you?"

"No, I will sleep with you, stupid man. I have already done this. I am asking if I must fuck you for these privileges." She rolled her eyes derisively at Priya. "Is he always so dense?"

I stifled a laugh. "You'll never be under any obligation to 'fuck me,' as you aptly put it. You'll enjoy free will to do as you please. It's your life. Not mine. But I have another disclosure."

"More rules?"

"Not so much a rule as a limitation. My companions can only travel a certain distance from me unless they fall in battle and are resurrected out of range. Well, that second part is a guess. I actually don't know how it will work."

"So, I cannot leave your side... forever?" Her eyebrows shot up.

"Not to worry. It's not actually that restrictive. There is a box in my interface I can click to allow you to roam as you wish and in exchange for your commitment, I promise you, it'll be checked at all times. I'm only telling you I have the power to make it so you can only travel so far. I believe in transparency."

Desini stared ahead and pulled her hand away to rest it in her lap. Silence ensued for a few minutes before she spoke again. "It is quite a commitment, 'forever.'"

I nodded, understanding.

"This morning has filled me with an excitement I haven't felt since I first set out on my own, before I learned of the dark nature of men in the kingdom. The warmth of companionship and the prospect of not traveling in silence with only Pickney for company entices me.

"As I told you, the mishon do not weigh opportunities lightly. I have always admired the stories of adventurers—the risks they take in the quest for glory, fame, and service to the goddess—when that applies." She turned her gaze from the road and leveled it on me. "It does apply to you, and this provides me the chance to do good in a world where I've witnessed so much darkness." She slapped her knees and gave a single nod. "I will follow the calling of the goddess. It's settled. Call on me when in need, Gemini. We are now family."

"You're sure?" I asked. "You don't have to be bound to continue on with us."

She glanced at her new half-elf friend then back at me. "Distribute the points."

Priya's lust came on a wave.

"Um, okay. Don't you want to discuss their allocations?"

"I thought you knew of these things." Impatience practically bled from her eyes. "I'm a fighter, yes? Give me what most benefits a fighter." Desini disappeared through the slit in the tarp. "Priya, come."

I distributed Desini's attributes, with a final moment's hesitation before distributing the sixth point.

*While non-players can increase their attributes through labor, they may also purchase attribute upgrades from trainers in Enora. But Enoran trainers can spend only five attribute points per trainee.*

*Players do not share this attribute cap. While you can spend more than five attribute points on behalf of your companions, doing so will cause the companion to be permanently bound to you.*

*To bind a companion to you, the companion must have a disposition of endeared or better toward you.*

*Fallen non-players who are bound to you will resurrect in your last spawn point if they are not revived after a battle. If you fall in battle, bound companions will continue to fight until your enemies are vanquished or the companions fall. If you have a foundational structure or pay for a room at an*

*inn, you can leave the non-player behind at your choosing,
but you will still be bound.*
*While bonds between non-players are broken by permanent
death, this player-to-non-player bond is permanent.*
*Be aware: There is no limit to the number of NPCs who can
be bound to you, as long as they maintain the requisite
disposition of endeared or better upon bonding. You may
bind a non-player of endeared or higher disposition without
permission.*
*You may only break this bond by killing the non-player with
your own hands.*
*Binding cannot be undone.*
***Are you sure you wish to spend further attribute
points and permanently bind Desini Sherre
to you?***
***Yes/No***

I bound a second woman to my life. I was responsible for Desini Sherre, now, too.

Next to my own stats:

*Strength:* 9
*Dexterity:* 2 1
*Intelligence:* 1
*Wisdom:* 1
*Constitution:* 1 3
*Charisma:* 1 0

Desini was a *machine.*

***Desini Sherre***
*Mishon*

Level 17 Fighter

**Attributes:**

Strength: 24

Dexterity: 19

Intelligence: 7*

Wisdom: 6*

Constitution: 26

Charisma: 42*

**Combat Skills**

Melee: 14

**Defensive Skills:**

Dodge: 44

**Weapon Skills**

Unarmed: 14

Blunt: 14

Bonuses:

Resist Magic Attacks: 5

Resist Charm Effects: 10

**Affinities:**

Languages:

Common

Dwarfish

Elven

Gnomish

Mishon

**Professions:**

Stonework: Skill Rank 13

Woodworking: Skill Rank 11

Horsemanship: Skill Rank 22

Swordsmanship: Skill Rank 7

Cooking: 50

Skinning: 11

*Disposition: Endeared*
**Magic:**
*Light Magic:* 20%
*Shadow Magic:* 15%
*Nature Magic:* 55%

After Constitution and Strength, I boosted her Dexterity by six points. I'd have liked to have given her more, but with a Constitution of 26, she now enjoyed an HP pool of 340 without equipment bonuses. When she geared up, she'd receive 27 more Constitution, doubling her hit points. The number seemed high when compared to my own, as it should be for a tank of higher level.

Desini was officially a meat shield.

I slowly added points. Desini grunted in the cart. She was adjusting for the physiological changes as I made them.

I chuckled each time.

Then something whacked the back of my head. I turned and found Priya's face pushing through the canvas, glaring at me.

"Quit playing around and finish!"

I gazed over my shoulder. "That's what she said."

Her forehead crinkled as she processed my words. "Ah, I see. You are purporting that in all your virility you have bedded a woman who said these words." The flap closed. "So juvenile."

I chuckled and finished the distributions, then turned back to planning mode. Whether I liked burning time on it while Roshan waited, Desini and I would need to spar each night, to get her dodge skill capped. I wasn't big on standing in front of her clumsy sword, but the decreased pain I'd experienced in dueling with Guiles convinced me it was a small sacrifice to level her weapon skill.

A hint of jealousy poked my mind as noises from the back grew louder, but I reminded myself I was in a game world, and besides, if Priya and Roshan were cool with sharing, I needed to not be a dick. Tuning out Priya's low moans, I peered at the world of Enora, and let the presence of a new tank outfitted and ready for battle warm me against the cool, rainy air. She'd learned multiple skills during the increases, so I'd study them.

The road ahead was becoming muddy under the heavy rain, but it led in the direction I most wanted to go—toward Roshan.

19

The road remained *eerily* quiet the entire afternoon and late into evening. To pass the time and fill the spooky silence, I shared the tale of how I'd met Roshan at the lake in the Dark Wood and then Priya, underground. Desini's rapt attention throughout the tale expressed just how long she'd been without companionship.

The mishon estimated we were most likely to catch up to Roshan on the road between our next stop, Warrington, and the city to its northeast, Trowlsby, if we maintained pace and rode around the clock. It depended on how long her captors stayed in Warrington.

But she wasn't counting for the levels Priya and I would need to gain to play it safe. When I explained that we expected level sixteen or better enemies surrounding our lost mage companion, the mishon was receptive to any idea that involved swinging her sword. I relieved her of the reigns at sundown when she'd cited fatigue from her workout with Priya earlier in the day and crawled into the cart to have a catnap.

'Catnap' was literally her word. I'd never take such liberties.

Priya leaned next to me on the cart after Desini departed. We sat in companionable silence and I noticed her hand rested on her belly. Had she done that before? She'd been pregnant for all of two days, still I sensed her calm acceptance of the turn of events. Though it helped me relax to know she was so comfortable, I still hadn't quite reached her level of chill about having a kid. I couldn't hide the associated emotions that came with the thoughts of fatherhood, but to her credit, she didn't bring them up.

A few hours after the sun went down, when Desini still hadn't returned, Priya had kissed my ear and ventured into the wagon. Though suppressed by the sounds of the driving rain, occasional giggles came from the back of the cart. I had learned from Roshan that women in different cultures in Enora enjoyed each other from early in their womanhood, but I wondered whether our new companion was more oriented toward women as a whole. I didn't care either way, but I had to acknowledge I had hormonal itches for the mishon. My wonderment as to what she might be like would have to remain just that... wonderment. All I needed was more trouble.

I smiled at their giggling in the back as I perused my interface, but a while later, I experienced an emotion I'd abated with technology in my earth life.

Loneliness.

I didn't want to pull Pickney off the road to sleep and lose time, and Desini and I sure wouldn't do any weapons training in the downpour, so I summoned Click.

True to her usual grouchy disposition after a long absence, she'd stumbled back and forth on the bench before curling up and setting her chin on my leg. I smiled down and rubbed her smooth flesh hairs as I guided the horse with the other hand. Not that it needed guiding.

After about an hour, Click perked up at a rustling sound and poked her head toward the back of the wagon.

"Click!" I heard Priya call. "Come here, baby! Meet Desini!"

Click scurried through the split in the canvas, her pudgy belly getting caught on the lip and her hind legs pumping wildly in the air until her front ones pulled her through. Judging from the lack of commotion, I assumed that the introductions went well. Click didn't come back.

*Figures.*

Not that I blamed her. Sit out here with rain spatter or snuggle between what were probably two warm, naked women. No-brainer.

In the middle of the night, when the yawn attacks became annoying, I scanned my map and analyzed the terrain surrounding us on either side of the road as the fog of war vanished. Unlike the time I'd spent in the Dark Wood, sections of the map revealed wider areas as they became visible and we progressed north. On foot in the Dark Wood, the map only revealed as far as my eyes could see.

I spotted a crooked blue line at the edge of the fog of war on my map.

*That must be the river Desini mentioned.*

At the realization that the water source was close, my legs twitched for movement. I eased Pickney and the wagon to the side of the road and reached into the back for the skins situated just inside. They bounced on my chest and back as I made for the river.

I shouldered my bow on the opposite side and cast Inner Illumination to make locating a break in the rocks easier. As I marched into the woods, rustles in the undergrowth prompted me to rip my bow off my shoulder. I had an arrow nocked so fast, I impressed myself. Then a little black head popped up nearby, and I spied unmistakable, fleshy hairs vibrating in the rain.

"I thought you were keeping the ladies warm." My pet bared her teeth and uttered the rapid-fire noise for which she was named. "Yeah, okay. At least *you* prefer my company when it means exploring." I clicked my tongue at her. "Let's go."

I checked a prompt as we set off together.

*You have reached Rank 3 in Light Magic.*

The cast of Inner illumination had gained me another skill point.

I let Click locate and lead me down the best path to the river. The static sound of the water lapping against the banks was subtle and relaxing, despite the heavy rain. Thick rush whooshed against my chest piece as I slipped sideways around dense foliage and pushed along. Click had an easier time, because of her low-to-the-ground profile.

We arrived at the river in ten minutes, though it'd seemed closer on the map. I'd have to start using a consistent zoom level on the tool to predict distances. Maybe there was some way to show a legend and ruler. Id' check later.

I slipped out of my clothes and dipped half a foot.

Though the air had been warm most days I'd spent in Enora, the rain had left the river icy. It would be bathwater only in function, not in sensation. The best way to acclimate was to get it over with, so I jumped.

"Bwah! Ah, fuck!"

My body adjusted quickly enough, but the initial immersion sucked.

I scrubbed myself as best I could without soap then stepped out, refreshed. The rain prickled at my skin but was warmer than the river.

I'd just slid my legs into my pants when rattling from my pet reached my ears. In those clicks, I heard, "Danger!" as if she'd spoken English.

Still bare chested, I threw on my quiver and grabbed my bow.

"What is it?"

Click crouched about thirty yards ahead of me, her flesh hairs standing on end. I tiptoed through the soaking grass lining either side of the river bank and perked up my ears to listen for activity, but the rain proved too loud to distinguish sounds. As I bent and drew closer to my pet, I clicked my tongue.

"What is it?" I repeated.

I followed her sightline through the shrubbery to a curve in the river that drew its flow back to the southeast. Motion caught my eye, and I eased forward another step to peek past the branches blocking my view.

A figure hunched down by the river. Its wet coat was thick, with long hairs of black and gray, much like Click's coloring. Its head raised up from the water and a long snout pointed in our direction.

I ran a check.

### Plains Wolf
*Level 12 Beast*

"What do you think, bud, can you stand for a little XP? Wanna stretch your claws?"

My pet's head rose, and she grinned as quiet clicking emanated from her throat.

"You're so violent-natured. I like that about you."

A little solo grinding wouldn't hurt. Desini was the highest level of us all, at 17. If I battled with her and Priya in a group, I assumed there'd be a combat XP penalty applied. Click didn't cause a penalty, so why not?

Still acclimating to my new world, I took a quick peek at my ranged abilities to prepare for a fight.

### Ranged Combat Skills
### Perforating Arrow

*Ranged Attack*

*Adds 3-5 damage to ranged attacks.*

*Cost: 35 Mana*

*Cast Time: Instant. Longer draws use more mana but cause more damage.*

*Cool-down: 15 seconds*

### Vine Entrapment

*Spell*

*Level 9*

*Call forth vines from the ground to bind your enemies.*

*Cost: 25 Mana*

*Cast Time: Three seconds*

*Cool-down: N/A*

**Can be cast by any class with Affinity:* **Nature Spells**

*This spell has diminished returns when casting on the same being.*

While I was tooling, I turned on a combat logging option I'd avoided during the Dark Levels, lest it distract me and I end up dead. Now that I'd survived, I wanted to capture the more in-depth math for later analysis.

I donned my chest piece and made sure it was fasted all the way around the sides. Then I ticked my head toward the wolf. "Get to it then!"

Click launched out of the shrubs.

Standing, I found myself astonished at the speed she carried her portly body across the distance. I stretched out my hand and casted the new spell Zhara had gifted me two days before. A green glow bloomed around my fingers.

The wolf's head jerked up from the water again, but this time it charged toward my porcupunk pet. Some vague notion picked at my brain as I watched my pet's oversized-hedgehog-like body close the distance.

The wolf screeched to a halt as thick roots erupted from the muddy soil and surrounded its legs. Its shoulders flexed as it struggled against the vines pinning it to the ground. I pumped my fist in victory, but only once.

Whipping an arrow from the quiver tied to my hip, I fired at the wolf just as Click arrived and lunged for its throat. I missed.

*+1 Bow Skill*
*Your bow skill is now rank 16*
*You have learned the skill:* **Drilling Arrow**
*Skill Cost: 25 Mana*
*Cast time: Three seconds*
*Damage: 200% weapon damage*
*+1 Ranged Attack*
*Your ranged attack is now rank 25*

The wolf lowered its head and rammed my pet as the porcupunk launched into the air. Their foreheads collided and, though she'd been the one in motion, Click took the worst of the effect as she'd weighed half as much.

*Click: -21 HP*

I had to admit, it was a nice move. The vines snapped and retreated into the ground as Click rolled off to one side. My porcupunk recovered as the wolf turned in my direction and sniffed the air.

I thought to check Click's stats, but before I opened my interface they appeared on their own.

***Click***
*Porcupunk*
*Level 10 Pet*
***Attributes:***
*Strength: 10*
*Dexterity: 7*
*Intelligence: 3*
*Wisdom: 2*
*Constitution: 11*
*HP: 99*
*Mana: 120*
*Stamina: 120*
*Skills:*
***Spike:***
*Level 2*
*Your porcupunk flips onto its back and slips spikes from beneath its flesh hairs to puncture enemies.*
***Bite*** *(Auto)*
*Level 3*

*Your pet bites the underside of your enemy, attracting its aggression.*

### *Hobble:*

*Level 10*

*Your pet tears at your enemy's leg or underside, slowing its movement speed.*

Whoa! I can just think about the stats and they appear? What did I do? I willed the text away and brought it up again, excited by the streamlined mechanic. With the mental note made that I would further investigate—RTFM! — I returned my attention to the reason I'd pulled up Click's stats.

Her hit points showed ninety-nine.

They reengaged. Clicks rattled, and growls filled the air above the rain's persistent patters. I brought up another arrow.

*Click: -9 HP*

*Plains Wolf: -11 HP*

Click had lopped off about ten percent of the wolf's health.

The two animals circled each other, showing the full breadths of their dangerous teeth. I drew back my bowstring but held fast to allow my energy to surge through my fingers and into the arrow. It would burn more mana, but the extended draw of my ranged ability would inflict more damage and allowed Click to piss the wolf off further so I wouldn't gain aggro and bring it charging at me when the projectile landed.

### *Perforating Arrow*

*An armor-piercing ability with an effective range of fifty yards.*
*Loses damage with distance traveled*
*Adds 3-5 damage to ranged attacks*
*Cost: 35 Mana*
*Cast Time: Instant. Longer draws channel more mana but cause more damage.*
*Cool-down: 15 seconds*

When Click landed a bite, blood spurted from the wolf's neck.

*Plains Wolf: - 15 HP*

*Click: + 25 aggression*

I loosed the arrow.

A yelp filled the air as my projectile pierced the wolf's thick hide on its front haunch, in the center of the meaty muscle, causing it to flop onto its face. A purple explosion of light gleamed on impact and glowed for a moment.

*Critical Hit!*
*Base Damage: 17 x 2 for 34 damage!*
*Damage Modifier: Dexterity 16 x .05 = +8 Damage*
*Plains Wolf: -42 HP*

*+1 Ranged Attack*
*Your Ranged attack skill has increased to 26.*

Okay, math was cool and all, but I would never be that

much of a dweeb. I ticked the extended combat log option down one notch.

The beast recovered but found itself unable to put weight on the leg though its health bar showed it still maintained about 40% of its reserves. Click quickly seized the advantage, leaping onto the animal's back and tearing viciously at the thick mane where its neck met it back.

*Plains Wolf: -11*
*Plains Wolf: -11*
*(Bleed)*
*Plains Wolf: -2 HP*

I readied another arrow, focusing on my other ranged skill.

### Drilling Arrow
*200% Ranged Weapon Damage*
*Cost: 25 Mana*
*Cast Time: 3 Seconds*
*Cool-down: 30 Seconds*

This would drain my mana pool down to about 20%, and I'd need to let it recover before I could entrap the wolf or fire another of my arrow skills, but I didn't plan on its survival.

As I readied the arrow, expecting a forward notch in my yellow XP bar after release, the wolf surprised me when it craned its neck back, reared its snout into the air, and howled.

That little pricking of nerves in my brain from moments ago rang like an old school telephone.

*Wolves are pack animals.*

Just up the rise from where Click tore at the wolf, a blur of white motion charged downhill through the trees at blinding speed. I focused on my pet and redirected her to the oncoming threat.

"Bite! Bite!"

Click launched off the unfinished target and acquired the second as I released my third arrow. Our first target died in a flash of yellow.

The second wolf lowered its head as it charged, but this time my pet was ready. She rolled into a ball and slid under the beast, ripping at its belly with silvery teeth as its momentum carried it right over her.

*Bite!*

*Plains Wolf: -17 HP*

Click spun around, sliding in the wet grass of the hillside, then leapt toward the wolf. She bit its hind leg before it could turn.

*Hobble!*
*Additional Effect: Plains Wolf movement speed slowed*
*by 15%*
*Additional Effect: Bleed*

*-5 HP*
*-5 HP*

Blood flowed to the ground beneath its belly as I withdrew another arrow. We'd whipped around to handle the new threat like an Indy car on fresh tires.

Then my breath caught as I spotted two more streams of motion raging down the hill.

They split off—one charged toward Click and the other hauled ass toward me. I knew Click would have her hands full with one healthy wolf plus the one she'd sliced under the belly. I'd have to handle the one charging at me solo.

Focusing on the width of the canine's shoulders, I disabled all combat messages. At the very least, I needed to slow the beast. A well-placed arrow might do the trick if it pierced the wolf's face, but if my shot wasn't perfect, I'd be in real trouble. I wasn't that damned good, yet.

An image of me dying and resurrecting alone at Breeder's place, with my companions a day's journey away informed me what a stupid decision this had been. I'd just picked a fight without my party in the most perilous world outside of hell. I hadn't even thought to bring my bag, just those stupid water skins. So, I didn't have a health potion. There would be no second chances.

*I have got to do better!*

Would've, could've, should've.

My hand quivered under the strain of the nocked and drawn arrow. The rain fell in sheets, and I blinked furiously to keep water out of my eyes as my target's massive haunches pumped hard in my direction. The wolf's long claws threw wet clumps in the air behind as it bore down. The tendons in my draw fingers crackled in my ears with their itch to release, but I had no intention of firing until I saw the animal's irises.

Yellow energy flowed through my fingers and into the arrow as I readied Drilling Arrow. Even with my slow mana recovery, I'd gotten back above twenty-five percent. That would have to be enough.

Wouldn't it?

My interface broke my focus as Click's health bar drained to about half. If I rushed, maybe...

I released as the wolf closed the final steps between us. The arrow sailed wide of my intended mark, but still pierced its left shoulder and filled it with exploding yellow light. The wolf stumbled and slid as it tried to find purchase on wet, high grass. In a display of deft agility, it kept its feet and plowed forward.

At the last moment, I dropped to the ground and rolled under its front paws, stealing a tactic out of my pet's play-book. The wolf tumbled over me as I rolled beneath it and back to my feet. I slipped and slid on the wet surface, but stabilized by throwing my arms out. My bow rattled to the wet earth. Then I reached for my daggers.

*You have changed your class to Assassin.*

Without so much as a glance backward, I tore off toward Click's battle against the other two wolves. A class switch meant I'd have to deal with a universal ability cool down before my assassin skills became available, so every second would count. Though I'd learned stealth before becoming an assassin, Enora had seen fit to include the ability in my global cool-downs, so I was stuck until they abated.

Again, Enora was a bitch, sometimes.

I glared at the timer and pumped my legs until the muscles ached, knowing the wolf I'd tripped up would soon recover and zoom up on my six. I eyed my abilities bar to watch as the horizontal line graying them out slowly revealed their color as it climbed each ability's square from bottom to top.

*Global Cool-down: 12 seconds*

I huffed and puffed, trying to force deeper gulps of air into my lungs as I heard, or maybe imagined, the wolf bearing down from behind. Luckily the points I'd put into constitution and my +1 Stamina buff, along with the fact I'd been standing in place while firing arrows, meant I ran with more than 50% of my stamina available. But there was no balancing my stamina meter by slowing my pace because the wolf would surely catch me. A swift end to this confrontation was my only hope. If I lived long enough to use my assassin skills, they'd burn what stamina I had left.

*Stamina: 175*

To buy myself an extra second, I turned hard in front of the trunk of a wide tree. I almost lost my footing in the wet grass, but flinging my arms out to the side and flailing a couple times helped steady me.

*Global Cool-down: 9 seconds*

Time crept. My legs kicked in slow motion. My quads burned, and my feet threatened to slide in the muck with every stride. I sensed death as it closed from behind. Recalling a tactic I'd used when I evaded a dinosaur in the Dark Wood days earlier, I sheathed one dagger, grabbed a sapling, then planted my heels as I slid across soaked pine straw in a semi-circle. I launched in a new direction. And face planted.

*Come on!*

A glance ventured over my shoulder revealed that the injured wolf faltered when it tried to run and scurry around the tree trunk from the side where I'd appeared so it could cut me off, but the sudden turn shifted its weight onto its bum shoulder, and I bent backward as it slid right by. Its yip rose above the rain as it recovered its footing and turned to pursue. I scurried to my feet and sped away.

About thirty yards ahead, Click fought for her life against the two wolves, one on either side of her, nipping at her from both directions as she clicked furiously and kept them at a distance with short lunges. I blinked at the wolf on Click's right.

### Plains Wolf
*Level 10 Beast*

*Level 10. Perfect. That's my bitch, right there.*

*Stamina: 125*
*Global Cool-down: 6 seconds.*

If my stamina ran out, I'd slide to the ground huffing and puffing as the wolf behind made me its dinner. That yellow bar ticked down quickly now as my exertion level caught up with me and the diminishing returns kicked in. Ignoring it, I glared ahead.

Click would only last so long.

*Pet Health: 19%*

I ran hard down the incline, ignoring the wet surface, risking an out-of-control slide into the fray.

*Stamina: 110*

A meter blinked red.

*Pet Health 10%*
*Global Cool-down: 4 seconds*

*Now!* I focused on Click and sent a mental command. *Disengage!*

Click lunged away from the wolves as one bore down on her backside, narrowly evading the bite that would've finished her. Turning toward me, her body warbled as she sprinted as fast as her legs would carry her. The two wolves tore off in her direction, toward me. The wolf behind me growled furiously, and I risked a glance over my shoulders just as it lunged into the air. Click was ten feet away, the other two wolves ready to pounce as we all came together.

*Cool-down: 1 second*
*Stamina: 93*
*Pet Health: 9%*

*Dismiss!*

Click faded from existence as the global cool-down expired.

I envisioned a cloud and stepped through it while focusing on the last wolf to have engaged Click.

*Shadow Merge.*

I vanished.

Two wolves careened into one another. An arrow lodged in one's shoulder caused a heavy limp, the other bled from the wound Click left in its stomach as it tore downhill after her. I reappeared behind the healthy wolf I'd inspected a moment earlier, dagger in-hand. If I wanted to do this right, those other two wolves couldn't get to me when they realized they'd collided with each other and not my pet.

They were both a higher level than I. They might spot me or break my stealth by sniffing me out. So, as much as I would've liked to wait for my stamina to tick back up as I prowled around, I'd be damned if I stood idle.

I shoved my daggers into their sheaths and cocked my eye at the wet tufts of hair on the animal before me. I lunged.

My stealth broke as I grabbed the back of the wolf's mane and threw my weight on top of it. Holding on for my life as it twisted its head and bucked, I pushed energy through the hands gripping its mane, willing myself to hold on as the progress bar rolled across my screen.

*Stamina: 67*

Considering my low stamina, it was a good thing that *Pacify Beast* used *mana*.

The other two wolves turned toward our struggle, but I didn't spare them any attention. This was my last chance to stay alive, and I had to focus on my skill cast if I didn't want to wake up a half-day's travel south of here in a town where people might want to ask me questions about a corpse I left in the street. Besides, having my flesh ripped away wasn't so attractive a prospect.

Wet hairs slipped through my grip, and I tumbled to the earth. The other two wolves stopped and circled at a wide berth as I lay on my back, daggers now withdrawn and pointed in each's direction. I huffed madly, the sky above me spinning as rain poured onto my face.

"You're not getting me without a load of pain, fuckers."

The Level 10 wolf turned and paced toward me from the front as my daggers pointed out to each side. Its huge snout sniffed. Three was too many. I was finished. I closed my eyes, waiting for the unfathomable pain of having my flesh ripped to pieces.

But nothing happened. I blinked my eyes open and found the wolf still just standing there.

Text appeared at the bottom center of my HUD.

*You have pacified Plains Wolf.*
*Level 10*
*Plains Wolf is now your pet.*

I peered at an injured wolf, turned my gaze on my new companion, and sent a mental command.

*Kill that one.*

My rejuvenated, healthy new pet lunged at the wolf with the belly wound and growled furiously as it shook its mane between its teeth. The wolf who'd received an arrow in its shoulder backed away, confused, easing from the conflict, apparently unsure of what to do.

So I pushed myself onto one knee, grabbed the blade of one dagger, and threw it. The blade lodged itself into the wolf's eye. A sick pop signaled the end of the battle as my final adversary fell, and my new pet relaxed its jaws as its new enemy dropped to the ground with a gaping, bloody hole in its throat.

*Despite the odds, your thrown weapons skill has increased to rank 4.*

*Lucky bastard.*

I scoffed. Then I chuckled. Then, the laughter burst forth. I flopped into the mud, gulping air and rain drops down my throat, staring at the sky, as the wolf's big head appeared over me.

I spoke between huffs. "Hey buddy, thanks. I'm Gemini."

The wolf licked my face.

Since my stamina was slower than molasses in recovering when it got that low, I lay on my back, feeling the cool rain pelting my face. My back was covered in mud and grass that had slipped beneath my chest piece, so I dipped back into the river. The wolf wandered in a kind of loose patrol while I scrubbed for the second time. This time, the water cooled my flesh in the best way.

## 20

As I started my second bath, I found scratches across an arm from my encounter against the wolf. In the adrenaline-fueled rush of combat, I'd hardly even noticed them.

*Adrenal simulation. Crazy A.I.*

The beast I'd rolled under must have clawed me. Another reason the wounds had gone unnoticed is I'd disabled my combat log to focus on my target. While my HUD displayed floating numerals above the heads of my enemies and pets during combat to represent gains and losses, the only way to see my own real-time changes in health was using the log. A quick check of my interface revealed a solution in the form of a scrolling real-time reflection of damage taken at the top center of the screen. It even showed me a little test readout when I activated it.

Since I hadn't brought a health potion, I left the scratches to heal on their own. The healing process seemed slow though I saw no icons representing any debuffs. I chastised myself for leaving my bag behind, with a stern reminder that noobs don't live long in Enora.

Luckily, the minor wounds faded as my HP recovered in the next couple minutes.

*If Roshan were here, she'd have fixed me right up with her Flash Heal or Light Heal.*

My fear for Roshan was furthered by the prevailing sense I'd failed her. After she'd saved me in the Dark Wood when I fell in battle, before my soul could be sucked away, no less. Then I'd left her flailing in the wind, instead of clicking two buttons in my interface.

*Two little ticks.*

My mistakes consumed me as my new pet led me out of the forest. Like Click, the wolf knew where I wanted to go, which was one way Enora ignored realism.

We stepped out of the tree line and onto the grassy rise forming the shoulder of the road, only having missed the cart by about fifty yards. I peered left, to the South, and spotted its dim form beyond the curtains of rain that soaked me again as I stepped out from beneath the cover of the trees.

I'd allowed my vision spell to expire lest I come to rely on it. One never knew when an enemy might silence me and render spells useless. My eyes adjusted to darkness like they did in the old world and it lent me a sense of normalcy to use them.

"That's us, buddy."

The wolf matched my meandering pace as we walked toward the cart.

A low growl rose among the pouring raindrops, and I peered down. The wolf hunched low, now creeping toward the cart, its nose crinkling, but I wondered if it could detect anything other than damp, muddy grass.

"Do you smell a kitty? That's Desini." I laughed at my horrible joke. It broke my self-deprecating thoughts. She'd probably kill me if she heard that and knew about cats in my world. Desini smelled no different than Priya or me as far as I'd noticed. She smelled kind of flowery, in a kind of contradiction to her muscular form.

The wolf growled again, louder this time.

I raised my head and squinted through the rain, and I cast Inner Illumination. My heart jumped into my throat at the sight of two huddled masses lying in the road.

*Oh, no! I left them exposed! They slept warm and cozy in the cart, and I didn't tell them I was leaving. What are we? At a La Quinta?*

"Go!" I yelled at the wolf over the rain.

He took off, his paws spewing mud against my pants as he tore across the slippery terrain as if it didn't faze him. I followed while bringing up my HUD.

I feared when I flipped to my Companions tab that I'd find my friends represented as bloody, wet heaps, or dimmed corpses because they'd died and resurrected out of range. I almost slipped in the mud as I slid to a halt.

The image representing my half-wood-elf companion revealed her curled up like a baby pushing soft breaths through her nose. My chest filled with an airy elation as a breath I hadn't realized I was holding exploded from my mouth. Desini also seemed fine.

*Are the images outdated? Have they not refreshed?*

I peered at the masses in the road just as the wolf arrived. They weren't my people.

The horse harnessed to the wagon shuffled as the wolf approached. It occurred to me that I'd grabbed the water skins and left without considering the animal's collapsible shelter, but I hadn't planned on a fight to the death with a pack of wolves. Either way, in the downpour, I found yet another reason to curse myself. Desini cared for the animal in a way I hadn't, and I could've taken the opportunity to win her affections by covering Pickney.

The wolf ignored the equine giant with the mud-covered white coat I'd seen Desini wash and brush the previous evening before.

I gripped my bow and blinked rain from my eyes as my new beast sniffed one mass, then paced to the second. It nudged at the second with his nose, then turned and peered back at me.

The horse nickered as I rambled past and I ran a hand along its thick body. It seemed to calm when the wolf showed it no interest.

I shoved the first figure's shoulder with my boot. It rolled sideways on the muddy road and flopped onto its back. A man with a bald head who wore several earrings on his right ear stared into death's oblivion. His throat gaped in a wide slit from ear-to-ear.

*That's the guy who bowed out when we killed his boss in town.*

My shoulders dropped, and I threw the other figure a cursory glance, but no more. My thoughts jumped to the occupants of the cart.

*Please...*

It didn't matter that my interface showed them alive and well, cuddled together. I had to lay eyes on them before I would relax. Jumping up onto the rider's bench, I noticed a muddy patch the rain hadn't yet washed away. My heart pounding against my ribs, I peered through the slit in the cover. A tear of relief welled up in one eye as a smile exploded across my face. Priya, my half-wood-elf, dark caster lay in the embrace of her new mishon companion.

"Oh, thank you," I said to the world that was Enora. "Thank you. I'll never leave them again."

"Mmm," Desini moaned. She scooted her pelvis closer to Priya, causing the shorter woman to smile in her slumber. Her tail twitched and rolled over her hips to land on the half-elf's waist. I withdrew my head from the slit and climbed down, off the bench. My boots splatted in the mud.

I set my hands on my hips and stood between the two corpses as I assessed the scene.

*Where did you come from, what were you doing, and... how did you end up dead?*

My head jerked in all directions, seeking a culprit in the storm. All I found was the tree line and rocks that lined one side of the road and the opened fields leading to more forest on the other.

The women wouldn't have been sleeping if they'd had anything to do with this. So who?

I knelt and set two fingers beneath the chin of the man closest to the riding bench and pushed his head back.

"Clean cut, one blade. Deep. Quick. What do you think, boy?"

The wolf paced next to me and sniffed the corpse.

I peered at the soles of the dead man's boots and glanced over my shoulder.

"Looks like this one was about to mount the bench but never made it." I swiveled my head and peered at the other form. A compact blade lay near him in the mud. "Maybe he'd planned to cut his way through the back. Like they planned to take us from both sides."

I patted his chest and split open his patterned leather coat. A thick wool shirt that must have itched to high heaven was all I found beneath. It was soaked in blood to his belly, his life force having spewed from an artery in his neck, forming a V in the undergarment. I yanked his belt.

*You have found:*
**Iron Sword of Maiming**
*Level 9*
*Slot: Weapon*
*Type: One-handed Sword*
*Quality: Uncommon*
*Durability: 37 of 50*
*14-17 Damage*
*+2 bleed effect when dual wielding*

*Hmm, it didn't ask if I wanted to change to fighter.*

Sliding his coat aside revealed a second, identical sword on another sheath. I withdrew the swords and held them up in the rain, getting a better look.

*Not bad. No nicks or dents. Could use a sharpening.*

I gripped and swung them, checking their balance.

*You have changed your class to Assassin.*
*You have learned the skill:* **Dual-Wield: Swords**
**Dual-Wield: Swords**
*Allows a combatant to wield two, one-handed swords*
*Off-hand weapons suffer 40% accuracy and damage*
*penalties. Efficiency increases with weapon skill rank.*
*Your dual-wielding rank is now 1.*

So, in Enora, dual-wielding applied to particular weapons. If I wielded two daggers, stat advantages applied to that weapon type. Now, I could also dual-wield swords, and my success would be determined by my sword skill. That probably meant I'd have to gain another ability if I wanted to wield two maces, etc.

"Hey, bud," I said to the wolf. "Prowl around the cart and the nearby trees. See what you can find, heh?"

A low growl emitted from the wolf as he set off behind the cart with his nose low to the muddy earth, his wide-set ears perked high.

*Pet Stance: Patrol*

As I watched its thick body covered in mangy spiked hair disappear around the cart, I mused at how kick ass it was to have a wolf. While I loved Click for the part she played in getting me through the Dark Levels, a wolf was a fucking wolf.

I patted the dead man's sleeves and pants legs. Something jingled—a pouch strung to the right side of his belt, near where I'd found the second sword.

The raging static of rain softened in my ears as I paced back to his companion while loosening the drawstring and shoving two fingers into the pouch. Cool metal graced my fingertips. I shook it next to my ear and coins jingled. I tied the pouch to my belt and knelt next to the other corpse.

*Yup, he's one of the guys from town, too.*

I matched the knife caked in mud beside him to an empty sheath on his belt. A similar blade sat in a sheath on his opposite hip. After patting him down in vain from shoulder to shins, I paced back up the muddy road to the spot where the wolf and I had exited the woods to retrieve the water skins. I set them on the riding bench just as Priya's blonde head popped through the canvas slit.

"Gem?" she uttered, knuckling sleep from an eye. "Why have we stopped? You tired? Should I steer?"

"I'm in one piece, but things are amiss."

She perked up, pushing the canvas to either side. Aside from the cloth she'd tied around her lower pieces and knotted at one hip, she was naked as the day she was born.

"Amiss?"

She crossed her arms beneath her breasts and rubbed her shoulders. Rain splatter bounced off the canvas and misted her flesh. My woods woman shivered. Her eyes fell on the water skins. An eyebrow ticked up.

"You going for water?"

My face scrunched up. "I already went. Then I came back to find this."

She leaned forward, and her eyes flared open. "Is that a man?" She crawled over the edge of the cart and onto the bench, covering herself as if the corpse would see. "A dead man?"

"You'll catch a cold."

*Hmm. Will she?* That was an interesting question.

She ignored me. "Where did he come from? I'm glad you came back before he..." She glared at me. "You left us here without telling us?"

The awe painted on her face made my head drop. "I didn't realize the mistake until it was too late, Priya. I'm sorry. I just didn't think it through. Getting water while you slept was, well..."

Priya sighed as she glared down at the corpse. "Learn your lessons." She punched my shoulder.

"I will. I swear it. When I saw them there, I... I panicked. I thought my heart would stop at the thought of you and Desini..."

The half-elf's expression softened. "At least you returned before things turned for the worse. Solara guides us, still."

"That's the thing. I didn't kill him." I thrust out a finger. "Nor him."

Priya scurried across the bench, one knee barely missing the clop of mud I assumed had come from a dead man's boot, then peered around the side of the cart. "You didn't... then who did?"

I shrugged. "I have my suspicions, but they make little sense. Clean throat cuts."

"The elf?"

"Yeah. But I had this strong sense he stays close to town for a reason. Like he's hiding out. Maybe sent a friend."

"Are there any more dead people?"

"Just the two, the best I can see."

The horse grunted, and purple light grabbed my attention. Priya dropped her arms from her chest and twisted them into claws as she sneered. Electricity crackled between her fingers as they became washed in its glow.

The wolf growled at her. I showed Priya my palms.

"Whoa! Whoa! He's with me. My new pet! My new pet!"

Suspicion crossed Priya's features, then they morphed into something else as she glanced around. Maybe confusion. The glow surrounding her hands slipped away.

"Where's Clicky?"

*Clicky?*

"I dismissed her."

"Hmph. What would Click think of your new pet?"

"I doubt Click will ever know the difference." I turned and peered into the glowing yellow eyes of my wolf. "All clear?"

The wolf didn't answer, but I took that it'd returned with an air of calm that the surrounding area was devoid of threats. Priya's eyes locked on the corpse again as rain coursed down her blonde curls and sent little rivers down her bare shoulders and arms.

I gripped her knee, diverting her attention from the

dead. "I think we're safe, for now. If you have to sit out here, at least put on your robe. It's made for the weather."

She dropped her butt on the wet bench, either oblivious or uncaring about wetting her tied cloth, then she leaned down and held out an open hand. Her voice adopted a soothing tone as she lowered its timbre and spoke to the animal.

"Submit my friend, and we shall conquer the world."

She'd first enamored herself to Click with the same soothing tone, in the forest, though the words were different. They reflected a new disposition, entirely.

The wolf peered up at me and took a hesitant step forward. Priya's back was suddenly washed in a golden glow reflecting off the tarp behind her.

"Did you activate your ward?" I asked.

Priya raised a shoulder in a half-shrug. "I figured it couldn't hurt. Why?"

I shook my head. "I didn't realize it was an active ability."

She clicked her tongue as she reached her outstretched fingers toward the wolf as it placed its front paws on the bench. Though she spoke to me, she never broke her gaze with the animal. "Now you know."

"You might as well get used to her," I said, scratching the beast's wet head between its ears. "She's with me for the long haul."

"I sure am," Priya said in the same, soothing tone.

The wolf sniffed her fingers and lowered its head.

"You're wet, baby," Priya crooned. "We should wash that mud off your paws and bring you inside." She tilted her head up. "Why wouldn't Click know about your wolf?"

"What? Oh! Click! I doubt I can summon two pets at the same time. It's unlikely they'll ever meet."

"That's strange. Why couldn't you have two pets at the same time?"

*Again, game mechanics. Same conundrum. Time for a new lie.*

"I'm not sure how it works. I have this strange sense that, when I summon the pets from the um... spirit world, they form a special bubble of sorts here. To summon Click, I have to empty the space occupied by this one. Here, I'll try."

Priya perked up, her eyes awash in that curious light that came when venturing into new territory and exploring new experiences.

She crossed her arms, still showing no sign she'd reach for her clothes and cover herself against the mist splashing off the canvas cover of the cart.

I brought up my interface to watch for messages and raised my hand. Focusing on the bench next to Priya, I peered at Click. A message popped up.

*You must dismiss **Unnamed Wolf** to summon another pet.*

"Yeah, I got a prompt. I have to dismiss the wolf first."

Priya slapped her hands on her knees, and I sensed her disappointment at not having gotten a show. "Well, I guess you can't have everything."

I peered down at the wolf. Water tamped down its mane, causing the black top coat on its back to shimmer in the glow of my Inner Illumination spell. The white hair beneath was dingy.

"That gives me an idea, though."

I dismissed the wolf. Priya perked up again and seemed to enjoy the display. The wolf peered down at its legs as they became transparent. Then it peered up at me and whined.

"Aww," Priya said. "He didn't want to leave us. Such a mean master, you are."

"Bah." Raising my hand, I aimed it at the spot next to her on the bench. As a glow traced and engulfed my fingers, Priya leaned backward and flared her eyelids. "What do you think? I'm going to dismiss you, as well?"

Her mouth gaped as she pawed her chest. "Can you do that?"

I shook my head and chuckled. "No, Priya, it doesn't work like that. Only *pets* can be dismissed. You aren't my pet. You're my fucking soul mate."

Her mouth closed and her eyelids dropped. "I like it when you call me your fuc—!" Priya turned as the glow in my hand faded and the wolf materialized on the bench next to her. She jumped and slid toward the end of the bench. But then she giggled and lost her hand in the wolf's fur.

It's dry, clean fur.

"How about that?" I asked. "Dry and clean. That's awesome."

There was a rustling behind Priya, followed by a "Mew!"

My eyes jerked to the parting canvas just fast enough to see Desini's face disappear back into the wagon. Her voice bellowed from inside.

"Fear not, my love! I will run through this beast!"

I guessed she addressed Priya.

Metal rubbed leather from beyond the tarp as she unsheathed her short sword.

"Don't stab my wolf!" I called. "It's my pet!"

Though the wolf's lips drew back as its instinct warned of danger, Priya kept her firm grasp of its mane and the ward glowed anew. It was almost comical. The wolf stood taller than me on his hind legs. The word *beast* was a more than adequate moniker. But its tongue lolled from its lips as it sighted the glow emanating from behind Priya.

"Shhh, baby. That's your sister, Desini. Be calm, my love." To my utter shock, Priya leaned forward and kissed the wolf right on its nose. The wolf's teeth vanished and it licked its upper lip twice. It then tilted its head to one side and licked Priya on the chin. She chuckled and pushed its snout down. The animal pawed at her hand.

The tarp peeled to one side, and one of Desini's green eyes appeared in the slit.

"It's okay, babe. Come meet... um... wolf."

Desini leaned out, and her nose crinkled up as she sniffed the air.

*How did she don that breastplate so fast?*

I'd never seen the sniffing gesture before and, as she leaned through the tarp, her head sliding over Priya's shoulder, I was struck by how she *moved* like a hesitant cat. While Priya's lines were angled with her elven heritage, Desini was rounder in the cheeks, her lips a little thinner, and she had a cute little knob for her chin that jutted out just slightly. Priya's chin had a subtle dimple.

My mind returned to the face missing from this team.

Priya's eyes flickered at me for a second, and she gave me a subtle nod of understanding. Then she turned her head and pressed her full lips against Desini's cheek. "Come, he is our friend." Pulling the wolf forward by the hair beneath its neck, she stroked its haunches.

"Merrrr," Desini hummed as her nose closed on the wolf's. "Is it true?" Her nose twitched a few times. The wolf's nose twitched in much the same way.

I had to suppress a laugh. It occurred how unlikely it

was either of them could attack the wolf, anyway. It wouldn't make any sense if my pets could take friendly fire. Then again...

"Are you our new companion?" Desini raised her hand and brushed the wolf's hair. It lowered its head to allow the affection. A half-smile crept across her lips as she turned to peer at me. "Your blessings abound, master." Then she jerked back. "What is that?"

*Oh, that! No big deal. Just a dead body.*

Priya and I explained the corpses were a mystery. I unsheathed my swords and displayed them.

> *You are now dual-wielding swords.*
> *Your sword dual-wielding skill is rank 1.*

"Everything else was junk, but these are in good shape." I tossed her the pouch tied to my belt.

Desini snatched it in a blur of motion. The contents jungled as she tinkered with her fingertips, then turned it over, emptying coins into her palm. Her lips moved as she counted. "Gemini, there are three gold and thirteen silvers here. This is no small amount of currency. Either they have robbed others on the road..."

Priya finished the thought with a sneer. "Or they were paid to murder us." Her head turned. "How have we made more enemies?"

I shook my head. "They're the men from town who tried to rob us."

"Then where are their horses?" Priya asked. "We've been riding all night. If the town isn't close..."

"Hmmm," Desini hummed.

"What is it?" I asked.

"I travel with the daughter of an immortal guardian of

the Tree of Solara and a being able to make others stronger with his mind. There are others who have this knowledge." She shook her head. "I guess it was not until now that I realized I'd bound myself to the two people in the region most likely to be assassinated by those in power." Her green eyes flickered toward me and a transparent layer within her eyes flipped up, her pupil growing as she peered.

I read no fear there, but I felt like she was measuring me. "You okay?"

Desini stared for another long moment before she hummed again. "Mmm. My lifelong yearning for adventure bears fruit. It matters not who these men are, only that my sword is prepared for the next ones."

"Agreed," I said.

"We should train before the sun rises and then proceed to town, if it pleases you, master."

"I can get down with that."

They both threw me confused expressions.

## 21

A looming wall of gray stone bricks rose into view as our cart crested the final hill leading down into the valley encompassing the town of Warrington. Though we'd seen just two corpses and no signs of life on the road the day before, riders on horseback, covered carts like our own, and peasants wearing homespun rags with sacks hung over their shoulders queued at the guardhouse as we approached.

Priya rode shotgun as Pickney nudged our cart forward. We chattered nervously for half an hour before we reached the guards. Desini sat inside the cart running a soft cloth over the new short sword for about the tenth time since Breeder sold it to us, though she'd trained with it only once, and that was about three polishes ago. Last I'd peeked, the wolf snoozed with its head nestled against the mishon's hip.

Our greeting guard wore only a day's stubble and the clothes beneath his chain mail lacked the dingy sweat stains wed become accustomed to in Brumhill. My mind conjured images of cities ahead, gleaming in their brilliance, with high-level guards and shops galore. I inspected him as we approached.

***Jensen Plowes***
*Human*
*Level 14 Fighter*
*Gate Guard, Warrington*
*Disposition: Neutral*

'Disposition' was new. I hadn't received that detail in Brumhill, and I wondered if I'd made an interface change of which I wasn't aware or if I'd advanced somehow. I hadn't gained a level.

*Strange. Maybe Enora updated something.*

His accent came off as Cockney.

"What's your business? You come from Brumhill or the farms?"

"Hello, sir," I said. "We're coming from Brumhill."

"Brumhill, aye. Have you been to Warrington before? I ain't seen you around." His eyes flicked over to Priya, who wore her robe with the top clasp fastened and her knees together.

"We're new. Our companion trades here."

"Where's your companion?"

I pulled the tarp to one side, winding the view into the back. "Desini?"

The feline woman poked her head out, the shoulders of her chest armor gleaming in the returned sunshine. After our sparring session, she'd taken it off, but only because she returned to the furs for a nap. She clutched the scruff of the wolf to keep it pinned down, but the animal showed little resistance.

The guard smirked. "Aye, I remember this one. Messenger, right? What's with the getup? Here to start a war, kitty?"

Desini bowed her head slightly, but after just two days with her, I knew the glimmer in her eyes conveyed she was no one's fucking kitty. The complexity of her expressions were yet another reminder of how Enora's evolution engine made for a new level of realism.

"After our visit, I will journey into the wilds for advancement."

"Adventuring, then?" The guard scratched his head and peered at me like this was the most interesting news he'd heard all day. "Well, all right then. I could see why you might want to take that up. Not sure who you think is going to train up your skills, but why not?" He gazed at her for a moment, his lips turned into the curve of a half-smile. When she didn't respond, he returned to his casual tone. "Well, you understand the rules, *kitty*. Leave your weapons in the cart. Keep your nose clean, do your business through the back, and keep out of the common areas, lest trouble be roused. Out by nightfall, right?"

"That's right," Desini replied. She lowered her tone. "Out by nightfall."

The guard hadn't been half the asshole as the guy in Brumhill. The tone he carried was much more civil, even helpful. Coupled with the words from Leira about how she'd been protecting Desini by asking her to use the back door of the Crescent Moon—lest she get accosted by the Brumhill guards—I found his disposition preferable.

Hell, he hadn't spit once.

"All right, move it in before the line grows." He waved his silver-gloved hand as he lowered his voice to a mutter. "Damned harvest season. Got 'em coming from all directions the second the rain stops."

"Thanks." I flicked Pickney's reigns.

After we passed through the gate, Desini directed us to the right, up an alley between the stone buildings and the high wall. I noted how the other carts followed the main road as we peeled off. Dust clouds kicked up by Pickney's clopping hooves puffed into the air. We meandered to the corner of the wall and turned to follow the one running north to south.

*Quest Completed!*
### *Mishon Security*
*You guided Desini safely to Warrington.*
*Reward: 5,500 XP*

A few decrepit stalls leaned unoccupied against the dingy rear facades of drab brick buildings. Desini explained these vendors didn't keep daylight hours, but the ones on the main thoroughfare would be hard at it by this time. I wondered what salespeople didn't keep daylight hours but kept my questions to myself. We only had until dark.

As we climbed down from the cart, I threw the bag of holding over my left shoulder. Desini stood close, her eyes shifting around the alleys as she spoke.

"I will ask around town about sightings of your mage companion while you go to the university to complete Leira's quest."

As she spoke, I'd rummaged through my inventory, reacquainting myself with the contents. I was eyeing the interface when I replied. "I don't like leaving you alone in this place."

"It is I who have frequented this town, master. You are the stranger. My contacts will harbor me should trouble arise. The guards tolerate no violence within the city walls, and penalties are harsh for violations. Those who align themselves against my kind will not lay hands upon me in the light of day."

"I'd still prefer you came to the university."

She shook her head. "It seems I should spend more time teaching you recent history."

Desini explained Mages and wizards at the university distrusted non-humans because of a beast uprising against Warrington and the King's lands in the east just twenty years before. They were the trainers who refused skill advancement services to her kind.

"Though we took no part in these uprisings, my people paid the prices imposed by human fears. Our villages were raided, and entire family lines lost when we resisted. Now it's been twenty years, master. These sentiments are ingrained into the populations of these smaller towns, but Warrington is not as bad as Brumhill, and Trowlsby is even better."

"You're not a beast," I said. "How they miss that is beyond me."

"The Dryads who led these revolts weren't beasts, either," Desini replied. "Though their Basilisk pets who murdered many fit the bill." She threw out her arms and turned. "Still, see you leaves or bark of a dryad? Do you spy the horns or spikes of a deadly beast?" Then she wagged her tail in my face.

What I saw was a physical specimen who'd gotten a raw deal, until now.

"Okay, can you use party chat?" I asked.

Her blank stare answered. I explained.

Desini had planned to draw us a map to the place where we'd pick up the crystal from hell. Then I peered at my quest log and thumped the heel of my hand against my forehead. An empty check box reminded me the system would paint a neat yellow line that would guide us to the quest location. Since I hadn't used the function since I'd been in the Dark Wood, I'd forgotten all about the feature.

It would have been nice to make some coin to gear ourselves. Most game worlds offered myriad quests, and I was wondering if I hadn't missed a secret, a trick to get access to quest chains that would help us progress faster. Our newest quest offered no monetary reward.

### *Secure the Entropy Crystal*
*The mysterious Mora has implored you to dispose of the Entropy Crystal.*
*Reward: 17,500 XP*
*Title for completing quest chain: Guardian of the Light*

Was this the downfall of a real-time, unique quest-spawning system?

I'd entered Brumhill as a fresh Level 10 hoping I'd be overwhelmed with chances to advance, just to find low-level guards and few people walking the streets. Where most games would've filled the place with NPCs to offer resource gathering quests and the like, Enora's experience seemed the opposite. I wasn't sure this was a good thing. I had a mage to rescue—for the third time.

Priya nudged my shoulder. "If you stared more blankly at the world before us, I might think you'd been stricken by Fowl Plague and lost your faculties, Gem."

I probably wasn't the best person to joke with about terminal diseases, but it wasn't like I could tell Priya that. "I was thinking how we might pick up tasks to earn come coin." I turned my gaze on her. "Something you should understand about me—I'm a gear whore. I like keeping myself upgraded and updated so that I can spend extended periods grinding XP."

Priya's emotions came to me on a wave accentuated by her words. "You are but a Level 10, and it confuses me that you have such preferences and strategies. It's as if you've adventured before."

"I guess Solara blessed me with intuition." It sounded like a shitty excuse, but it was all I had at the moment.

Priya surprised me with an emotional pulse I recognized as relief and an enthusiastic nod, but it was Desini who answered.

"It must be so, Priya. We should not question the gifts bestowed us by our goddess. Gemini is such a gift."

Priya nodded acquiescence.

I gripped both their shoulders. "Regardless of my blessings, we'll want to keep our gear upgraded, and I don't know how far 4 gold, 12 silvers will go. The guard at the gate was a Level 14 fighter. The guard at Brumhill was only a Level 4 and had no class selected. That ten-level gap gives me the impression we should've been adventuring in the wilds between Brumhill and here."

Priya's face twisted into confusion. "I don't understand. Are you saying that people's levels change as you move through the world?"

I nodded, tapped my nose, and pointed at her. Her confused gaze told me she didn't get it.

*All things, in time.*

It also meant I had to try to explain common game design without incurring a penalty. Evolution or not, the game developers' staples lingered behind when Enora took over. I allowed myself a few seconds of contemplation and tried to consider how Enora managed level control in a world where people evolved.

"As we progress further to the north, people are of higher levels because they beat back the beasts who venture into their territory. This keeps the population quelled and from leveling. If a level twelve human—"

"Or mishon."

*Shit.*

"Yes, definitely. If a level twelve mishon—"

"Or an elf."

*Gods dammit.*

"If a Level 12 *being* kills a Level 12 wolf, it gains experience and ranks up. The wolf's energy gets absorbed by Enora and reproduced."

Priya shot a finger at me. "Like the squirrels!"

"Right! So, the individuals advance to a certain level, but since they're fighting the same level beasts, they get diminished rewards for defeating them. Killing them becomes too easy, and that's how Solara creates balance."

Desini nodded. "You must earn what you receive in life. This is why adventurers travel north."

I returned the nod. "Exactly. Humans—Elves, mishon, et cetera—who want to level up have to travel where there are higher level beasts. Does that make sense, Priya?"

"You are very perceptive. This idea of natural progression rings true in my mind. Besides, it would be hard to gather power to oneself anywhere near Zhara's forest. The creatures are of a lower level as you said."

*Except for the Vellick who climbed out of a tree and attacked us yesterday.*

I decided not to voice that thought aloud.

"Before I met you, I never remembered gaining a level, and I think this is because the animals I hunted were no longer a challenge. Do you think Solara truly provides for us in this way? Creates balance in the world?"

"Yup. You're a sharp cookie."

An eyebrow flicked up. "I would think a cookie would have to be over-baked and misshapen to have an edge. And what has this to do with what I said? Ah!" She raised a finger. "Another one of your stupid expressions, right?" She nodded without waiting for a reply. "You should either teach their meanings or stop using them right away. Otherwise, you will become annoying." She patted my shoulder twice.

Desini gave a curt nod of agreement.

"Fine. I'll do better."

"I'm ready," Desini said, throwing her own sack across her shoulder. "I admit I feel hesitant about leaving my new friends. Just try not to draw attention to yourselves and meet me back here when you have secured the crystal."

She bowed her head slightly and was off without further fanfare, her tail waving high in her wake. Priya glanced up at me and shrugged. I matched the expression and smiled.

"You ready to take on a new town?"

## 22

Priya slipped her arm inside the bend of my elbow as we stepped out of the shadows and onto Warrington's main concourse. Our boots clicked on cobblestones as we transitioned from the dusty alley. We stopped within milliseconds of each other to peer up the road.

Priya's mouth dropped open slightly. She started to say something, then pressed her lips back together.

The cobblestone paths were lined on either side by single- and double-story stone buildings. There were no bricks in their walls, just sheets of chiseled stone. The difficulty that would've been involved moving the stone slates reminded me of the mystery of Stonehenge. However they'd moved them, the labor must've been extensive. Did the shop owners foot the bills themselves? Was there a tax system? Slaves?

"I've not seen the likes of this," Priya muttered.

"It's kind of impressive, isn't it?"

She cocked her head to one side, pushing a blonde lock over an almost elven ear. "No. Save for the people bustling across the roads, it seems lifeless. Dry. Except for the rails to which the horses are tied, there's so little wood. Few trees."

"Hmm. Thanks for sharing. It's interesting to see the world through your eyes—as someone who grew up surrounded by a living, breathing ecosystem. I forget humanity's tendency to push nature away from itself."

*Even in Enora.*

I nudged her forward as we paced in the general direction of the university.

"My heart aches for the people who cast nature out." She gripped my arm and pulled me closer so our hips bumped as we strolled. "Tell me we will not live in this way. Tell me when we have a hearth together that it will not be fashioned in such cold disregard."

"Heh. Priya, if you, Roshan, and Desini are there, I can't imagine how it would be. You all seem to share a legacy built around nature. I hope that someday, when we have a home, it will reflect you. I—" I almost said I'd seen my share of cities but caught myself at the last second. My amnesia story would've gone to shit in a hurry with such a blunder and, if I thought it was hard explaining level progressions through areas... sheesh. "Sure, I'll make that promise."

A flicker in her expression told me she caught my hesitation, but she left it alone.

I glanced up, and a woman in an ankle-length yellow dress passed us. Long brown curls flowed from under a matching shallow-brimmed hat. Her lips turned up in a smile at the sight of Priya leaning into me as we walked.

"Priya, you said people in Brumhill never treated you like they treat Desini or Guiles."

She shook her head. ""I think I received enough essence from my human forebears that people don't recognize the elven side of me, but I would wear it with pride if they dared to question it."

"I have little doubt of that."

"Besides, I don't think elves are held in such low regard. Creatures perceived as beasts seem to be at the root of their bigotry. Guiles hides for other reasons he didn't explain. Either way, a low-profile suits. Roshan's return outweighs considerations of the self."

"Your adoration shows high character. Roshan is the real deal."

"I like this turn of phrase. Real deal." She nodded. "And you're too kind. Forever may I warm your bedroll."

"Ha."

"Why do you laugh?"

I looked down at her, focusing on those perfect sea blue eyes. "There's no way I would let you settle for a bedroll. You'll sleep in a bed covered by rose petals someday."

A pink hue flushed her face. Then it turned red. Then, magenta. She lowered her tone and gripped my arm tighter. "I don't know how I could deserve someone who respects one of so few accomplishments."

I opened my mouth to tell her it was because she was wonderful, but she cut me off, her tone rising into something of a growl.

"I will burn down your enemies before you and warm you in sleep whenever you desire. If it be your wish, I will birth you 100 warriors of Zhara's line for your army. If you desire few children, I will bring you beasts to submit to your will and warm your feet. I will cast out those who show you anything but adoration and protect you until I am cast to my grave beneath the sands of Enora."

"Um... wow."

*Rose petals, indeed.*

"I pledge this to you," she said.

I thumbed aside a twisting golden lock and kissed her temple.

"Stop!" A voice yelled in the distance. "Murderer! Stop him!"

Our heads jerked and swiveled. A figure swathed in black tore into the road from a two-story building on the right. Its boots kicked up dust as it shoved people aside, hauling ass in our direction. Squinting against the sunlight, I spied a long dagger in one hand. I reached for my quiver and shrugged the shoulder that usually held my bow, but my fingertips found only my naked belt and my shoulder was empty. My weapons sat inside my inventory and, though I didn't leave them in the cart as the guard at the gate had ordered, I'd figured concealing them was good enough. Revealing them might cause trouble, so I balled up my fists in case the figure drew too close.

"Move, Gemini." Priya stepped forward and formed claws with her fingers.

I wasn't sure I liked this idea. I looked around for guards, but saw none. We were in a place where higher-levels were commonplace, and Priya's low spell skills might not prove effective. I inspected the incoming figure.

### Murderer
#### Level 13

A single burst of her energy pulse might not stop a level 13 and, at the speed he was moving, I doubted she'd get a second shot off if she missed.

A numbing sensation coursed through my hand and up my forearm as I grabbed her wrist. "I don't know if we should get involved. Remember what Desini said about keeping a low profile."

Priya's emotions reached me before her eyes did, but the disdain I found in them was equally impactful. "You would have me stand idle as a killer flees from justice?" She cocked her chin toward her target.

Syrupy red fluid coated his dagger. The figure slammed into a man with wild gray hair who'd been pacing hunched and slow off to one side.

That pissed me off.

"Charge it up. Focus. Hit hard."

A nearby woman careened as the figure shoved her aside and a net sack slipped from her grasp to the cobblestones. Tubular fruit like elongated oranges rolled in many directions as she yelled out in surprise.

The figure was just a few paces from Priya when a ball of crackling energy jetted from her palm, slammed into the figure's chest, and halted his forward motion in its tracks. His feet swept out from under him with the forceful impact and his body thumped to the cobblestones like the sack of fruit.

Patrons who'd cleared a path flooded in behind the figure and eyed the scene.

Priya took a tentative step forward. I hurried ahead.

"Did you kill him?"

"How would I know?" She shook her head, staring down at her handiwork.

The answer appeared in my HUD.

***Unknown Male***

*Human*

*Level 11*

*HP: 85/190*

**Stunned**

"Guiles said you wouldn't be able to stun people with that until you reached the next rank."

Priya shrugged, but my jaw dropped when I realized I'd only known because of my familiarity with the emotion accompanying the gesture. She was standing behind me!

*That will prove fucking useful. I just know it.*

When the figure moaned and writhed, I breathed a sigh of relief. The dagger clattered into the corner as I shoved it away with the sole of one boot. The man's narrow shoulders rocked from side to side as he ran long fingers over burned skin beneath the charred hole in the center of his dark robe.

"Stay down, or I'll keep you down." I flicked a warning finger.

"I'd like to see you try, squirt." The figure grunted and glared up at me.

"Then get up. I dare you."

Rolling to one side, the figure tried to push himself onto his elbows, but then he moaned in pain and dropped onto his back, kicking up a plume of dust.

"Hold there! In the name of The King!" Silver plate gleamed between the bodies of onlookers as guards pushed through the emerging crowd. "You there! Halt!"

*Shit.*

## 23

Something clutched my arm. I turned, expecting to find Priya. Instead, a stout, cloaked figure tugged, urging me to follow. After a short glance toward the guards rushing through the crowd with their hands on pommels, I did. He gripped Priya's arm with his other hand as he towed us into a side alley like a teacher leading two combative teens to the principal.

Hushed growls conveyed a male voice. "Rare souls! Rare, indeed! Come! Come with me. The guards won't take kindly to the use of offensive spells within the walls." The face escaped the hood's shadow as he looked up and wide purple irises gazed back at me. "They take exception to those who enforce the law without license."

"I didn't want a murderer to get away." I shrugged with my free shoulder.

"You? Ha-ha." He gave us a yank forward. "By my perceptions, it seemed your caster friend decided his fate. Ha-ha. You stood behind her."

I tried to jerk my arm away in an egotistical display of contempt, but his grasp was stony.

"No, no, none of that. Come. Belay your pride. You must be far from the trouble when the guards arrive. This way, this way."

We whipped around a corner and stopped. The diminutive figure released us.

"You can never be too careful. Never too careful, indeed." He shook a finger for emphasis. "Come."

We turned another corner, into a doorway. The old man waved two digits like antennae in front of a heavy door and a bolt threw. After a shared glance, Priya, and I followed him across the threshold. Random beams of daylight flooded through windows on either side of long shelves lining the front wall. The rest of the space was cast in shadows.

"I am Prantu. Welcome to my place."

"Thanks?"

Prantu's head reached the center of my chest, and he was a full head shorter than Priya. He slid off his hood, revealing a balding head covered only by a few twisted gray wires of hair. Cords of taut muscles stretched on either side of a goiter that hid his Adam's apple. Engulfed by his robe, his torso wasn't discernible.

I jerked as he set his palm in the center of Priya's chest.

"Hey!" I reached to thrust him away.

The other hand rose, extending the same two knotted fingers that unlocked the door. My muscles seized and ran cold. My hand froze in its grasping gesture.

"Be still, friend."

The lone muscles I controlled were my eyeballs. I'd experienced this before. Last time had been at Zhara's hand in the Dark Wood.

Despite the restraints, I was able to inspect him.

### *Prantu*
*Human*
*Level ?? Shadow Wizard*
*Disposition: Friendly*

Tendrils of dark energy snaked around his fingers, slithered over Priya's red robe, and crept in all directions. She reared her head back as she stared down at them, but made no move to evade. They formed a pool that washed her form in darkness. Once her robe was awash in black, the short wizard grabbed a lock of her golden hair and another wave streamed through her locks, washing them in a glossier black that reminded me of Roshan's.

He gripped the lock for a long moment, staring into Priya's eyes as if searching for the key to her soul. I thought I saw the hint of a smile on the corners of his mouth. "Blessed one." He lowered his head in a slight bow, then turned to face me.

My clothes were masked the same way moments later.

Prantu released me. Pins and needles crept through my arms as if they'd fallen asleep. I shook them, trying to return circulation to my muscles. My shoulder dropped as if they'd gone from stone to flesh.

"How the hell did you do that?"

"No matter. I am Prantu—did I say that already?" He tapped his chin with an elongated, crooked finger of knotted joints as he peered up, through his eyelids. "Yes. Yes, I said that. You are?"

"Gemini."

"Ah! Such a strong name. Unusual."

Priya introduced herself.

"Lies," he muttered.

My head jerked around. "What? Did you say—"

"Pssst!" He admonished me. "Quiet." He raised the same crooked finger in the air between them. So swollen was the digit's tip, I expected it to glow like E.T.'s. His words came in a distant tone. "I'd almost forgotten."

"Forgotten? Forgotten what?" I asked.

"The contradiction." He gazed at the ceiling as if he conversed with a voice inside his head. "Yes. Washed in the Light, born of Solara's own energy, but her blood carries the essence of shadow." Prantu's arms stretched shakily in her direction. "Do you mind if I have a closer look? So much time has passed."

A cloud appeared in the eye closest to me and swirled.

"Closer?" she asked before I could tell him to go and promptly fuck himself.

"I felt you coming from..." his voice trailed off.

"This is starting to weird me out, dude."

The ancient man dropped his finger and turned to me. "And you!" The finger was inches from my nose now. "How is it someone so devoid of Enora's scent comes to breathe?"

"Say what?"

"You are not Enoran. An aura surrounds you I don't recognize."

"He is Shénhuà," Priya said as if this simple matter would fall as common to his ear.

Something popped in the old man's neck as his head jerked back.

*Blurt it out to a stranger, why don't you?*

"Shénhuà? Shénhuà, you say?" He pulled me down by the collar of my leather chest piece. I whiffed mint and age.

"Yes! That explains it!" He turned, his eyes rolling toward the ceiling as in in consideration. He thrust a thumb over his shoulder. "Priya, go to the basin in the corner there, and use the blue crystal to cleanse your hands."

"Why would she—?"

"She cast magic on the concourse. They will want to check her registration." His eyes flicked between us. "She is unregistered." Met with two confused glances, he continued. "Hmph. Let me tell you what will happen.

"The guards will go to the university and call upon the mages to track her by her magic essence. That would prove... unfortunate."

I recalled Zhara had gifted me such a spell that I had to cast every twenty-four hours. I'd cast it upon waking and planned to make it a daily habit.

### See the Light
*Spell*
*Duration: 24 hours*
*Mana Cost: N/A*
*Cool-down: N/A*

*You now recognize those bathed in the power of the Light by an aura. Stronger auras represent a higher affinity in Light Magic.*

Was there a shadow magic equivalent?

"There were many witnesses to her casting. When they detect magic on your companion—and they will, considering her immense affinity—they'll check her fingers. When they find she is not licensed with the Magister's Guild via the registry kept at the university, they'll interrogate her under the assumption she's a spy of the Shadow Coven. She would not enjoy this, I assure you. A simple cleansing is easier. Yes, much easier."

"Shadow Coven?"

Prantu thrust a finger toward the opposite side of the shop. "Blue crystal, young Priya. Time is short. Don't worry, you won't be left out."

She shrugged and crossed to the basin. The old man watched her go, and when the blue glow shimmered on the far wall, nodded.

"Shénhuà. You can advance her skills?"

"While I wasn't sure I should share what seemed like vital information about myself with a total stranger, he'd pulled us off the street and seemed to be saving us from real trouble... if all he'd said was true. "Yes, I can raise Priya's attributes. But you're getting ahead of yourself, Prantu. Treat me like I'm ignorant. Which guild?"

"You really were born just five days ago." He flashed me a crooked smile. "I never thought I'd see such a being in my lifetime. If only we had more time to chat. Oh, well.

"The Magister's Guild of Rubal is the body that licenses trainers who do what you do—with limitations. They register magic users, by order of the king. The guild also maintains a registry of all persons who request attribute increase from all over the kingdom. They keep tabs on hunters and any other classes who gain experience and come for advancement. All but adventurers."

"Why adventurers?"

"Hmm, the longer version, then." He shrugged. "Good, good. That's just fine. You should learn all you can, Shén-huà. The road ahead is long and perilous. How blessed am I that you ventured by?"

Seems we left a lot of people feeling blessed.

"Thank you." I wasn't sure how else to answer.

"I assume you haven't heard of the Demon Wars and the resulting blight in the Eastern Kingdom?"

Actually, I had. Roshan had educated me when explaining why her magic skills were suppressed where she came from—why her family had hidden her magic affinity and a priest had secretly taken her as protégé.

"The one where the mage read incantations from a book of power and flooded the land with demons? Seems I heard a word or two."

Prantu appraised me and nodded. "Yes, superb. What you might not realize—reading that incantation required one-hundred levels of power."

"Wait, you're telling me this mage—"

"Arturus, if you're into details. He was a warlock. A dark caster, not unlike myself, but corrupted by Hokrahm."

"Arturus was over Level 100?"

"Indeed." The old man nodded. "To imagine the torment of the people of that land, to understand the sheer destruction they witnessed, the millions of lives lost...." He shrugged. "Once the demon invasion was quelled, the East saw fit to outlaw magic. I've always thought such suppression of the natural gifts bestowed by Solara to be but a trifling effort. Balance will come, and the stronger oppression, the more violent the compensation by the oppressed." He shook his head. "Though many decades have passed, I fear the East has not seen an end to its strife. There will be those who train in secret and gain power while the rest are suppressed, much like what has happened here."

"What happened here?"

"Imagine a king who hears of demon invasions and blight on the continent an ocean away. This was the plight of his grace" —he spat on his shop floor— "King Constance Luttrell, our current king's grandfather. The tales of blight, famine, and violence beyond comprehension, wiping millions of souls from Enora, were heavy news."

The dark wizard peered at me for a long moment, one curly eyebrow raised high, as if he expected me to imagine the scene. "If not for the mages of the warring Eastern Clans setting aside their differences to rise and bind the demon armies into crystals of imprisonment, I posit all of Enora might have fallen prey to the words of a single caster."

*Holy shit. Complete turmoil.*

Did Enora purge the players *because* of what happened in the East? Was Arturus a player?

Prantu was awaiting a response.

I cleared my throat. "I can imagine a million ways the king might react to something like that."

"React, he did. But imagine the reaction in The East. After the mages joined forces to send the demons back to the underworld, what do you think the warlords did?"

I frowned. Roshan had given me the answer, though it wasn't until now I was seeing the whole picture for the atrocity it was. "They banished magic from the realm and, let me guess, destroyed the mages."

"How is that for gratitude, Gemini?"

"It fucking sucks."

"What the hell?" Priya barked from the far corner of the shop. I'd forgotten she'd been listening. My lingo was really rubbing off.

"They systemically wiped them from existence. How ironic that warlords who warred for millennia for the tiniest expansions of their strongholds found common ground when they realized the threat of a thousand mages to their influence. If only the mages had seen sooner."

"So, the warlords wiped out the mages."

"Methodically. They didn't provide battlefields upon

which to fight. Instead, they slit their throats as they slept. Those who came together were met with the overwhelming force of the combined warlord armies. Humans cannot be banished to the underworld, so the casters could only resist so much. Had they banded together and taken the fight to their leaders... well, who would have known?"

"So, what did Luttrell do?" I asked. "The grandfather kings?"

He spat again... he really didn't like that guy.

"His grace took what he considered a more civil approach. While the Magister's Guild had been a private, self-governing body in those days, the king thought it wise to monitor the progressions of those who gained power. He didn't want another warlock wreaking the same havoc in the West as had been unleashed in the East.

"The guild had other ideas, specifically as to its autonomy. It was a body with a thousand years of tradition, with a university at its seat and smaller colleges throughout the realm. Luttrell didn't care. He absorbed the guild and the university into his bureaucracy and decreed the registry's creation. All attribute training was to be reported and logged. Failure to report attribute increases came with stiff penalties, up to death.

"The guild was—and still is—primarily composed of those with magic affinities. After all, they were the ones with the power to raise attributes."

"What about weapon trainers? Do they have to keep registries?"

"Any fool can learn a weapon skill well enough to teach it. Swing a sword at a tree enough times and you appreciate its weight. Besides, it takes a lot of swords to overthrow a king, and Luttrell the Senior had enough swordsmen of his own. Magic is much less predictable and weapon skills are less valuable to someone who can't increase the attributes required to wield them effectively."

"Right, if they can't raise their attributes, their levels are worthless and their weapon skills cap. How did the mages respond to the takeover of their guild?"

"We took it poorly," he said.

"I'll bet. If I were a—Wait! *We?*"

"You trusted me with your secret. I see no reason not to trust you with mine, especially considering you have so much at risk. As you will see, my stakes are also high."

"I'm all ears."

"A contingent of my brethren and I defied the king. We refused to adhere to the policies instilled by his royal highness" —he spat— "and went on strike. Since our services helped feed the guild and the university, we wielded power beyond magic." Prantu winked. "Economic prowess is as crucial as any to the throne.

"Luttrell saw the decrease in royal taxes as a betrayal and ordered any mage or wizard who refused to perform his or her royal duty, as overseen by royal authority, be subject to lavation."

"What's lavation?" Priya asked.

I hadn't even seen her appear next to me.

"It purges mana from magical beings."

"What the fuck?" I asked. "Purged? You can take someone's mana away?"

Prantu nodded. "Lavation is a multi-faceted process using casters from all the elemental disciplines. Though a mana pool itself cannot be expunged—thank Solara—lavation reduces one to its base value. In addition, the memories of the afflicted were wiped clean, resulting in the loss of all learned abilities. Of course, without one's memories, they lose their levels, as well."

*Lose their fucking levels? That's harsh!*

"You're saying the mages who refused to do the king's bidding were returned to Level 1 and had their memories stolen?"

The old man's face scrunched into a sad expression. "I wish it stopped there. It would've been better to return to Level 1 and have a fresh start. No, I'm afraid Luttrell the Third was not so forgiving a soul as our current king.

"Beings with magical affinities have always been treated with some renown. The citizens of Rubal historically looked up to us as protectors from the terrors of the underworld. Murdering the mages would've caused outrage from which the kingdom might not recover, so the king gathered his wealthy subjects and devised a different plan.

"My brethren of the highest affinities were distributed to the land owners to serve them. After all, they showed little resistance, since they were clean slates and did not understand who they were. My understanding is they were retrained for their required functions and kept well."

"What functions?"

"Earth magic to help crops grow. Security. I can think of one-hundred uses, but we lack time for such stories."

I turned to find Priya's face a deep red. Her jaws bulged with the clinching of her teeth.

"Did the rest fall in line?"

"I didn't." Prantu said. "Mages—and wizards like me—fled the university system, refusing to be subject to government bureaucracy. Those of us who lacked the courage to suffer lavation bided our time and served the population as we always had. But when the king installed price controls so only the children of his rich subjects could afford attribute expansion, we drew the line.

"Many of us came from meager beginnings and it was only our affinity for magic that allowed us the comforts of guild life. We longed to raise up others of less privilege. It was a central tenant of our organization. Solara gifted the world with magic, and we saw the king's proposed limitations as a curse. Our goddess created the world and decided its limitations to maintain balance."

"You mean the five-level limit on attribute advancement?"

"Yes." He raised his hands and shrugged. "If the goddess saw fit to limit a magic being's access to another's pool, who was the king to further limit it? Did he deem himself wiser than the Goddess of Life and the Light?"

"Pool?" Priya asked.

Prantu shook his head and peered at Priya. Her forehead wrinkled. His attention lingered on her for a long moment, soaking up her features, but it was a far cry from the kinds of ganders she'd suffered at the hands of town guards lately. It was like he searched for a missing mole. When he finished weirding me out, he continued. "The two of you have much to learn." He raised his crooked finger and pointed at us. "But learn, you must! Hmm?"

We both nodded.

"Your spirit pool is unending. It's the source of energy used to increase your attributes. When experience provides you with levels, it increases the size of your spirit pool, just like mana but without class- or attribute-based variation. As you will later learn, spirit can also be used for other magical purposes, but for now, just understand the amount made available at each level is a constant in all beings. This is how we know this is the goddess's doing. It is a perfect system, unvarying."

*It's a mathematical equation forming a game mechanic to keep the NPCs of the world from leveling so high that the players would be overwhelmed from the moment they entered Enora. They've attributed it to their goddess. In a sense, they're right.*

"I understand," I said. "But are you saying that spirit pools are also affected by lavation?"

Priya also nodded her understanding.

"Ah, a sharp one." He nodded. "Spirit pool depths is determined by level."

"Your tone indicates you're ready to move on, and we have a quest to get to. But tell me one thing. If you ran, why are you this close to the university?"

"Because I can disguise myself from the Wahrsagers."

"What the hell is a Wahrsager?"

"They are also called scryers, but that word is insufficient. They are like dogs who track a being's magical scent. Except they don't use a sense so rudimentary as smell."

"This is why you had Priya cleanse her fingers."

"They have one here, of which I am aware. Wahrsagers are very rare, and I do not believe their abilities were born of Solara, but a darker power."

"Hokrahm?" I asked.

"You know the Dark One's name. It's a start, I guess. The Wahrsagers' abilities serve little purpose other than to betray the users of magic. I understand they are quite prevalent in the east, beyond the ocean where magic is outlawed."

"They sound like assholes," I muttered.

"My inclination is to concur. But I digress. To escape the Wahrsagers, we travelled to the far edges of the continent, and some of us faced the perils of the sea. For twenty years, we lived low and used alchemy to hide our essences from the mercenaries of our king. We smuggled ancient texts from the university shelves—which angered both the king and the traitorous complacent who remained in the guild— and our powers blossomed while in hiding. Then, fifteen years ago, we reconvened to form the Shadow Coven."

"Which brings us back around to why Priya shouldn't cast in public."

Prantu returned the nod. "You show good focus, Shén-huà. If she was just another caster, their discovery that she is not a member of the university or the guild and that the attributes you have given her are not registered, would bring them to torture her until she named her skill trainer. Then they would subject her to lavation and send her to the king for reassignment to a noble."

Priya gulped and raised a hand to her throat.

"Lavation." I furrowed my eyebrows as the room seemed to tilt a little on its axis. A bolt flashed in my brain, and I stumbled backward. Priya reached out to clutch my arm.

"What is it, Gemini?" Prantu asked, his gaze dancing between my eyes. "A vision?"

"Vision? What?" I shook my head to clear it. "No, it's not that. It's just..."

"What is it, love?" Priya raised an eyebrow. "Why are you looking at me like I might melt?"

"Ah." Prantu nodded. "You see much, Shénhuà." Then he muttered. "A little later than I'd have thought, really."

"Gemini? What's he talking about?"

"I don't believe it." I shook my head.

"But you do, my new friend. You are Shénhuà. You must learn to trust your wisdom, for heavy is your burden."

He cast his eyes on Priya's angular elven features for a long moment. "The heaviest."

"Okay!" Priya barked. "That's it! I'm going to punch people! I am *not* known for my patience!"

"Then you'd better learn some." Prantu raised a cautionary eyebrow. Then his face relaxed, and he shook his head. "The power you hold inside threatens your legacy if you don't." As Prantu's face stretched into a crooked smile, Priya's infuriation washed over me. "My, how you've changed."

"What? I've changed?" Priya dropped the hand that had been perched around her neck. "You crazy old—"

"He's not crazy, Priya."

He knows her. Like Leira did. Leira, the shopkeeper who lives under Zhara's domain in the shithole town of Brumhill. Leira, who once served at the University.

I turned to Prantu. "How did she escape?"

Prantu shrugged like the answer was obvious. "If you know Priya's origins, you likely know the answer to that query, Shénhuà."

"This sucks," I said.

Prantu nodded.

Priya reared back and punched me in the shoulder. In other circumstances, I might have chastised her, but I hardly noticed. I wasn't stringing her along to frustrate her, I just didn't want to play messenger with news that would shake her very foundation. I'd as soon have sent it on parchment with Desini.

Priya's hand slid up to her chest and clutched at her robe as she took a faltering step backward. She'd finally taken stock of my emotional disposition.

I took a deep breath, but it did little to cleanse my lungs or my mind. Slipping my arm over Priya's shoulder, I kissed her cheek and hoped it would help calm her before I dropped the bombshell. She allowed the gesture of intimacy without resistance.

"Zhara brought you to the forest to hide you. She wanted to protect you from the king's Wahrsagers. That's why you don't remember your previous life. You aren't a simple girl from a forest. Your memory and your mana pool were wiped."

24

The Light of Babylon had been so much simpler. We partied up, killed stuff, bought or crafted better gear to supplement what didn't drop off the bosses, stocked our guild house, then we rinsed and repeated. In those ways, it was just like every other game out there. My five days in Enora took a shit on all those antiquated ideas about gaming.

What I'd have given to be banging a hammer against an anvil.

On one hand, the unfolding events were so random—like the way the guard and his bandit friends showed up outside The Crescent Moon when they erroneously thought they sniffed the potential for easy money. In another way, the story—*my* story—unfolded as if I were on a guided adventure like quests in LOB, except the lore, the ever-important backstories, were all up in my fucking grill. They were immediate, crucial to the companions who served with me, and downright taxing.

*Because it just so happens, I sense Priya's emotions. Gah!*

In LOB, I sought quests, met their requirements, turned them in, and got my reward.

In Enora, punishment followed poor decisions. My companion got kidnapped because I fucked the pooch, requiring that I traipse across an unfamiliar land to recover her because my sanity seemed to hinge on it. People believed I was some kind of mystic. I had brain-shaking sex with a beautiful half-elf—and got her pregnant—just to find out she was a traitor to the crown whose memory was wiped clean decades before.

*Quest Update:*
### *Not on the Up-And-Up*
*Complete: You have figured out the true nature of Zhara's relationship with Priya Skyy.*
*Complete: Prantu has revealed crucial elements of Priya's past.*
*Next Objective: Probe further to confirm your suspicions and complete the quest.*

This was getting to be a bit fucking much, if I was being honest, but any lingering doubts about whether people would play Enora online long enough for me to enjoy my new life were wiped out. I'd harbored this subconscious worry that the game would last about twenty years and then they'd shut down the servers. I didn't know if they had plans for me if that happened, and Nokuro Takemoto had been vague on that point. But now I knew this game would sell like mad. It didn't get any more genuine, and the A.I. could still patch when it needed to and make it even better. People would play it for decades, maybe even half a century. In Enora time, that was one hundred fifty years.

I wasn't going anywhere for a while.

We sat in the back room of Prantu's shop, sipping tea as Priya's world turned upside down.

"Did she hold a special role with the university?" I sipped tea to quench my parched mouth.

Prantu huffed a harsh breath of air. "Does your penis hold a special role within your body?"

My head jerked back. "I can name two, right off."

Prantu thrust his thumb to the side. "She was our penis."

I might have spit tea if it weren't for Priya's emotions bouncing in eleven directions.

"That's a horrible metaphor." But it was funny as hell.

"Priya was the High Chancellor of the university."

"Damn, baby," I muttered. "Sounds like you were top dog."

Priya turned green.

"What better leader of an organization based on magic than the daughter of an immortal? A leader who doesn't age?"

"What?" Priya barked. "Did you just say... I...?"

*Oh, flying twat hammers.*

"I said, you don't age."

Priya's eyes flared wide. "Not *that*. The other thing. Something about the *daughter* of an immortal?"

Leaning back in his chair, his attention lingered on her for a prolonged moment. "I'm sorry, Priya. I know this all comes at quite the shock."

*King of understatement.*

*Quest Completed!*
### *Not on the Up-And-Up*
*Complete: Prantu has confirmed that Zhara is Priya Skyy's mother. You also learned that Priya Skyy was the High*

*Chancellor of Warrington University and is a fugitive from*
*royal justice.*
*Rewards:*
*XP: 17,500*
*One full level.*
*Congratulations!*
*You have reached level 11!*
*+1 Dexterity*
*+1 Constitution*
*You have two attribute points to spend.*
*Congratulations!*
*You have reached level 12!*
*+1 Dexterity*
*+1 Constitution*
*You have four attribute points to spend.*
*Congratulations!*
*You have reached level 13!*
*+1 Dexterity*
*+1 Constitution*
*You have six attribute points to spend.*

"What was that all about?" Priya asked.

"I leveled." I lowered my voice. "Three times."

"Three times? How in Hokrahm's hell did you level three times? And why did you have to do it now when I can't be happy for you?"

*I'd just been wondering if I was ever going to level again!*

"Sorry, babe. It wasn't something I could control and, with your emotions flooding me, I'm not finding much joy in it, either."

"It was about me, wasn't it?" Priya leaned across the

untouched teacup resting on the table. "That's the only reason I could think of that…" She leaned back and folded her arms across her chest. "Your guilt speaks volumes, but I have no room for it. Dismiss your emotions so I can deal with mine."

*Easy-peasy. No problem. Right.*

My companion was awash in a new light cast by knowledge of her past. Minutes earlier, she'd been my companion, my friend, and the future mother of my child. Then Enora flipped that pancake. Now, my brain quaked with questions and realizations.

Holy crap. Priya was much older than I. She didn't age. The woods weren't her home. She was once the most powerful woman of magic in the region. Oh, and did I mention Solara's right hand was her fucking *mother?*

The list of Zhara's deceptions grew. When we'd prepared to make love the first time, she'd claimed to cast a spell that would keep Priya from bleeding her virginity. But what was the likelihood Priya had been a virgin if she was a non-aging immortal who led the university of magic… or whatever they called it?

I couldn't care less, but that Zhara would spin such a yarn just to cover her tracks? Well, the guardian of the Tree of Solara was a calculating bitch. Did she know we'd learn the truth?

*Sure, she did.*

What if someone recognized Priya? Well, that was less likely considering the passage of decades. Those old enough to remember her would really have to look at her. Then again, she kind of stood out.

*My girlfriend is hot shit.*

"When did you smuggle her out of Warrington?" I asked.

Priya's eyes jerked to me, then to Prantu. He nodded in answer to her unasked query.

"It was I. After they relieved her of her mana and spirit and reduced her to Level 1, they locked Delphine in her quarters until the mages could replenish their spirits."

"Delphine? Was that my name?"

"Indeed, my very old friend." Prantu nodded. "Forgive my saying so, but I am so taken by your emergence. I missed your influence in my life over these forty years. Your name is one of reverence among us in the Shadow Coven."

"I'm honored," Priya said in an emotionless monotone. A tear slipped over her eyelid and streaked down her face.

With some effort I suppressed her emotions so I didn't start in.

"If you smuggled her out forty years ago, why does her age only show as twenty years in my interface?"

"A simple illusion. Zhara's doing, no doubt." Prantu waved his hand.

That explained the asterisk next to her age, but that punctuation was a puzzle I couldn't have solved at the time. The A.I. had screwed with me, given me a lock to which there was no key.

"Why would Zhara claim Priya was her niece?"

Prantu peered at the tea cup in his lap. "When I returned you to her, she said she would cast you into the Wood after a short time and set guardians upon you so you had as little exposure to her as possible. There are stories of the cleansed recalling their pasts after some time. A familiar face might trigger it, a place one had seen before. In a being with such powerful affinities as yourself, the lie that Zhara was your aunt was likely a small part of a constructed narrative to keep you from recalling your life."

"But it was me who grew tired of her hovering." Priya

shook her head. "I insisted on going into the forest, she just picked the..."

Prantu nodded understanding. I got it, too. Zhara had driven her away and dropped her next to a magical treant named Magellan.

"I longed to check in on you over the years, but I dared not return to the forest. The Matron was so soaked in anger for what happened to her beloved child, she threatened curses on any from her daughter's former life if they dared enter her domain. I remember her saying a century of preparation had been washed away by the foolish inclinations of a paranoid human ruler. She promised retribution. I wouldn't invite that fate upon myself or the coven."

"A century?" Priya said, swiping tears away and dislodging my hand. "How fuckin' old am I?"

Prantu peered at the ceiling and his lips moved silently. "By my count, one hundred fifty-seven."

"That seems exact," I said.

Prantu smiled, still staring into Priya's eyes. "Delphine was my friend. I served her gratefully as the head of the Shadow Magic curriculum. We shared many meals together." He reached across and set the back of his hand on the small round table between them. Priya eyed it for a moment and then set her hand in it. A light glow appeared around his fingers and spread to hers. As it crept up her arm, my muscles relaxed as Priya's emotions waned.

*Wait just a second, here. Is he... Did he... Aww, man. I didn't need... Aww, man!*

"I just earned three levels, and this is *still* not my day," I muttered. "I hate this world."

Prantu continued, unabated. "Solara has decided the time for you to reassert yourself in this world has come. I'm sure your companion plays no small part in her decision. A mystic, indeed. Zhara obeys the goddess's command. It can't be easy for her, either, to give up her lone child. But that was probably the deal."

"What deal?" I asked.

"Solara granted Zhara a child. It's not my place to guess the goddess's reasons. Nor should you."

I grumbled, but Prantu continued as if he hadn't heard.

"A tumultuous road filled with enemies awaits. But one day, maybe after the old man before you has returned to Solara's shining bosom, a member of the coven will come and offer aid. I will see to it."

Priya sniffled and spoke through tears. "I welcome your friendship and theirs."

Prantu bowed his head in reverence. Then he turned to me. "It is best not to draw attention to yourselves while you are in town. What is your business? May I assist?"

I explained we were here to retrieve the entropy crystal.

"How appropriate." Prantu laughed and shook his head in derision. "One of the very objects in which the mages of the East imprisoned the demon invaders so long ago. Only such a pair as you should be entrusted with it."

"I'm only Level 13," I muttered to myself.

"Indeed," Prantu agreed. "There's work to do. When you have secured the crystal, I suggest you take it to Zhara."

Priya and I locked gazes as we spoke in unison. "We can't."

"Can't? You must."

"The days when others control my destiny are over." Priya shook her head. "We'll get this crystal because it's the right thing to do. But we're on a quest to save our companion, a priestess of Light Magic. After that, who knows? But we'll deal with the crystal when we've done what we've come to do."

Prantu shot up faster than I'd have expected was possible. "Be cautious. You are the daughter of the Guardian of The Tree of Solara. Your companion is the only known mystic in Enora, of which I'm aware. If word reached the Governor of Knall or King Luttrell that a being of such unlimited potential treads his realm and has not bent the knee, you will both be hunted. I cannot overstate what enemies to the crown you both are. I implore you! Act like it!"

A chill ran up my spine as yet another, simpler realization struck me.

"Can Priya even walk into the university if mages are scouring the town for her and can detect her magic affinity? Will we find portraits of her on the wall?"

"As to your second question, all memories of her and other supposed traitors were ordered banished by the king's grandfather." Prantu smiled, revealing all his aged teeth. "As to the first, what better place to hide?" The wizard rose. "Come."

We moved into the shop proper, then he passed behind a thin wooden display with crystals encased in glass. He tapped the top of it.

"Shénhuà. Shénhuà, indeed. Historic times are these. Change has come to the world." He shook his head. "Quite the shift in circumstances. Come, come over here, young man."

I peered down at the small, multi-colored crystals lining the counter. Each seemed to glow as I shifted my attention to it. Every time one brightened, a strange, cool sensation crept across my scalp as if a breeze fluffed my hair.

"They beckon to you," Prantu said. "I must keep them in this case, or they will eat away my power."

"Why would they do that?" Priya asked.

"Because they draw their energy from the Light and I, like you, draw my power from Enora's shadow essences. Exposure to these crystals for long periods will neutralize my abilities. If they were socketed in armor or weapons, their power would be channeled and I'd be safe, but until they are seated, they must be contained by wards."

"Yours seems like a strange choice of a profession," I said. "Like Superman selling Kryptonite rocks."

They stared at me.

"How does one with amnesia upon waking in the wood have such strange words?" Priya asked. "Who is this Superman? What is this Kryptonite?"

"A man with a cape who flies through the sky, and the remnants of his exploded world that are poison to him. It's a fable. Amnesia doesn't mean I don't remember common things."

*Warning: You are in violation of the Player's Agreement. If you continue to speak of lore derived outside Enora, you will be penalized one third of all earned XP, including the loss of levels associated with the penalty. Filters are being adjusted to ensure NPCs do not hear these words in the future.*

*Forbidden words*

**Superman**

**Kryptonite**

I'd just been about to use a 'never mind' phrase when I stopped and considered the woman standing before me.

*Fine. I won't continue the conversation, but I will not treat her like some kind of fucking robot, Enora. If you can hear me, know that. If I lose levels to keep shit real with my shorty, then I'll do it. If you want other players to enjoy this place, I respectfully request you lighten the fuck up a little and understand people will use common words. You don't have to shit on them to turn on your filters, right? The game should adjust, not the players. If you think Nokuro is going to keep you plugged in with an attitude like this, you're sorely mistaken.*

There was no response to my thoughts.

Priya bailed me out. "I could see how you might remember stories without recalling their sources. I've heard of such things, although usually associated with demonic possession."

"There is no demon in him, child." Prantu nodded. "This I see. Besides, I'm sure you've used expressions of which you know not their origins, right?"

"Point taken." She grasped my hand. "What a perfect pairing. Two amnesiacs."

Text flooded the lower half of my HUD and my face went slack.

### G3m1n1 Fowler

*Your trouble ticket has been accepted. The A.I. will review this occurrence and adjust accordingly. You might not notice any changes made because of this trouble ticket.*

*Thank you for playing **Enora Online**.*

*Well, cool. That's not so bad. Wait! She's listening to my thoughts! Or maybe because I directed my thoughts her way, she was able to hear me. Who knows?*

"The shroud I cast on your clothing and hair will last for a while, but don't linger in the city. Retrieve the entropy crystal. Take it with you." Prantu rubbed his temples with his crooked fingers and muttered, "Damn thing's been giving me headaches. 'Wondered what in Enora that was."

If the entropy crystal was giving him headaches when he didn't even approach the university, the demon prison must have put off some serious vibes. It was weird a Shadow caster got headaches from what I thought would be a Shadow object. I made a mental note to drop it into the void of my magic bag and leave it there. Something told me it was less likely to be detected or cause problems in one of my inventory slots.

*Come to think of it, a soul-bound bag might be the best place in the world for that crystal, since it resurrects where I do, and no one can access the container without my permission.*

Priya said, "Thank you for your aid, Lord Prantu."

"You are welcome, Priya, but I'm no lord." He chuckled. "Give my regards to Zhara, next you see her. I'm convinced she meant the best for you and hope you will not hold her deceptions against her."

Priya's curt nod lent little agreement. No way. She wasn't ready to forgive, and I didn't blame her. The vibe coming off her at the mere mention of Zhara's name slithered darkly down my spine.

Prantu led us out through the front of the shop, but as I passed across the threshold, he grabbed my sleeve and yanked me back toward him, surprising me with his strength.

"You are forgetting something. Maybe you should spend points in Intelligence at your next opportunity."

"I thought Intelligence was just—"

He thumped my forehead. "You focus on the wrong thing!" He grunted derision. "I tell you, you are forgetting something, and you focus on my jest about attribute expenditure!"

"Okay! Okay! WTF man?"

"To what place are you bound, Shénhuà?"

*Breeder's place. Shit.*

"Would you mind if we bound here, in case something untoward happens to us?" I asked.

"Hmm. What a grand and novel idea." He rapped a knuckle on my forehead, reminding me how Leira had treated her defiant customer when we'd first entered her shop. "You must stay focused. You are the protector of a descendant of the Light."

Before we left, he pointed us toward the university barracks then slid back into the shop.

"What a fortunate encounter," Priya said.

"Yeah, but one thing he didn't say stands out."

"What's that?" She interlocked her fingers with mine.

"Shadow Magic is not inherently evil. It's all true. Roshan and you could grow together and teach each other. Balance each other. The path being laid out for us is no mistake. Zhara really knew what she was doing."

"Hmph."

I stopped and turned, gripping her shoulders.

"Priya, let it go. Not because you're wrong, but because it will eat you up inside." I threw a thumb over my shoulder. "I sensed everything you did in there. I despise things about Zhara, too. But your mother protected you for a reason. She went to great measures to keep your memory at bay. We should trust someone that old and wise knows what she's doing. Our destinies are joined, and I become more convinced every day that a path is being laid to fulfill them by a higher power than your mother."

"You really believe Solara is taking a particular interest in us despite the number of people in this world?"

"The daughter of her right hand would be of particular

interest to her. Do you think my presence in your life is a coincidence?"

Priya's jaw worked overtime.

I sighed. "If you need proof, take Roshan. We barely know her, and yet this sense that we can't live without her pervades. That is *not* normal!"

Priya's facial muscles were loose now, and her eyes gazed through me.

"My animosity will serve only to make my spirit dark and turn my Shadow magic toward evil."

*Wow. That's further than my mind went.*

"I will endeavor to forgive so that I might move forward in the Light." She locked her gaze with mine and gave a curt nod. "Gemini Fowler, when you are not fetching water or forgetting to bind yourself to people and places, you are wise beyond your years."

I laughed, as what she'd said was tragically true.

*I have to do better.*

I n the interest of improving, I multi-tasked, putting my map on the left side of my HUD and my character pane on the right. While Priya and I navigated, following the yellow quest line running down the middle of the path through a garden with flowering bushes and miniature trees resembling palms, I allocated my new points to Constitution and Dexterity, two to the former, four to the latter. I chuckled about Prantu's joke that I should add Intelligence.

But I'd be pissed if I tried a caster class later and found out it made me smarter. I didn't feel slow, but I'd made my share of stupid mistakes!

The university popped up on my map, just ahead and around a corner.

As we made the final turn, the building's spires came into view, rising high above the tops of stone dwellings and blocking the rest of the campus from view. While the grounds were not exactly sprawling, the university itself was a work of wonder. Its gothic architecture and wroughtiron gates seemed out of place in such a mid-level town. I theorized it might have been built before the larger cities I'd heard about blossomed.

"'Tis creepy." Priya pulled back the hood on her robe so the sheen of her shiny hair, turned black by Prantu's spell, glimmered in the sunlight.

"I could see how you'd think so. It's dingy and colorless, but it's also mammoth. It's interesting how the buildings throughout the town blocked these spires from view. Kind of strange we didn't see them sooner."

"I have a creeping sensation in my belly."

"We shouldn't dilly-dally then."

"What?" She threw me a confused glance.

"We should go straight to the barracks and not linger."

"Dilly... dally... It sounds silly." She shook her head. "No, it's not meant for a man's lips. You won't speak these words again."

"You're bossy. C'mon. Let's get the crystal then get the hell out. We still have other business before we break camp."

"Agreed."

"That long building, the three-story one, is the mage's barracks."

"I see the line," she said impatiently.

The massive wooden doors were adorned with wrought-iron plates and hinges and held open by thick hooks bolted to the wall. A long yellow carpet with red trim stretched toward a massive circular desk in the center. As we approached, I peered up and across the structure's breadth. It seemed larger by magnitudes than it'd appeared on the outside.

*These are barracks? It looks like a royal library.*

A single attendant sat at the desk, a monocle squeezed against his eye by his facial muscles. Though I had a perfect yellow line pointing my direction around the desk, it might have been unwise for two strangers to waltz past unannounced.

So, we would announce.

He peered down at a thin book as we approached. Figures in all varieties of colorful robes milled all around us in the wide hall that stretched three stories to an open ceiling. What I'd first mistook for glass up there shimmered with little ripples of energy rolling across the opening.

*That barrier is magic.*

"Yes? What's your business?" the monocled man asked.

"We've been sent to speak with Master Mora," Priya said.

"Master?" the man chuckled. "While Mora is a talented magician in her own right, she certainly does not have the years required to be a master. Master means something different here than wherever you come from, child." His head tilted to one side. "Say, do I know you?"

"If you've ever been to Brumhill, I sell skins there," Priya said.

The lie was so convincing and sudden, I almost believed it. That was the thing about lies, the closer they resembled the truth, the harder they were to detect. Priya had sold skins to vendors in Brumhill in her lone exposures to the outside world since her seclusion. I guessed Zhara wasn't concerned about her short trips to the town. Then again, she might not have known about them.

*Bullshit. She had Leira.*

"I've never had the pleasure. Though it's just a day south, I've never had reason to visit." He shrugged and jerked a finger toward a staircase on the far right. "Second landing. Third door on the right." He glanced at Priya. "Are you sure you're not from the College?"

"Me?" Priya's eyebrows ticked, and she pointed a finger at her own chest? "No. I'm just a simple girl from the woods near Brumhill."

"I see. Forgive me. I must have misread a sense I was getting from you."

"It's not a problem. I get that all the time." Her gaze flickered toward the stairs.

I thanked the attendant for his help, then we scooted out of the central area before he decided to inspect us. When I considered the innumerable stacks of books we passed, I couldn't imagine what the library inside the university proper must have held.

Wide stone stairs curled upward in a spiral. We ascended to the second floor, but as we stepped across the threshold and into the hallway, Priya stopped and doubled over.

"Ugh," she moaned.

"Are you okay? Is it the baby?" I gripped her arm.

"It's only been days since you impregnated me, *fool*." Still doubled-over, dangling black hairs streamed across her face as she threw me a derisive glare.

I set a hand on her back. "Are you okay, then?"

"Yes. Just, ugh." She stood straight and her already milky smooth complexion had faded to grey paste.

I shivered.

*Is it cold in here?*

My mind suddenly flashed to the underground dungeon where I'd first met Priya. As Roshan and I had closed in on Crohl's lair, the air grew chillier. Roshan explained to me that my new affinity for the Light made it so demons or certain dark casters would bring an aura of cold I'd adapt to as I gained levels.

"Do you want me to go? Maybe you should wait outside."

She gripped my hand and lifted it away. Shaking her head, she drew a deep breath into her lungs and shook her head. She whispered, "I'm the great Delphine of the amazing university of... whatever. I'm okay." She squeezed the hand.

I'd played enough VMMORPGs to be taken aback by the senses of this world, but the way my body responded to stimuli, the way the scent of whatever they used to clean the dormitories of the barracks tickled at my nose hairs, took the cake.

As we reached our destination, I raised my fist to knock but hesitated with my knuckles inches from the door and flashed Priya a look. She nodded, then I rapped on the thick wood.

Something clanked inside the room, like a metal tray or table rattling to the floor. I smiled at Priya. Perhaps we'd surprised the occupant. But instead of returning my smile, Priya double over again, wrapping an arm around her stomach. A fresh slithering chill crawled through the nerves in my neck.

I stepped back from the door and stared at the vertical waves of grain on its polished wood face. Then, to my surprise, Priya reached out, took the knob in hand, and twisted, shoving the door violently open and leaping inside.

My heart jumped at the sight of a woman sprawled on a round rug in the center of the floor, blood dripping from a wound near her temple. An iron candle holder lay next to her and a book sat open on its pages by a knocked over shiny metal tray that seemed out of place in Enora.

*Motion, in the corner!*

My hands trembled as a black figure emerged from the

shadows, its jagged hand cupping diamond-cut, smoky glass. Long, curved fingernails extended into the air around the crystal. It's pointed chin rounded into a low-hanging tip and narrow yellow eyes glared back at us. All I needed was a little dramatic score to round things out, and I'd have given the scene five stars for creepiness.

"That's the crystal." Priya growled.

"Gee, ya think?"

I inspected the creature.

### *Lesser Vile Demon*
*Level 14*

"Oh, I'm sure. Don't you feel the energy coming off of it?"

Since Priya and I shared an emotional bond and spoke the same language, I was a little surprised my sarcasm hadn't come across on either channel.

"So, it *was* making you sick?"

"No, it's him." She thrust out an accusatory finger at the demon.

*If she has shadow affinity, why should a dark demon make her sick?*

My teeth chattered as I eyed a swung-open window on the opposite side of the room. A chair was tipped onto the wood floor beneath its frame. I adopted the best authoritative tone one could between clicking teeth. "You're not leaving with that crystal, demon." Role-playing had never really been my jam, and the tinny timbre of my voice left something to be desired.

My daggers sat inside my magic bag. I might not have wanted to pull them out on a crowded street when the figure had erupted onto the scene before we met Prantu, but seeing as there weren't witnesses in the barracks room, I was functioning like a gamer again.

Priya's Lightning spell was mana-intensive, and even though her Wisdom allowed for decent mana regeneration, I didn't want to dump her resources if I could handle this demon bastard more quietly. More importantly, I now knew there were people out there who could home in on her magical essence.

"No lightning," I muttered.

Instead of the wave of disappointment I expected, I got a simple nod of confirmation and understanding. The way she stood with her hand at her midsection with her face wound up in distress, I wasn't sure Priya could've spread her hands to cast the spell, anyway.

*Either she has to get out of here, or that demon does.*

The demon lurched sideways and made for the window. I yanked the daggers from the bag and lurched forward to cut off its angle, sending it creeping back into the corner. It massaged the crystal in its hands, as if it didn't want to engage me and damage it.

*Sorry, asshole, I'm the hero of this story, and I'm taking that crystal with me.*

Then the demon lunged forward.

I swept my daggers across the air in front of me, and it threw up its free arm to defend while cowering away. It was testing my range, feeling me out. Motion caught my eye, and I glanced over at Priya to find her hands held low, just to the sides of her waist, with her palms facing the ceiling. Wisps of purple smoke rose from her palms, reminding me of the machinations of the orb in which she'd once been imprisoned.

*That's not the lightning spell.*

The demon cut the silence with a shriek, causing me to

cringe. I swung a dagger, ripping at its forearm, forcing it back, but it dodged my second strike and turned its claws on me.

*You strike Lesser Vile Demon*

*Lesser Vile Demon*
*-20 HP*

I toned down the combat log details, but then pain shrieked from my abdomen as the vile bastard swiped upward. Droplets of my blood splayed through the air. I'd been distracted while I removed the distraction. I doubled over as my abs burned, growling as I held my arm against my stomach. The demon's eyes glowed brighter.

*Oh, this world is too real! Too real!*

*Critical Hit!*
*Burning Claw*
*-93 HP*

I glanced at my health bar

*147 HP Remaining*

The wiry minion swayed on its crooked legs as its stony black lips spread into a cracked smile. It's croaky voice ground against my ears like a high-pitched squeal. "This is the possession of the master. You will leave it to me, or you will die."

A red droplet indicating a bleeding effect appeared beneath my health bar.

*-15 HP (Bleed)*
*132 HP*

In the already-dark corner behind him, a tiny black spot emerged. It was so devoid of light or color, it stood out even among dark shadows.

*-16 HP (Bleed)*
*116 HP*

My stomach muscles seized and throbbed as hot blood seeped from the gashes. Curling my arm and rejecting the pain coursing through my gut, I raised a dagger and flung it with all the strength I had.

*Dagger throw hits!*
*(Glancing)*

*Lesser Vile Demon*
*-8 HP*

*Thrown Weapon skill has increased to Level 4.*
*-15 HP (Bleed)*
*101 HP*

The demon's eyes flared wide as it reacted a second too late. Although the throw hadn't been well-aimed and the blade missed the dark bastard, the pommel caught him right on the bridge of his nose and he lumbered backward. Glowing green blood trickled from the wound as the crystal thumped to the ground and bounced toward Priya.

The black dot behind the creature expanded into a swirling vortex, sucking the wind out of the room. Its draw wasn't enough to pull me forward, but its proximity to the demon presented the dark bastard with a new distraction.

*-16 HP (Bleed)*
*85 HP*

"No," it growled. "The crystal is ours. Caym must have it." It struggled forward, fighting the draw of the void.

*-15 HP (Bleed)*
*70 HP*

Hand cradling my gut, I lunged forward and thrust my foot into its chest, sending him flailing into the gaping black hole. My forward momentum carried me to the blackness's edge, and I froze as I caught sight of the other side of this portal to hell.

Dark images chewed on my sanity. A grim warrior with burning embers for eyes wielded a great flaming sword as he stood on a cliff overlooking a lava lake filled with screaming souls reaching for a black sky. Electric worms of fire writhed in the sockets where their eyes had once been. The blade pointed toward me and a voice—not spoken, but cast into my mind—rendered a dark invitation.

*We have unfinished business, Gemini Fowler. You know where to find me. Come when you are ready, but don't wait too long, lest I send my minions to retrieve you.*

*-16 HP (Bleed)*
*54 HP*

Something clutched my shoulders, the sensation barely registering on my numb body. It was as though it came from another world, tugging me backward as the void shrank to a pinprick, and then popped out of existence.

"Caym," I muttered.

"Did you say Caym?" Priya turned me and tugged my leather plate. "Oh, gods, Gemini. You're losing so much blood."

The demon's claws left three gaping wounds in my abs. Blood trickled in slow rivers to my pants, below.

My health meter flashed.

*15 HP (Bleed)*
*39 HP*

"Too much bleed. I'm going to respawn if..." I fell backward, landing hard on my ass and felt an extra eruption of blood spurt from my wounds as my flesh was doused in its warmth. "Get a health potion from my bag."

*-16 HP*
*23 HP*

Priya legs crept in slow motion as she lunged toward my bag. Darkness pulsed across the room, matching a thump in my temples. The walls twirled around me, and it pulsed again.

My eyes rolled up into my head and I muttered, "Meet me at Prantu's sh..."

26

The remnant chill of the demon's dark presence and my loss of blood evaporated in a blanket of glowing warmth as white light engulfed me. Though I expected to wake in the back room of the dimly lit crystal shop a few blocks from the barracks, I was instead greeted by the welcome sight of Priya's sea-blue eyes. My health bar was up to 75%.

Priya patted my cheek and dashed away, crossing the room. A grunt garnered my attention, and I turned to find my companion kneeling, giving aid to the woman I'd mistaken for dead in the center of the room. Priya clutched one of her arms, and I scurried over to grab the other. Echoes of the wounds in my stomach ground the muscles there as I got to my feet.

As we sat the woman up, Priya used a finger to brush aside dark hairs that had fallen across her face.

I scanned the text at the bottom of my HUD.

Mora casts Flash Heal II
+150 XP

*+15 HP (HOT)*

Even in her injured state, she'd managed a well-timed heal. The spell added a heal-over-time effect.

*+15 HP (HOT)*

Mora looked at us through unfocused eyes. A sheen covering the pale flesh of her cheeks and forehead reflected the natural light through the window. Bloodshot sclera circled brown irises. She raised a hand to her head, tapped it, and sneered at the blood on her fingertips.

"Are you okay?" Priya asked. "What can we—"

The mage answered with a dismissive wave. A glow bloomed around the fingers of the same hand, then a touch to the wound staunched the bleeding and sealed the gash. Though she couldn't yet be in her forties, her voice creaked as if with age. "Demons fight dirty." Mora threw her hands up, beckoning us to help her to her feet.

To my surprise, Priya's sarcasm came faster than my own. "Yes, so unexpected."

*She's in a mood.*

Mora ignored the snipe. "Little bugger snuck in as I snoozed. Seems my paranoia about falling asleep with that dark artifact around proved justified. Been awake for days, casting spells and sipping poultices to keep myself awake, but I guess my body got the better of me."

"Gotta sleep some time." I shrugged.

Mora released our hands as she got her feet under her.

"Thank you, kindly." When an effort to press the wrinkles out of her robe proved futile, she sighed. Turning her gaze on me, she cocked her head to the side and winked her eyes. "Not a bad health pool for your level, but do you find the added points in Dexterity prove worth it in the grand scheme?"

"Apparently not, when fighting lesser vile demons. Thank you for the heal, you saved me some trouble, there."

"If you call death trouble, yes, I'd say I saved you *some trouble.*"

*She doesn't know you re-spawn, idiot.*

"Right. Thank you for saving my life."

She waved the sentiment away with a cranky grunt.

"It's you who serves, young man. I just wonder at the logic of the lower constitution. Bah. Damage classes—always focused on maximum D.P.S. at the expense of survivability." Mora's body weaved with each step as she stumbled over to stand in the spot the demon had vacated. A hand shot out, and she steadied herself against the wall. It took me two lunging steps to reach her, but by the time I had, she stood straight again.

"You good?"

"I'm fine."

"Are you sure? You want to sit over here?" I picked up the fallen chair near the window.

"I'm fine, I say. It's not the injury. Just misfortune. Vertigo. Stuff's plagued me since I was a teenager. Comes on when I'm hassled."

*An NPC with vertigo. Okay, you win, Nokuro.*

A mouse scurried across the wood floor and onto the center of the carpet. Mora knelt, holding out a hand. The animal stopped and turned toward her, its tiny pink nose twitching, then it scurried across the rug and up, into her hand. Standing straight again, she ran two fingers down its back. "I assume Leira sent you for the crystal?"

I followed Mora's gaze to my elven companion.

Priya tossed the smoky crystal in her hand as if testing

its weight. The act of fiddling with something that could unleash a bunch of demons on the town brought an extra thump that resonated from my chest to my throat. I didn't have to say anything for Priya to get the picture.

"Ooh. Yeah." She clutched it in one fist. "Sorry."

Her earlier abdominal distress was absent, even as she clutched the crystal. I deduced that it'd indeed been the lesser demon who'd been the source.

"Yes, we're here for the crystal." She tossed it to me, and as I snagged it out of the air, a golden flash surrounded her, the number 12 appeared, and zipped into the corner where the void had swirled just moments before, passing through Mora.

Priya shot me a thumbs up. "Ding!"

"Nice." I winked.

Mora raised an eyebrow.

"Did you level, young lady?"

Priya nodded, but suppressed the smile as if this were common.

Mora muttered, "Congrats."

*You have completed a quest!*
### *Retrieve the Entropy Crystal*
*You have retrieved the Entropy Crystal.*
*Reward: 12,500 XP*
*Complete the Entropy Crystal quest chain to earn the title:*
*Guardian of the Light.*
*Your companion Priya Skyy has reached Level 11!*
*Priya has four unspent attribute points.*
*Since Priya's disposition to you is Beloved, you may spend four of her attribute points.*

I guessed all that discovery XP gained while traveling

between here and Brumhill must have really added up because I was already about 70% into my next level.

*XP: 5500/8000*

Mora eyed the crystal I pinched between the tips of my fingers like it was coated in poison. I dropped it inside my bag and resisted the urge to wipe my fingers on my pants leg.

"Good riddance to that dark thing," Mora said. "Lodge it somewhere deep in the earth or secure it in a magic container where the demon lords will not sense it. Then bury that dark bruise on the Light."

"Speaking of demon lords," Priya said, "you said a familiar name when you almost died."

"Caym," I added. "I saw him in that black void you cast."

"Call not the name of a demon lord, lest he should appear," Mora said. "That foul creature has plagued the lands north of the Seran Hinterlands for so many ages, they burn. What's the significance of his name to you?"

"One of his bastard minions held me prisoner."

Mora perked up. "Now there's one you don't hear every day!"

*All in a day's business.*

I shrugged. Four days ago was ancient news.

The mage folded her arms across her chest. "Bah! You act like it's no big deal." She adopted a higher pitch. "She says, 'One of his bastard minions held me prisoner.' And then *you* shrug like it's commonplace." When she realized we had little to say on the topic, her tone regulated. "Well, I figure if you clip the wings of a demon underlord on not one, but two occasions, you're all right in my book. You got names, or would you like me to call you *'unknown human'* and *'unknown half-elf?'*"

"I'm Gemini. That's Priya."

"I am Mora, Frost Mage of the First Order of Mages."

"Frost mage? So, you can hurl icicles and shit?" I asked.

"I can *hurl* ice in many forms, young man, but I can't imagine an effective way to pelt enemies with feces." Mora paused and tapped her finger to her chin. "Though that might be useful at some of our debates in the guild chambers." She cackled.

Our senses of humor weren't up to the task, of late.

"Well, I'm not sure why Leira chose you, but I figure with the essence bleeding off this one" —she threw a thumb at Priya, though she spoke to me— "I have a theory. Tell me, are you her bodyguard?"

"My lady," Priya said in a regal tone, "Gemini is the—"

"Best bodyguard this side of the King's Royal Seat," I interrupted.

"All evidence to the contrary, considering I had to save your arse!" Mora cackled again.

"Well, my charge was still standing," I replied.

"Ha! I like this one. It's okay, kiddie—whoever you are. Rich parents? A family name to protect? Either way, it's of no importance to me, just so you get rid of that blasted gem." She leaned forward. "But at your level, you're probably not the best of anything yet, unless you have a great cock beneath your trousers and a desire to please that surpasses common men. Is that what you mean by guarding her body?"

Priya blushed.

When she peered down at my junk, I felt myself suddenly wanting to turn and cover it, but I resisted and instead, stood proudly.

"Speaking of your pants, they're covered in blood. That won't do you any favors." Again, she tapped her lips. "Tell you what, Let's get a cleansing crystal so you can clean that up." She traipsed across the room, her gait more study now, then reached into the drawer of a simple hutch. "Hmm, yes, this will work."

The cleansing crystal came arcing toward me, and I snatched it out of the air. The blood that splattered on my boots when I killed the poser in Brumhill had vanished on its own. I wondered if NPC blood didn't.

"You have shadow magic?"

"Not really," I said. "Just the affinity for it."

"Then you must cleanse him." She flicked a finger in Priya's direction. "It emanates from you."

"Does it? Why is it everyone detects this in me?" she asked. "I knew I had affinities, but—"

*That makes me wonder why Roshan didn't sense shadow magic in her. Was it her low level? Maybe the chill we'd both felt in Crohl's layer had dissipated with his removal so we hadn't noticed a lingering chill with Priya? If so, why don't I feel it anymore? Or could her relationship to the Light mask it? Zhara's influence? Gah!*

"It amazes me how little people know of themselves. What, did you grow up in a forest?"

We shared a glance, Priya's cheeks flushed pink, and I sent her an emotion of foreboding equating to a shake of my head.

"Perhaps I've lived a somewhat sheltered life."

If I could say anything about Priya, it was that she acclimated.

"Right." Mora sniffed the air. "And yet your own attributes indicate experience. Tell me, why have you selected no class?"

Priya shrugged.

Mora's eyes blinked in succession, and I realized she possessed what Leira had called *The Eye.*

"Hmm. Your level is high enough. Your energy is no trifle. Whoever trained you should have had you select a discipline."

If Breeder had carried something for dark casters, that little problem would've been solved. I committed to buying her a weapon before we left Warrington, but I'd take heed of Prantu's warning and not give away that I was Priya's trainer. Mora might be an ally to the outcast Leira, but she was still affiliated with the university who registered adventurers and regulated the industry.

A random thought that they'd need satellite offices all over to control it blipped through my mind and left as easily as it came.

"Priya's new to all this, having recently lost her parents. Her trainers probably didn't take her seriously. I mean, look at her."

Mora eyed me suspiciously. Her tone matched. "Yes, I suppose a pretty face and a figure suited to whore in the king's own court could hinder. Your trainer probably saw easy gold. I take offense at it, especially considering how you beam dark energy... and light, for that matter. At least your attributes align with your affinities. I will give your trainer that."

I beamed with pride. Priya smirked.

"Since you're still casting Dark Void to rid us of demons when you should be folding them into piles of crushed bone, my advice is to treat your advancement with seriousness."

"I like the sound of that!" I barked.

Mora ran a finger down the side of Priya's face, but my woman was ice daggers. She didn't so much as flinch.

"Your half-breed blood will not serve you in some human realms," Mora whispered, "but it splits your Dark and Light affinities in a way I have rarely seen. Promise me you will select a class and move forward in your studies."

"I'll try to select a class, but I have no idea how to do that, my lady."

"I am no *lady*! Unlike the rest of these entitled fools, I came to the university because of high affinities and dead parents. We're alike, in that way. Orphans, the two of us!

"My inheritance bought my spot, and they kept all of it. Equip a suitable weapon with a proper trainer so your class can be selected for you. All they need do is search your interface. But they should've known that! Where was this trainer? Brumhill? One of the backstreet, unregistered fools?"

Where I was afraid she'd implicate me as her trainer with a shift of her eyes, Priya locked her gaze on the woman. "I'm afraid I don't know what you mean." She flashed a knowing smile. "Trainer? I increased all my attributes the hard way."

Mora laughed. "Go back and tell him he's an idiot for me."

My nose twitched.

"I will certainly tell him." Priya smiled grandly.

"Better yet, register your skill with the guild and return with your chosen weapon. You'll need a guard to escort you to carry it in town, but that shouldn't be a problem. I'd be happy to train you myself and help you select a class." She lowered her tone. "Someone of such strong affinities shouldn't be interacting with backstreet trainers of ill repute, anyway." She gripped Priya's palm.

"I'll take it under advisement." Priya patted the back of Mora's hand.

"Good. Get Gemini cleaned up and extricate that foul crystal from my room. Cleanse your hands, too. I don't want the mages catching wind of my harboring the dark vessel. They'll take exception to my luring a demon into the barracks."

"Picky sorts, huh?" I joked.

Mora cackled.

*You have received the second quest in the **Entropy Crystal** quest chain!*

**Dispatch the Entropy Crystal**

*Find a way to permanently dispose of or hide the Entropy Crystal*

*Reward: 12,500 XP*

*Complete the Entropy Crystal quest chain to earn the title: Guardian of the Light.*

"How many demons could fit into one crystal?" I asked. "I mean, they're demon prisons, right?"

"Pray you never find out, Gemini. In the wrong hands, it will summon horrors the likes of which you cannot imagine. Ensure it doesn't."

"Seems like a lot of responsibility for such a low level as me," I said, using her words against her, but with good humor.

She thrust a finger toward the door. "Then go talk to some shop owners, take quests, and level up!"

"Shop owners. Right. Okay, then."

"Were you also born of a rock?" Mora asked. She didn't wait for an answer. After a quick look in her small mirror—I suppose to ensure there was no blood on her robe—she used a cloth to clean around her temple.

She flung her door open when Priya finished running the cleansing crystal over my pants. "Go out the side entrance and turn left. You can cross to the western wall then walk back alleys to the shopping district. Start with a man named Bensin at the tannery. He always has a use for animal skins. Perhaps you can hunt some."

*Ooh, finally, some simple quests.*

## 27

I f I'd learned anything from my recent undoings, it was to expedite spending my and Priya's attribute points. I never hesitated in other games, but Enora had sucked me into a different frame of mind. I hadn't been willing to risk it in Mora's room, so I'd waited until we were near the western city wall.

"Strength," Priya said.

"No."

"Gemini, I want more strength."

"Why, so you can toss Desini around in your bedroll?" I smiled from one side of my face. "Your strength is as high as mine."

"Maybe I want to toss *you* around my bedroll," she squeezed my hand. "Come on, one more point."

"No. Strength isn't for casters. Maybe when you reach twenty and get a profession."

"Who made you the boss?"

I hesitated for a tick.

"Solara herself, when she empowered me to do for you what would cost others thousands and thousands of gold."

"Shit," Priya said. "Yeah, okay. Can't argue with the goddess, I guess. You're still kind of a dick, though."

"I'm not sure I like how much you're picking up my lingo."

"Deal with it, doze bag."

"Close."

She punched my shoulder.

I quickly spent two points on Priya's Intelligence, one on Constitution, and one on Wisdom.

***Priya Skyy***
*Half-Elf*
*Level 11*
*(No class)*
### ***Attributes***
*Strength: 8**
*Dexterity: 3**
*Intelligence: 20*
*Wisdom: 13*
*Constitution: 17*
*Charisma: 8**
### **Combat Skills**
*Ranged: 14*
*Unarmed: 1*
*Blunt: 3*
*Melee: 5*
### ***Defensive Skills:***
*Dodge: 4*
### ***Weapon Skills***
*Bow: 14**
*Blunt: 7*
### ***Spells:***

### Shadow Void

Level 8

Required Affinity: Shadow Magic

The caster opens a portal to the underworld and banishes chaotically aligned creatures within two levels into the void.

Cast Time: 3 seconds

Cost: 100 Mana

Cool-down:" 30 Minutes

### Sleep

Level 9

Required Affinity: Shadow Magic

The caster calls forth dark essence to force a single adversary to slumber.

Damage will end the effect.

### Mystic Sight

Level 10

All Magic Schools

Cast Time: 5 seconds

Cool-down: 24 Hours

The caster views a 100-yard area from up to one mile away and reveals the location on the map.

### Occupational Skills

Not to be confused with combat professions, occupational skills allow people to earn a wage, run a business, build foundations, or create weapons, armor, and potions to supplement adventuring.

Carpentry: 18

Forestry: 41

Skinning: 15

Cooking: 17

### Affinities:

Shadow Magic: 100%

*Elemental Magic: 57%*
*Languages:*
*Elven*
*Common*

We passed a blacksmith, an herbalist—I made a mental note to return when the clock weighed less and learn to make health potions—and finally came to an open-air shelter with a single wall in the back and a ceiling fashioned of wood planks but supported by rough, stacked-stone blocks.

A nose-assaulting scent wafted its way to us a block before we arrived. It wasn't until I noticed the hung skins curing around the perimeter that I realized this was the tanner of whom Mora had spoken.

Bulky and wide, he also stood four inches taller than me. He bent and ran a long knife across a pelt stretched on a tree stump.

"Are you Bensin?"

"Maybe." He didn't bother turning. "Who are you?"

"I'm Gemini."

The knife scraped, and little flecks of accumulated gunk rolled off the edge of the skin. "Strange name."

"And this is Priya."

"Hello," she said.

Shooting a quick glance over his shoulder at the source of my companion's voice, he flung the knife into a stump, wiped his hands on his apron, and presented Priya with a wide, charming smile filled with better teeth than I would've expected. His blondish-red beard was trimmed close enough to showcase a strong jaw and ass-shaped chin. His large eyes shone blue, and a single knot in one side of the bridge of his nose told a tale of a past conflict. From his defined shoulders and the way his chest cut to his waist in a perfect V, I assumed the conflict hadn't ended well for the other fella.

"I'm Bensin, all right. A pleasure to meet you"." He diverted his glance to me for only a moment. "Both."

Priya's cheeks colored a little.

I didn't like it.

"I'd shake your hands, but it would get messy. Now, what can I do for a pretty thing like you?"

"Mora said you might have need of skins and be short on help," I answered, although I wasn't the pretty thing he referenced. "We hunt from time to time."

The smile grew wider, and his eyes took on a distant gaze over my shoulder. "Ah, yeah... Mora the Mage. I like that one. Good company."

*Ugh.*

"Okay, well, it's your lucky day. Tell ya what, I keep a list of going prices for skins. If you'll peel them off the carcasses and bring 'em to me, I'll do the rest and pay you according to the list price... subject to market changes."

"Of course." I smirked on one side.

"Try to keep 'em in one or two pieces. Oh, and if you're crazy enough, I pay a premium for Grizzly pelts. I export 'em to Trowlsby and auction 'em off. Rich ones up there pay a premium for furs."

"You have fucking auction houses?" I blurted.

"Trading posts? Yeah. Sure. They're specialty-specific, though. Gotta get to a bigger town 'n this one if you want to use 'em, but yeah."

Okay, so not auction houses, but trading posts broken down by craft. I had to see those for myself.

*You have been offered a quest:*

**_A Grizzly Endeavor_**
_Bring a Grizzly Pelt to Bensin in Warrington._
_Reward: 8 gold_
_3,500 XP_
_Additional reward per pelt, 2 Gold_
_1,500 XP_
_(Unlimited turn-ins)_

_Cool, hopefully Priya can teach me the skinning skill._
I accepted the quest.

"If you don't mind copying that to your interface, it's my only one. He held out a leather skin with text carved into it, in Common.

"I'm also running really low on deer skins, so I'm paying a little more than usual for those."

_You have been offered a quest:_
**_Deer, Direly_**
_Bring Three Deerskins to Bensin in Warrington_
_Reward: 3 gold_
_2,500 XP_
_Repeatable_
_Accept?_
_Yes/No_

_You have been offered a quest:_
**_Kill the Wabbit_**
_Bring three rabbit skins to Bensin in Warrington_
_Reward: 1 gold_
_2,000 XP_
_Repeatable_
_Accept?_
_Yes/No_

*You have been offered a quest:*
### ***Wolf It Down***
*Bring three wolves down to Bensin in Warrington*
*Reward: 2 gold*
*3,000 XP*
*Repeatable*
*Accept?*
*Yes/No*

The slew of quests promised some leveling. I didn't want Roshan getting too great a lead on us, but I'd need at least two levels to be ready for what we faced. I flipped through my quest interface and brought up what I thought of as my main quest.

### ***Rescue Roshan***
*(Recommended Level 16)*
*Rescue Roshan before the guards can deliver her to the*
*Governor in Millbury Peaks.*
*Reward: 18,000 XP*
*25 Gold*
*A Foundation Stone*

If Enora Online recommended Level 16 for the quest, and it followed the leads of other VMMORPGs—but I couldn't fucking count on it—then I might find enemies guarding Roshan as high as Level 18. A two-level spread above the recommended level was pretty typical, and fighting enemies two levels higher than me was usually a tad more challenging. When balancing XP rewards with difficulty, my previous gaming experience proved that doing all the quests and completing them when I was at the recommended level was the most efficient way to advance.

However, this quest boasted an unlisted criterion I had no way of gauging—Time.

Roshan was being taken to the Governor of Knall, and my quest was to intercept her before she arrived. The quest log gave no indication of when that arrival would take place. There was no countdown timer or anything, which really pissed me off.

If I wanted Roshan to be part of what was now my life, I had to bind her to me. But if I strolled up to a convoy, into a stronghold, or whatever, and I was too low level to defeat the enemies guarding her, it might end up not just costing me the unique quest, but also Roshan.

That wasn't acceptable. I needed levels. They needed to come fast. Two companions stood ready to help me, and I could take on slightly higher-leveled opponents, but they were both greener than grass in April.

I peered through my interface at the perfect specimen eyeing my companion like a lollipop he wanted to suck on. I ran a check—let's say for giggles.

***Bensin***

*Human*

*Level 37 Tanner*

*Disposition: Neutral*

*Must be nice to be a Level 37 anything.*

"Hey, Bensin?"

"Hmm?" His disinterested expression gave me the impression he begrudged me diverting his attention from Priya.

"Anyone else in town who might need materials or help?"

He shook his head. "Actually..."

I raised an eyebrow and eyed *him* hungrily. You know, hungry for quests.

"It's a lady over on the east side, close to the south gate, third house from the end." He winked at me and muttered. "Had occasion to visit her there twice, if ya take my meaning." His voice returned to a normal speaking tone. "She's been prattling on for months now about her need to hire an adventurer to go to Greycutter Downs and snatch a family heirloom back from this rascal." He eyed Priya. "I'd get it myself, but I've got a backlog of orders and that place is crawling with meanies."

"Uh-huh," Priya muttered.

"Anyway, name's Looli Graples. Good tits, sweet face, you can't miss her. Her place doubles as her business. She'll be out on her stoop, selling the foodstuffs she fashions from local produce just for people like you. Maybe ya go talk to her and tell her I sent ya. Might even set me up for a return trip. I scratch your back, you scratch mine kind of thing."

"What's a Greycutter?" I asked.

"A bird. Wide wingspan, big head. The Downs is an old port that went belly-up ages ago. Short while back, a pirate band moved in and took it up. Then the pirate bay turned into a thief haven. Guess there wasn't much booty on the seas, so they hit the roads to the north and south."

"Wait. Are you saying the reason the roads are dangerous is these assholes in Greycutter Downs?"

He shrugged his massive shoulders. "About sums it up, yeah. No great secret, really."

*Greycutter Downs. That seems like a bigger deal than some heirloom. Hmm.*

"Why doesn't someone get a crew together and just go clear them out, if they're so bad for business between towns?"

"Ha! You're not the brightest sort, are ya?" Flipping the skin he'd been smoothing down off the stump, he sat and beckoned me closer with a finger wag. He peered in both directions then spoke in a conspiratorial tone. "See, the governor likes to control what comes and goes through his territory. Trowlsby, to the north, they pay his taxes because he can send men down there to make trouble if they don't. He offers his protection, they pay the fees.

"Unlike Trowlsby, Warrington and Brumhill don't like to pay his *personal* taxes on top of what they pay the king. Since the governor is just a little too far north to be spending his gold to send people, this far south—especially to towns that don't like to pay for the privilege—he don't regulate the roads."

*Though he'll send a few to collect a woman he had kidnapped from across the ocean. This guy doesn't know shit.*

"If we want him to clear out the thieves, we gotta pay the taxes. But see, our Mayor got a stony head. Stands up real straight when he walks, if you get what I mean. He ain't about to bend the knee to the king's regent. After all, he's an *elected official.*

"After you talk to the lady Looli Graples, run just up the road there and talk to him. He might even be close by. It wouldn't be an easy go, but if you have friends, you might clear out that riffraff." He furrowed his eyebrows. "Unless you got love for the governor or something."

"No, it's just the opposite. So, you're saying if I clear out these folks, it might help the towns down here by making the roads safer, and I might make friends while sticking it to the governor in a big way?"

"That about sums 'er up, chief."

"That sounds superb to me. Thanks."

"Hey, I live to serve, Chimney, or whatever your name was." He clicked his tongue at Priya and matched it with a wink. "You be careful out there, now. Wouldn't do to have you scratch up that pretty mug."

"I'll do my best," Priya said.

She fell in next to me as we paced across town. "Do you think we should get rid of the crystal first?"

I checked my quest log.

*You have been offered a quest:*
### *Lovely Looli*
*Speak to Looli Graples about her family heirloom.*
*Reward: 500 XP*
*You have been offered a quest:*
### *Den of Thieves*
*Speak to Warrington's Mayor about the thieves at Greycutter Downs.*
*Reward: 500 XP*

*One-thousand XP just for finding them. Accepted and accepted!*

"Are you going to tell me what you're doing in your interface? Why the smile? What about the crystal?"

I wrapped my arm around her shoulder in plain view of the tanner and planted a kiss on top of her head.

"Priya, honey. I'm working on it so I can answer your question. Give me a minute."

"Of course. I just didn't know—"

"It's fine. I'm just trying to figure out the best way forward. We picked up a bunch of quests to help us level.

But there's also the question of time. If Roshan's too far ahead, we might have to risk going after her now."

"Roshan is my priority. I don't care about these little details."

"Details..." I trailed off.

*Fuck it.*

I opened party chat.

> *Party: [G3m1n1:] Hey Desini, you there?*

She didn't answer. I wondered how her interface might be configured that she didn't see the message.

> *Party [Priya:] Guess she's not watching.*

"Why are you party chatting when you're walking right next to me?"

> *Party [Priya:] Because I think it's cool. Before a couple nights ago, I had no idea there was such a thing. This will be a great way to pass secret messages when we're around others.*
> *Party: [G3m1n1:] True. Dammit, now you've got me doing it.*

I turned to Priya's companion page, remembering what Mora had said about her classless status. I focused on the text above the image of her.

> *No Class Selected*

When I focused on the words, a tool tip appeared, confirming what I already knew.

*Equip the weapon of the desired class in your companion's
hand to select a class.*

"We need to find you a weapon and discover a class."

"What do you mean, discover?"

I took a moment to organize the words that would best
explain the concept. Then I nodded to myself.

"I don't know what classes there are." I left out the part
about them being suspiciously absent from my player
manual and how I thought Enora liked forcing me to
discover everything on my own. "Something about
weapons, I guess some unique energy, identifies them as the
weapons of a given class. I think you would make a good
shadow caster, like Prantu and Mora, and it would be really
great to have someone like you to deal damage at range.
Where Desini is tall and better-suited to be a front-line
fighter with her long reach, you're built to stand back and
rain hell down on our enemies. That's why I give her
strength and mold you more toward your natural affinities."

"I like the sound of that! Rain hell down on enemies!"
Priya's eyelids vanished as her eyes flared wide.

*She probably didn't hear a word that came after that.*

"I'll bet you do. Anyway, we need to find you a weapon
to identify a good damage dealing caster class."

I scanned my inventory slots for anything that might fit
the bill. I'd been through all the items there—most of which
I'd forgotten to sell to Breeder. My eyes fell on a symbol
representing a small glass orb. I selected it and it appeared
in my hand.

"I wonder if this—"

"I never want to see that thing again," Priya said.

"Zhara cast out Crohl, it should be safe."

I hadn't seen an option to choose a class for her when

Priya held the orb the first day we met, but she hadn't been my companion at the time.

"I would not deign to touch this thing."

"Priya, if it will help you discov—"

She thrust a finger at the globe that was once her prison.

"Not. This. Thing." She sped her pace and walked ahead of me.

*I guess she's said it three times and made her peace. Damn.*

I shoved the globe back into the bag. I didn't need reminding Priya was not some random NPC built of ones and zeroes by some human on earth.

*Most of the time, I like that.*

"There's bound to be a weapon vendor in town, even if they won't let you carry them. Maybe they deliver them to the gate or something."

"What about the blacksmith we passed near Bensin?"

I didn't like that she remembered the flirting tanner's name.

"No, I think we'd want something more of wooden construction for a caster."

Priya slowed her paced and walked next to me. "How would you know this thing? That it would need to be of wood instead of metal?"

*Oh, because I've played so many of the games, it's like second nature. They all do it that way.*

"Call it a feeling. Roshan is a caster, and she wielded a scepter of wood and then a staff."

"I don't think I'm a staff person. I'm a bit on the slighter side."

"You mean you're short."

"Prick." She pursed her lips.

"You fucking adore me."

"Do you still have her scepter?"

I shook my head. "I do, but I don't think that's the kind of caster you want to be. It's for healers."

"Ah, but we currently have no healer. If I learn to heal until we have rescued Roshan, wouldn't that be prudent?"

*Shit, I hadn't even thought of that.*

"It wouldn't do anything for the shadow magic skills that are most likely to help us offensively, but now that you mention it, perhaps it's not such a bad idea. It might even help level your Light magic, to balance your shadow later. Or some shit. Who knows?" A memory flashed in my mind. What had I seen when selecting Desini's class? "Whoa, let me check something."

She nodded, and we stopped walking.

I opened the Companion Tab and focused on tool tips, but wasn't finding what I needed. I checked my logs, selected yesterday's date, then scrolled to when we selected Desini's class.

*Unlike players, companions cannot change classes.*
*At Level 20, companions can choose a single combat profession.*
*Profession options for this companion at level twenty are:*
### Warrior
### Marauder
### Shadow Knight
### Blade Dancer
### Paladin

"I don't think the scepter will work out. It's possible you can learn generic healing spells, even as an offensive caster, but I don't understand how that works yet. So, for now, I'd rather we find you something that best expresses your affinities and highest potential. You can't pick a healing class, or you'll be stuck with it."

I expected arguments about how strange it is someone can't choose their own class and was prepared to joke that Solara was a bitch sometimes. As often was the case, Priya surprised me with her answer.

"This makes sense to me. We'll find something that better allows me to rain hell down on our enemies." She pointed. "I believe this is the dwelling Bensin described. There is the woman on her stoop."

"How did you know?"

Priya shrugged. "The tits. They're perfect."

The single-story stone hut sat third from the end, as Bensin said. The woman standing in front lingered behind two tables cut of thin wood, set on the stony edges of her porch. The scents of fruits and cooked meats swirled on a wrap-around breeze.

There were no other patrons.

The woman Priya presumed was Looli Graples wore a casual forest green bell-sleeved blouse that hung off her shoulders and cut across just beneath her neckline. Her skirt resembled denim and her hair was drawn back by a swatch of cloth matching her blouse. Smooth tan skin covered the angular features of her face with the slightest hints of crow's feet evident as she squinted out at us, regardless of the fact she stood in the shade of her porch.

"Looli Graples?" I raised my hand in greeting.

"Yes?" She raised a hand in return. "That's me. Is the law after me again?"

"I'm sorry, what?"

She smiled. "I was having a go at you. Sorry."

Priya and I laughed. "No need to apologize. I was slow

on the uptake." I raised our clasped hands. "This is Priya." Priya gave a little bow. "I'm Gemini."

"Pleased to meet you both." She bowed twice, in-turn. "I'm Looli—but I guess we already said that. So, are you looking for delicacies?"

I scanned the food spread atop cloths of varying colors. After running a quick scan of each item, two stood out.

***Peach wrap***
*Price: 50 coppers*
*+5 Mana regeneration per tick*
*Duration: one hour*
***Melon Berry***
*Price: 75 coppers*
*+3 to intelligence*
*Duration: One hour*

I saw nothing that would help me with Dexterity boosts or Desini with strength or Constitution, but the bonuses for Priya would be worth the expense, especially at those prices. I told her we'd take five of each and stowed them in my bag before raising our real business.

Our funds were 4 gold, 7 silvers, 90 coppers after the purchase. Wow, maybe I had more money than I'd thought, but while food was cheap, Desini's plate, my quiver, and Priya's under armor had been painfully pricey.

"The tanner across town told us you were looking for someone to snatch a family heirloom from Greycutter Downs."

"Ah!" She set her hands on her hips and threw her head back. "It seems someone is trying to make up for his lack of attention of late." She peered at us as if waiting for some kind of response before finally raising her shoulder in a half-shrug. "Guess a cold shoulder served, after all. Not that you should worry yourselves with such trivialities."

"Okay?" I said.

Looli's smile lit up the shade. "Ha-ha. You're cute."

I returned the smile. Priya did not.

*Payback was a bitch.*

"So, the heirloom?"

"Ah, yes! My uncle would pay you handsomely if you return my mother's betrothal dress to me. Truth be told, I have no desire to be betrothed, but he thinks the return of the dress would change my mind. Some men are single-minded."

Priya nodded. "I know, sister."

"Don't suppose I should hold it against him. He's just trying to see his sister's child cared for. But I'm no chick anymore, and it grows tiresome, sometimes." Looli thrust a hand over her shoulder. "He's inside, wrapping fruit, but he has offered an open reward of two gold and your choice of five food items."

*You have completed a quest:*
### *Lovely Looli*
*You spoke to Looli about her family heirloom.*
*Reward: 500 XP*

"Two gold is no drop in the lake," Priya said.

*Party: [G3m1n1:] It's not a windfall, either. Risking our asses for two gold would usually be out of the question. But we'll take this on because something tells me the wider quest to clear out the former pirates will make it worth the trip.*
*Party: [Priya:] I told you this would come in handy.*

*You have been offered a quest:*
### *Looli's Lace*
*Retrieve Looli's Mother's Binding Dress.*
*Reward: 2 Gold*
*2,000 XP*
*5 foodstuffs of your choice*

I bowed slightly. "I'd be glad to search for your mother's dress."

"Excellent. He will be so pleased. I must admit, I would be warmed by its return, as well. I miss my mother, and it would make me feel closer to her memory."

"We're thrilled to help," Priya said in her most enthusiastic tone. "Leave it to us!"

"Can you tell me where I'd find the mayor?" I asked.

"Yes. My uncle is inside. Would you like me to fetch him?"

"Your uncle is the mayor?"

"I guess that simple-brained tanner didn't mention it, huh?" Her lips twisted up on one side.

"He said the mayor might be nearby."

"I swear to Solara he has the social skills of a trout, but at least it's made up for in brawn. Ah, well. I'll summon my uncle."

She disappeared through the door and a minute later the mayor appeared. The tanner might have lacked social skills, but his description of the man with the straight back hit the mark.

After introductions and our explanation, he raised his hand and looked up and down the street.

"Come, come. Let's not talk on the road." We followed him around the corner between two row houses, and he peered up to ensure every window was battened.

"Why the secrecy?" I asked.

"The governor has spies. Dirty, no good..." he trailed off. "Anyway! Best leave politics to me. Meantime, I have long sought a brave adventurer to go and clear the Downs." After a quick surmising of us, he peered back at the road. "It isn't just you, is it?"

"No," I said.

"Oh, no offense or anything. Just, well..."

I nodded. Priya threw a suspicious squint.

"Trade has declined since the bandits started their dark enterprise on the roads. I suppose the dried-up port and lack of sea traffic turned them to land, and it's we who pay the price for their debauchery."

*You have completed:*
### Den of Thieves
*You spoke to Warrington's Mayor about the thieves at*
*Greycutter Downs.*
*Reward: 500 XP*

"Right. It's usually the innocents who pay for the crimes of others."

"You speak true, adventurer. Clearing out the Greycutter Downs might restore our fishing trade. I have many here who scrape by but would otherwise prosper if they could cast their lines and nets in that inlet."

"Any idea of the bandit numbers?"

"No, but if you take out their leader, the aptly named Blackbard, I'd bet the rest of them scurry away like the rats they are."

"Blackbard?" I'd heard this name in Brumhill from the phony guard who'd had the sense to walk away—and later showed up dead on the road. He'd said that Blackbard didn't appreciate failure, or something along those lines.

"A nickname combining his disposition with his love of the lute, I believe. So, what do you think? Ten gold to wipe out or drive off the lot?"

*You have been offered a quest:*
### *Den of Thieves: Part 2*
*Dispatch 6 thieves at Greycutter Downs.*
*Kill Blackbard.*
*Reward: 7,500 XP*
*10 Gold*

"My team will be happy to wipe them out." I leaned forward, lowered my voice, and gave my throat a creaky quality. "All of them."

*He wouldn't get the reference, but I'd always wanted to say that. Even if the movie sucked.*

"Right." He slid a subtle step backward. "If there's nothing else, I should relieve Looli so she can man the front. People come with endless issues and complaints when I dare stand out in the open, so I wrap the fruit in concealment, you understand."

"Before you go, can you tell me where I might find a weapon shop or woodworker who deals in caster weapons?"

"Of course. Turn back up the road to the right then keep straight until the dirt turns to cobblestones—I'm afraid we haven't had funds to expand our infrastructure this far down— you'll see Merk's place on the right. He doesn't hang a sign, but you'll know it by the wooden statue of the king outside. Merk is a patriot. Be wary of speaking against the king or his regents."

"Thanks for the warning."

W e found Merk's shop right where the mayor indicated.

If we reigned at Greycutter downs and kept an eye out for animals to skin, we stood to make twelve gold plus the rewards for the pelts. It would be great if we leveled into new gear and upgraded before rushing after Roshan. So, my desire to arm Priya with a bonus-infused weapon trumped my desire to save coin, and I went in ready to spend what was in my bag.

Merk stood about my height and, while taut, his muscles were more wiry than huge. He wore a long beard dominated by gray with a few struggling remnants of black mixed in. He'd polished up a wooden buckle for his belt with the image of a bird. It seemed he ended about half his sentences in rhetorical questions as he explained the buckle's significance.

"It's a Greycutter, don't you know? The symbol of Warrington for as long as anyone remembers, do ya kin? In the Spring, the people gather for a festival to celebrate the birds as they roost on the wall for a few weeks before returning to the inlet. I think it's an excuse to partake of the dwarven ale come down from the mountains after a long winter, but who could say with any certainty?" He slapped my shoulder good and hard as he turned to a wall of shelves.

"Who knows, indeed," I agreed in an even tone, flashing an eye-roll at Priya.

She snickered.

*Party: [Priya:] You're bad.*

"So, a caster's weapon, you say?"

"Right. My companion here is selecting a class today."

Merk spun around, his eyes wide, all his teeth showing. "A class, you say? Well! Isn't it a blessed day for thee, young lady?" He bent his elbow and feigned a low jab. "Setting out to adventure, eh? By Solara's will shall you grow strong in service to the king!" He clapped his hands together and rubbed them furiously. "Have ye an idea what class you desire? Something in healing? Wind magic, mayhap?"

"I was thinking something complimentary to Shadow magic," she said, throwing him a dark-magic-kind-of-brooding-expression I found absolutely adorable.

He matched the expression, though less adorably. "The dark stuff then!" He lowered his tone in a mock growl. "By the king's grace! I might have just the thing for ye."

He spun and pulled a wooden pole with a loop carved in the top that stood about two feet tall in his grasp. He handed it to Priya.

"Try that, young miss."

Priya grasped it.

### *Nightmare Cudgel*
*Level 11*

*Slot: Weapon*
*Type: One-handed club*
*Quality: Uncommon*
*Durability: 20 of 20*
*Damage: 12-21*
*+5 Damage from shadow magic spells*
*+2 Intellect*
*+2 Constitution*
*Binds on Equip*
*Chance on hit: Terrify the enemy so they flee for three seconds.*

*Hmm, soul-binding. Doesn't look like a cudgel to me, though. Aren't those like canes or something?*

I noted how it didn't offer her a class selection when she equipped the weapon and suspected this was because she didn't yet own it.

"I feel the power of this weapon surging into me." Priya turned toward Merk and adopted negotiation tone. "What is your desired price for this item?"

I thought about how Desini's high-ranked negotiation skills might have been good here. I intervened before he could name a price.

"And what classes might equip this?"

Merk rubbed his chin. "Hmm. Dark Mage. Thaumaturge. Necromancer."

"Necromancer?" I blurted out.

"Yes, but I believe those dark devils to be a specialty profession one would select after Level 30, if it pleases ye. By then, they wouldn't bother with this... umm... fine piece." He picked up his tone. "But it would serve the lady's level very well, indeed!"

I focused on his earlier words.

*Specialty Professions. Level 30. Good to know.*

Priya gazed at me in confusion.

"Necromancers raise the bones of the dead to fight with them," I explained.

Her lips pinched together, so they were almost invisible. "This sounds powerful, but disrespectful to the dead."

Merk nodded. "A dark school, indeed. Shadow mage, however, provides for powerful offensive spells. In my adventuring days, we had one in my party who advanced to Level 20 and became a Black Mage. Her power was exceptional." He barked laughter. "Many times did our tank have problems keeping monster hate, I will tell you!"

"Which means you also have to control your damage output, Priya. You can't just cast and cast, over and over. Timing would be important, and understanding burst damage. Do you think you might enjoy that? It's methodical while also powerful."

"That sounds very attractive to me." Priya nodded enthusiastically. "Now, as to price?"

"Let's get a feel for a few others before we decide," I said.

Priya agreed, eager to get her hands on other weapons. But everything else was too far below her level to be effective or too high for her to equip.

"Okay," I said. "How much?"

Merk rubbed his chin again and peered at the weapon fashioned of wood. "I can let it go for 55 silvers."

"I will give you 45 for it," Priya said.

"Fifty is as low as I can go, ma'am."

"Sold!" I said. Compared to what we'd bought from Breeder, this wooden stuff was cheap. Maybe competition in the larger town forced prices down.

Merk was hesitant to buy up the inventory from my bag,

citing overstock and disinterest in the items I showed him, so I walked out with the same predicament—a lack of inventory space. Oh well, I'd dump shit rather than burning time to search for vendors to buy it.

I paid Merk and asked if he knew the quickest path to Greycutter Downs.

"Oh, quite a place to start an adventure. I hope you plan to level her skills before you venture into Blackbard's territory."

"We do."

"Good!" He slapped my shoulder again. "The merchants of Warrington would be grateful to travel the roads again. It's half a day's journey to the east. Follow the river until you come to the high hills to the north, then follow them to the great sea. You cannot miss it."

*At least a day lost.*

We thanked him and set off for the cart to meet up with Desini, from whom I was eager to hear news.

When we reached the cart, we found her inside, curled up into a ball with her muscular back facing us. That explained why she hadn't answered out party chat. Priya and I smiled at each other. But I also wondered how wise it was for someone who might not fit in so well among humans to sleep in her cart half nude. Of course, she was confident enough to travel the town without us in order to gather information, and I was the stranger here.

"Mmmmrrrrrr," she rolled onto her back, revealing things. I scanned the seams cloth of running along a top corner of the canvas cover out of respect. "Sleep snuck up on me. I spent some copper on food. It's over there in the corner."

"Good!" Priya barked. "I'm starving, and his lordship here wouldn't let me partake of the fruits he bought, insisting I save them for battle." She eyed me. "You don't feed us often enough."

Food was well and good, but... "I will endeavor to better nourish your lovely body." I turned my words on Desini. "Do you have news about Roshan?"

"Oh, yesssss. As luck would have it, the party who brought her here only set out just after sunrise this morning. They are only a few hours ahead of us. My contact informs me they have plans to stop in Trowlsby to the north, which is fantastic news."

"Why is that good news? Will they be there long enough for us to catch up?"

"Yes. As her captors represent the governor, those lickers of boot heels in Trowlsby will insist on lavishing them in fineries and presenting the best accommodations. I have little doubt they will stay at least a couple days."

"How in the world did you learn all that?"

Her lips spread into a smile as she sat up, half-bare. I kept my gaze locked on hers.

"I brought delicacies from an associate in Trowlsby to a guard at the north wall. He is not so pig-headed as most humans. I provided him with two silvers and a promise of more salted lamb my next pass through town. He traded the information."

"You are very resourceful, my Desini," Priya said. "I would like very much to reward you for your services."

"Can you two keep it in your pants for half a day?"

"Oh, look, Desini!" Priya held out her hand and snapped her fingers at me.

"What? Oh! right!" I reached into my bag and dropped the cudgel in her hand.

Desini stared at it. "This is a dwarf's cane?"

Priya laughed. "No, you silly mishon! It is a Nightmare Cudgel! It has bonus attributes and makes me powerful!"

Desini's confused expression jumped to me.

"It's a shadow caster's weapon. Priya is going to select her class. She wanted you to be here to mark the moment."

Desini's back shot straight as her hands went to her cheek. She clapped them and crawled on her knees to pull Priya into a hug.

"This news fills me with chills of excitement! We will adventure long together, shadow caster!"

*It's like she got engaged or something instead of preparing to face a violent lifestyle. At least they aren't prissy. Well, too prissy, anyway.*

"Are you ready?" I asked.

Their lips were pressed together.

I sighed.

Their lips smacked as Priya pulled away then nodded at me, a huge smile on her face. Probably for multiple reasons.

"What do I need to do?" she asked.

"Nothing. Just hold it."

*Priya has equipped:*

**Nightmare Cudgel**

*You have discovered a new class!*

**Shadow Mage**

*You have discovered a new class!*

**Thaumaturge**

*You may choose one of two classes for your companion.*
*Do you wish to select Priya's class now?*

As Thaumaturge was the class that led to the possibility of becoming a necromancer, and Priya was nauseated by the thought of that, I chose shadow mage. At Level 20, she might become a black mage.

*Are you sure you wish to select **Shadow Mage** for Priya's starter class?*
*This decision is permanent. Consider this carefully.*

"Shadow Mage then, Priya?"

"What does it do for me?"

"According to the tool tip, you can cast ice, fire, and shadow spells. But if you select this, no Necromancer later."

"Blah!" She stuck her tongue out. "It is against nature! Select Shadow Mage!"

"Congratulations, you are now a Shadow Mage."

"Ooh! I have a prompt!" Priya's eyes flickered and then she clapped her hands. I received what I assumed was a similar system output.

*Priya has learned the nature spell:*
### Thunder
*Level 10*
*Required Affinity: Elemental Magic or Shadow Magic*
*Cast a storm overhead of multiple enemies causing 13-20 damage.*
*Cast Time: 3 Seconds*
*Mana Cost: 50 mana*
*Cool-down: Not applicable*

*Priya has learned the nature spell:*
### Ice Storm
*Level 10*
*Required Affinity: Elemental Magic or Shadow Magic*

*Cast a storm of ice over multiple enemies causing 13-17 damage.*
*Additional effect: Chill*
*Chill: Slow enemy movement speed by 30%*
*Cast Time: Channeled Spell*
*Mana Cost: 45 Mana*
*Cool-down: 30 seconds.*

*Priya has learned the nature spell:*
### ***Fire Flash***
*Level 11*
*Required Affinity: **Shadow Magic***
*Project a burst of fire before a single enemy causing 15-31 damage.*
*Cast Time: Instant*
*Mana cost: 40 Mana*
*Cool-down: Not applicable*

"I can cast all these things?" Priya asked, her eyes wide.

"Well, not inside town!" I joked.

"Thank you, Gemini." She kissed me. "How your presence matures me!" She kissed me again and leveled her gaze on me.

"Yeah, sure. You talk all that shit when we're hanging out, but then I do something for you, and I'm *the man* again."

"I cannot make sense of your words, but I give you leave to use them to your heart's contentment!"

"Well, thanks."

"You are welcome! Now! Take me to where I can destroy things!"

I peered over Priya's shoulder. The arched eyebrow on Desini's face was priceless.

"Ready to level your sword skills?" I asked the feline-like goddess.

"Mmmmrrrrrr."

We rolled into a thicket of trees east of Warrington and followed a trail marked with narrow trenches from cart wheels. Our group passed a couple of farms with clucking chickens and animals resembling cows with short, twisted horns, but no one came out of the well-kept but aged single-story homesteads, which suited us fine. We didn't have time for social interaction, as much as I itched to get to know my new world better.

About two hours later, as we left the lush crescent and entered low hills, a survey of the overgrown terrain ahead informed us we'd have to leave the cart behind.

Though Desini spent most of her time on the roads between towns in her life as a messenger, she was no stranger to hiding the cart on short notice. After a brief discussion, we decided we'd camouflage it, continue on foot, and give the animal some rest from pulling the weight. I doubted we'd move any slower.

Desini strapped packs on the animal's back. We stopped at a stream half an hour later to water the horse while we ate. Though I'd spent a couple nights inside the cart, I'd paid little mind to the saddlebags she'd folded into one corner of the interior, but now that they adorned the powerful horse's back, it occurred to me we had extra storage space so that my bag's capacity was less a problem. Still, I wouldn't want to overload the beast if the idea was to give him some recovery time from pulling all of us on a cart, and I'd keep an open mind as far as discarding less valuable items, if it came to that. When I mentioned the subject to Desini, though, she laughed and patted the horse's thick haunches.

"Pickney is a powerful boy, but seven years old. You could pack enough for five plate-clad warriors and provisions for weeks on him and he would tow your load without a grunt." She patted him again and cooed. "He is my sweet boy."

The horse nickered in response to her loving tone.

The salted meat Desini picked up in Warrington had a spicy finish that left its ghost on my tongue as it filled my ravenous belly. Back in real life, I'd always been the kind to eat only when I was hungry—a tendency that followed me into Enora. I noticed almost zero fatigue when I went long stretches without food. I wondered if it was even possible for me to starve to death. Though my stomach growled from time to time, and food was rewarding when it hit my gut, it often wasn't until I ingested sustenance that I realized just how hungry I'd been.

Priya and Desini shared a different outlook and constantly reached into Desini's bag for the next snack. It really did seem like I was starving them.

Having passed the rocky egress emptying into an open plateau, we splashed across another shallow stream to a grassy hillside leading down into a valley. I stopped to absorb the amazing vista to the east, where the wide river Merk had mentioned flowed.

It took about two hours to cross a sprawling valley, and the trek back up to the next ridge took until nightfall. Though the air was cool at that elevation after the sun went down, we forewent a fire, wrapped up the horse in a blanket, and arranged our furs so the three of us slept on two of them and the third lay atop us. We stared up at the wonder of millions of stars as we tangled our legs and arms across each other for warmth and drifted off to sleep.

Shuffling sounds disturbed my slumber the next morning. My eyes blinked open to find Desini leaning over me with a finger pressed to her pinched lips. The horse nickered from somewhere behind her.

"I've spotted a pair of men. They are dressed similarly to the dead ones on the road and might have originated from the place we seek. The cloud cover shrouds the sun, so if we use the trees in the valley for additional cover, we could take them by surprise."

A field commander couldn't have asked for a more efficient report.

"Well, do you want me to get up so I can look, or do the two of you plan on handling it yourselves?" I peered up at her, then down at the hand she held across my chest.

Desini blushed for an instant before sliding her arm away.

"That way, master."

I followed her sightline to the bottom of the hill where a grove of trees and underbrush descended into the crease in the valley then climbed back up the next hill. The sun hadn't reached the crest of the next rise, so the trees cast only a thin shadow. I squinted.

"I don't see anything." Desini dropped on her belly next to me and pointed from my eye level. I squinted for a few heartbeats. Two dots moved among the trees. "How in the world did you see that?"

"Your human eyes are weak."

"I'm the one who spotted them," Priya said. "I'm half-human."

"Then your elven eyes are even better than mine." Desini said. "What do you want, a fruit roll in reward?"

"Chew me, clever ass." Priya bent down and slapped Desini's hard butt.

"It's *bite* me and *smart* ass." I chuckled.

"I will never get the hang of your words. So, what do you think, should we torture them for information?"

"Torture?" I asked. "What kind of monster are you?"

"The kind who wants my Roshan back."

Desini said, "We should fight them to increase our skills and XP. This would seem most prudent. I very much look forward to wielding my sword."

"Yeah, we need all the help we can get if we're going to take on Roshan's captors. There's no time like the present." I flicked a finger at Priya. "No torture."

"I like this expression," Desini said. "*There is no time like the present.* I will live by these words."

"I could think of worse ones," I said, "like, 'chew me, clever ass.'"

"Your wit is without end," Priya grumbled.

I shrugged my bow over my shoulder. Priya stood in her robe—which had returned to its regular red color as we slept and Prantu's glamour wore off—wearing a stony gaze and clutching her cudgel in a white-knuckled grasp.

Desini's breastplate and strapped-on thigh protectors would soon gleam in the risen sun. The pommel of her sheathed sword sprouted over her shoulder.

"Long have I dreamed of this day," Priya said. "I never knew I held such desires until I saw my beloveds lay waste to thieves in the wood of my home. Now," she rubbed her palms together as if to warm them up, "I long to burn my enemies."

*They're itching to fuck something up. I like it.*

"Let's go."

I led them down the hill, using a line of trees to conceal our approach while asking Priya to watch the hill opposite us for reinforcements or scouts, since she apparently had the best set of eyes. And ears, for that matter.

The horse trailed far behind since Desini wasn't pulling its reigns, but she assured me it would follow. When I was close enough, I inspected the two travelers.

### Human Bandit
*Level 15*

### Human Bandit
*Level 15*

"This is fine. They're a few levels higher than Priya, so maybe her OP casting will be mitigated by that so she doesn't draw too much hate."

I drew confused gazes.

"Let me try again. Since Priya's spells do a lot of damage *for her level,* maybe the fact that they're four level higher will increase their resistances. If they resist some of the damage, they could become less angry at Priya, so Desini can keep their attention."

Desini clicked her tongue. "I don't know why you don't just say things this way in the first place."

"Adapt," I said. "I'll always talk in code. My way is brief and will be useful during combat."

"Oh. I see. You're right, Master. What is OP?"

"It means overpowered."

"I will commit this to memory."

"Me too," Priya nodded. "My lovely tactician." She smacked my backside—another habit of mine she'd adopted.

"Let's review your Fighter abilities, Desini."

### Slice Achilles
*Slash your enemies' legs, slowing their movement speed and causing bleed damage.*

*2-5 Damage*

*2 bleeding damage per second*

### *Charge*

*Charge forward up to 1 5 yards, knocking your target down and stunning them.*

*2-4 Damage*

*Additional effect: Stun*

*Stun effect: 4 seconds*

### *Swipe*

*Swing your sword at the enemies in front of you.*

*Strikes up to three enemies.*

*9-1 1 Damage per enemy*

### *Howl*

*Provoke your enemy into attacking you.*

*Cost: 1 2 Stamina*

*Cast Time: Instant*

*Cool-down: 1 0 seconds*

"Use your abilities like we discussed on the road. Before long, it will come easily as would picking up a stick. You'll want to build an effective rotation. We'll modify it as needed."

"Rotation? My order of skills, yes?"

"Yes. For instance, you should probably open battles with Charge. This will disable one of your opponents for a few seconds so you and we" —I nodded at Priya— "can focus on beating the other one down. When the first one recovers, try using Swipe to hit both. The higher damage should keep him pissed off at you as he returns to the fray. Remember, your primary role is to keep your enemies so threatened by you that they don't turn their attention on us."

"Yes, master." Her eyes were locked on me, focused. "I will spread my wrath between them when the second one rises."

"If either of them turns toward us, use Slice Achilles to slow them down and then use Howl to provoke them into attacking you."

"This sounds like magic!" Desini barked, nodding at Priya.

"Shh, they'll hear us."

She nodded.

"It's kind of like magic, because it charms them into attacking you instead of us, but it uses stamina. Watch your stamina bar. Try to keep it above half, if you can, but not at the cost of them coming after your party. Got it?"

Desini rattled off what I'd said back to me. "Charge to stun the first one. When he falls, attack the second. You will join in. When the first stands up, use Swipe to anger them both. If any show the poor judgment to turn a back to me, use Slice Achilles to slow them, then howl to bring them back." She nodded curtly. "I will make these fools furious at me. I like this tricky strategy."

"That's good. You'll be using it for the rest of your long life."

She gave a curt nod then turned a pair of fierce, hateful eyes on her targets. "I am ready to kill these men."

My chin dropped. I gazed at Priya, but she wore a distant gaze. She maintained the white-knuckled grasp on her cudgel. I reached out and gripped the strained hand.

"Priya?"

She jerked. "Huh?"

"It's okay. I'll be right beside you in case one of them gets stupid and charges you. Ready to talk about your role?"

Priya took a quick breath, closed her eyes for a second, then nodded. "Yes."

"When the first one falls, cast Fire Flash on the one standing by focusing on it in your interface. Once you practice and get a sense for how the cast feels, you should be able to use it with simple thoughts. You know how I envision a purple cloud to leap through space, like Guiles taught me?"

She nodded.

"It's similar to that."

"This is how I cast Lightning Pulse, Gemini. I never focused on my interface."

"Oh. Well, that's impressive. But you practiced on Guiles's target dummies first, right? For now, just keep the abilities up on your interface in case they don't come as naturally, and feel how the dark energy flows through you.

"Count off a few seconds and cast again. If either of them moves toward you, try out Ice Storm. That will slow both of them if you can target the area under their feet. At least, I assume it will create a circle under their feet. I guess we'll see."

She nodded. "Fire Flash and then Ice Storm, but only if they move toward us."

"Yes."

"What of my other spells? Thunder? Sleep?"

"If we had more opponents, I might pick a target for you to put to sleep, but it isn't necessary with just two ordinary MOBs like these."

"Mob?" Priya asked.

"Um... short for enemies."

"But it sounds nothing like 'enemy.'"

I scowled. She shrugged. Emotions equal to a hug came across the airwaves.

"I want our tank to practice handling aggro on multiple targets. I think Desini is powerful and will keep them angry."

"Excellent."

I smiled, feeling the familiar surge of my adrenals prefacing combat. My party was about to fight together for the first time. "You guys excited?"

They both nodded, but Priya still seemed a little off.

I gripped her arm. "If you get nervous, back up and we'll finish them. There's no shame in just surviving. Okay?"

She smiled widely and nodded. "Thank you. I'm sorry, I just—"

"Burn them down." I waved a hand and kissed her forehead.

"Will Click or Wolfie be helping?" Priya asked.

I shook my head. "I want the three of us to get as many skill points as possible. If I summon a pet, they'll fall faster. By making the fight a little longer, we increase the odds of leveling weapon and magic skill ranks. I haven't noticed an XP penalty for using pets, but you and I are probably going to suffer because Desini is higher level than us."

Desini peered down at her boots. "I'm sorry master."

"Dude, there's nothing to be sorry for. Having you kicks the most high of asses."

I wanted to run a thumb across her cheek for reinforcement, but opted for a light punch of her shoulder instead. She smiled and nodded.

We scooted to the edge of the tree line and halted next to a maple. I leaned toward Desini as we knelt and bounced on the balls of our feet. I nudged her with my shoulder. "You should have some indicator with your Charge skill that turns green or changes from gray to colorful when they're in range. Just go when you do. We'll be right here behind you." I reached out and pressed a healing potion into her free hand. "We don't have a healer. I don't expect they'll put you in any real danger, but if they do, suck that down. I'll be watching your health and call out if I think you need it. Just don't be nervous. And if you make a mistake, don't worry."

"I see why she loves you," Desini said in a soft voice.

A lump caught in my throat.

I'd been poised to thank her when her gaze flicked up and to the right, then her mouth dropped open, and she zipped away from the trees, closing the distance to the bandits in a hot second. Her shoulder slammed into her target, flattening him.

"Damn!" Priya barked.

*Desini uses Charge.*
*Human Bandit is stunned.*

*Human Bandit*
*-17 HP*

I activated my expanded combat log with a mental command. I wanted to see my tank's damage output calculation. Maybe I was just selective about when to be a dweeb.

Desini turned on the other opponent who fumbled with his sheathed blade. As my new tank's sword swung, catching the man across his leather chest armor, I nocked an arrow.

*Desini attacks Human Bandit with Sword of the Defender.*
*24 Damage*

*Damage Modifier: Strength x 0.5 = 12 additional damage*
*Bonus: Two levels higher than opponent*
*Base Damage 24 x .2 = 4.8 Damage*

*Human Bandit*
*-31 HP*

*Desini's Sword skill has increased to rank 13.*

Knowing the information was logged, I focused my combat log back down to the minimum display.

*Desini*
*-17 HP*
*643 HP remaining*

I'd forgotten about the sick constitution buffs Desini received from the plate Breeder sold us. What would've been a pool of 340 HP was increased to 660—almost double. I reminded myself to buy Breeder an ale when next I saw him. Though Desini wouldn't do a lot of damage, that wasn't her function. She was there to be a meat shield.

"No good, dirty beast!" the standing bandit yelled, bringing his sword around for a second strike.

*Oh yeah, those are the right words to get her worked up.*

Since I wanted to give Desini a couple more seconds to garner hate, I quickly eyed the weapons the bandits carried, starting with the standing.

**Steel Short Sword**
Level 12
Slot: Weapon
Type: One-handed Sword

*Physical Damage: 11-18*
*Quality: Common*
*Durability: 12 of 17*
*Damage: 15-23*

Although I planned on leveling my assassin skills for interior combat situations, I'd stuck with woodsman for outdoors. After all, Guiles had recommended it, and I had a tank.

Wanting to gauge the distance and adjust my aim before I spent my limited mana pool, I fired a simple shot. The Silver-Tailed Swallow Arrow Zhara had gifted me flew fast and true.

### ***Silver-Tailed Swallow Arrow*** *hits!*

*Human Bandit*
*-31 HP*

*Your ranged attack skill has increased to rank 27.*

The NPC grunted as his body turned under the impact of the arrow, then he switched stances and balanced his sword in his grip as if he hadn't missed a beat. The arrow jostled in the shoulder of his off-hand. They hadn't looked all that tough. He seemed more confident than his ragged attire would've led me to think he'd be.

An orange glow surrounded Priya's weapon, and my interface showed her casting progress across a horizontal bar. Instead of a fireball zooming toward the target as I'd expected, a short wall of fire materialized and exploded in front of him. I stared in wonder as his flesh burned and blistered. Desini jumped back and covered her face from the explosion, but then shot a glance at Priya and her jaw dropped open.

*Priya casts **Flash Fire***

*Human Bandit*
*-21 HP*

*Priya's fire spells skill has increased to rank 2.*

*Hmm. Twenty-one damage and she has hardly even ranked the skill. Not a bad start.*

The victim of my tank's charge attack climbed to his feet.

I yelled, "Focus, Desini!"

Desini shuffled her feet and leaned to dodge an incoming attack. As a second came on its heels from the newly engaged target, she slid away fluidly and it was I who became distracted. I stood idle, an arrow nocked loosely to my string, in awe of her natural dance of avoidance, the way her flexible spine allowed her to bend in ways a human couldn't. She didn't even seem to need her sword to avoid the thrusts of the lower level characters.

*Can you imagine if she had a shield? Mental note: Get Desini a shield.*

After an agile dodge where Desini swung her hips to pivot away from an overhead attack, she spun and swept her sword up, across the target's body, then across in a horizontal arc. Blood spurted from her target's neck. My interface reported:

*Critical Hit!*

*Human Bandit*
*-47 HP!*

*Desini's sword skill has increased to rank 19.*
*Desini's sword skill has increased to rank 20.*

Her enemy fell to one knee as the other came around to attack. Desini didn't see the attack coming until it was almost upon her, but her spine folded backward so deeply, the glancing blow slid off of her breastplate. The cat-like woman surprised me again when she used the momentum to bring herself upright in a swiveling arc to reply with her pommel to his face, distracting her attacker and—

A wall of fire exploded next to the man teetering on his knees, blowing him onto his back. His face shriveled as I glanced at his health bar.

*Empty.*

*Priya has killed Level 15 Human Bandit.*
*Priya gains 138 XP*
*Priya's fire spells skill has climbed to rank 3.*
*You gain 149 XP*
*Desini gains 201 XP*

Priya's cudgel glowed again, then another Fire Flash hit the second attacker, who brought his head around. His attention flicked to Priya, and a sneer crossed his face. He launched away from Desini, bellowing as he charged, sword raised high in both hands, long tangles of black hair flowing behind him.

"Turn not your back on me, little man!"

Desini turned and roared! The enemy stopped short of us, his cheeks flooded red, and he whipped around. She swiped at him with her sword as he reentered the fray. Blood sprayed from his chest as he brought his weapon around. I glanced at his health bar and guessed it was at about 20 percent.

"Priya, see his health?"

"Yes!"

"Now, cast liberally and burn him down. If he comes at you, I'll finish him."

She nodded but didn't answer.

I prepared a Drilling Arrow in case we needed a finisher. While I was pleased I'd only had to fire a single arrow during the skirmish so far and hadn't even grazed my mana pool, I wanted to be prepared to drop this asshole if Priya pissed him off. I doubted she would, with the low damage resulting from the meager skill rank, but fire hurt.

Priya sneered, her face glowed, and her cheeks shone a healthy shade of pink as she raised the cudgel and burned that mother-humper down.

*Priya has killed Level 15 Human Bandit.*
*Priya gains 141 XP*
*Priya's fire spells skill has increased to rank 5.*
*You gain 155 XP*
*Desini gains 209 XP*

My smile stretched until it tugged both ears while Priya raised her fists in silent victory. Desini's state was... different.

Sword dangling in one hand, her shoulders hung low as she peered down at the fallen men. The sun beyond her cast this side of her plate in shadow and a fiery halo around her orangish hair.

Priya lowered her arms and inched closer to me, but her

gaze, too, was set on Desini.

My elven friend had either picked up on my emotions or, like me, was seeing something new about our most recent companion in the way she stood there, eyeing the dead. We watched in silence as I contemplated how the beautiful mishon might be reacting to falling her first two victims. I suddenly wished we shared a similar emotional bond.

Had I overestimated her excitement? Was the reality of what she'd done—

Desini raised her sword high, gripped the pommel with both hands, rose onto her tiptoes, and then slammed the point of the blade through the neck of the last man to fall, into the earth beneath.

"For your sins against my kind, you devil!" Again, she raised the sword and brought it down. A sickening thump combined with a meaty pop.

Priya raised a hand to her mouth and leaned closer to me.

Desini screamed in rage. "I will have the heads of all your kind! All who do evil to the defenseless! All who treat mine like fodder for your exploits!" Again she thrust the weapon, this time brutalizing his chest. "Die!"

Then she turned the weapon in her hand and hacked at the corpse. Blood sprayed into her face and splashed onto her chest plate and shorts.

The bandit's head rolled away. For a moment, I thought she'd go to work on the other one, but she thrust the sword into the earth with one hand, knelt so she could lean her head against the pommel, then muttered low words I couldn't hear.

Priya and I shared a glance and an uneasy smile. She pulled the neck of my armor down kissed my cheek. "You have unveiled my destiny... and hers."

## 29

Spine protruded from the headless corpse like a sickening antenna as Priya and Desini stood behind me, chattering excitedly. I patted him down.

"You move so quickly, Desini! I am so impressed by your reflexes!"

"And you cast your hot fire with such accuracy!"

"It is so, exhilarating! I love combat!" Priya exclaimed.

*Nerds.*

**Leather Vest of Defense**
*Level 14*
*Slot: Chest*
*Type: Armor*
*Quality: Uncommon*
*Durability: 48 of 50*
*+3 Defense against melee attacks*
*+1% chance to dodge*

I slipped the vest into my bag for future use. The 1%

chance to dodge would be great as an assassin, though the stats on my current piece were better for ranged damage.

### *Iron Short Sword*
*Level 11*
*Slot: Weapon*
*Type: One-handed sword*
*Quality: Common*
*Durability: 11 of 15*
*Damage: 8-11*
*+1 Melee Damage*

I slid the sword into one of my sheaths and tossed aside one of the Level 9 Iron Swords of Maiming I'd retrieved from the corpses on the road.

"That sword is not acceptable?" Priya asked.

"It's trash. I'd throw it in the saddlebags and try to sell it for a few coppers later, but who knows what we'll find ahead. You'd think someone with—"

*What? Game experience? Yeah, that will play well, dumbass.*

"Well," I continued, "you'd just think I'd know better than to let my inventory pile up."

"I will endeavor to remind you when we return. Gemini," Desini said. "I will go and negotiate prices on your equipment."

A red Jackson Pollock painted the back of her gear. I remembered how the chalices and plate Roshan and I found in a low-level dungeon had outfitted Desini. A nagging thought about the presence of those items in a low-level dungeon and how things didn't always seem on the up-and-up where my advancement was concerned rushed through my mind.

But I was tired of second-guessing. For once, I would enjoy the moment—the victory with my new team.

"I have little doubt you'll fetch three times the price I would, ma'am." I said as I continued patting down the second corpse.

*Medium health potion x 2*
*Restores 60 HP upon consumption*

I eyed my cat-like companion's health in the rectangular box where I set my party interface, on the left side of my field of vision. It was back up to ninety percent, and she hadn't used the health potion I'd given her. Other than a single cut on one hand that closed as I watched, they'd barely grazed her.

That rocked. Those extra points I put into her dexterity turned out to be a good idea. Dodging saved her HP. It'd been a lucky guess that a creature who appeared so dexterous would gain benefit from an increase in that stat. Most games wouldn't have acknowledged the dexterity at all, preferring constitution and strength for a tanking class. It was possible Enora saw my logic and adapted. I wouldn't put it past the A.I.

Either way, I took no small amount of pride in the decision.

"Desini, pocket these vials with the other health potion I gave you."

"Should we not distribute them?"

"Why, do you plan on letting someone attack Priya?"

She cocked her head to one side.

"What?"

I gripped the sides of her breast place and pulled her close so our faces were inches apart. It was time for a little soldier talk, even if I needed to keep it gentle. "What you just did exceeded my expectations. You held aggro, you pulled back the man who charged at us when you saw him move, and I was very impressed." I tapped her temple. "Now, I need you to absorb the measure of your responsibility while we're not in combat.

"I have entrusted you with the most important role in our party, Desini. Priya and I are your damage dealers. We are the ones who will bring down your enemies. So, your job is to always be alert. Always probe your environment for threats so when they come, you pick them up and get them good and pissed off at you."

I gripped Desini's hand that held the health potion.

"You are our greatest advantage because you are so many levels higher and naturally powerful. It helps you to keep enemies focused on you. But as we level higher, we will catch up to you because the amount of experience you need to advance becomes greater and greater from level to level. Our power will grow stronger, we will do more damage, and your job will become harder. So, it's vital that you practice your skills, get used to them, figure out the best order of their use, and ensure you keep enemies around you. You with me so far?"

Desini nodded, and her intent gaze confirmed.

"When we have a healer, Roshan will be primarily focused on you. She will gather a lot of aggro healing you so you can keep enemies away from us. Priya will piss them off, and they will charge her if you don't keep them aggro'd. As a damage-dealer from hell, she will be good practice for you. Keep her enemies at bay, and she won't need the health potions."

"Which means, since I am the target of all enemy damage, I am the one who should hold the potions."

"Exactly." I clapped her shoulder.

"Tell me what I could have done better, Gemini. I'm eager to serve with distinction."

The last thing I wanted to do was discourage Desini, but something in the way her gaze locked on me, the way she hung on every word, told me she could handle all the criticism I could dish out. Early in our fighting careers was the perfect time to coach.

"When he came at us," I pointed at one corpse. "you provoked and drew him back. That was very well-timed. But if you would have used Slice Achilles to slow his pace, he would never have even gotten close to us. I think what you did worked fine, but try it the other way next time. The pursuit of perfection requires experimentation."

"The way you talk," Priya said.

"Is perfect," Desini replied. She nodded curtly. "Next time, I will make my enemies bleed for daring to turn their backs."

"I love it." I kissed her cheek.

"Thank you." She stepped past Priya and checked on her horse. "It is good, how you teach me, master."

"What should I change, Gem? How might I improve?" Priya smiled at me.

"Keep using Fire Flash as your staple spell, time your casts, and try not to do too much damage in too short a period. You drew this one" —I nudged the corpse with the toe of my boot for emphasis— "toward us with your consecutive uses of Fire Flash, so maybe count off an extra second or two between casts. Apparently, it wasn't just the damage that pulled him, but the pain of your fire. I'm still guessing."

"Burn our enemies at a more reasonable rate." Her eyes flared. "This surging energy makes me flow with such excitement. It is like I am channeling Solara's fire, itself!"

"Also be mindful of the spells you haven't used yet. You'll want to break them out and start your own experiments."

I chuckled as she turned and pranced toward Desini and Pickney, but the laughter caught in my throat as her words cycled back through my mind.

*Channeling Solara's fire, itself.*

The woman who would be a mother to my child was over 100 years old and a magical creature beyond what her level dictated. I let people think I was a mythic with special abilities because it had suited their own narratives and complemented their own lore. Whether drawing that kind of attention was a mistake, only time would tell.

But Priya? I had the nagging feeling she was part of something bigger than the rest of us. That woman's destiny was intertwined with this continent's, which was only a small piece of the massive world I'd seen when I first zoomed out my map what seemed like weeks ago. Hard to believe it had only been days. I wondered if there were others like her spread out across that space for other players to enjoy similar stories. My narrative was a gift, whether I was being led forward, or not.

"This shit is fun," I muttered.

The way Priya's eyes had flared when she spoke of channeling Enora's power and the almost sensual energy she projected at having burned down her enemies gave me pause. Memories flashed of her scowling face—cute though it was—as she unleashed lightning hell upon the men threatening Desini on the road, the same way she'd pounded the spell into the dark figure in Warrington. I sensed her burning desire to unleash her anger and a confusion born of Zhara's betrayal, King Constantine Luttrell's erasure of her mind, and years of solitude in the forest.

Priya might be a sweet half-elf, but she would become powerful. Hell, she'd already been that, many years before. I might be a fine companion for her, and I certainly planned to be, but she needed someone who could truly balance her emotions instead of just sharing them.

*She needs Roshan.*

The young healer's maturity was unquestionable. The calming influence she exhibited in our first dungeon together suddenly seemed crucial to our success. The unwavering belief in the Light she wielded would serve us all by keeping us grounded, but confident. But if my suspicions were correct and the battles we'd fight on this continent would have a wider impact on the world, Priya would need Roshan most of all.

A mental swipe of my interface brought up the grayed-out picture of the woman we'd lost at the inn in Brumhill. With focus, I gave color to the image and gazed into the oversized eyes that turned slightly down on the outside corners.

*Roshan. Our balancer. Our conscience. I'm coming, and I'll kill anyone who stands in my way.*

Priya was still gazing at me, but her face had changed. "Your thoughts were of Roshan, just then."

"Yes."

"I dream about her." She flicked one fingernail against the other as she gazed down. "I sense your resolve, and I share it."

"Then let's keep moving, I want to get to Greycutter. We didn't get much XP here. That's the problem with having a higher-level tank—XP penalties. So, we will make up for it by killing as many enemies as we can."

"I like the sound of this," Desini said. "I shall lead us forward from now on, if it suits you, master."

*Master. She's devoted.*

"It suits me just fine, as do you, my prized student."

Desini stopped, her eyes wide. Bowing low, she showed me the top of her head. "I will fight for you until my death."

## 30

A couple hours later, we exited a cluster of pines and were greeted by the sound of rushing water. Just down the hill, a river flowed toward the sea in the east. White suds bathed shining black rocks along the opposite shore. Except for the strange stones, it reminded me of a creek I used to play around near an apartment complex when I was a kid, except wider. I'd seen my first snake swimming down that creek, an image fastened to my brain.

"Bear." Priya thrust out a finger.

I peered to the northeast and, sure enough, a brown bear with massive haunches and a wide, round face sat along the bank of the river, both paws prying open a fish's silvery scales, its gaping jowls stripping the pink flesh inside.

***Greycutter Grizzly***
*Level 16*
Disposition: Aggressive

*Just short of Desini's level. Probably lots of H.P. Might take a little time to bring him down.*

The grizzly peered up at us. It was cute, for a beast of its size. Too bad it would have to die.

"What do you think Desini? Ready for some real combat?"

Desini's eyes flashed wide. "Against a bear? Will that not be very painful?"

"I don't mean to trivialize your role, but *no pain, no gain*. The small health potion I gave you will replenish about twenty percent of your health. I would use that one first and keep the medium ones in reserve. You can use those if it gets you down to thirty-five percent, then we'll burn him down and let some of your HP recover naturally."

I reached into my bag and handed Priya a Melon Berry I'd bought from Tooli.

### Melon Berry
*+3 intelligence*
*Duration: One hour*

"That'll give you another level's worth of INT. The extra damage per cast will bring him down a little faster. Just remember not to overdo it. Let Desini keep him angry."

Priya took the strange fruit wrap and nibbled it. Her eyebrows ticked up, she smiled, then she shoved the fruit into her mouth. "Mmm. It's good."

She eyed the bag.

"No," I said.

She dropped her shoulders. "Ugh!"

I pulled out the last strip of deer jerky given me on the day I arrived in Enora and offered it to Desini.

"This will boost your stamina and give you a little more health to work with."

Desini scowled at it and shook her head.

"No, thank you, master." She turned toward the horse.

"What do you mean, 'no, thank you'?"

"If I am to fight a grizzly bear," she said without looking back, "I will use my food. In town, I noticed that since I have become an adventurer, food benefits are visible in my interface. I think you will approve."

She withdrew a small piece of cloth and turned back. She presented the unwrapped food for my analysis.

### Stone Ground Wheat
*+1% health every two seconds for 30 seconds*
*+2 Stamina for one hour*

"You've been holding out on me."

"It is a simple staple when you live on the road. I often chewed it as I traveled, but before it just looked like ground sprouted wheat. Now, it is a boon!"

"Right. A buff. Now chew it so we can attack."

A roar behind me and the expressions on my companions' faces brought me to whip around and yank my bow off my shoulder. The bear tore up the hill toward us, at a furious clip. It reminded me of the way my pudgy-but-strong porcupunk hauled its butt around.

"Go, Desini! Eat it now, charge that fucker, and use Roar to get it angry!"

Desini launched into action as Priya ran over to me.

"Stay calm, babe. Raise your weapon and get ready. Once she roars, you can cast."

Priya nodded, but fear burned in her eyes as she glared toward the looming threat, just like when we'd taken on the two bandits. But it was so unlike the Priya I'd known the last few days. Then realization dawned. Desini was the source of that aching gaze. It was our new tank she was worried about.

Well, Priya would have to harden the fuck up. My job was to make sure she did.

"Focus on your job and worry less about Desini." I thrust a finger out. "She doesn't look too worried to me."

Nocking an arrow as I heard the bellowing roar that had no business coming from Desini's lips, I aimed. The string gave a satisfying creak as I drew the arrow back, holding it near my ear. Yellow energy filled my hand and streamed into the arrow.

The grizzly raised onto its hind legs, swiping with both hands as it plunged toward Desini. The damn thing had to be nine feet tall. The glow of Priya's cudgel rose on my right. Just as her Fire Blast seared the bear's chest and Desini's sword swung around to take a chunk out of its shoulder, I sent an arrow zipping across the distance. It caught the grizzly right in the side of the head and it roared.

*Desini attacks Greycutter Grizzly.*

*Greycutter Grizzly*
*-17 HP*

*Priya casts Flash Fire.*

*Greycutter Grizzly*
*-21 HP*

*Priya's Fire Spells skill has is now rank 4.*
*Your Drilling Arrow strikes Greycutter Grizzly.*

*Greycutter Grizzly*
*-37 HP*

*+1 Ranged Skill*

Red text over Desini's head revealed damage as the bear swiped its paw across her chest!

*-31 HP*

That was fine. With over 600 HP, that was little more than a glancing blow.

But the other paw swiped upward, lifted Desini off the ground, then tossed her like a trout. The mishon flailed her arms in wild circles, and her sword went flying.

*Greycutter Grizzly uses* **Feral Sweep.**
*Desini*
*-109 HP*
*Desini is disarmed.*

Almost twenty percent of her health in one attack. This wasn't good.

"Baa!" Her wind escaped as she thumped hard onto her back. She blinked a couple times as the bear dropped to all fours to pursue.

"Desini! On your feet! Get your weapon!"

I cast Entangling Roots to stop the bear in its tracks, but I knew it wouldn't last long since it was higher level.

"Priya! Ice Storm! Now!"

I readied an arrow just as the grizzly broke free of my vines. They'd lasted only a couple seconds. I really needed to rank up my nature skills.

Desini rolled and scurried on her hands and knees before the grizzly had a chance to fall onto her.

I unleashed my arrow, having charged it with more mana than I'd intended.

*Your Drilling Arrow strikes Greycutter Grizzly.*

*Greycutter Grizzly*
*-47 HP*

...but for what I lost in the resource, I gained in damage done.

*If only it'd been a crit, but slim chance with it being higher level.*

The glow surrounding Priya's cudgel bloomed blue instead of orange, then a dark gray cloud appeared above the grizzly's lumbering form. Desini finally got to her feet, and though I'd thought the bear would close before she grasped her sword, ice pellets rained from the sky, and it halted.

*Priya casts Ice Storm.*
*Greycutter Grizzly is **slowed**.*

Blue waves shimmered outward from the center of ice pellets striking the bear's thick coat. The beast glared down at its foot and struggled to raise it. Then it raised the other and a clump of ground came up with its claws.

I readied another arrow, and Desini grabbed her sword then rolled away from a heavy claw swipe with impressive agility. When she gained her footing, her sword lashed out in a vicious swing that sliced up the grizzly's belly and right through its chin. A stream of gushing blood splattered in a line across Desini's breastplate and face. She spat and stepped forward as a blast of fire exploded before the massive beast.

I was thrilled with the way the battle went, though the powerful bear's attacks had toppled my tank on four occasions. The agility with which she recovered as she bounced to her feet each time was awe-inspiring, and she never dropped her sword a second time. Desini might not be a cat, but she sure moved like one. Her food kept her health propped up enough that she'd only expended the small health potion, despite the power of the initial strike that threw her to the ground.

Priya timed her spells perfectly and never pulled the grizzly's attention away from her tank. We all got some vital skill-ups and a nice bit of XP for the kill.

"Babe?" I asked.

"Yes?" She said as she clasped hands with Desini.

"Were you watching the damage output on your interface during that fight?"

Priya nodded, and a hint of pink colored her cheeks. "I figured out that, if I watch how much pain my spell inflicts, I can better control damage and make sure Desini keeps the bear's focus. Also, delaying my casts allows my mana pool to recover slightly, and my energy is more consistent. It gives me this airy sensation in my chest in my early casts, and I better maintain that sensation by waiting. Calculating? Is that the word?"

I nodded. "That is, indeed, the word. There seems to be no end to the surprises you keep in store for me, woman."

There was definitely pink in her cheeks this time.

Besides the crucial practice and my satisfaction at seeing how my partners in crime performed when things weren't easy, I also experienced that bright flash of light I loved.

Priya yelled, "Ding!"

*That was fast.*

*You have reached Level 14!*
*+1 Dexterity*
*+1 Constitution*

*You have learned the skill:*
***Perforating Arrow*** *(Rank Two)*
*An armor-piercing ability with an effective range of sixty yards*
*Loses damage with additional distance traveled*
*Adds 11-15 damage to ranged attacks.*
*Skill Cost: 40 Mana*
*Cast Time: Instant*
*Longer draws use more mana but cause more damage.*
*Cool-down: 15 seconds*

"Awesome!" I yelled in victory. My log showed we'd gained a significant amount of discovery experience as we'd crossed the valleys and hillsides over the previous day. Though I couldn't figure out why Priya hadn't leveled, since we gained our last ones simultaneously, she was very close to doing so. She was still a few hundred XP from advancement.

I was Level 14 now. The quest to save Roshan recommended Level 16, and though Desini was Level 17, I worried about Priya. She was still too low at Level 11—and squishy from a health perspective—and I feared we might meet more resistance than the quest suggested inside the gates of a city. Since I had no idea how we would fare or what we were up against, it made sense to complete these quests, stack our attributes as much as possible, then go in guns blazing. We had a couple days.

I reached into my bag for a piece I'd won from our first battle together, in the hills before we arrived in Greycutter.

***Leather Vest of Defense***
*Level 14*
*Slot: Chest*
*Type: Armor*
*Quality: Uncommon*
*Durability: 48 of 50*
*+3 Defense against melee attacks*
*+1% chance to dodge*

Happy with damage output against the higher-level beast, I spent two points on Intelligence to increase my mana pool. I had two offensive skills that used mana— Drilling Arrow and Perforating Arrow. Besides, someday I'd want to wield spells, and Roshan had already set me on the path to Light Magic. But when I spent the two points, I became woozy. Roshan had mentioned such a sensation when I'd leveled the same attribute. I likened it to the lifting of a fog, like my mind felt lighter.

*Shit!*

***G3m1n1 Fowler***
*Shénhuà*
*Level 14 Woodsman*
**Attributes:**
*Strength: 6*
*Dexterity: 30*

*Intelligence: 3*
*Wisdom: 1*
*Constitution: 28*
*Charisma: 10*
**Combat Skills:**
*Ranged: 24*
*Unarmed: 1*
*Melee: 13*
*Dual-Wield: 6*
**Defensive Skills:**
*Dodge: 5*
**Weapon Skills:**
*Bow: 17*
*Blunt: 7*
*Dagger: 30*
*Thrown: 2*

Priya guided me as I skinned the bear, and my skill climbed five points by the time I was done. In other games, I just hovered over a button to skin a beast. But in Enora, the experience required cutting and realism all the way down to the scent. Another unique facet was that I'd never received more than a single point in the skill per animal. The longer I worked at separating the bear pelt from its carcass, the more points I got. The ticks seemed to come when Priya showed me how to detach it from different parts of the body as well. To my credit, I only gagged once and never vomited.

We gutted the beast under Desini's guidance. We set aside its intestines in all their grossness, then sliced away at its meat. The coppery scent was overwhelming.

I still had limited capacity in my bag, but we soaked a few chunks in the river and wrapped them on the inner side of bearskin scraps to stow them there, instead of making a bloody mess of the packs hanging from the horse's back. After all, it was a magic bag. It didn't have an inside to get dirty... just a void from which I drew items. Plus, it preserved things.

I was surprised to find myself only covered in grizzly blood up to my elbows when we finished. That one pelt would get us more XP and a little coin when we returned to town, and Desini said she would show me how to cook up the bear steaks when we camped on our return trip.

The blood gave me an excuse to coax my skinning teacher into the river so we could bathe together. Then things turned to another natural tendency. For a while, she arched her back beneath me on a reflective black slab of rock as we enjoyed a perfect rhythm. I tattooed that image on my brain.

Desini stood watch. I think my tank was hoping to take on an enemy solo as Priya and I enjoyed each other. When we'd dressed and returned to her, she smiled grandly.

"The two of you make love sweetly, but with such hunger."

"If ever you have a man again, Desini, you should try him. He'll treat you with respect and give you great pleasure."

Warmth flooded my face.

Desini's response gave no indication, either way.

"Hmm, yes. Sweet indeed." She swept her gaze toward the grass for a moment and muttered. "Not what I've known of human men."

That was a damper. The half elf's lips pinched into a white line, but she relaxed them again when Desini looked up.

"We must continue to advance if we are to retrieve your

healer, yes?" Desini asked, reclaiming her fighter's smile, filled with her pointed canines.

"Absolutely," Priya said with her enthusiastic smile.

Before nightfall, we came upon a herd of deer. Literally, a herd. I knew it would be like shooting fish in a barrel to engage with my bow and Priya's spells, but I felt pressed to get to Greycutter Downs. It was Desini's voice who shone a light on the conundrum.

"You seek to advance, but you focus on what will be more intelligent prey at Greycutter Downs. Would it not benefit us to level up with these creatures so that we might be better prepared for human prey this evening?"

Her logic was sound. We killed and skinned four of them. Though she'd been right and we could've bagged more with a few lightning pulse spells bouncing around, Desini put a halt to it, reminding us of our time constraints and that it was good to leave what we might not be able to carry on the way back.

To save time, the three of us skinned. We kept from getting messy this time as we peeled away the outer skin from the inner muscle. When I stepped away for a stretch while my companions worked, I was surprised to find I gained skill points just by observing their technique! It was about time Enora gave something up without making me want to stab myself in the eye for it!

My skinning skill was up to 17 by the time they finished.

The glowing golden quest line painted a path for us to follow, and we soon spotted the rocky outcropping Merk had described. We crept along quietly, keeping ourselves in the shadows of the rocks cast by the moon above. A trail formed where the grass ended and proof of recurring footfalls revealed itself. I scanned the area ahead and spotted light shimmering in the distance.

"That's the inlet," I whispered. "Hard to see anything beyond the drop off ahead."

"Should I use my Mystic Sight spell?" Priya asked.

"I forgot all about that spell! Yes! Let me get my map open." I opened the map with a thought. "Okay, cast away."

Priya raised a hand, then a purplish hue surrounded her fingers. My chest thumped when her eyes rolled up into her head, but she nodded, so I knew she was okay. But it was still spooky.

"See the buildings? There are men down there."

Not only did Priya's spell show her the scene below the drop-off, and not only did my map clear the Fog of War where she'd cast, but my interface carved out a translucent square in which I shared her vision! "Babe..."

The perspective twirled in a slow circle as if she'd done this a million times. She spotted a man in leather similar to gear worn by the two we'd taken down in the hills. He leaned against a wall, sitting on a worn crate, arms folded across his chest with a spear leaning next to him as he snoozed. A quiet ping snagged my focus. A tiny red X appeared on my map.

"It's marking enemies," I whispered.

Priya didn't respond as she focused on the task at hand. She swung her perspective as if she were pivoting in the center of her spell's area of effect. The effect blurred beyond the point of its influence, like we gazed at a translucent barrier.

The lookout snoozed on a rocky rise that crept down another trail to a lower area, where men slept in bedrolls outside a small building. Orange embers of a forgotten fire at the sleepers' feet glowed in the cold breeze coming off the inlet.

"Priya, show me the guy on the rise again. Can you turn around?"

"Yes," she said, her voice distant. "But my cast is about to expire."

She turned her spell's perspective to face the man. I tried to inspect him, but it didn't work.

*Oh, well, you can't have everything.*

"Can you zoom out, like to a sky view?"

Priya squeezed her eyes closed tighter, and the perspective shifted, rising from the ground and causing me a moment of vertigo. She mumbled in awe, "It's like I'm a bird, flying."

On the opposite side of the shack, another lookout snoozed.

The square vanished.

"I'm sorry, Gemini."

"For what? That was epic!"

"Oh. Well, good!"

"Shh!" Desini admonished us. "Perhaps you should have opted to be a Necromancer someday if you would raise slumbering bones, anyway."

Her meaning took a second to register. "Are you saying we would wake the dead?"

"Is this not what I said? Did you not learn to creep over branches in all that time in the forest?"

"What? Three days? I'm not a Ninja."

Priya and I glanced at Desini, then at each other. Our shoulders rose to shrug in sync. I opened party chat.

*Party [Gemini:] Okay. I want to try something. Can you two open your maps?*

They both blinked in succession and nodded.

*Party [Gemini:] Good. Do you see the red Xs?*

They nodded again.
I tapped the X with my mind and it turned black. That was really awesome.

*Party [Gemini:] Did you see that?*
*Party [Priya:] Yes.*
*Party [Gemini:] That's our first target.*

Desini smiled a wicked smile.

*Party [Desini:] I will run him through before his eyes open.*
*Party [Gemini:] Actually, I think I have a more efficient plan.*
*Party [Desini:] You will change tactics?*
*Party [Gemini:] Yeah. Stealth time.*

## 31

I clutched my daggers and waited out my global abilities' cool-downs as I slowly descended a beaten path beneath the moonlight. I was ecstatic to find increases in my stealth ability made me less reliant on shadows to stay concealed, as indicated by the steady blackness of the eye symbol on my right-hand side. Due to the stationary nature of Priya's seeing spell, it was a mystery how many people might be inside the building near the campfire or the larger one near the dock. Although I knew my elven trainer from Brumhill would have doubts about my using assassin skills, I needed to keep things quiet as I executed the plan Desini, Priya, and I had hashed out. I'd gained three levels since he'd trained me, and my stamina had bloomed an extra sixty points.

I reviewed the two primary abilities I'd use.

***Sneak Attack*** (*1st Tier*)
*Skill Cost: 30 Stamina*
*Cast Time: Instant*
*Damage: 300% Weapon Damage*

*+15% chance of Critical Hit for 5 seconds*
*(Requires Stealth)*

### Spine Snap

*Skill Cost: 30 Stamina*
*Cast Time: Instant*
*Damage: 200% Weapon Damage*
*10% chance of bleed effect causing 2 damage per second for*
*10 seconds*

Heart thumping against my ribs, I rolled my feet slowly from heel to toe, remembering patience was the order of the day if I didn't want to incite a riot. I was practically on top of the first guard before his eyes so much as twitched.

### Unknown Fighter
*Level 14*

*Fighter.* These men had selected classes, which meant someone had trained them, maybe only five attribute points each. I couldn't tell, but if they weren't fully trained as to attributes, they'd be weaker. Hopefully, that meant less constitution. I wished the A.I. would tell me.

*Pain in my ass.*

I slipped closer to the guard then clapped a hand over his mouth as I put my daggers to work.

*You* **Sneak Attack** *the fighter.*
*Critical hit!*

*Fighter*
*-51 HP*

The resulting groan as I plunged my knife into his back caused me to jerk, but I didn't think it had been loud enough to alert the other guard over the breeze from the inlet. I ripped the dagger away, then slammed it into the side of his neck, silencing him. Blood spilled from his lips, and I pulled my hand away from his mouth. Murder was a messy business.

*You **Spine Snap** the fighter with your off-hand dagger.*
*Critical hit!*

*Fighter*
*-60 HP*
*(Bleed)*
*-11 HP*

*You stab the fighter with your dagger.*
*Critical hit!*
*Mortal Wound!*

*Fighter*
*-61 HP*
*(Bleed)*
*-7 HP*

*You have defeated a Level 14 fighter.*
*475 XP*
*+10 Reputation with Warrington*
*Current Reputation: Neutral*
*10/200*

*Awesome. Faction rep.*
The guard's eyes rolled back in his head as he slouched

and slid off his box. I gripped his vest and lowered him to the loose earth. I theorized my Sneak Attack and the guard's lack of ready defenses had greatly increased the possibility of a critical hit because consecutive *crits* weren't commonplace. It was nice knowing that initiative counted for something.

A quick glance at my interface confirmed my suspicion about the XP gained from the kill. The enemies we'd vanquished early that morning had granted us less experience, though their levels had been similar. A glance at my companion tab showed Priya was still Level 11. Since she and Desini were still on the far end of the path, waiting in the shadows of the outcropping, they hadn't shared in the experience gain.

The guard had lost 190 HP. At level 14, that meant ten points max had been spent toward his constitution. Not a full spread, so he wasn't trained up, especially since he'd likely earned some of that naturally. That bode well for our chances with the others and lent doubt whether Blackbard had the ability to train his people. It was the first time in a game world where I'd seen NPCs suffer for a lack of training. The shit was pretty original.

A cursory glance at his possessions revealed nothing helpful, so I dropped them on the ground. I didn't want to lose the loot if the corpse vanished, but I didn't want to waste the inventory space by carrying them. The horse should be able to traverse the trail down here later with no problems. My stealth skill reached the end of its cool-down, and I reengaged it.

I crept around in the shadows until I sighted the men sleeping at the bottom of the short hill. Satisfied they were still none the wiser, I snuck over to the second guard on the opposite side of the shack and verified my stamina had recovered. The way he leaned sideways and slumbered with one shoulder against the outer wall, I had a plain view of his back. Something darker than the surrounding flesh on his neck caught my attention. I inched toward him and peered down.

*A bird tattoo.*

I recalled Merk's buckle with the Greycutter bird for which the area was named, and this tattoo seemed to match it. The sprawling wings spread down the bottom of his neck, and a long beak ran up his spine to disappear behind his ragged, knife-cut hair. I guessed was a local who'd been recruited by the former pirate band turned road thieves. Maybe a former fisherman.

*Nice ink, bud.*

And the tattoo would make a great target.

Though I got no indicator of a critical hit, the gurgling sound as my blade slipped into his flesh combined with an audible pop told me I'd severed his spine. Just for good measure, I followed-up with a backstab.

He slumped to the ground. I patted him down, then raced over to the trail where I raised my hand to signal my companions.

"Alarm! Raise the alarm!" a voice cried from behind me.

I turned to find a man gripping a spear as he rushed down the hill, away from me, toward the slumbering men sleeping below.

*Shit! We missed a patrol!*

As Priya and Desini came into view at the far end of the trail, I waved my arm furiously. They sprinted toward me as I ran to the edge of the drop-off, where the steep trail declined to the sleeping crew below. I reengaged stealth—or I tried to, but it didn't work.

*He spotted you! You're in combat mode!*

There were six men. A quick glance at each revealed they were all between Levels 12 and 15.

*Okay, okay.*

Still struggling to shed their bedrolls, the men reached for their various weapons. It was almost comical, watching one of the Level 12s trip and tumble face-first.

I scurried down the trail toward the guard who'd sounded the alarm, since he was the closest.

"Hey, fuck face. What? You need all these guys to take on one dude? I'm right here, shit head."

The guard raised his spear and charged toward me.

I jumped through the puff of purple smoke with more confidence than ever before as he closed the last few steps in my direction. Instead of stabbing him when I materialized at his back, I slipped off to one side and started up the hill. I'd never intended to attack. I just needed to get into stealth, and Shadow Merge required a target to activate.

When I reached the top of the hill and peered back to find the guard turning in circles, seeking me out, my first inclination was to switch to my bow and try to injure a few bandits before they reached the crest, but then I had the element of surprise if I stayed in the shadows, provided I remained still enough.

Just as Desini and Priya rounded the curve in the trail leading around the shack, two men reached the crest of the hill about ten feet from me. Three men trailed them as one near the campfire raised a bow and nocked an arrow.

*Shit.*

Desini burst forward, slamming one bandit to the ground as the other swung at her. Priya stopped at the curve of the trail near the corner of the shack and cast from about thirty feet away—the outside range of her spell.

*Perfect.*

As Desini engaged the second man, I had a decision to make. The global cool-down if I changed my class would render me less effective, especially against the higher-level MOBs. If I attacked the level twelve Desini engaged, and we downed him, I would reveal myself, showing my back to the higher-level men coming up the hill.

Most concerning was the Level 15 archer at the bottom of the hill. If he climbed and spotted Priya, that ranged battle might get ugly.

I slipped down the hill, past the charging men, sweeping a wide path around the archer and hoping he wouldn't spot me. The sounds of metal striking metal floated to me from behind as Desini grunted. Explosions filled the night—Priya's Fire Flash. A soldier screamed.

As I closed on the archer and raised my dagger, he ran up the hill. I fell in behind him, but with the movement speed penalty while I was shrouded, it quickly became clear he would see Priya before I could Sneak Attack him. I noted the small building in the distance, closer to the water, with a small window through which a soft light emanated. I thought it far enough that no one inside would've heard anything over the sounds of the waves near the shore, but I glanced in that direction just to be sure.

We already had our hands full.

*Party:* [G3m1n1:] *Priya, you've got an archer coming up the hill.*

Though she wasn't visible from the incline, an ear-shattering roar told me Desini had just drawn aggro to keep her assaulter away from Priya. With four men surrounding her, it would get hairy in a short second, despite her higher level.

I closed on the archer just as he drew back his arrow,

and I swallowed a lump when I realized he wasn't aiming at Desini.

Priya was the only other option. I wouldn't reach him, and the glow surrounding his hand told me he was about to unload a special ability into his arrow before firing at my caster.

My *squishy* girlfriend caster.

I was about to just break stealth so I'd be fast enough to stab him with a simple strike when his shoulders slumped and his arrow dropped to the ground. He kept his clutch on the bow, somehow.

*WTF?*

Three little Zs appeared over his head. A low hum emitted from him as I approached.

*Snores.*

Priya put him to sleep!

> *Party: [G3m1n1:] Good job! Holy shit!*
> *Party: [Priya:] I'm stone like that.*
> *Party: [G3m1n1:] You rock like that.*
> *Party: [Priya:] Piss off. I'm busy.*

The archer was best left to waver on his feet since we were outnumbered and Desini would need help, so I crested the hill and assessed the battle. Blood poured from somewhere beneath her chest armor and down her arm. Any relief I'd felt when Priya put the archer to sleep vanished at the sight. Four men surrounded her, swinging their swords, jabbing their spears. Her feline dance mesmerized as she ducked, pivoted, twisted, and swung. I didn't understand how she swayed her hips like that, at just the right moments to dodge the incoming spear jabs, while swinging her sword to deflect incoming blows from the others.

She was supposed to be a noob.

I cursed myself for not summoning one of my pets. Now I'd have to break stealth to do it, and I reasoned my damage bonuses attacking from my shroud would be worth waiting for.

Despite her natural dodges, blows landed, and Desini faltered backward every few seconds, giving ground and then cutting wide arcs with her sword to keep her enemies at bay. I peered up at her health bar to find it less than half full. Her sword flashed in the moonlight as she swung in a circle and sliced at all her attackers as I closed in.

*Swipe skill... nice.*

A flash of fire exploded in the face of one of the Level 15s, causing him to fall back for a second. Turning his attention to Priya, he lunged. Desini swept her sword at his legs and sliced him open so a splatter of blood spat to the ground.

*Slice Achilles!*

He continued toward Priya, but his movement speed was crippled as he dragged one leg behind him. Desini roared to reacquire his attention.

I scanned the group around Desini, eyeing the lowest level enemy then creeping behind him. As my Sneak Attack pounded his shoulder blade, he lunged forward, shook violently for a moment, then raised his sword to attack Desini again. I activated backstab, aiming for his spine, but I missed an inch to the right. That didn't mean I failed to garner his attention. Turning, he drew back his spear.

I tensed, raising my daggers, hoping to parry the spear when he jabbed. He lunged. I parried then twirled around, swinging both my daggers toward his neck. Blood splattered, but he kept thrusting. The spear found purchase in my thigh, and I cried out as electric pain shot through my leg. Blood spurted, and 20% of my health vanished.

*Vanished...*

I stepped through space and time, thankful the cooldown on *Shadow Merge* had expired. I activated Sneak Attack, slit a long gash parallel to the man's spine, then shoved his ass with my boot for good measure. He rolled down the hill. A shock of pain slithered up my back, and I tumbled to the ground as a hulking Level 16 stepped over me.

My health was down to 35% and I had a bleed effect going, to boot.

Raising his sword in a reverse grip, he aimed at plunging it through me and smiled through a stream of blood pouring from his nose and across his teeth.

I was kind of pissed off. I'd done nothing to grab this man's aggro from Desini, except kill one of his friends. Once again, Enora was showing me my experience in other games had little to do with this world.

A tattering sound surrounded us as a chill filled the air.

The man standing over me peered up at the sky as frozen pellets littered the ground. Somehow, I was untouched by the falling ice, but as I watched in awe it sliced at his skin, each impact turning his flesh blue. Slits opened revealing red meat. Rolling up to my backside then swiveling onto my knees, I thrust my dagger up and into his abdomen just as the blade of a sword ripped through his chest, missing my face by inches.

"Ah!" I rolled backward and scurried to my feet. Desini ripped her blade out of the man's back.

*Priya freezes and slows him, and Desini runs him through. Those two just saved my ass.*

Another attacker was down, just beyond Desini. Two melee fighters remained, Levels 15 and 16. In the distance, Priya's hands raised in the air. Blue light engulfed her body, channeling the final seconds of her Ice Storm spell.

I tried to sneak up on the 16, but I couldn't access Stealth in combat mode. My Merge skill was still on cool-down, so I lunged forward and activated Backstab. My knife landed in the higher-level's kidneys, but he stepped forward, swung around, and struck me in the side of the head with the pommel of his sword.

The world spun as another flash of fire burst into the night, dropping the Level 15 on Desini's left to the ground, where he clutched his face, writhed in pain, then lay still.

My gaze flicked to the party interface, and I found Desini's health was down to 15%.

"Desini! Potion! Now!"

Blood running down her cheeks from a gash across her forehead, her eyes went wide as they flickered to me. A potion appeared in her hand and she chugged it. Her health jumped back up to 35% as I rolled to my feet. Not as much HP recovery as I'd have liked. Now her potion use was on cool-down.

The man who'd struck with his pommel had returned his attention to my tank, so I raised my hand. A blue glow surrounded it. Moments later, a portly black and white animal with long flesh hairs jostling on its back peered at me in the darkness.

*It clicked.*

"Kill something," I said.

Click turned and scaled the back of the man who'd pommeled me as I scurried to my feet.

*Yeah, that shit is on now.*

My health was at 29%, but I saw no bleed effects. The advantage was suddenly ours, at four-to-one.

*I like those odds.*

If only things were ever that easy.

"Gemini!" Priya's finger jutted toward the space behind me. As I turned, I found the archer nocking a new arrow, aimed at her. I lunged at him just as Desini roared her provoke spell, but the archer was out of range, and we were both too late. The arrow sailed across the air, slammed into Priya's neck, and sent her tumbling to the ground.

Just before she fell, messages erupted in red text above her head:

*Critical hit!*

*Mortal Wound!*

"Ahhh!" I screamed as I closed the final few steps and launched myself into the air. The archer tried to turn his bow on me, but I threw my arms around his waist as our bodies collided and sent him crashing to the ground. The mother fucker gasped as the air left his lungs.

I pushed myself to my knees. In primal rage, I activated Combat Flurry. My arms zipped in an onslaught of blurry strikes. His arms came up and I stabbed them furiously. Then I swung around them, stabbing him in the neck and face, over and over until his own mother wouldn't have recognized him. Blood spewed onto my arms, hands, and face as I punched with the blades like Guiles had taught me. The archer's health meter dropped to zero as critical hit messages flooded my field of vision.

Huffing and puffing, with my stamina meter suddenly blinking red, I turned to find Desini slamming her sword against that of her enemy in hard, overhanded arcs. Click jumped down from his shoulder as my tank beat the man down, closer to the ground with each strike as horror painted his face. A gaping hole in his neck revealed the damage my pet had thrown in.

As Desini's target fell, she twirled her sword with a flourish then marched to the man and growled as she stood over him. He raised his hands as I turned my attention to Priya.

A green skull and crossbones blinked next to her health bar as her H.P. dipped below five percent. When she died, she'd re-spawn at Prantu's place. I had nothing for the poison that mangled stack of bloody meat behind me had inflicted upon her. It was my first experience with poison in Enora.

I crawled toward her.

"Priya! It's okay, Priya. We'll come back for you at—"

Desini thrust her sword down with a fearsome howl. Her victim gurgled out a final yelp and died.

A golden light filled the night air across Priya's body and her health jumped to 100%.

*Your companion Priya Skyy has reached Level 12!*
*Priya has gained four attribute points.*
*With Beloved status, you may spend four attribute points on*
*Priya.*

I huffed and puffed wildly as I rolled onto my back. Despite my lack of wind, I laughed into the dark sky. Moments later, Priya stood over me.

"Is something funny?"

I laughed harder, gripping my belly as my stamina replenished itself.

"That fucking hurt!" She rubbed the spot in her neck

where the arrow had impaled her. It had vanished. "That was really close! Why are you laughing?"

"I'm sorry," I gurgled through the laughter. "I'm sorry."

She sneered at me, banged me in the chest armor with her cudgel, and stuck her tongue out.

Then she smiled.

*I guess the second mortal wound is easier, especially if you survive it.*

"Should we search the bodies?" Desini asked.

"Always. Drop everything on the ground, then we'll load the horse up when we leave, assuming these guys don't re-spawn. That sort of thing seems to be touch and go. I haven't figured out how it works."

Desini shrugged as if this made perfect sense. "Solara takes their energy when they die and decides when to take what is left behind. Who are we to wonder?"

"Someone is more worldly than I," Priya said. "You sure you don't want to trade me for her, *master?*"

I spoke to Desini as if Priya hadn't fired her snark cannon. "If you see a better sword, take it. Leave the crap."

Desini nodded, but I thought I spied a shade of pink in her round cheeks.

I peered down at the inlet and again spotted a dim light projecting through a window in the building preceding the rickety pier.

"I'm guessing that's where we'll find the boss. I can move down there unseen. Stay in the shadows. I'll do recon, then we'll come up with an infiltration plan." I peered at

Priya for confirmation, but she stared off toward the water, rubbing her neck. I grasped her hand.

"I'm fine. I just..." She blinked a few times.

I pursed my lips, realizing she'd been sarcastic to distract herself from the trauma.

"I think it's the kind of thing we get used to, after a time. Sometimes things go sideways. We should make every effort to stay on our feet, but experience will help with that as much as anything. Remember, it'll be better when we have a healer. In the meantime, I gave you four points of Constitution because that scared the shit out of me."

"Your words reassure me, Gem. Thank you."

I squeezed her hand then set off down the steep incline toward the pier.

Though the building's boards were muted by age, the scent was unmistakable. The structure must have once been a fishery.

The breeze brought muttering off the inlet. On the east side, I spotted crates stacked on the outer wall and stepped closer to investigate. I expected them to be flimsy and weather-beaten, but they were just the opposite. Though a layer of salt and sea muck covered their outer edges, the insides still smelled of wood. A moment of reasoning revealed the contents had been prizes of the attacks on travelers along the roads, mostly garments.

After a quick look across the pier to ensure I'd missed no scouts or patrols, I quietly stacked the crates beneath a dingy window and engaged my stealth. Stepping up, I peered through the filthy glass.

An oil lamp inside cast the space in a dim glow at this end of the long building. Rows of metal troughs confirmed this had once been used for fish processing. I thought about how awesome it would be if the people of Warrington could reclaim this place and add the fish back into their diets. It might be a boon for my party's reputation in the area. That could get us special pricing with the vendors. Also, I'd bet fishing was an occupation in this game. Gods knew it had everything else.

"Two is not enough," a burly man with a long, curly black beard said as I peered inside. His voice traveled through the cracks in wood surrounding the window. "Governor Zane wants us to take it up a notch. The more trouble we make, the better. Have Guntil and his group returned?"

*Guntil, the guy I killed in Brumhill.*

"All five unaccounted for, boss. They're two days late."

*Had his compatriots who fled our conflict decided not to come back?*

"That's unlike him."

"We haven't heard from Rupert and Jorel, either."

The bearded man tapped his fingers on a worn wooden tabletop and sipped from a mug. I spied a small keg with a spout plunged into one end nearby on a table near the wall. Just across from it, on the other side of the window, leaned a fat-bodied instrument with shining wood on its face, polished to a high sheen.

*A lute.*

I recalled Roshan telling me she'd played when she was younger. That might make a nice gift.

"Someone on the road is taking matters into their own hands, I think," the curly bearded man I assumed was Blackbard said. "If the governor gets wind we aren't slowing trade, we could become of disuse. He might seek other options. How many do we have left to stir things up?"

So, these aren't pirates, they're mercenaries. Mayor Graples in Warrington had mentioned the trade deficit. It seemed this Governor Zane, who I suspected was the Governor of Knall, really did want his taxes.

"We have the eight outside and ten harassing the travelers on the road north of Warrington, to Trowlsby."

"If we've lost Guntil and his men, and Rupert and Jorel do not return, we will have to go to Trowlsby and recruit more from the affected guilds."

I could tell by his strong concern for his men that Blackbard was a conscientious individual.

"The governor might get wind of such efforts, Blackbard. Perhaps we should try Brumhill. Surely some of those—"

"What?" Blackbeard interrupted. "Peasants?"

"Well, yes. A hungry man will work harder and has fewer... moral limitations."

"Bah!" Blackbard waved his hand dismissively. "We need men with muscle on their bones. Otherwise, we end up feeding them for weeks before we can send them out!" He banged the side of his fist on the table a few times.

I blinked each eye in succession.

***Blackbard***

*Human*

*Level 20 Bard*

*You have completed a quest!*

***Blackbard?***

*You have confirmed Blackbard is the leader of the bandits who have been terrorizing the roads.*

*Reward: 1,000 XP*

*So, Bard is actually a profession in Enora. No one's done that in forever. I wonder what the subclass is?*

I inspected Blackbard's companion.

### *Chims*
*Fire Mage*
*Level 18*

Rustling nearby caused me to turn my head. Priya and Desini knelt beside the crate. Though it was a tribute to their subtle steps that they got so close without my noticing them, my heart thumped in my chest. I let out a long, slow breath.

"Go and rouse five men. I want them to find our people and report. Tell them not to bother travelers for now. Just find out what happened to our teams."

"Sure, boss."

Boots clicked on loose planks as the mage made for the exit.

I slipped off the crate and knelt next to my team. I whispered, and it still felt too loud with only lapping water in the distance for sound cover.

"The mage is coming out. We need to take him down fast and then focus on Blackbard."

Desini nodded.

Priya did not. "Perhaps I should sleep this mage so you can shove a dagger into his throat."

"He might have magic resistance. My checks don't show me that. If you fail the cast, he will sound the alarm, then we'll have an 18 and a 20 on us."

Priya wrinkled up her lips. "Level 20. This is high. Perhaps we have overstepped."

I answered her with one word. "Roshan." Priya nodded, and doubt morphed into determination on her features.

Buff icons from food effects still appeared below their avatars on my party interface. I outlined my plan.

I activated Stealth so I could watch the mage. With his high level compared to mine, I stuck to the shadow cast by the building against the moonlight to ensure Desini drew first blood. The mage turned left out of the building and paced toward the sleeping rolls where the men had been only moments ago... before we killed them. He used a staff of dark wood like a walking stick as he ascended, tapping the ground at intervals.

Desini circled to fall in behind him at a safe distance. My mishon friend's cat-like agility made for such silent movement that I wondered fleetingly what kind of assassin she might have made. Then I recalled how she'd avoided the strokes of four men swinging swords and jabbing at her with spears.

*Tank. Definitely tank.*

When the mage approached the ashes where the campfire had been, he peered left and right, looking for Blackbard's men.

*Party: [G3m1n1:] Now!*

Desini lunged forward as he pivoted and thrust her sword at his chest.

The mage spun in a circle, his robe flailing, shrouding his form as his hands rose into the air and glowed orange. Desini slid right past him on one side as he twirled and bumped her with his hip. She stumbled and recovered, but we were already blown.

"Blackbard! Intruders!"

"Click!" I yelled. "Go!"

My porcupunk launched from the shadows of the fishery. The mage raised his staff, and a meter appeared over his head though it didn't reveal what he was casting.

*Shit.*

My pet slid to a halt and began to rock side-to-side.

*Party: [G3m1n1:] Dammit. He put Click to sleep. Go! Kill!*

Clattering inside the fishery traveled to my ears across the port breeze, and I measured my distance to the mage. Sticking to the shadows as Blackbard circled around, I waited for my chance to lunge.

The weapon the pirate leader clutched was not made of metal, but of wood and strings. He held the lute to his considerable belly and began to fingerpick notes. As I approached, he strummed a finishing chord, then an unseen energy slammed into Desini's back.

She tumbled forward but gripped the mage's robe before she fell, pulling him to the ground with her. As they struggled, rolling in a meshing of cloth robe and metal armor, black and purple circles surrounded Blackbard's head. He peered around to his left, then the other direction at the sight of the incoming spell, but I'd had Priya conceal herself from view among the rocks. She had line-of-sight to the pirate, but she kept her hands low, behind the cover of stone, and it had worked.

Blackbard resisted the Sleep spell. Charging forward, he strummed the strings several times. Above his head I saw text flash and rise toward the top of my interface.

*Ballad of the Sea*

A red bar appeared above his and the mage's heads and grew an inch to the right.

A health buff.

I pulled my daggers back and activated Sneak Attack.

"Ahh!" Blackbeard screamed as one of my blades entered his shoulder. I readied the other for a Spine Snap, but he spun around with an agility I wouldn't have given him credit for and stunned me with an elbow. As I tried to regain my feet, he reached into his belt, withdrew a long wooden object with a fat head, then clocked my temple.

A hollow *thunk!* rang through my head as I thudded to the ground. Blackbard lunged and stomped his boots down inches from my head as I rolled.

"Ahhhh!" A bellow pierced the night.

Blackbard spun around then charged.

I struggled to sit up and caught sight of the mage running up the hill where we'd massacred his cohorts, trying to avoid Desini's blows. Blackbard brought up the rear of the trio.

The mage threw his arm up to protect himself from an explosion of fire that halted his ascent. Desini swung her sword at the mage's leg and connected.

*Slice Achilles.*

The mage limped to casting range, but Desini bore down on him.

Priya's casting bar appeared over her avatar icon in my HUD as she prepared to strike with her fire spell again.

The mage whipped around, swirled his arms out in front of him, and vanished in a cloud of smoke I could barely see against the night.

Priya's cast halted.

*WTF?*

My interface gave me the name of the ability.

*Flash*

The mage reappeared at the bottom of the hill, twenty-five feet from where he'd stood before. Blackbard stopped next to him, and they both stared up at Desini.

I struggled to my feet and fell to one knee. The smack to my temple had affected my equilibrium. The world spun, then steadied again.

Blackbard strummed his strings, and the mage sneered as one of his hands glowed. Words appeared over the bard's head.

*Weakness Crescendo*

When the strumming ended, text appeared over Desini's head and floated toward the sky.

*Attack Down*

*Hmph. Shit.*
A massive ball of fire charged up the hill from the mage's hand then crashed into Desini's chest. She faltered, stepping backward, then steadied and continued her run toward them. The mage charged up another spell and Blackbard fingerpicked his strings.

With a final determined grip on my bearings, I sprinted toward both.

A Fire Flash slammed into Blackbard's face. The bard bellowed as he flailed and stumbled on his heels. "Where is that mage?"

"Behind us, above the rocks!" his mage barked.

Blackbard turned and searched for Priya as the glow around the mage's hand intensified. Desini charged across the remaining distance then slammed the mage to the ground She turned toward Blackbard as he located Priya and strummed. Desini provoked him to turn his attention back to her, but—

*Resisted*

*Shit!*

The unseen force slammed into Priya, and she swayed back against the rocks. I needed to close faster, or this whole thing would turn to shit in a hurry—as if it hadn't already.

Desini swung her sword, connecting with Blackbard's shoulder and causing him to cry out. His health bar was at 70%, but the mage's was at 30% tops.

"Focus on the caster!" I yelled.

Better to take out the glass tiger so we could all focus our energy on the bard.

Though his staff lay on the ground a few feet away, the mage thrust his hands into the air. A bright flash impacted Desini, knocking her backward and onto her ass.

*Desini*

*249 HP Remaining*

"We shall do the same!" Blackbard screamed. His eyes glowed with ferocity under the moonlight as the mage rolled to his feet, then both faced Priya in the rocks above. Her hands flailed in a circle, a white trail of light circling her that I hadn't seen before as her casting bar filled on my interface.

Blackbard strummed his lute. The caster built a new ball of fire. Bars filled above their heads.

Desini moaned and rubbed her forehead, trying to reach for the sword that had clattered to the ground.

Lightning crackled as thunder roared directly above us.

Two bolts from the air a slammed down onto the mage and Blackbard, interrupting one's song and the other's cast. I lunged at the mage with both daggers and activated Spine Snap!

The mage howled. Two streams of blood ejected from beneath his robe when I ripped my daggers away from his flesh and muscle. As he dropped to his knees, I swung around and swiped at Blackbard's throat. He dodged and swung his lute at me. Ducking beneath it, I slammed one of my blades into his knee. He dropped, then rolled onto his back. The lute fell free. I kicked it to one side, and the strings gave an audible thrum.

A gurgle brought my head around to find Desini shoving her sword deep into the soft flesh between the mage's shoulder and neck.

"You die in the name of your fellow man's sins, *pig!*"

My chest rose and fell as I dropped my weight onto Blackbard, pinning his shoulders beneath my knees. "What do you think of that, motherfucker?"

"I think you've made an enemy who'll chase you for the rest of your pathetic life, boy." He grinned, revealing teeth painted with blood.

"That's the way Gemini digs it, bitch!" I slammed my daggers into his eyes and bore down. An audible pop was followed by a spurting of white and red fluid draining down his face. When I ripped my daggers free, their tips were covered in bloody soil.

I rolled off of the dead bard, huffing and puffing to get my breath.

*I need to do something about my stamina.*

Priya's red robe flailed behind her as she circled the rock, descending toward us. Desini sat next to me, her head lowered, her tail lying dormant on the dirt behind her. She set her hands on her knees and huffed.

"You okay?" I asked.

She closed her eyes and nodded a few times. "Let not my appearance mislead you, teacher. My new life suits me, and I revel in victory. I long for my next victim." She inhaled deeply after the expenditure of words. Her stamina bar ticked in mass gulps that made me jealous.

I shoved her shoulder and, when she looked at me, I smiled. "This is what it's all about, baby."

Then I checked her attributes.

***Desini Sherre***
*Mishon*
*Level 17 Fighter*
***Attributes:***
*Strength: 24**
*Dexterity: 19**
*Intelligence: 7**
*Wisdom: 6**
*Constitution: 25**
*Charisma: 42**
***Combat Skills:***
*Melee: 14*
***Defensive Skills:***
*Dodge: 44*
*Melee Defense: 47**
***Weapon Skills:***
*Swords: 19*
*Unarmed: 14*
*Blunt: 14*
*Bonuses:*

*Resist Magic Attacks: 5*
*Resist Charm Effects: 10*
***Affinities:***
*Languages:*
*Common*
*Dwarvish*
*Elven*
*Gnomish*
*Mishon*
*Disposition: Beloved*
*Magic:*
*Light Magic: 20%*
*Shadow Magic: 15%*
*Nature Magic: 55%*

*Beloved.*

So, when she'd said I was her beloved teacher, she'd meant it literally. I guessed my words earlier that day, letting her know I respected her as a student—regardless of the fact she seemed to do a lot of teaching, herself—had a great effect. My devotion to Desini was growing, but considering the way I'd become so enamored with Roshan and Priya, and considering the trauma men of my race had weighed upon the mishon, I didn't want to let myself become a source of distress or confusion for her.

*You have completed the objectives for:*
***Den of Thieves: Part 2***
*Kill 6 thieves at Greycutter Downs: Completed*
*Kill Blackbard: Completed*
*Reward: 5,500 XP*
*Title: Savior of Commerce*
*Return to the Mayor in Warrington for your reward.*

That XP would push Desini over the threshold to the next level if we didn't end up being assaulted on the way back to Warrington. Even though Priya wouldn't have lost XP like I had when I died in Brumhill—it's good to be an NPC, I guess—the idea that she'd have respawned at Prantu's shop if she died and wait a day for us weighed on me. But I'd given her Constitution points, and that was all I could do at the moment.

Clicking echoed off the rocks nearby, and I turned to find my porcupunk's coal eyes staring up at me.

"You have a good nap?" I asked.

She clicked her disapproval of my joke. I scratched her head.

"First order of business, loot these assholes."

The rustling of Priya's robe signaled her return. "A fine battle, yes?" She smiled as if she'd just won an Olympic medal. I thought she might clap her hands. Her health was full and her mana was recovering.

Desini rolled the mage onto his back and patted him down. "A rewarding victory."

Items struck the earth next to him with a rhythmic repetition that made me wonder if she hadn't done this sort of thing before I met her. She tossed me his staff.

"No doubt you will want to keep that in reserve for our lover." She threw a glance at Priya, whose eyes widened and flicked to the staff with hunger.

***Dark Staff of Storms***
*Level 15*
*Quality: Rare*
*Durability: 71 of 75*
*7-10 Melee Damage*
*+10-15 Shadow Magic Damage*

*+5 Damage to nature spells*
*+50 Mana*

I eyed the staff's stats and agreed. It would be quite the weapon for Priya when she Reached 15, assuming we didn't find something better before then. I might have gotten more excited about it, as her expression indicated she was, but I expected equipment to upgrade at a pace Commensurate with the difficulty of the enemies we faced. But its text was blue, which meant it didn't suck.

**Fine Lute**
*Level 20*
*Slot: Weapon*
*Type: Ranged Instrument*
*Quality: Rare*
*Durability: 72 of 75*
*17-23 Magic Damage*
*+5 health from healing spells*

*You have discovered a new Profession:*
**Bard**
*The Bard is a support class dividing time between damage and healing while also buffing party members.*
*Bards learn songs instead of spells.*
*Available at Level 20*
*Starter Class Requirement: Woodsman*

"Awesome, we've learned a profession," I said.

"I like music very much," Priya said. "The only songs I heard in Zhara's forest came from birds and frogs, but when I bartered in town, I stopped to hear music drifting out of the Brumhill Tavern. I dared not enter, as my au—mother warned me against dangers for a young woman such as myself, you understand." Her eyes flicked nervously at Desini as if she hadn't considered just how well *she* might understand. "But how I loved to sit outside and listen."

"Maybe I'll learn songs to play for you someday," I said. I'd played guitar in my former life, so this instrument-weapon hybrid actually held some potential.

"I would like that."

### Blackbard's Belt Pouch
*You have received:*
*14 gold, 27 silvers, 48 coppers*
*You have received:*
### Medium Healing Potion *x 2*
*Heals 20% of imbiber's total HP instantly*

At risk of having Priya fall down, I leveled my tone so it reflected no excitement. "We picked up some coin." Then I turned to my tank. "Sorry, Desini. It doesn't look like any of the swords are upgrades. Blackbard's stick is a piece of shit, too. Looks like his lute was his main weapon."

"I am fond of my weapon, Gemini. It draws much blood." She spat on the burnt flesh of the mage's corpse. "I do not require fancy items."

"Your enthusiasm for violence warms my soul. Both of you."

The similarities of their concerned expressions made me laugh.

"Ha! I was being facetious." Their faces twisted further. "Facetious... joking around."

"I'm not so sure you were." Priya shook her head. "Adventure boils your blood for fuel. I can feel it."

"Oh, we're even then."

"How is that so?"

"Because I've seen the excitement in your eyes when a foe falls. I've seen the way you light up when someone levels. We're cut from the same cloth, and you know it. There's no shame in it."

"Well, then. Is there more loot?"

"Again, you're just like me." I tossed her a gold piece, which she snatched from the air with both hands.

"Fourteen of those."

"We're rich!" Priya cried.

Desini chuckled and shook her head but did not respond.

All the crates outside and in the fishery were empty. We checked the building near where the men had been sleeping, and it answered a question I hadn't voiced aloud but had subconsciously entertained. I'd wondered if the bandits preferred sleeping in the open air, especially since they'd once been pirates. Maybe it was the scent of salt water on the breeze.

But from just outside the rickety door hanging from two rusted hinges, we discovered the real reasons—a gaping hole about six feet in diameter punctured a roof that might otherwise collapse at any moment, moldy inner walls, and a stench that punched me in the nose. It smelled like a mortuary, sans formaldehyde. Like someone left cracked eggs to rot in a sauna.

"Gods, if catfish wore diapers, it would smell like that!" I waved my hands furiously in front of my face as I lumbered backward.

"Cat... fish?" Priya asked.

Okay, so no catfish in Enora. Good. I couldn't stand the shit, anyway.

A crumbling wardrobe sat in the far corner of the

stinking structure. The thought of crossing to it made me want to gag. But I had to man up. There might be something nice in there.

After two rounds of retreat and intense puking, I finally swung the doors open. One ripped away from it hinges and landed on my boot, but I ignored the pain as the assault on my olfactory sense took precedence. As if that hadn't been shitty enough, Looli's dress was stashed in a trunk inside the wardrobe, and I had to pry it open with the blade of a dagger. Luckily, I had no food left to regurgitate by that point. After a final dry heave on the way out, I hit the glorious pay dirt that was the thick sea air.

"Your bravery abounds," Desini said. "Grrrrrr." She leaned her head back and waved a hand in front of her face.

Priya nodded, her nose pinched between her thumb and finger although she stood twenty feet away and upwind. "I'm so glad I didn't have to perform that function."

"You will bathe before you sleep on my bedroll," Desini said. "Do not come too close, either. I fear that odor might cause me harm."

*You have met the requirements for the quest:*
### Looli's Lace
*Retrieve Looli's Mother's Binding Dress: Completed*
*Reward: 2 Gold*
*2000 XP*
*5 foodstuffs of your choice*
*Return the betrothal dress to Looli in Warrington to collect your reward.*


### Debuff:
### Piu!
*You stink!*

*-10 Charisma*
*Duration: Until you don't stink*

"That's fucking helpful," I muttered. I held up the dress. "Hey, it's two gold and a mess of XP. I wasn't about to pass it up."

Priya's face scrunched tighter, her thumb and forefinger turning her nose white against pink cheeks. She took a step backward.

"There is no amount of gold worthy of that scent."

"Hey! You said we were rich because we had fourteen gold! We get two more, and it's not good enough for you? You behave like *you* went in there and gave up your lunch!"

Priya smirked but didn't lower her hand. Her voice came out nasal and pinched... literally. "That is silly. If I'd gone in there, I would be the one kneeling at your feet hacking up my contents. I might even have re-spawned." She waved a hand. "I still might."

"Fair enough." I laughed, but it caught in my throat as an uncontrolled whiff of the dress slammed into my olfactory sense.

Desini took another step back. "We will not wait until we return to the river. You will go to the salt water and bathe," She thrust a finger toward the inlet pier as an involuntary smile of disgust crossed her face. "I could become sick. You could kill the horse. I will adventure no more until you have expelled that scent of demon filth from you."

Priya nodded agreement, still pinching her nose so hard I thought it might bleed.

Clicking came on the stinking air and I glanced around until I located Click, standing beyond Priya beneath some bushes. Her nose was buried in the soil.

I dropped the dress, sneered, then paced toward the fishery.

"Wait."

I turned and Desini threw the dress.

"Take it with you and pray the scent washes away. Else you will be out two gold." She wiped the hand that touched the dress in the grass.

"Who's in charge here?" I snatched the dress from the air.

"Until you rid our party of that scent, it will be me. I am higher level, do not force me to smite you." Desini smiled, but I thought I saw a hint of seriousness flash in her eyes. "Or slice your achilles and leave you behind."

"Won't the salt water ruin the dress?"

"I care not. Blame it on that riffraff." She gestured at the two corpses. "Did you promise her a perfectly maintained item? Do you think this woman would expect it pristine? I doubt it. Now, go." She thrust a long finger toward the sea.

The mishon was probably right. Looli didn't seem to be in any hurry to actually use the dress for its intended purpose.

I returned twice from the water before they let me stay. I had to admit, the salty-kind-of-clean on my skin left me rejuvenated. It must have shown on my face because Desini stripped and dove in as well.

"I must now erase this scent from my nose."

By the time we strolled out of Greycutter, we were much-improved in experience as well as from an olfactory perspective. I peeked through the window into the stench house a final time, but for the life of me, I could not figure out the source of that nose-hair-melting odor.

Then it hit me.

This quest was just waiting for an adventurer to come

along and grab it from Looli. It hadn't been marked unique, which meant other players might someday come here for the dress.

*An A.I. with a sense of humor. That's a dirty trick, Enora. But you're fucking funny. Twisted, but funny.*

I sniffed the dress, satisfied Looli would be happy enough to have it back.

We stashed any undamaged leather armor from our opponents' corpses into the horse's pack for sale later.

Hours later, we passed the tree line where we'd killed the two outgoing thieves in our first combat as a true team. At this point, it held a bit of nostalgia for me. Greycutter had been fun in the most screwed up of ways. Having almost been separated from Priya reminded me of my combat with the wolves and how I'd almost gotten my ass kicked. The lesson was that Enora was a bitch and required my complete focus.

I had to work for it.

But that was fine. I'd work for it, and I planned to be a powerful bastard. But before I flew, as the saying went, I needed to eat my eggs.

When we returned to the river where we killed the bear, we searched for others to no avail. I wouldn't have minded picking up a few turn-ins for that quest. But we came across our herd of deer again, which I interpreted as a stroke of luck until I realized I wasn't thinking like a gamer... yet again. Of course, the herd was there. They were designed to be there. They re-spawned there.

We killed four more to ensure that we could manage two extra turn-ins for the repeatable quest. I got clocked good in the head by a hoof and had to take a few to recover, but all-in-all, we did well and made good time. But then the weight of the day's activities bore down on Desini and me.

My shoulders slumped, my legs ached, and my eyelids drooped. I dozed, snapped awake, and snoozed again until the sun came up.

I peered down at a warm slither of fur against my knee and smiled. Desini's tail wrapped over both Priya and me, as if keeping us close.

33

After hitching the horse back to the cart, we rolled back into Warrington. I stopped at Looli's to return the heirloom and report to the Mayor. I showed him the lute as proof of completion. The blood stains added to the effect.

"You actually did it?" the mayor asked. "They're gone?"

"We overheard Blackbard stating there are stragglers on the road north of Warrington, but they shouldn't be too much to handle. Maybe you can send a posse. If I run into them on my way, I might be able to help, but I won't be returning anytime soon."

"I understand. I'll see what I can do about the others, but if I send guards out to Greycutter Downs so the bandits return home to cold, hard steel, it will be just as effective."

I smiled at him. "That's why you're the mayor. That's a much better idea than mine."

He held out a small purse. "Per our agreement."

You have completed the quest:<br>Den of Thieves: Part 2

*Rewards:*
*5,500 XP*
*5 Gold*
Title: ***The Savior of Commerce***
*You have reached Level 15!*
*+1 Dexterity*
*+1 Constitution*
*Congratulations! Now that you have reached Level 15, you gain three elective attribute points per level.*
*You have three new attribute points to distribute.*
*+200 Reputation with Warrington*
*New reputation status: Esteemed*
*Next reputation threshold: Revered*
*60/1000*

Wow! More attribute points! That kicked ass!

I confirmed that Priya and Desini received credit for the quests so they wouldn't have to come turn the quests in separately. Next, I again dropped two elective points into Intelligence to grow my mana pool for use with my woodsman skills and one into Constitution. Then I performed an expanded interface check and read every line to see who I'd become.

**G3m1n1 Fowler**
*Shénhuà*
*Level 15 Woodsman*
**Attributes:**
Strength: 6
Dexterity: 31
Intelligence: 5
Wisdom: 1
Constitution: 30

Charisma: 10
**Combat Skills**:
Ranged: 31
Unarmed: 1
Melee: 13
Ranged Attack Power: 312
**Defensive Skills:**
Dodge: 5
**Weapon Skills:**
Bow: 17
Blunt: 7
Dagger: 33
Thrown: 2
**Spells:**
**Inner illumination**
Level 5
Affinity Required: Light Magic
Allows the caster to see in dark environments
Mana Cost: 35
Cool-down: N/A
**Vine Entrapment**
Level 9
Call forth vines from the ground to bind your enemies.
Cost: 25 Mana
Cast Time: Three seconds
Cool-down: N/A
*Can be cast by any class with Affinity: Nature Spells
This spell has diminished returns when casting on the same being.
**Ranged Combat Skills:**
**Perforating Arrow** (Rank Two)
Skill Cost: 40 Mana

*Cast Time: Instant.*

*Longer draws use more mana but cause more damage.*

*Damage: Normal weapon damage plus 11-15 physical*

### ***Drilling Arrow***

*+200% Ranged Weapon Damage*

*Cost: 25 Mana*

*Cast Time: 3 Seconds*

*Cool-down: 30 Seconds*

### ***Melee Combat Skills***

### ***Dual-Wield: Swords*** *(Passive)*

*Allows a combatant to wield two swords.*

*Off-hand weapons suffer a 40% accuracy and damage penalty. This penalty is decreased as weapon skill rank increases.*

### ***Spine Snap***

*A vicious attack performed while stealth is active, causing 350% main-hand damage*

*Sneak Attack (1st Tier)*

*Skill Cost: 30 Stamina*

*Cast Time: Instant*

*Damage: 300% Weapon Damage*

*+15% chance of Critical Hit for 5 seconds*

*(Requires Stealth)*

### ***Occupational Skills:***

*Not to be confused with combat professions, occupational skills allow people to earn a wage, run a business, build foundation structures, or create weapons, armor, and potions to supplement adventuring.*

*Skinning: 17*

*Butchery: 4*

### **Affinities:**

*Languages:*

*All Neutral and lawful languages*
*Common*
*Elven*
*Mishon*
*Fortwan*
*Magic:*
*Light Magic:* 100
*Shadow Magic:* 100
*Nature Magic:* 100

My next stop was to visit the tanner. Since the ladies 'made preparations for our trip North' instead of accompanying me, Bensin was disappointed at not seeing the blonde eye candy. I knew what Desini and Priya were actually doing. Even if they wanted some personal time away from me, I wasn't offended. Let them play. It maintained morale. As to Bensin, I counteracted his disappointment with the skins. His stock appeared barren, and I was happy to oblige.

At 3 gold for as many deer skins, I turned in six, earning 5,000 more XP and another 6 gold coins. He happily took the bear pelt off my hands for the promised reward of 8 gold, and we received 3,500 XP, which meant, wherever she was, Desini had just been washed in light and reached Level 18. I hoped she'd been in the throes of some dirty sex with a certain half-elf when it happened. She'd earned it.

As much as I would've loved to visit another vendor and seek out some better gear, my thoughts of Roshan's absence crept through me like an intensifying nausea.

I dumped the gear we'd been stashing in my bag and the horse's saddlebags for a pittance since Desini was otherwise occupied, and we were on a timetable . I netted 3 gold, 10 silvers for the lot, bringing our stash to 29 gold, 49 silvers, and 48 coppers.

Unlike Brumhill, the guards in Warrington carried less of a chip on their shoulders, and there was enough traffic coming from the farms and other surrounding industries that they kept busy. We slid out of town with little difficulty.

It was hours past noon by the time we were on the road again. Though I'd slept fitfully the night before, turning in all the quests had given me my second wind, so Priya and Desini slept in the cart as I steered us out of Warrington and set across the grasslands leading north toward Trowlsby.

Things were looking up. I'd hit the recommended level for the quest to rescue Roshan, and the three of us were getting acclimated to fighting together. I closed my eyes and let the sun—roughly a third larger than the one on earth—bathe my face in its warmth.

The thunder began an hour later, followed by driving rain. It seemed every new encounter with that godforsaken road came with the wet stuff.

We traveled for two days in incessant storms. On the second day, nearing the end of our journey, Desini sat next to me beneath the meager shelter on the front bench as Priya napped in the back.

"You are becoming impatient."

"Why do you say that? What did I say?"

"You say nothing. You do nothing. You haven't offended. This is why it seems you've changed."

"I'm sorry if I'm being weird."

"I just said you didn't offend." Desini grasped my hand. "Priya has explained the depth of this special bond you share with Roshan, filling in the emotional gaps you omit from your tales. She has told me of the special look you had in your eye, and how Roshan shared it with you, but you didn't deign to have relations together, although you slept nude and adjacent. This would be strange behavior unless there was something deeper. Do you understand what I'm saying?"

"That we wanted our first time to be special?"

She squeezed her eyes closed and shook her head. "If you want to be simple, you could say that. My words would be different."

"How so?" I was interested to learn more about Desini, and this moment struck me as an opportunity.

"Were the two of you savoring your time together, knowing that when you pulled the cork from the bottle of your passion, you would drink vigorously?" She didn't wait for an answer. "The taste always changes after the first sip. Change comes with physical relations; a corner is turned. These deeper connections lend a comfort to love, but we always remember our early passion. It is to be primed and savored. Do my words make sense to you?"

"Very much. I've been trying to figure out what it is about Roshan that has me constantly on edge."

"Hmph! Her absence?"

"Does it make you or Priya assume I value you less?"

To this, Desini chuckled. "Men possess such egos. The belief they carry so much sway over our beating hearts. To compare ourselves with Roshan is ridiculous. I am Desini. Priya is Priya. Roshan is Roshan. Priya holds Roshan in high regard, so I I'm certain I will. We don't all measure our value by how you feel about us."

And thus, I was reminded of the primary difference between NPCs of other games and the ones in Enora. These women might show me a certain level of adoration, and that trait might have been sewn into their digital genes by the programmers, but they also valued themselves and each other.

"What is different about Roshan?" Desini asked.

"It's not how she's different from anyone that makes me ache for her. She carries herself with such dignity. Such maturity. She'll be an anchor for this group, a disciplined caster to help balance Priya's cast-first-and-ask-questions-later disposition. Her council is wise and unbiased. When I miss the forest for the trees, she'll be a strong partner."

"More strange words from you." Desini laughed, a hacking sound like she was coughing up a hairball. "I don't doubt that you endeared her to you like us." She turned on the bench and faced me. "I am no longer alone, master. I've found a new sense of purpose." Tears welled in her eyes. "During my childhood, people viewed adventure as a respectable vocation, as they have for many generations. We lost much, and I never presumed such an opportunity would befall me." She swiped a tear away then pressed her lips to my cheek for a long moment. "Today you knew that Priya and I made excuses to enjoy each other's company."

I shrugged.

"This is what I mean. You give so much and take little. You teach us with such patience. The other commonality between men of all races is jealousy. Yet, I see none of this in you."

"Then you should have seen me glare lasers at the tanner in town who was undressing Priya with his eyes."

"What are lasers?" She shook her head. "Never mind. The question I have is, did you gaze thusly because you were overcome with jealousy? Because you expected Priya might run off with him and give him pleasure?" She cocked an eyebrow at me but answered the question herself. "No.

It's because you are protective of your companion. She's important to you. Family. A beloved."

*Shit, she's right.*

I nodded.

She replied in kind. "You beat yourself up for your mistakes but don't repeat them. You bear down on yourself so you remember the lessons you learn. Yet you remind me to use my Slice Achilles ability when I slip up with such patience in your words. There's only one person in our party unsure about your motivations and your underlying essence, Gemini. That's you."

"Thank you."

"Don't thank me in this dismissive way." She pried my hand from her knee and dropped it on my leg. Then she cupped it. "Decide what you'll take from this world and what you'll give. What will be your legacy? What are your limits? How far will you go to meet your objectives and what will you sacrifice to do so?

"You are a good man, master. We see that in you. Use all of us as your anchors like we use you so you don't drift from who you are meant to be—our leader."

Desini surprised me when she pressed her lips against mine and ran her soft hands across my cheeks. "You have treated me with such kindness, master. Other men possess no place in my heart. But to you shall I ever be indebted. I pledge my fealty and will fight by your side for all the days I draw breath."

My heart swelled. I huffed a few times to keep the emotions at bay. Then I nodded. "You're my friend. And, as you've shown just now, it's you who is my teacher."

Desini opened her mouth to say something, but pressed her lips together and shook the thought away. Then she cocked her head toward the back. "Keep Priya warm for a while. I'll steer. The storms slow our pace, and we'll need to move fast when we arrive in Trowlsby. Rest well and make up for lost sleep, for we will need our leader at his sharpest."

I hugged Desini with one arm and kissed her temple. When I crawled into the bedroll with Priya, I slept like a corpse.

## 34

If Warrington sprawled when compared to the meager Township of Brumhill, Trowlsby was a metropolis. I knew when the high walls came into view that this was a major hub in this part of the kingdom. If Enora held up to her predecessors, I would find spell trainers, vendors galore, occupation guilds like blacksmiths, tanners, and carpenters, and who knew what else.

But the excitement I'd felt when first I'd walked into Brumhill, when first seeing people outside the Dark Wood, was gone. The punch had become a tickle. I came with a lone purpose—reconnaissance and recovery of my prized friend.

Per Desini's suggestion, I paid forty silvers to the gate guard to bypass common hardships of contraband searches and harassment. A corrupt guard might employ loose definitions of 'contraband' to elicit more coin, so it was best to pay a reasonable sum up front and avoid the mess. The fact the man took it might've been indicator enough we'd made the right choice. She assured me that once we were inside, we shouldn't run into trouble because the larger city had a live-and-let-live attitude, as long as 'beast people' kept to their place. Because Desini still wasn't eligible for a bed at the inn, we wouldn't take one. Inns hadn't been great lately, anyway. There were camps where people slept in their vehicles, safe inside the city walls. The grassy area with sandy white trails where we parked reminded me of RV campgrounds in my former world.

Desini slipped away from the cart just after noon and told us she would locate Roshan. She had a suspicion our Light priestess would be kept near the city council's hall. "The local politicians will want to keep in the good graces of the governor by extending all courtesies to his men and securing his eastern prize."

From the intel Desini had gained in Warrington, the men transporting her had business to conduct here before moving on, and they would need to resupply before taking the week-long trek to the northwest, to the governor's seat of power, in Nashtolm. When they set out, they'd have to be ready to take on what she'd called the Plague Barrens—a challenge that demanded power, numbers, or both.

As Priya and I marched around town, my map revealed the different districts. For each, we received some discovery XP.

*You have discovered the Occupational District.*
*150 XP*
*You have Discovered the Medical District.*
*150 XP*
*You have discovered the Military Training Grounds.*
*150 XP*

In one area of the latter, I spied training dummies lined up in an open, grassy area. The gamer in me longed to go over there to train up my skills and perfect my attack rotations, but they might be for exclusive military or city guard use and, judging from the guards patrolling the streets in plate armor polished to a high sheen and carrying unblemished swords, spears, and battle axes, I didn't want to piss anyone off.

### *City Guard*
*Human*
*Level 40 Warrior*

Way out of my league. The guards didn't seem unfriendly, returning my nods of acknowledgment, even if they didn't exactly smile, but their eyes were very friendly to Priya. Their more-than-casual glances until she'd passed out of their sight reminded me of how Desini had categorized me in the cart the night before.

*You are a good man, Gemini.*

I didn't watch over my shoulder to see if guards checked Priya's backside because her words made me want to be better than a jealous thug.

One wonderful surprise I hadn't expected—or even considered—when trying to survive the hardcore levels at the beginning of my life in Enora had been that I might discover classes by entering their guilds in the Military Zone.

*You have discovered the Profession: **Necromancer***
*You have discovered the Profession: **White Mage***
*You have discovered the Profession: **Paladin***
*You have discovered the Profession: **Monk***

*You have discovered the Profession:* ***Wizard***

What I didn't see, unfortunately, was a guild for rogues or hunters, but I didn't plan on sticking around if and when I managed to grab Roshan. When that happened, we were going to get the hell out. The White Mage trainer—White Mages just seemed like nicer people if I'm being honest—verified that Level 20 was the cutoff where subclasses stopped leveling simultaneously.

If I wanted to have access to multiple specialized combat classes, I would have to pick a combat profession at 20, level it, then switch to the other, pick up at Level 20, and level it separately. It was unlikely I would level a starter class once I had a combat profession, but who knew? At Level 30, a starter class might obtain a skill that complimented the skill sets of a combat profession.

*I wouldn't put it past this freaking world.*

Credit was due, though. I'd never seen a game world before where you could level everything to 20 at the same time to get a taste of what you liked before picking an advanced class. It was kind of cool. The tradeoff was that other players would have to roll new characters until they reached Level 10 without dying.

The Occupational District was heaven on Enora.



I not only found a blacksmithing guild, a tanner's guild, and a carpenter's guild, but also an alchemist's guild. Again, I wasn't taking a lot of time to sightsee, but I bought a couple axes at the carpenter's guild and stuffed them in my bag, which was now emptier since I'd unloaded so much crap in Warrington.

***Simple Axe***

*A tool for cutting trees and sometimes enemies*

*Level 5*

*2-5 Physical Damage*

***Apprentice's Axe***

*Level 10*

*4-7 Physical Damage*

I also added some new skinning knives to replace the simple ones Priya had given me in the forest she'd called home.

Desini forced me to promise I would restrict my purchases until she was with me, but I figured a few couldn't hurt.

The cost to unlock the forestry profession with the trainer was only 50 silvers, and it was available to anyone Level 5 or higher. This served as another reminder that Enora wasn't designed to center only on players. No players would ever visit this place before Level 10 because they had to survive the Dark Levels first.

I'd wondered a few times what might have happened if I'd tried to leave the forest before Level 10. I'd almost done it at 9 and been attacked at the border. Then I'd reached 10 and crossed the threshold into the lands around Brumhill. Would other players run into the adversity like that if they tried to leave their starting areas before Level 10?

A woman smiled as she passed us by, swinging a rather large-headed baby on one hip. When she passed, I turned and looked at the back of the baby's smooth head.

*That little thing is an NPC. Wow. Now that brings home the idea that these non-players actually procreate to populate Enora.* I cocked my head to one side as another thought slapped me. *Will our baby be considered an NPC or a player?*

We wandered into the Council's Glen by total mistake. Ignoring the signs, I'd led Priya out of the carpenter's guild and climbed the cobblestone path up a hill and was alerted to the discovery.

*You have discovered the* **Council's Castle**
*150 XP*

I hadn't considered all this bonus XP would add up so quickly, but when combined with the quest turn-ins in Warrington, it did. Priya was engulfed in light and leveled as we entered the new sector of Trowlsby.

"'Grats!" a passerby said.

"Congratulations, young lady!" Another said as she passed us by on the way down the hill.

"Wow, you're an adventurer! Solara bless you!"

"Strange, they can see you level within the city?" I asked. Until now, only companions could see that.

I brought up my interface and dropped three more points into Priya's constitution since it didn't award her as many HP as mine, and one more point in Intelligence. Her mana pool had yet to fall to critical levels during combat, but I would leave room for Wisdom soon, when life got more difficult and she'd have to spend more of the resource. Recovery was as important as overall mana during longer battles.

***Priya Skyy***
*Half-Elf*
*Level 13*
*(No class)*
**Attributes**
*Strength: 8**

Dexterity: 3*

Intelligence: 23

Wisdom: 13

Constitution: 22

Charisma: 8*

### Combat Skills

Ranged: 14

Unarmed: 1

Blunt: 3

Melee: 5

Fire Spells: 13

### Defensive Skills

Dodge: 4

### Weapon Skills

Bow: 14*

Blunt: 7

### Spells

### Shadow Void

Level 8

Required Affinity: **Shadow Magic**

The caster opens a portal to the underworld and banishes chaotically aligned creatures within two levels into the void.

Cast Time: 3 seconds

Cost: 100 Mana

Cool-down:" 30 Minutes

### Sleep

Level 9

Required Affinity: **Shadow Magic**

The caster calls forth dark essence to force a single adversary to slumber.

Damage will end the effect.

### Mystic Sight

*Level 10*
*All Magic Schools*
*Cast Time: 5 seconds*
*Cool-down: 24 Hours*
*The caster views a 100-yard area from up to one mile away and reveals the location on the map.*

### *Thunder*

*Level 10*
*Required Affinity:* **Shadow Magic**
*Cast a storm overhead of multiple enemies causing 13-20 damage.*
*Cast Time: 3 Seconds*
*Mana Cost: 50 Mana*
*Cool-down: Not applicable*

### *Ice Storm*

*Level 10*
*Required Affinity:* **Shadow Magic**
*Cast a storm of ice over multiple enemies causing 13-17 damage.*
*Additional effect: Chill*
*Chill: Slow enemy movement speed by 30%*
*Cast Time: 3 seconds*
*Mana Cost: 45 Mana*
*Cool-down: 30 seconds.*

### *Fireflash*

*Level 11*
*Required Affinity:* **Shadow Magic**
*Project a burst of fire before a single enemy causing 15-19 damage.*
*Cast Time: Instant*
*Mana cost: 40 Mana*
*Cool-down: Not applicable*

### *Occupational Skills*

*Not to be confused with combat professions, occupational skills allow people to earn a wage, run a business, build foundation structures, or create weapons, armor, and potions to supplement adventuring.*

Carpentry: 18
Forestry: 41
Skinning: 35
Cooking: 17

### *Affinities:*

Shadow Magic: 100%
Elemental Magic: 57%
Languages:
Elven
Common

Priya's blush was absolute as she curled her arm inside mine and chuckled in response to all the attention she'd gotten upon leveling.

"I'm never going to get used to having so many people around, and this is embarrassing."

I laughed, but it caught in my throat as I peered through my interface, across the wide-open plaza before the castle serving as home to the Council. Thick gray bricks composed the wall of the structure, with a drawbridge—complete with a moat—at its foot. High atop the bastions, guards patrolled east-to-west. Long spears standing taller than they did rocked with each step as they marched like toy soldiers.

An area cut out of the brick, shaped like a dome, was what caught my attention, though.

"Priya?"

She perked up. "Yes, love?"

"I need you to come with me." I grabbed her hand and pulled her forward.

"I come willingly, but where are we going?" she asked as I jerked her forward.

I pulled her around to the side of a small building. "I need your eyes."

She glared at me like I'd lost my mind.

I pinched her chin, turned it toward the castle, then pointed a finger, so it directed her attention exactly where I wanted it to go. "See that little cut out in the wall? The one with the hanging banners inside?"

She nodded and squinted against the daylight.

"Oh, my." She cupped her hand over her mouth. "Can it be?"

"Can you cast Mystic Sight and show me?" I scanned around us to make sure no one was watching.

I hid Priya from view while she cast the spell. Her eyes rolled into her head in that creepy way. A translucent metal rectangle was drawn on my interface and I focused on it as her line-of-sight took me to the drawbridge, up the stony brick surface, and past guards marching back and forth. The camera perspective drawn by her eyes stopped and zoomed. The space behind the curved section of wall was cut into a tower, like some fairy tale. Judging from the posters of a bed and a basin sitting against the west wall, it was definitely living quarters. Perhaps it belonged to the captain of the watch or a councilman.

Colorful tapestries hung on the wall inside, but I focused on the figure standing on the balcony, gazing out across the district, wearing a green-and-yellow robe that flowed down her back but split in front to show long, athletic, coppery legs. Long locks of shining black hair reflected the sunlight and, courtesy of the Mystic Sight spell, I could just make out the unmistakable face.

Priya swiped away a tear.

There, at the top of the most heavily fortified section of Trowlsby, in a tower near the top of the castle, with uncounted high-level guards pacing the walkways below and manning the only way in or out, was Roshan.

# ALSO BY ARLO ADAMS

Gemini's adventure continues in Enora Online Book 3: *The Plague Barrens.* You can get it on amazon by searching for B07NTMD8FM

If you haven't already signed up for my release newsletter, make sure to head over to our wicked-cool, motion-based sign-up page and join us so I can let you know when new books arrive!

Go to https://enora.online to sign up!

We'll also share artwork from the world of Enora with you!

# CONNECT VIA TWITTER!

Although most social media is a time suck I can't afford if I want to write more books, you can follow me on Twitter by clicking the icon below.